Summer at the
Scottish Castle

Summer at the Scottish Castle

Rachel Bowdler

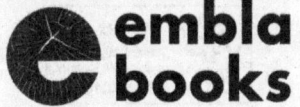

First published in Great Britain in 2023 by

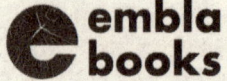
embla books

An imprint of Bonnier Books UK
5th Floor, HYLO, 105 Bunhill Row,
London, EC1Y 8LZ

A CIP catalogue record for this book is available from the British Library.

ISBN: 9781471415265

Also available as an ebook and an audiobook

2

This book is typeset using Atomik ePublisher
Printed and bound in Great Britain by Clays Ltd, Elcograf S.p.A.

The authorised representative in the EEA is Bonnier Books
UK (Ireland) Limited.
Registered office address: Floor 3, Block 3, Miesian Plaza,
Dublin 2, D02 Y754, Ireland
compliance@bonnierbooks.ie
www.bonnierbooks.co.uk

For Ivy,
moji lásku

Chapter One

The hydrangea shrubs were Jessamine's best hiding place yet, even if she did have to contend with a leafy branch tickling the inside of her nostril. She batted it away, pinching the bridge of her hay fever-ravished nose to trap a sneeze, and huddled further into the leaves. Lilac petals fell at her feet and droplets of last night's rain dampened her dress.

The clicking of Petra's tall heels across the garden path grew louder. Through teary eyes and a gap in the shrub, Jessamine caught a glimpse of her personal assistant's sharp, impatient features as she approached.

Jessamine held her breath when Petra neared – and released it in relief when she sauntered straight past the hydrangeas, her pointy nose jabbing the air with a hauteur that seemed permanent, innate, on her narrow features. A moment later, Petra disappeared around the corner and circled back towards the castle, where Jessamine should have been, too.

Though it was childish to hide, she simply didn't have the energy for her assistant-slash-chaperone today. They'd been travelling up and down the country for weeks, attending business meetings and charity events and dinner parties to save face after Jessamine's rather public divorce, and she was wiped out. Then, the article had been released by gossip magazine, *Splendour*. She'd been expecting it, but nothing had quite prepared her for the sight of her distraught features plastered all over the internet. And if the immortalised 'meltdown' – as labelled by journalist Emily Kingsley – wasn't terrible enough, Robert had accused 'the ice queen' of cheating on him throughout their relationship,

1

claiming she wouldn't have children with him because she was cold-hearted and unable to love anyone but herself. All lies, of course. Robert was the one always away on business trips, coming home smelling of other women's perfume. When she'd pulled him up on it, she was labelled jealous, paranoid, ridiculous. All she'd asked of him afterwards was that he sign the divorce papers, because God forbid she spend another day married to him. Naturally, though, he hadn't been able to leave peacefully, and she'd become the talk of the town: *Poor Robert, having to put up with her. I bet she was an utter nightmare. I never quite took to her anyway. There was something off all along. He could do much better than a loopy, cheating so-and-so. Has she no shame?*

Mother had thought it an apt time for her to get away from London, and Jessamine had rather quickly agreed. Their ancestral castle, Rosemire – left to Jessamine in her father's will, because apparently Mother had no interest in adding an 'old-fashioned tourist trap in the middle of nowhere' to her hefty collection of inherited properties – was as good a place to hide as any, especially since it had been left forgotten for years. *Until it blows over*, Mother had said. But accusations of being a promiscuous, conceited, hysterical, manipulative shrew were unlikely to blow over anytime soon. Certainly not for a peeress with a reputation to uphold. Mother wasn't talking to her at all, and besides politely telling her to naff off, hadn't bothered with Jessamine since the dinner party at the Chelten Estate weeks prior, where it had all gone wrong. Where Jessamine had finally exploded after months of coaxing Robert into signing the divorce papers and listening to his veiled insults about how she should be crawling on her knees, begging for both forgiveness and another chance. It had been their first reunion since the divorce, and no doubt not their last, since they were bound to the same social circles. Jessamine had been civil, focusing her attention on her own group of 'friends' – people who mysteriously stopped talking to her not long afterwards – and doing her best to look as though she was having fun. Robert hadn't liked that. Just to ensure she didn't come out of the other side looking *too* happy about their separation, he'd accused her of flirting with one of the servers in front of all of their friends. No mention, of course, of his own myriad affairs throughout their unhappy marriage.

Jessamine hadn't been able to stop her rage that time. Not after four years of living with his muttered remarks about the way she dressed; how she was embarrassing him by talking too much or not enough. Four years of looking the other way when he flirted with any woman with a pulse. So, she'd thrown her glass of champagne all over him, and then his friend's glass just for good measure. And, all right, she'd gone off on a bit of a tangent about how toxic it all was: Robert, himself; the gossip; the superficial nature of their lifestyle; the unimportance of wealth when one had no morals. Now, she was the mentally unstable, bitter, cheating ex-wife who liked to make a scene while poor Robert just wanted to move on. To make sure it stayed that way, he'd done the interview with *Splendour* and 'dished the dirt' on their tumultuous marriage. Who would people believe? A handsome, charming baron everybody quite fancied, or the frumpy wife who had made a scene at a civilised, elegant dinner party? No matter that Jessamine spent her days working with charities to make a positive impact. It would always be the woman's fault.

So, here she was, in the heart of the Scottish Highlands, where the scandal couldn't reach her. But her assistant could. There was still work to be done, after all. The problem was, Jessamine just wanted one day to herself. One day to lick her wounds in private. One day to—

'You're flattening my tulips.'

The gruff brogue cutting through delicate birdsong startled her. She'd been so focused on avoiding Petra that she hadn't even noticed the rusty-haired man kneeling on the other side of the path, a pair of shears in his grubby-gloved hands.

The gardener, she presumed, having noticed him pruning the rose bushes yesterday in the same green apron and tatty clothes. She'd wished him a good morning then, but he hadn't answered. She'd supposed he hadn't heard her, but judging from the tense set of his jaw and the heavy, furrowed brows casting shadows over his eyes, she was beginning to wonder if he had purposely ignored her. The thought made her feel uneasy. Surely the article hadn't reached this tiny village. Jessamine had already had trouble connecting to the Wi-Fi, and she'd only managed to find a phone signal at random spots in the castle – usually by hanging out of a window or turret.

'I beg your pardon?' she asked, almost choking on another intrusive leaf in the process. She stepped away, her dress snagging on a branch, but she didn't have a chance to free herself.

'My tulips.' He gestured to her feet with his shears, the silver winking against watery sunlight. He stood, then stepped closer. 'You're flattening them.'

She frowned, wincing when she looked down to find the buttery yellow petals squashed beneath her tasselled leather loafers. 'Oh. Sorry. I—'

'Hang on.' The gardener stepped onto the grass, reaching towards Jessamine with his shears. Her hackles rose at the sudden, unsolicited proximity. Was he trying to *cut* her *dress*?

It was pure instinct to slap his hand away before he tried.

'Excuse me!' she snapped, placing her hands on her hips. 'What, exactly, do you think you're doing with those shears?'

He recoiled, face flushing pink as he cradled his gardening tool to his torso defensively. '*Oi!* No need for that. I was only trying to cut the bloody bush so you wouldn't tear your dress! Jesus.'

Embarrassment echoed through Jessamine. She bowed her head, shielding her watery eyes as the low spring sun bled through the clouds. The hem of her dress was still knotted in the branch, causing a tear in the chiffon.

He'd been trying to help.

Still, she was too stubborn to apologise now. 'Well, you should have warned me. You can't just go around approaching women with sharp objects. What was I supposed to think?'

The gardener's broad chest rippled with an impatient sigh, his lips pressed into a thin line beneath coppery, grey-peppered stubble. 'I didn't realise I looked like a suspect in *Midsomer Murders*. Just get off my tulips, will you? You're killing them.'

'They're not *your* tulips,' she retorted, though she unhooked her dress carefully and hopped back onto the path. He had already retreated, kneeling over a line of weeds. The shears were left abandoned at his side; instead, he yanked dandelions from the ground with his hands.

'I bloody well planted them, thanks very much. Honestly, you seasonal staff.' Bitterness soaked his words and thickened his Scottish accent. 'You think you can do what you want, don't you? Just walk in and leave your rubbish all over the place, ruin my flowers, prance about, and let other people clean up your mess.'

'I'm not—' She frowned, clamping down on her words. She should have told him who she was, should have embarrassed him the way he had her, but the fewer people who knew about her stay, the better. She hadn't been recognised or badgered by castle visitors or locals yet, and that had been her only respite from it all. In fact, nobody had given her a second glance. People tended to hover when they knew there was a countess around, newspaper reporters and photographers included. Since the divorce, it had been non-stop, and the recent series of unfortunate events had only added fuel to the fire. She was in hiding. She would remain that way, even for the sake of rude gardeners who needed to be knocked down a peg or two.

Still, she narrowed her eyes, annoyance flickering in her chest. She wouldn't be belittled by someone who'd clearly woken up on the wrong side of the bed, regardless of her low profile. Not a chance. '*You*, on the other hand, are quite delightful,' she said.

He threw her a daggers look over his shoulder. 'I assume you're one of the tour guides. Just keep the bloody visitors off the grass, will you?'

'You're very possessive of the gardens,' she noted, tugging at her blazer self-consciously. She supposed she *did* blend in with the black-uniformed tour guides scattered around the castle grounds today. It hadn't been planned but it seemed an effective disguise. 'You do know the grass doesn't *actually* belong to you.'

He huffed absently at that. 'Since I spend most of my days tending to it, I think it's fair to ask that you show it a wee bit of respect.'

Jessamine cleared her throat uncomfortably. In all her life, nobody had ever acted this way around her. Even now, they pasted false smiles on their faces, until her back was turned and they had the chance to criticise her in hushed whispers. Robert and her mother's remarks had always been bitterly passive-aggressive. This man seemed not to care at all how he came across: all barbed bluntness.

The people-pleaser in her squirmed. She didn't enjoy being disliked, even if it was refreshing to be mistaken as a normal person with a normal job. In another life, perhaps she *would* have been a seasonal tour guide, or maybe even a grumpy gardener like him.

Then again, the thought of all that dirt under her fingernails made her shudder.

'Fine,' she said. 'I'm sorry about the way I reacted. It was only done in self-defence.'

His shoulders stiffened beneath his thick, muddied shirt as he tugged another weed from a small crack in the path. 'Don't you have tours to guide? Flowers to butcher?'

She shook her head in disbelief. 'When one offers you an apology, it is polite to accept it properly.'

He yanked off his gloves, offering her a blank expression as he stood up. His large, softly rounded frame left her in his shadow. 'Apology accepted. I suppose I should have asked before trying to help.' His words were forced through clenched teeth, but he at least met her eye. 'I'd work on your self-defence skills, though. If a nastier bloke comes at you with a pair of shears, you'll have to do more than give him a slap on the hand.'

'Oh, I know exactly where to aim, thank you,' she crooned, glancing at his crotch and then immediately wishing she hadn't. She wiped her clammy palms on her dress – a habit her mother would have donned 'most unladylike', if her mother was speaking to her at all, that was – and worked desperately to avoid his gaze. 'I'm sorry for ruining the flowers.'

He smirked crookedly. 'Apology accepted, I s'pose. It's nothing to cry about, though, love.'

The sudden softness in his voice gave her whiplash, and her tone turned even steelier to overcompensate. 'I *beg* your pardon?'

'You look a bit teary.' He pointed in her vague direction. 'Didn't mean to upset you.'

'Oh, as if *you* could impact my mood. It's hay fever.' She sniffed through a congested nose, pulling her embroidered handkerchief from her breast pocket and dabbing her itchy eyes.

'Probably shouldn't get up close and personal with my hydrangeas, then. Hiding from the kids?' Knowingly, the gardener gestured towards the castle, where a group of school children had just spilt out of a giant black coach. A school trip. Jessamine would not be getting any peace today, after all, unless she hid in her room in the east wing, where Petra could easily find her.

She hummed in agreement, crossing her arms. As grumpy and irritable as he'd been, it was strange, new, to be treated like a normal person; to be spoken to like a person at all. Besides, it had been a long time since she'd had to be anything but polite, while a growling tiger, forever tamed, slumbered in her stomach. It was nice to argue about flowers and not the circumstances of her divorce.

Her nose grew stuffy again in the pollen-rife wind, the smell of freshly cut grass taking her somewhere else for a moment. When was the last time she'd noticed her surroundings? Noticed the sun or the flowers, or the way strangers could start conversations? Her life was always sparkling champagne and camera flashes and stiff handshakes with people whose names she'd forget in an hour.

But there was nothing stiff about the gardener – that she could see, anyway. She didn't want to think about the double entendre there, nor did she want to hazard another glance in *that* southerly direction. He was the type of man she'd never look twice at if she was walking down the street, but that might be a mistake: when she gazed past the tuft of reddish-grey curls, she found faint laughter lines half-hidden by fuzzy facial hair, constellations of freckles across both apple cheeks, and a soft, upturned mouth full of charm that he didn't necessarily seem aware of. Or maybe she was just underestimating his ego, since he clearly had a fire in him that he refused to tamp out for her sake.

'I didn't catch your name,' she said in an effort to distract herself as much as him.

'Mac,' he said. 'Going to file a complaint to your manager about the nasty gardener, are you?' His green-blue eyes now sparkled with good humour. Teasing. He was teasing her.

'Maybe I will.' Her brow twitched with the challenge, but he didn't have time to rise to it. The sound of clacking heels returned, and quickly, now. A moment later, the golden-brown crown of Petra's head bobbed over the hedges around the corner. Dread twanged through Jessamine like a plucked violin string as she was thrust back into the real world, where gardeners were just people she passed on her way to dinner parties while either her mother or Petra told her what to do, what to wear, where to go, how to chew her food.

'Mrs Townsend?' Petra's high-pitched voice reminded Jessamine of rusty car brakes, and the use of her husband's surname didn't soften the blow.

Mac looked towards the sound, and for a moment she thought the ruse was over. But then he wiped his damp brow. 'Bloody hell. Thought gardens were supposed to be peaceful.'

She sucked in a breath. 'I should get back . . . to tour guiding. Because I'm a tour guide.'

A wrinkle of mirth formed between his low brows. 'Aye. Enjoy, then.'

On wobbly legs, she ran in the opposite direction of Petra's calls, towards the throng of children lining up by the castle's portcullis. She weaved through them in the hopes they'd hide her as effectively as the hydrangeas had, then wandered around the corner towards the birds of prey annexe.

The shadows of the long archway spanning the side of the castle's west wing concealed her, her distorted reflection following in the long stained-glass windows.

Until a small, dark ball of fluff stopped her in her tracks.

Rufus, Jessamine's three-legged rescue cat and the only living creature she could stand to be around for longer than an hour, prowled – or rather, hopped – around by the conservatory, still unable to accept that he had no chance of catching the birds fluttering above. So far, he'd taken to Scotland far better than Jessamine had.

She softened and knelt. 'Hello, Rufus.'

She felt quite special when Rufus let her pick him up and even nudged his head against her cheek, as though he knew she needed the comfort. It had taken him a while to warm to her, and he and Robert had shared a mutual dislike when they'd all lived together, but Rufus had stuck by her, nonetheless – probably as glad to see the back of her ex-husband as she was.

'I'm not sure how much longer I can do this castle thing,' she whispered into his fur. 'What do you think? Do you like it here?'

Rufus mewed, as though saying, 'yes' which was no surprise, since he had most definitely been fed scraps by visitors enjoying outdoor picnics. He scrambled to be put down, as though well aware that a busload of schoolchildren had come to fuss over him with ham sandwiches. She let him go, running a hand through his dark fur before bidding him goodbye. Apparently, Rufus was running away from her while *she* ran away from everyone else. Typical, really.

'Mrs Townsend!' The name was screeched, and Jessamine pressed her back into the cold stone wall in defeat. She'd been found, and apparently her maiden name was too difficult a change for Petra to adjust to. Even the newspapers called Jessamine the '*Wife of Baron Townsend*' more often than her own, higher-ranking title: The Countess of Cheshire. Sometimes, it felt as though all the meaningless names would engulf her, smother her, and one day Jessamine wouldn't exist at all. She would only ever be defined in terms of ownership: what she owned, and who owned her.

'Mrs Townsend!' Petra was out of breath, clutching her phone in one hand and a diary-planner in the other as she approached. 'There you are! Thank goodness.'

Jessamine merely forced a smile and straightened herself out. 'Oh, hello, Petra,' she said. 'Have you been looking for me?'

Chapter Two

'I am not late! I am not late!' Mac, who was very late, rasped out between shallow breaths. His heart sank at the displeased expression on Linda Murphy's face, her lips pursed with impatience as she waited at the sage-green door of the gardener's cottage.

He stopped at the gate, anyway, feeling as though his lungs were caving in. Not only was he late, he was also sweaty. It poured down his back in rivulets, causing his shirt to stick to his skin. He swiped his forehead, wishing he'd kept to his New Year's resolution of going to the gym just once in his thirty-three years of life.

The social worker sniffed, tapping her foot. 'Mr Douglas, I'm certain you told me that you work on these premises as well as living on them.'

'Aye, I do.' He straightened up, unbolting the rusted gate and making his way up the garden path.

'Then it's quite impressive you still manage to be late.'

'I'm a man of many talents.' It was a joke, but if Linda found it funny, she showed no hint of it. He sighed and pulled his keys out of his pocket then unlocked the door. 'I'm awfully sorry, Linda. Time got away from me.'

'I worry sometimes that you don't take this seriously enough.'

Panic lanced through him at that, sobering him as he let her into the cottage. 'I do take this seriously. I always will. Arran is the most important thing to me.'

'Good.' She looked incongruous in his hallway, her pristine blazer a depressing shade of grey against the silly rainbow-hued pom-pom decorations Mac had made with Arran for last year's Pride and the gaudy, fleur-de-lis patterned wallpaper of Rosemire's previous resident gardener. 'Then you won't keep me waiting again, will you?'

'Of course not.' Mac rubbed the sweat off his neck and cringed as he caught a glimpse of himself in the mirror by the coat stand. His face had turned beetroot-red beneath his stubble, his auburn and grey-streaked hair matted and unkempt. Not quite the picture of an excellent, well-put-together foster father that he'd been going for when he'd got ready this morning, but it was hard to stay clean when he spent his days digging through soil. 'Can I offer you a drink?'

'Tea, please. One sugar, plenty of milk.'

Mac hid his shudder – weak tea disgusted him – behind a smile as he motioned to the sunken, tatty couch in the living room. He'd at least managed to clean up this time. On her last visit, Linda had turned up without warning at the very same time that Arran's rabbit, Pickle, had somehow gnawed through his hutch upstairs and decided to ransack the place. Needless to say, it hadn't ended well. 'Please take a seat. I'll be with you in a moment.'

'Lovely,' she said before getting comfortable on the old armchair by the unlit fireplace.

In the safety of the hallway, Mac let out a breath before heading into the kitchen to put the kettle on. As it boiled, he wiped himself down with an old tea towel and prayed desperately that his armpits were not as visibly wet as they felt. He grabbed a button-down shirt from a pile of unironed laundry to cover them, slinging it over his shoulder as he made the drinks. With trembling fingers, he emptied a packet of chocolate digestives onto the fanciest plate he could find – his mother's, which he had meant to give back last week after devouring a plate of her homemade shortbread.

And then he tried to figure out how to juggle all of these things in two hands. In the end, he threw on his wrinkled flannel shirt and placed the drinks and biscuits on a tray before carefully carrying them into the living room. Linda hadn't moved from the armchair, her dark eyes following him behind rectangular-framed glasses.

'Here we go.' Mac set the tray down on the coffee table and then sat on the sofa across from her, trying to figure out how to get back in her good books. Finally, he commented, 'You're looking well, Linda. Been away?'

'No. Went on the sunbed.' She helped herself to a digestive. 'Are we resorting to flattery now?'

Mac shrugged, smoothing down his hair. She sometimes made him feel like a criminal sitting handcuffed in an interrogation room, though he had done nothing wrong. 'Is it working?'

'Can't fault you for trying.' She drummed her fingers against the arm of her chair. 'Let's get down to business, shall we? How's Arran doing?'

Gulping, he laced his fingers together awkwardly. 'Brilliant.'

She raised a brow, as though unconvinced, then pulled out a notepad and pen. 'No outbursts?'

'I mean, he's a kid. All kids have outbursts, especially ones—' *Like us*, he had almost said. He trapped those words, found their replacement. 'Especially in situations like his. It's nothing I can't handle.'

'How frequently?'

'Not very. Once or twice a week.'

Linda's expression turned sympathetic, as though that was very frequent, which Mac found hard to believe. He remembered how difficult he'd been as a child, even when he'd been placed in the most loving home possible. Being exposed to so much abandonment and uncertainty wasn't something a kid could just forget once they were given a real family. Mac still felt the ache of his childhood even now, thirty years on.

Linda had told Mac of Arran's past when he'd started fostering him. She'd told him that he'd been found abandoned on a bus. His parents had come forward afterwards, two teenagers who couldn't handle it because the baby wouldn't stop crying. They'd never come back for him. Never tried again.

Mac's own story wasn't too dissimilar, though he'd been taken in by social services at the age of one, when his biological mother couldn't afford to feed him. Mac had apparently been living in a dank apartment in Glasgow, freezing in the winters and always hungry, until a neighbour had reported his mother to social services after seeing the state of things. Mac didn't hold it against his mum, but he had no interest in knowing her, either. She had never tried to turn it around, had never come back for him, and it had left him flitting between unfamiliar, intimidating homes with strangers for the next five years. A miserable time, and one he didn't like to think about. He was just glad he didn't remember – it was easier to detach himself that way. His story was exactly that: a story. He had no images or a face to pin to the words. It was terrible, but it wasn't him. Wasn't who he was now. He'd been chosen by a *real* mother, one he could trust, one that gave him a comfortable home and a new life. The reason he could be happy.

He wanted that for Arran. He never wanted Arran to wonder why he wasn't wanted, because he was. Mac wanted him with every fibre of his being.

'Look, I've been taking him to youth clubs and karate classes and all sorts. A few outbursts aren't a measure of anything important. We're dealing with them.' He furrowed his brows, heart pounding against his ribs now. It was like this every time. Like he was waiting for the moment that somebody ripped Arran away from him because he wasn't good enough, even though he knew Arran was his child in every way but a biological one. He knew it as certainly as he knew that bluebells only bloomed from April to May, and that he should expect rain after a sunny spell because he lived in Scotland. The knowledge was ingrained in him, not taught, but learned all the same. Arran was his.

'It's a wee cause for concern, Mac,' she said. Apparently, they were on first-name terms now, which only left more dread twisting in his stomach. 'We want Arran to be settled.'

'He's been in and out of foster homes for twelve years,' he replied through clenched teeth. 'It's going to take time.'

'I'm not attacking you. I'm not saying that you're doing anything wrong. But you've been fostering Arran for over a year now, and he still seems to be struggling. I just wonder if he might be better suited somewhere else.'

A flash of red burned behind his eyes, sending fire through his veins. *Somewhere else*. Not here. He couldn't imagine Arran not living here now. He couldn't imagine not dropping him off at school every morning and picking him up each afternoon, couldn't imagine not saying goodnight to him before he went to bed, or not buying him a new book every time he went into the village. 'Like where?'

Linda shrugged. 'Maybe with a larger family, where he'd have siblings to lean on.'

'Will all due respect, Linda, I've been in homes myself with other kids, and so has Arran. They can be OK, but they can also be lonelier and more difficult to live in than places like this. Arran isn't like other kids his age. He has a couple of friends at school and that's it. He doesn't like busy places much. He likes doing his own thing, having his own space. He has that here.'

'All right.' Linda raised a hand, and a twinge of regret flickered on her features. 'I understand what you're saying, I really do. I would just hate to think of Arran missing out. It's always going to be trial and error until we find the right fit. Most of our parents only foster their child for around a year.'

'Arran isn't missing out on anything.' Mac's fingers curled into his palms, jaw tensed to the point of aching. He'd built a home here for Arran. How could a virtual stranger walk into it and tell him that it wasn't enough? 'I would like to keep fostering him. Uprooting his life now, when he's just started high school . . . it wouldn't be right. Surely you can see that.'

She nodded, leaning back and sipping her tea. 'You feel very strongly about this. You do know that this is temporary?'

'Does it have to be?' He had never dared ask before, but he was angry now, and perhaps ready. 'What if I adopted him?'

She softened. 'I certainly wouldn't discourage you from trying. For what it's worth, I do think you're doing a good job. Exceptional in comparison to most single foster fathers, especially with a child like Arran. I just wouldn't like to give you false hope. If you do decide to pursue this, you need to make sure it's what's best for Arran, not you. And you need to be prepared for the possibility that it might not work out the way you hope.'

Mac glared at a stale crumb of toast on the coffee table. He hadn't expected it to be like this; that he'd want to keep Arran forever. He'd become a foster parent to help children who were like he was before he'd been adopted, to show them that love was out there. But Arran had made a home with Mac, and he didn't want to tear that home down now. He'd liked building it too much.

'Think about it.' Linda stood, leaving her still steaming, barely touched tea on the table by the biscuits. 'I'll schedule a meeting with you and Arran in the next couple of months. I should tell you that we do have a few couples looking to adopt an older child at the moment, though. If you're serious about this, now's the time to make a move.'

'Right.' He followed her into the hallway, his shoulders hunched, hands in his pockets. 'Thanks for stopping by.'

Sympathy lingered on Linda's features, and she patted Mac on the shoulder. 'Call me if you need anything.'

He agreed, waving goodbye as she left, though he knew he wouldn't call her. Afterwards, in the silence of the cottage, he watched his coffee go cold and wondered if he'd made a mistake in becoming a foster father. It could very well break him.

*

There was a three-legged cat on Mac's dinner table. It had been a long day, he could admit, but he couldn't remember ever adopting a cat, and certainly not one lacking a limb.

'Arran.' Mac's brows furrowed at the child, and then at the dark tabby, who seemed to regard him with just as much hostility, its gleaming green eyes slit and full of shadows.

'Yeah?' Arran didn't even look up, too busy feeding chunks of tuna to the cat. Mac wondered if he'd walked into a parallel universe. Ten minutes ago, he'd told Arran to do his homework. This was not homework. This was feeding a three-legged cat with a tin of tuna that had been left out for dinner.

'Arran,' he said again, just for good measure.

'What?'

'There's a cat on the table.'

'I know. Isn't he cute?'

'Arran.' Mac scraped his hand across his face then pinched the bridge of his nose as though it might keep his patience from escaping. 'Why is there a cat on the table?'

A shrug.

'Did it just appear out of thin air?' Mac grimaced when the cat started to lick itself, legs – well, *leg* – akimbo to reveal that the cat was most definitely male. He made a mental note to clean the surface down with anti-bacterial spray before they ate tonight.

'No. I found him outside. Didn't have a collar.'

'Right. Well, unfortunately, you can't just take amputee cats from the street and put them on my kitchen table. It probably belongs to someone.'

'Like who?' Arran narrowed his eyes in challenge. 'Nobody else lives here, and he can't be from the castle. Cats don't live in castles. Especially not three-legged ones.'

If this was a rule, it was news to Mac, and it seemed a bit of a blanket statement. He rolled his eyes and filled a saucepan with water before placing it on the unlit stove.

As he passed the cat, he was absolutely certain it hissed at him. 'They might do. Maybe he's a reincarnation of the first Lord Rosemire. You might be keeping him from his home.'

'If he lived in a castle, he wouldn't come here,' Arran argued – and Mac supposed he did have a point. The cottage was a little bit lacklustre in comparison to Rosemire Castle. Then again, nobody had lived in the castle in years, as far as he knew. It still had residential rooms for the owners, but Mac had never met them in his six years of working here and didn't wish to.

The Byrons had turfed out Mac's late grandfather from groundskeeping duties without warning after taking over sixty years ago, leaving the Douglas family in poverty for a little while. Mac had only decided to come back because Granddad had loved the gardens more than the castle itself, and he wanted to make sure they stayed as beautiful as they'd always been. It was Mac's way of remaining close to him, now that he was gone; a reminder of all those times he'd sat by his armchair as a child and listened to Granddad's stories of the castle. When he was in care, he'd never expected to have parents, let alone grandparents, but Granddad had treated Mac as though he had always been part of the family. As though he'd always been a Douglas.

'And ghosts don't possess cats,' Arran continued. 'They possess horses. Callum said so last week.'

'Well, if Callum said so . . .' Mac muttered under his breath. Arran believed just about everything his best friend said, once coming home with the theory that the world was contained within a polystyrene cup and the moon was just a hole poked in the top. *Callum said snow was just someone breaking up the polystyrene after putting us in the freezer.*

Mac no longer had the strength to argue. God only knew where the cat had come from, but judging by his glossy fur, it wasn't the street. He didn't belong here, no matter how much he made Arran happy. 'Look, the cat is welcome here tonight, if you keep him off surfaces we tend to eat on, but we need to put some posters up tomorrow on the way to school in case somebody's looking for him. We'll have to take him to the vets to see if he's microchipped, too. We don't want to be cat burglars.' He elbowed Arran and winked proudly. 'Get it? Cat burglars?'

'No,' Arran deadpanned, but begrudgingly removed the cat from the table and scattered the tuna on the floor instead.

'I was going to use that for dinner, by the way.'

'I know. I don't like tuna.'

'You liked it last week,' Mac grumbled, going back to pouring pasta into his pan of water. 'Go back to your homework, please. And get some old newspaper in case the cat decides to do its business in my house.'

'But Gherkin is hungry,' groused Arran, his shoulders sagging dramatically. He was well on his way to adolescent mood swings.

'Gherkin?' Mac repeated, amused, turning on the stove. *Gherkin* didn't look hungry. In fact, the soft belly under his fur almost put Mac's to shame. Further proof that somebody was probably missing him. 'What will Pickle say about this, anyway? He might not like cats.'

Another shrug. That was the conversation over, then, Mac supposed. Overpowered by a twelve-year-old and a cat in his own house. If Linda truly thought Arran didn't want to be here, she didn't know him at all.

Perhaps that was why Mac let Arran keep the cat for the night, pretending not to notice him feeding it pasta under the table when he thought Mac wasn't looking. In the end, he just wanted Arran to be happy. Even if that meant possibly abducting a cat in the process.

Chapter Three

Jessamine realised that her loneliness was sending her a little bit barmy at around the same time she started obsessing over owls. The daily birds-of-prey demonstration at lunchtime had just ended, the first one she'd had the time to attend since her arrival four days ago, and she hung back to admire the birds a little bit longer while the rest of the crowds dispersed. The demonstrator – Lauren, she'd introduced herself as at the beginning of the show – smiled wryly at Jessamine now, a barn owl still perched on her gloved arm. Funny that so many people worked here, in the castle where Jessamine now lived, and yet she knew none of them. She didn't even know if *they* knew her. They were so separated by the old walls, with the living quarters completely roped off from the visitor's exhibitions, that she sometimes forgot the castle was open to the public. As far as she knew, that had been the deal when the Byrons had bought it sixty years ago. Deemed an important historical site and celebrated as the home of the legendary Clan Rosemire, the castle was protected by the Scottish Castles Association, meaning only the residential areas belonged to her family.

'Would you like to hold him?' Lauren asked, extending her arm steadily. The owl only stared blankly, its feathers ruffling in the light breeze.

'Is that OK?' Jessamine couldn't help but step forward, eager. She'd wanted to volunteer earlier, but the children had been so excited that she hadn't dared ruin their moment. Besides, she was doing her best to blend in while she still could.

'Of course, ma'am.' A small smile graced Lauren's lips, and then her eyes widened. 'Is that the right way of addressing you, or is it "Your Highness"?'

Though disappointed, Jessamine pasted on her well-practised, polite smile – the one Mother had probably taught her to do well before she could walk. 'Definitely not. Just Jessamine is fine. I'm on holiday after all,' she whispered. 'Keeping a low profile at the moment.'

'Understood.' Lauren worried at her lip as though it was some sort of trick. 'You'll want a glove, ma'am . . . Jessamine, sorry.'

Warily, Jessamine took one from the basket beside Lauren, feeling as though she was being watched by the other birds in their cages. It was almost like she was at some sort of event again, only she found the beady eagle's eyes a little bit less judgemental than her usual peers'. The peregrine falcon *did* have a look of her mother, though: beak set in disapproval and feathers puffed up importantly.

The worn leather glove was warm and fleecy. Trying not to imagine all the other hands that had used it before hers, she wiggled her fingers and extended her arm. She noticed the barn owl hadn't been clipped to a lead like the other birds. 'Hasn't it ever tried to fly away?'

Lauren smirked. 'He lives in a castle. Would you?'

She had, more than once, back on her childhood estate, a grand manor house in Cheshire, but she didn't dare admit it.

'No, he's been here a very long time and has had plenty of training. He's a good boy.' Lauren stroked the owl's snowy chest lovingly before offering him out again.

Jessamine held her breath as the owl stepped onto her wrist. She laughed at the strange weight, the pressure and honour of being a sturdy perch. 'Does he have a name?'

'Bartholomew, the barn owl. You can stroke him, if you'd like. Just be very gentle.'

Jessamine did, slowly running her finger down the owl's warm, soft breast with instinctive wariness. It was a bit like

21

stroking Rufus, only Rufus did not possess the intimidating ability to stretch his wings and fly away at any moment. If anything, his three-leggedness made him much slower than most cats, meaning she could hold him hostage whenever she needed a cuddle. 'You're very cute, Bartholomew. It's nice to meet you.'

Lauren laughed. 'The pleasure is all his, I'm sure. He's in the company of a countess and doesn't even know it.'

Another pang of something unpleasant shot through Jessamine, her smile faltering no matter how she tried to keep it stapled there. 'I'm helping to plan for the spring fete in a few weeks, actually. I don't suppose you'd be willing to put on a few shows throughout the day?'

'Of course. I'd love to!' Lauren looked as though she truly meant it, blinking keenly. 'Will it be held here as usual?'

'Yes, the grounds will be full of stalls and fairground rides. Such beautiful gardens deserve to be used, after all. We wanted to raise funds for a few local charities, so they'll be taking part, too.' It was the least Jessamine could do: open her space to local charities and give them a spotlight. Most of her events were smaller, based in the city, so she was excited to work with new charities and hopefully give the village a nice weekend. The fete was held every year according to the groundskeeper, Bill, but this year, since the castle was being lived in for once, she had the opportunity to plan with Fort Aileen's little village committee and involve her own charities. She just hoped she could still hide at least until then.

'Sounds great. I'll be there.'

'Thank you, Lauren.' Though her manners had been taught, Jessamine's appreciation was sincere. She knew what she was asking, having castle workers volunteer more hours. She hadn't even ventured into the village just across the bridge to meet Fort Aileen's community, yet she was already asking things of them.

'My mum has been gushing about you non-stop since I told

her you were here. She's obsessed with royals and nobility and all that.' Lauren's cheeks pinkened, and she tucked a wiry strand of hair behind her ears. 'Sorry. I hope I'm not being rude. I've never met a countess before.'

Jessamine could feel a hot rash prickling along her neck. All these years, and she still felt uncomfortable in her own skin whenever her title was brought up. 'You should bring her to the fete. I'd love to meet her.'

'You wouldn't mind?'

Jessamine opened her mouth to say no, she wouldn't mind at all, but the words were silenced by a shrill call.

'Mrs Townsend!'

She startled, and the jolt caused Bartholomew to flap his wings. Letting out an unladylike screech, Jessamine ducked her head against the attack of feathers, forgetting that the owl was still perched on her arm.

'Oh, no!' Lauren shouted, her hands clapping over her mouth, and then Jessamine could no longer feel the pressure of talons gripping her glove. Bartholomew flew away in the direction of the gardens, a blot of white and brown against the grey and green landscape.

Jessamine didn't know what to do. She blew her ruffled fringe from her face, panic wrenching through her as she lost sight of the owl. Panic, and then anger. She whipped around and glared at Petra, whose loud voice had scared her in the first place.

'Dear me.' Petra tugged at the hem of her blazer as though *she* was the one dishevelled from the owl's panic. 'That was quite unexpected.'

Jessamine swallowed down a scoff. 'Maybe it's time we discussed using *inside* voices more often, Petra.'

'Apologies, Mrs Townsend. I didn't expect to find you with an owl on your arm.' Petra pursed her lips as though Jessamine was the one at fault. 'I only came out to tell you that your mother is planning a—'

'My mother can wait! We have an owl on the loose!'

'He shouldn't go too far.' Lauren was already stumbling towards the gardens, her brow furrowed with worry. From her pocket, she offered Jessamine a lead and kept one for herself. 'Let's just find him quickly. If I don't get him back, I'm in serious trouble.'

Jessamine nodded. 'I'll take the right side of the gardens.'

'But, Mrs Townsend—'

'For Christ's sake, not now, Petra! Don't you have meetings to schedule?' she hissed in annoyance. Though Petra couldn't help having a voice fit to scare an owl, Jessamine was at her wits' end. She couldn't even stroke a bloody bird without being interrupted to arrange an event or take a phone call or whatnot, and it was quickly growing tiring. Not to mention the constant reminder of her divorce and the ugliness that had followed. She was supposed to be taking a break from it all, so why Mother had insisted Petra trail along was beyond her.

Jessamine raced off before Petra could reply, still wearing the glove in case Bartholomew decided to return to her arm. She was just glad the visitors didn't seem to recognise her as she weaved through them by the front entrance. If it got back to her mother – or, worse, the gossip magazines – that the Countess of Cheshire had been spotted barrelling her way through the gardens of Rosemire in search of a barn owl, she would be made a laughing stock. Again.

And Jessamine was a little bit tired of being a laughing stock.

Mac rattled the rusted, padlocked gate in another futile attempt to pry it open. Frustration welled in him, though he had long since stopped believing the thing would ever budge. Every week, he tried to fight his way into the secret garden behind the ivy-and-vine infested bars. Every week, he failed. He'd even brought a hammer once to try to bash the padlock off, but years – decades, even – of rain and snow and hail and sunshine had welded the metal. He needed a key, and nobody he spoke to seemed to know where it was.

Of course, any sane person would have admitted defeat, but the sight of lifeless vegetation and overgrown, wilting shrubbery wasn't something Mac could accept. He wanted to fix it, wanted to bring colour to a garden hidden behind old stone walls and wrought iron. He could imagine clearing away the dead foliage and planting an apple tree, or perhaps a vegetable patch for visitors to enjoy. There was plenty of room for benches and picnic tables. It could be beautiful. He could *make* it beautiful.

He stepped back and scratched his unshaven stubble, his hands red and raw from gripping ruined metal so tightly. He was so distracted that he barely acknowledged the sound of shushing behind him at first. Then a voice whispered, 'Don't move,' and he frowned, whipping around on his heel.

The pretty, tulip-flattening tour guide he'd run into yesterday stood behind him, her arms raised as though pleading for mercy. She held some sort of blue rope.

'What?' Mac grunted, and then felt guilty for being so rude – again. He just despised tour guides. Especially the seasonal ones who had no respect for his bloody flowers. It was a little early in the year still, with Easter only just having passed, but in summer, Fort Aileen flooded with students and tourists who knew nothing about the history of the castle, nor cared. They left their litter all over the cobbled shopping streets and let their dogs and kids run free all over Mac's gardens. After years of watching his home be damaged, knowing his parents and grandparents had done just the same, he no longer had the patience for new, temporary faces.

'Quiet!' the tour guide scolded sharply, and then pointed at something above Mac. 'Come here and move slowly, otherwise you'll scare him off.'

Mac did, taking a step towards the tour guide, though he had no idea what was happening. It resulted in a jolt of pain cracking through his nose and rolling down his face. He'd stood on the bottom of the sweeping brush he'd been using to clear blossom from the paths with, and the wooden pole had swung into his head.

'Jesus fuck!' he thundered, clutching his nose as his eyes started tearing.

'No!'

Something fluttered behind Mac – and then swooped so closely over his head that he had to duck. He only made it out as it flew away into the pale blue April sky: a barn owl. It disappeared behind the large, twisted oak, where leaves were slowly blooming on the branches again.

'Splendid!' The tour guide's hands slapped to her sides, her features crumpled as though she had been the one who had come head-to-head with a bloody brush. 'You frightened him off again! Do you know how long I've been looking for him?'

Mac rubbed the swollen bridge of his nose a final time. 'Oh, well I do apologise, love. I wasn't aware there was a bloody barn owl behind me, was I?'

'I told you to move slowly!' She crossed her arms, her expression tight, stubborn, irritating. Mac had never known somebody so impossibly argumentative before – except maybe Arran.

'And I did until I stepped on a brush!' He kicked it away, the rough bristles scraping against concrete. His face was still throbbing, but for the sake of his pride he refused to acknowledge it. He had a feeling the tour guide would only delight in his pain.

'Did you see where it went?'

He shook his head. 'Somewhere behind the oak, I think.' Only then did the peculiarity of the situation dawn on him, and he drew his brows together. 'Why on earth are you chasing an owl?'

She was already turning her back to him, heading in the same direction as the owl had a few moments ago. 'I don't have time for this. Are you going to help me find him or not?'

'*Not*,' he snapped.

It was a mistake. When she turned to face him again, her face was thunder, her bright blue eyes turning grey and stormy. He almost wanted to shrink away, but with the mood he was in now, that wasn't going to happen. Instead, he straightened his spine, glaring, waiting.

'I beg your pardon?' she said, voice low. '*You're* the one who scared him away. It's the least you can do!'

'Are you sure about that, love?' His mouth curled into a smirk that felt wrong, oily, bitter, but he couldn't help it. She was driving him up the wall, causing problems for him twice in as many days. 'If I were an owl, I'd be trying to get as far away from you as possible, too.'

'You . . .' Stuttering, she stepped closer to him, jabbing her gloved finger into his shoulder firmly. He swayed on his heel, fiery humour igniting in his belly at the way her face turned red. He'd been pissed off before, but now she was on his level, he couldn't help but enjoy it.

'Hmm?' he asked expectantly. 'I'm what?'

'*You*' – another jab to his shoulder – 'are a supreme tosser.' She smiled proudly at her insult, and Mac had to trap a laugh.

Still, a twinge of discomfort shot through him. *Was* he being a tosser? He'd been a little bit brusque with her, but it felt justified at the time. Now he wasn't sure, and he wasn't in the habit of being this . . . *this*. He didn't know what the word was . . . Irritated, mostly, but in a little bit of an enjoyable way. Especially, since he was annoying her, too.

'I'm wounded.' He feigned nonchalance, clutching the left side of his chest. 'Really. Shouldn't you be off finding your escapee?'

She pursed her lips, nostrils flaring, but didn't move away. This close, he could smell her flowery perfume, feel her warmth, see where her ashy hair was intercepted by streaks of buttery blonde. It made him forget to be angry or arrogant or teasing. It made him forget to be anything at all.

Until she put space between them again, tugging on the hem of her blouse and clearing her throat. 'You're going to help me.' It wasn't a question anymore. And then: 'Please. I don't think Lauren will forgive me if I don't get him back.'

He understood, then. The owl was from the birds-of-prey annexe behind the castle. He took Arran to the demonstrations there almost every weekend and they knew Lauren well, now. He should have put it together sooner, what with the fact the tour guide wore one of the thick, brown gloves from Lauren's basket.

And the tour guide was right. He couldn't *not* help her, not when one of the castle's owls was missing. It seemed his flowers weren't the only thing she had wrecked this week.

'Lead the way,' he muttered finally. Satisfaction smoothed her expression, and then he was following her back through the gardens towards the giant oak. 'How did you lose it, anyway?'

'My a . . .' she faltered – or maybe her voice wasn't carrying to him with her back turned. 'He was on my arm, and something startled him.'

'Must have been something big to spook a bird of prey,' Mac noted, lengthening his strides until he was at her side. Most of the owls were used to being surrounded by large crowds of excited, screaming children hyped up on ice cream.

The tour guide only narrowed her eyes as she lifted her chin to the tree branches above them. Mac did the same but saw no sign of the owl. 'Are you sure it went this way?'

'Don't know. I was a wee bit busy being hit by a brush.'

A poorly stifled snort fell from her nose, which wrinkled in a way that made him want to laugh, too. Something else distracted him, though. Across the gardens, another tour was going on, with an older guide. 'Listen, I don't suppose you know anything about that gated-off garden back there, do you?'

'The one you were trying to break into, you mean?' She flashed him a knowing look. 'No. Why would I?'

Disappointment sank into his gut. The more he was told no, the more desperately he wanted to get into that garden. 'Thought knowing things was kind of your job. You wouldn't make a very good tour guide otherwise.'

'Right . . .' she agreed, worrying at her plump bottom lip. 'Well, I've never guided visitors into the garden. Sorry. Why were you trying to get in?'

He shrugged, scratching the back of his neck in an attempt to hide an embarrassed flush. 'Curiosity. It's a shame to waste a nice wee area. I'd like to work on it; make it pretty for visitors. Nobody seems to have the key, though.'

'I'll ask around.'

The offer took Mac aback, and he stopped in his tracks. 'Would you?'

She nodded as though it was nothing. 'There must be a key somewhere, mustn't there?'

'Cheers. I . . . er . . . appreciate that.' It only just occurred to him that, though he'd told her his name, she'd rushed off before he could ask hers. 'What's your name?'

'Oh, it's Jessa—' she clamped down on her lip again, brushing her fringe out of her eyes. 'It's Jess.'

'Jess.' He shoved his grubby hands in his pockets a little awkwardly. A moment ago, they'd been at one another's throats, and now they were strolling through the gardens, exchanging names. He couldn't keep up. 'Mine's Mac.'

'Yes, you told me. I'd say it's nice to meet you, but . . .'

He chuckled. 'Aye, likewise. We're not off to the best of starts, are we?'

She shook her head, amusement dancing in her eyes.

The sound of a plane flying overhead brought his attention back to the skies. A metal tail glinting against the sun disappeared behind the oak's leaves as they reached it.

And there, perched on a bronze statue of Lord Gaven John Rosemire, the fifth and last Rosemire heir . . . was the barn owl.

He stilled, his fingers curling around Jess's wrist quickly. Her skin was soft, warm, delicate. He tried not to notice the slight stir in his gut, a creature waking from a long, long slumber, as he pointed to the statue, depicting a hard-faced, square-jawed, muscular man wearing a kilt. Mac had often chased off pigeons sitting on Rosemire's head. It somehow always fell to Mac to clean up their droppings.

'Oh, thank God.' She let loose a relieved breath, preparing the lead. 'What do I do now?'

'Can't say I'm much of an owl expert myself. I could go and find Lauren.'

'What if he flies off again?'

The owl sat with a languid expression, his dark eyes a little too eerie and watchful for Mac's liking. Arran, on the other hand, would love him. In fact, he'd be taken in as another stray if Mac wasn't careful.

'What do owls eat? Grass?' Mac asked.

'Mice.'

There went that idea, then. He was beginning to like the owl less and less, and not just because of his gross dietary habits. He reminded Mac of a feathery Thomas the Tank Engine, with a flat face and cylindrical body. 'Don't suppose you have any lying around, then?'

'Not at the moment, no.' Her eyes pierced into him, icy and peeved. 'Maybe if I just . . .' She outstretched the lead and took slow, cautious steps towards the owl. Mac held his breath. 'Bartholomew,' she whispered. 'It's me, your old buddy. Be a dear and hop back onto my arm so I cannot be blamed for your disappearance. There's a good boy. Being free is overrated anyway.'

The corner of Mac's mouth pulled with a smirk. 'I didn't know you were an animal whisperer.'

'Not helping,' she ground out. But it might have been,

actually, because when Jess got close enough to come face to face with Lord Rosemire's bare nipple – apparently old Scottish nobles did not own shirts – Bartholomew hopped onto her gloved hand. Mac trapped a cheer, afraid anything might scare the owl again. Before it could take off, she clipped the lead to the black anklet around its feet.

'All right,' she said. 'Phew. Good boy. Now we just have to walk back through miles and miles of garden paths. It's fine. We can do that.'

'Aye, "paths" being the key word. Meaning, not my flowers,' Mac reminded Jess as she stepped onto a patch of daisy-speckled grass.

She risked sending a glare over her shoulder before taking slow and steady steps back onto the smooth flagstones.

He followed her towards the castle, rounding the next corner and falling onto the main walkway. It was lined with a few, sparse cherry-blossom trees, and a large fountain dripped sadly, fallen pink blossom floating on the water's surface. A few visitors were enjoying picnics on the lip of the fountain, and children gasped and pointed when they saw Bartholomew perched on Jess's arm.

'*Shh*. Don't scare him off,' Jess whispered, her voice kind now. He could imagine her giving them tours, all animated and engaging as she told them stories about the castle, and another faint flutter rose in Mac's belly. It had been a long time since it had last roused, so he couldn't be sure . . . but it felt an awful lot like attraction. Which was impossible and silly, of course, since they'd been bickering like enemies five minutes ago. Besides, Mac didn't have time for all . . . *that*. He had Arran to think of. He'd said goodbye to his dating life a long time ago, to focus on being a father.

They managed to survive until the castle's looming bricks came into view, the Scottish flag flapping against the breeze on the highest turret. Lauren waited by the portcullis, and she sagged with relief when she saw them.

'You found him.' She took Bartholomew gently, petting

his chest and leading him back towards the birds-of-prey annexe around the corner. 'Where was he?'

'Mac found him, actually,' Jess replied. 'He was on a statue.'

'Keeping our Lord Rosemire company,' Mac added.

'Well, thank you, both.' Lauren guided them inside, where an array of large falcons and hawks watched them from behind glass shelters. Bartholomew soon joined them in the corner, looking quite pleased with himself when he sat on his branch.

'I'm terribly sorry for letting him go,' Jess said, pulling off her glove and leaving it on the side. 'Honestly, I'm so embarrassed.'

'Oh, you needn't be, ma'am.' Lauren batted her hand, detaching him from the lead before shutting the cage. 'I'm just glad we found him.'

Mac frowned. 'What's this "ma'am" business about? Is there some weird castle-worker hierarchy happening now?'

The women shared a strange glance before Lauren answered, 'Oh, no, I'm just . . . trying out a new thing.' She did a curtsy, bowing her head. 'Sir. Ma'am. I thought it would make the kids feel like they're in a real castle. *Anyway*,' she finished. 'I need to prepare for the three o'clock display. I'll see you both later.'

'Yes, of course.' Jess ushered a bewildered Mac forward, and he waved Lauren goodbye before they both stepped outside again.

'Phew.' He laughed, wiping his forehead dramatically. 'Close call, eh?'

'Too close,' Jess agreed. Her gaze seemed to soften as it found his. 'Oh, gosh. A bruise is coming out.' She took his chin in her hands to tilt his head down, fingertips pressing lightly into his skin. The sudden contact stole his breath. 'I didn't realise you'd actually got hurt.'

He was so unused to being fussed over that it was instinct to pull away, replacing her delicate fingers with his rough ones. He regretted it instantly, and not just because her hands were warmer, softer. The bones around his nose were slightly tender and he winced. 'It's fine. Nothing a bit of ice won't fix.'

'It's not broken, is it?'

'Nah.' He hoped not, anyway. A crooked nose wouldn't make him much more attractive.

Concern still wrinkled her forehead. 'Maybe you should get checked out . . . just to be sure . . .'

'Not necessary, honestly,' he reassured. 'I'm fine. I'll see you later.'

'Wait. Mac.' Her voice kept his feet planted in front of her. She put her hands on her hips; the button of her blazer slipped undone to reveal a frilly, silk blouse beneath. He tried not to notice her curves, tried not to let himself like them. 'I must apologise for earlier. I haven't been acting very much like myself, and I feel terrible that you seem to keep bearing the brunt of that.'

The apology was just as surprising as everything else that had happened today. He couldn't help but smile – sincerely now, rather than teasing. 'No apology needed. You've not caught me in the best of moods, either. I'm not usually a tosser, as you put it. Or I try not to be, at least.'

There was a pause between them, and it felt important enough that Mac was almost afraid to breathe and break it. Finally, her cheeks swelled with a forgiving grin. 'Well, thank you for helping me find Bartholomew.'

'No worries. I should be getting back to work, though.'

'OK. Goodbye, then.'

He tipped his head, reluctant, somehow, to leave her. But he forced himself away, ignoring the strange fizzing in his belly. She was a pretty lass – gorgeous, actually – but it wasn't as though he could ask her out for coffee. She was a pain in the arse, a tour guide, an invader, and he had a twenty-four-seven job in the form of a moody twelve-year-old.

Still, he worked a little bit closer to the castle that afternoon just in case he caught another glimpse of her. Not that he wanted to, of course. He was just . . . curious.

So he told himself, anyway.

Chapter Four

'Did you say you had a letter about a trip in your bag?' Mac called from the living room, grimacing when he picked up Arran's grubby backpack. God only knew what he'd been doing with it – skidding down mudslides, by the looks of it. He pulled out the Marvel-themed flask to wash out later and then waited for Arran's reply. He knew better than to root through his bag without permission.

'Yeah,' was all Arran said, his voice floating in from the kitchen.

'Right. Can I check it, then?'

'Yep.'

'Don't overwhelm me with all this conversation,' Mac muttered under his breath, before unzipping the backpack. It was full of all sorts, from tattered workbooks to broken earphones to . . . Was that a dead leaf? He threw it out with a shake of his head and grabbed a crumpled wad of papers at the very bottom of the bag, unfolding the first one he came to.

It wasn't a letter. It was the missing-cat posters they'd made and printed together at the library this morning. The ones Arran had said he'd hand out and post around the village with his friends on his way home from school.

Frustration blazed through him, only fuelled by Gherkin's appearance from under the couch. He picked the cat up and kept him under his arm, grasping the posters with his free hand. Gherkin meowed in protest, his tail wafting against Mac's elbow as he marched into the kitchen, where Arran was playing Minecraft on his tablet. He didn't bother to look up, and Mac could only pause in the doorway, hesitant. He had to do this carefully, no matter how disappointed he was that Arran had lied to him.

'Can you switch that off a minute, kiddo?' he began finally, closing the door and letting Gherkin roam free.

Arran rolled his eyes and continued tapping on the screen. 'I'm in the middle of something important.'

'Now, please,' Mac ordered, voice firmer than he'd usually dare.

With a belligerent sigh, Arran turned the tablet off and slammed it on the table, glaring at Mac. Mac pursed his lips and sat across from him, watching Arran carefully as he placed the missing posters on the table between them.

Arran showed no sign of guilt. He only blinked and crossed his arms.

'I'm going to give you a chance to be honest with me,' Mac said carefully. 'This morning, when I asked you to distribute the missing-cat posters outside of school, did you do it?'

'Yeah.'

Mac's nostrils flared impatiently. 'Interesting. Would you like to explain why these posters were crumpled in the bottom of your bag, then?'

Arran shrugged.

Mac tapped the table with the fleshy tips of his fingers, where flecks of mud and grass stains still – and always – lingered. 'I don't want to be upset with you, Arran. Please don't give me a reason to be.'

Nothing. The kid had a poker face grown men would envy, Mac included.

He swallowed, rolling his tongue across his slightly crooked teeth as he debated his next move. It was times like these he felt out of his depth. If he shouted, he was just encouraging Arran to get angry and push him away. If he was too kind, too understanding, Arran would think his behaviour was acceptable. He aimed for some sort of middle-ground and hoped it would do.

'Right, well, I'm going to assume, then, that you lied to

me so that nobody would contact us and we'd be able to keep the cat. Am I warm?'

Blank stare.

'That's very deceitful of you, Arran. I'm disappointed.' Gherkin mewed by Mac's feet as though agreeing. 'Lying to me to have things your way isn't acceptable. Am I being clear?'

'I just want to keep him!' Arran argued finally, tugging on his pale brown curls. 'He found me, so why shouldn't I?'

Mac couldn't help but soften. 'Because he's not yours to keep, bud. Somebody is searching for their cat. Imagine how sad you'd be if somebody took Pickle from you just because they wanted to and made sure you'd never find him again.'

Arran's lower lip jutted at that, though he said nothing.

'It's time to find his owner. I want you to go and put a couple of posters up around the castle while it's still light, and then tomorrow we'll both go into the village to do the rest.'

'No!' Arran swept the posters off the table, causing Gherkin to scuttle away.

'Arran—' Mac began, but tears poured down Arran's face, and no end to the sentence came. He didn't have time to find one, either, as Arran stormed out, slamming the back door behind him. Mac knew better than to chase after him. He'd come back when he was ready, but following him now would only make things worse.

Mac watched Arran disappear from the kitchen window then bowed his head, exhaustion setting in. For just a moment, a kernel of doubt weighed in his stomach, and he wondered if Linda had been right yesterday. What if Mac wasn't the right person to take care of Arran? Maybe he needed more. Somebody who would buy him a bloody cat of his own and calm him down before the tantrums started.

He pushed the doubt away, letting it sink lower and lower until it was gone. Mac wasn't perfect, but he wasn't giving up. They'd find a way to manage together.

Claws tugging at the bottom of his jeans tore his attention

away, and he looked down to find Gherkin at his ankles, his green eyes round as though full of questions.

Mac sighed again and picked up the cat, scratching him under his black, whiskered chin. 'What are we going tae do, aye, Gherkin?'

Gherkin only meowed, as though saying, *You're on your own, mate*.

Jessamine had not climbed down a garden trellis since her teens, and she soon realised she was not quite as agile now that she was in her late twenties. Perhaps locking herself out on the balcony of the castle's second storey had been a little bit overdramatic, too, but dear lord, she just wanted to *breathe*. Wherever she turned, Petra was there. Always. This was supposed to be a break, and yet her personal assistant always found new work for her to do. Not to mention she hadn't had her Rufus cuddles today, as though not even he was willing to put up with her anymore.

So, yes, she'd crawled from the balcony like some sort of modern-day Juliet with no Romeo in sight, her thighs jiggling and hands shaking. Her palms were torn with cuts by the time she reached the ground, and she had to wave awkwardly at the man who served ice creams in his truck outside the castle. He was in the middle of putting away his awning, mouth agape in shock. She was just glad she'd worn trousers.

She didn't even know where she was going, but she crossed the bridge for the first time since arriving in Fort Aileen, the smell of rich coffee from the Rosemire tea room greeting her at the other end. The village beyond was nothing more than old gables, chimneys, and lights at the bottom of a hill that Jessamine was too afraid to venture down.

Tea. That's what she needed. Tea fixed everything.

Without Petra following at her heels, Jessamine felt bare; exposed. Would people recognise her? But when she walked in, a bell tinkling above the door, nobody looked up from their drinks or conversations. She sucked in a deep breath, joined the queue – and felt as though she was plummeting. One of the customers had their nose stuck into the newest issue of *Splendour*. Robert grinned at her from the glossy front page, his features as oily as his dark, gelled hair. Jessamine's vengeful face glowered in a small box in the corner, grainy and blurred and captioned: *Lady Byron, the Bunny Boiler?* She knew when it had been taken. The moment she'd thrown the champagne in Robert's face. The moment she'd realised that even after the divorce, she couldn't escape his snide, ridiculous ways of demeaning her. The article's headline was, *The truth about Sir Robert Townsend and Lady Jessamine Byron's short-lived marriage. Meltdowns, manipulation, and more.*

A lump formed in her throat. She tore her gaze away, skin stinging as though she'd been slapped. The customer hadn't looked up; they couldn't have recognised her. But still. It was haunting her, even here. She couldn't escape the labels Robert had thrust on her or the implications that Emily Kingsley had drawn from them in her cruel article.

Jessamine tried to distract herself by browsing the tea-room menu, which was written messily on a chalkboard. They had an array of herbal teas listed, as well as typical coffees, but her focus was drawn to the hot chocolate. She hadn't had hot chocolate since childhood, her mother eradicating it from her carefully monitored diet when her puppy fat didn't disappear with adolescence. It still hadn't, mind – a fact Philippa Byron despised. Robert had liked to drop the occasional hint for her to lose weight, too. Jessamine had grown to love her curves, anyway, having discovered beautiful, high-end, plus-size clothing brands and learning from her stylists in London how to find outfits that would flatter her shape.

It felt like a small rebellion, then, when the elderly man behind the counter asked for her order and Jessamine replied with, 'Could I have a hot chocolate, please?'

A nod. 'Whipped cream? Marshmallows?'

She brightened, desperate to drown her sorrows in a sugar fix. 'Ooh, yes please.'

'Anything else?' The questions were grumbled, but she pretended not to notice.

She browsed the display of cakes and biscuits, her mouth watering. 'I'll have a slice of Victoria sponge cake.'

He put the numbers into the till with slow, arthritic fingers, and only then did Jessamine realise that she hadn't brought her purse. *Idiot.*

'Five pound twenty.'

'Oh.' Flustered, Jessamine searched her pockets as though she might have money hiding somewhere she didn't know about. 'Oh, crumbs. I'm sorry. I seem to have—'

'Don't you know who she is, Hamish?' someone called from behind her. Jessamine turned, her cheeks aflame, to find a silver-haired woman pointing at her. 'That's the Countess of Cheshire. She's here living at Rosemire. My Lauren told me all about it.'

Jessamine's heart thundered against her ribcage, but she forced an amiable smile. The person reading the magazine still didn't look up, thank goodness. Hopefully, they were too invested in the other cheap stories-slash-lies featured in the issue, such as the Earl of So-and-So's hair transplant and Baroness Whatshername's secret affair with her dressmaker.

'You're Lauren's mother?' She remembered Lauren claiming that her mum had been 'gushing' about Jessamine, and this woman had the same dark eyes as the castle's birds-of-prey demonstrator.

The woman gasped, her glasses slipping across the bent bridge of her nose. 'She knows who I am, Margaret,' she said, nudging the woman she sat with.

'Bloody hell, Elsie! You're famous!' said Margaret, squinting through round lenses at Jessamine.

'I don't care if she's the Queen of Sheba. It's five pound twenty,' the grumpy man behind the counter said – Hamish, she assumed.

Jessamine winced. 'On second thoughts, I think I'll cancel that order, Hamish. I seem to have left my purse at home.'

'A countess, she says,' Hamish muttered to the group of customers behind her. 'She doesn't even have any money. If she's a countess, then I'm Sean bloody Connery.'

Elsie gave a scandalised tut, her silver curls bouncing. 'Oh, Hamish, do take a day off from being a moody old sod and give us a smile!'

Now almost everybody in the tea room was watching, and Jessamine wished she could shrink beneath one of the tables.

'Really, it's fine.' She wasn't sure who she was trying to reassure anymore.

Margaret rolled her eyes and stood up with her purse, almost tripping over a chair leg as she joined Jessamine at the counter. 'Here.' With a sniff, she threw a five-pound note and a one-pound coin onto the counter. 'Keep the change – a tip for such charming customer service.'

Mortified, Jessamine could only fight the urge to cover her face in her hands. 'Really, Margaret, that's not necessary. Thank you, but—'

Margaret batted her away with a liver-spotted hand. 'Nonsense, Miss Lady Countess Rosemire, Your Excellency. It's my treat. And never mind what those awful newspapers are saying. You're a lovely young woman.'

Jessamine wanted to argue, wanted to push the money back into the sweet old lady's hand, but she couldn't stand another moment of being under so much scrutiny. Never mind it was the first time anyone had taken her side since the divorce. Defeated and on the brink of tears, she made to thank Margaret again, but—

'Hang on just a minute. You're not one of those *Byrons*, are you?' Hamish asked. He spat her surname like it was venom on his tongue. Jessamine didn't know what he could possibly have against her family.

'Don't start on all that now. Let sleeping dogs lie, will you? The countess wasn't even born when her family bought Rosemire, for heaven's sake.' Margaret was already shuffling back to her table, batting him away.

Hamish shot Jessamine daggers above the cake counter. '*I* was.' He cut her a meagre slice and set it roughly onto a plate, shoving it at her without care.

'Er . . . could I please have it to go?' Jessamine didn't dare ask why Hamish held so much contempt for her family. She wasn't sure she wanted to know. In fact, she wanted to get out of the tea room as quickly as possible. If Margaret hadn't paid for her order, she would have left it on the counter and run away, never to return.

She swore that Hamish growled before transferring the cake to a brown paper bag. She'd be lucky if it was anything but crumbs at this rate. The hot-chocolate machine rumbled with the same ferocity as Hamish before he finally served it in a takeaway cup.

'Will that be all, m'lady? Have I to fan you and feed you while you sit on a throne, too?' He bowed mockingly.

Jessamine was beginning to quite dislike him. Still, she pretended that his joke was funny and flashed him a toothy smile. 'That won't be necessary today. Perhaps next time. Thank you, Hamish.'

She thanked Margaret again on the way out and said goodbye to Elsie, Robert's wobbly magazine portrait following her the entire time. 'And . . . if you could just maybe keep this quiet. I'm on holiday, you see. It's been a hard year.'

'Oh, of course! We shan't tell a soul!' Elsie said. 'You take care of yourself, now.'

Jessamine forced another appreciative grin then spilt outside and tried not to fall apart from both humiliation and anger.

Coming here had been a mistake. She couldn't run away from who she was. She was beginning to realise that now.

*

Jessamine wasn't ready to go back to the castle. Instead, she stayed on the other side of the bridge, finding a cluster of rocks to perch on that looked out over Loch Leannan. The sun sank behind the towering castle turrets, the wispy, pink clouds and amber sky reflected in the still water. It had been a while since Jessamine had found time to watch the day end, and, clutching her hot chocolate in her hands to keep warm, she sucked in the fresh, loamy air until her lungs ached.

She was alone. The thought hit her all at once, and she didn't know whether it was a blessing or a curse. She was alone, but she was always alone. She was alone, but she was never alone. Petra was always there, asking things of her. Her mother was always on the phone, demanding she do this and that. The current bout of silent treatment was the most peace she'd ever had. People bought her coffee and called her 'Your Excellence' as though she were a royal. But there was nobody to talk to, nobody who asked her how her day was, nobody she could tell about what had just happened in the tea room or even the true story behind her divorce. Everybody wished to believe the worst in her.

Her eyes pricked with tears, a lump forming in her throat. She had to stop pretending as though she had a terrible life because she was a countess. She had to. But she never got a moment to herself, and she was a tired, lonely divorcee with no real friends. She was ashamed and, for the last few days, the words from that article had stuck with her. The words *impossible to love* plastered above pictures of her face. There were crueller things in that interview. Things that should have hurt so much more than that. Lies that made her sound like an evil Disney villain. But these stuck with her. Perhaps because everybody in her life had always made her feel as though it was true.

She staunched the tears with her fingers. *Pull it together, Jessamine. You live in a bloody castle, for goodness' sake. You're happy. Robert doesn't matter.*

But she wasn't living so much as rattling around at the moment. She existed for the small intervals where she could sneak away and pretend to be an outsider, a normal person – like when the gardener, Mac, called her Jess and she could pretend that's who she was, or when her only mission was to walk down the meandering garden paths, or when she could watch visitors picnic on the grass and pretend she was one of them.

And here, now. She lived for this. A cheap hot chocolate with soggy, drowning marshmallows, and a dry piece of cake. The jam was sweet and made of blackberries, reminding her of the pie her favourite home-schooling tutor used to make with her at lunchtime, when her mother was at work and the house was quiet except for them.

A voice beside her broke through a sharp wave of nostalgia. 'You've got a moustache.'

Jessamine started, almost dropping her cake, but it was only a child watching her intently. His eyes were red-rimmed, face pale, and a mop of curls fell across his forehead. Though he was tall, his cheeks were still round, perhaps not yet a teenager.

Self-consciously, she wiped her upper lip and found whipped cream on her sleeve. 'Oops.' She smiled. 'Thank you.'

He sat beside her without invitation and threw a stone into the loch. 'This is my place, you know.'

'Oh.' She frowned. 'Is it?'

He nodded. 'I come here when I'm angry, but since you're sad, I suppose you can sit here, too.'

Jessamine put her cake back in the paper bag to give the boy her full attention. 'That's very kind of you. Thank you. What's your name?'

'You're not supposed to tell strangers your name.'

'All right. Well, I'm Jess. And now I'm not a stranger.'

The boy pursed his lips, frowning as though he'd been tricked. 'My name's Arran.'

Amused, she sipped her drink, huddling in on herself when a crisp breeze whistled through her thin blazer. 'Why are you angry, Arran?'

He only shrugged, scraping two stones together absently. 'Do your parents know you're here?'

'I'm twelve. I can go where I want to. Why are you sad?'

'I'm not sad,' she lied. Judging from Arran's look of doubt, it wasn't very convincing.

'Then you can't sit here.'

She raised her brows in surprise. 'Pardon?'

'If you're not sad, you'll have to sit somewhere else.' Sincerity burned in his gaze, and Jessamine couldn't help but smirk.

She shifted away from him until there was a space between them, the hot chocolate swishing in her cardboard cup. 'There we go.'

His face crinkled with disdain, but he said nothing else – only picked moss from the rocky banks of the loch, his brows and chin set stubbornly. Jessamine sensed he didn't want to talk, so she simply sipped her hot chocolate quietly and then offered him half of her cake. He refused.

'Would you like to be alone?' she asked, hoping the answer was no. Though the sky had darkened to a murky violet, she wasn't ready to go back to the castle yet. She had emails to attend to, events to plan, and the thought made her drink taste sour.

Arran shook his head, and that was that. She sat with him until the last slither of sun disappeared, and then he walked away without a goodbye. It was the most seen she'd felt in years.

Chapter Five

'Mrs Townsend!'

Jessamine gritted her teeth and hissed out an irritated huff. She was tired of hearing that name.

'Mrs Townsend!' Petra called again, her heels crunching against gravel as she neared.

Jessamine took a few soothing breaths before replying, 'Down here, Petra.'

She resumed sprinkling Rufus's favourite gourmet cat food around the shrubs as she waited, anxiety knotting in her gut. She hadn't seen Rufus in two days, and she was finding him more difficult to track down than Bartholomew the barn owl at this point.

'Where?' More scuttling about, and then: 'Oh, heavens! Mrs Townsend—'

'That's it.' Jessamine sat up and clapped her muddy hands together. 'My name is *Byron*, Petra. Jessamine *Byron*. If you can't deign to remember it, perhaps I might find a personal assistant who can.' Stunned, she lifted her hands to her mouth slowly as though she might find thorns growing there. 'Dear lord. I sounded just like my mother then, didn't I?'

Petra's freckled cheeks pinkened, and she smoothed down her skirt with shaky hands. 'Apologies, Ms Byron. I had forgotten . . .' Her trailing words were meek. Petra had never been meek in her life. The fact only caused more guilt. Petra *had* only started working for her a couple of years ago, and Jessamine had been Mrs Townsend the entire time she'd known her – until now.

'I, er . . . Are you quite all right down there?' Petra asked.

'No,' Jessamine muttered, sighing and hauling herself up. Her knees were damp and caked in soil, although it had been unseasonably warm and dry for late spring, the one saving grace of staying in Scotland so far. 'I can't seem to find Rufus. He hasn't been home for the past two nights.'

'The cat?'

'No, my bloody uncle,' Jessamine retorted sarcastically. 'Yes, the cat!'

Petra flinched, and Jessamine blew her fringe out of her eyes. Perhaps she was in a bit of a bad mood today. Considering her only friend, a three-legged cat, was missing, she had a phone call with her mother planned for later after a week of the cold shoulder, and her period coming early had left her crampy and bloated, it wasn't a good morning.

But it wasn't Petra's fault, not really. She knew that.

'I'm sorry,' she admitted gently. 'I'm just a bit all over the place. I shouldn't take it out on you.'

'I understand.' Petra shifted uncomfortably as though she wanted to say something else but wasn't sure how it would be received. 'I've noticed that you keep sneaking out of the castle. Is everything OK?'

No. Nothing has ever really felt OK, least of all now, Jessamine wanted to say, but that wasn't who she was. Her job was to smile and be grateful, elegant, and perhaps slightly detached like Mother. Not that it had got her very far in the end. Still, it was none of Petra's concern and Jessamine doubted she'd understand.

'Adjusting to new surroundings, I suppose,' she lied finally. 'What was it you needed?'

'Your mother emailed over the guest list she's decided on for the gala in June. I just need you to look over it.' Petra peeled a sheet of paper from her binder and handed it to Jessamine.

'Hang on. What gala?'

She blinked as though Jessamine had grown two heads. 'Your mother should have sent over the details, considering it's just over two months away . . .'

Jessamine gritted her teeth. 'My mother is not talking to me at the moment. Where, exactly, will this gala be held?'

'Well . . .' Petra cocked her head gingerly. 'Here.'

Jessamine swallowed. It was just like her mother to spring this on her. A scheme to win everybody over again, no doubt. To prove that she didn't have a defective daughter. To gloss over their problems by showing off their grand ancestral castle. One couldn't be an evil little wench if one was rich and wore a nice dress, after all.

Her stomach churned at the thought of being exposed to a castle full of people who were judging her. Laughing at her. She couldn't bear to so much as look at the guest list. She'd have no say in any of it either way. What Jessamine cared about, who she wished to surround herself with, what she had spent her life working for, didn't matter and never had. All that mattered was what other people thought.

'I truly thought she'd been planning with you,' Petra said softly.

Jessamine folded the list, half-tempted to rip it up and let the wind scatter the pieces. 'I'll discuss it with her later on. Thank you, Petra.'

Petra nodded and then seemed to hesitate. 'Would you like any help with your cat?'

With a forced smile that felt watery and wrong, Jessamine replied, 'No, thank you. It's a new area for him. I'm sure he's just found somebody else to feed him.' Or maybe Hamish from the tea room had kidnapped him, or one of the castle visitors had taken him home, she thought. Sharp anxiety sliced through her gut. She tried to hide it by glancing at her wristwatch. 'I'd better go back inside. Lots of meetings scheduled today.'

'Yes, Mrs Town—' Jessamine cut her off with a severe, warning look. 'Ms Byron,' Petra corrected.

'You know, you could just call me Jessamine.'

Petra only wrinkled her nose. Then again, Jessamine supposed, she might grow to hate her first name as much as her ex-husband's surname if Petra went around shouting it all day. Better they remained on a last-name basis for now.

It had taken Mac all morning to decide what to do with Gherkin. Arran hadn't spoken to him since the argument, not even a goodbye before he went to school, and Mac was at his wits' end. Finally, he decided it would be best to take the cat to the nearest vet and see if he was microchipped. Then Arran could say a final farewell tonight and, with any luck, the cat would be reunited with his true owners tomorrow.

He wandered up the stairs with a few pieces of cheese in his hand, finding Gherkin where he'd been curled up for the past few days – on Arran's windowsill. Since he had no cat carrier, he retrieved Pickle's rabbit crate from beneath Arran's bed, pausing when he heard the sound of jingling. Mac clenched his jaw as he slid the crate out, both against the dust bunnies he found and the fact that on top of the crate lay a brown, tweed collar. He could guess who it might belong to: the three-legged cat now hovering around his ankles, perhaps.

With pursed lips, he picked up the collar and twisted the name tag around. *Rufus* was etched into the gold paw print, though no address or phone number was given.

'Gherkin, my arse,' he muttered, looking down at the wide-eyed cat. 'Tell you what. My Arran's going to be in some trouble tonight, crafty sod he is.'

He dreaded to even think about it. A part of him wished he could be angry, but he only felt . . . betrayed. Twice now Arran had lied about the bloody cat. Mac was doing his best to create a safe home, an honest home, but Arran still had his guard up. He couldn't blame him. He couldn't even blame him for kidnapping a cat. Being a foster kid was lonely, and they all needed something to cling to. Jesus, Mac had spent his six years in care never letting go of a teddy bear named Walter that he'd been taken in with. It still lived on top of his old wardrobe at Mum's because even as a teenager, as an adult, he'd felt tethered to it. Like the old stitching and fluff was the very fabric of his existence, the plastic-button eyes and red bow tie an intrinsic part of who he was. The only thing he'd had when the rest of the world had forgotten him.

He wouldn't shout, he decided. There was no use in shouting. He would understand, because he did – and because Arran needed to know that, too.

'Come on, mate,' Mac muttered to Gherkin – *Rufus* – as he fastened the collar around his neck with a bit of cheddar as his lure. 'Let's see where you live.'

Rufus purred happily, and Mac left the remaining cheese in the crate, waiting for the cat to hop in. He did, a little bit squished but happy nonetheless, and Mac fastened the door. 'Off to the vet we go.' And then: 'Don't tell anyone I talk out loud to a cat, will you?'

Steadily, he left Arran's bedroom and made his way downstairs, setting Rufus down to pull on his jacket and grab his car keys from the hook. Outside, colour smattered the gardens as spring bloomed, the overcast sky looking, for once, out of place.

'Off we go,' he sing-songed as he locked his door. 'To the vet—'

'Mac?'

He turned around, finding Jess standing at his gate.

'Oh. Hi, Jess,' he greeted her slightly uncomfortably. 'Everything all right?'

'I don't suppose you've seen a three-legged cat around, have you? Mine has gone missing.'

Dread turned his stomach to lead. He glanced down at Rufus, fighting back a curse. The cat was hers. Of course it was. The universe was playing some sort of cosmic joke on him, throwing Jess in his path any way it could. If accidentally threatening her with garden shears or almost knocking himself out with a sweeping brush wasn't enough, he was also now the man who had involuntarily kidnapped her cat.

'Er . . .' Instinct had caused him to hide the crate behind

his back, and it made him feel sneaky, untrustworthy. He hated it. But how could he admit he had her cat? How could he tell Arran that Gherkin was gone without giving him chance to say goodbye? He at least deserved that, didn't he? Maybe tomorrow, Mac could find out where Jess lived and drop Rufus off on her doorstep.

'No. No, no cats here. Only me.' Of course, he'd forgotten that he couldn't lie for shit. He still gave his best shot, though, flashing an achingly wide grin Jess's way. 'What's the name of this missing cat?'

Maybe it was a different cat. Maybe several three-legged cats were roaming Fort Aileen, and they were talking about two completely different ones.

'Rufus,' she replied, and his irrational hope deflated and shrivelled like an old helium balloon. 'He has a tweed collar and a nametag. He's a dark tabby.'

Mac bit the inside of his cheek, unsure what to do next. 'Right. I'll, er, keep an eye out for him, then.'

Her brows pinched together, and it looked as though she wanted to say more. 'OK. Thank you, Mac.'

He hoped that would be the end of it, but she leaned against the fence and motioned to the cottage behind him. 'You live here, then?'

'Aye.' Awkwardly, he patted the weather-worn sign by his door that read, *Gardener's Cottage*.

'It's lovely.'

He hummed, his arm vibrating as Rufus began to stir in the carrier. He was never going to get away with this, and even if he did, he felt awful. He couldn't keep somebody's cat. Even if he was just waiting for Arran to say goodbye, it wasn't right. For all he knew, Jess could have kids of her own who were missing Rufus just as much.

He sighed in defeat, his stomach tightening. 'Look, Jess . . . I'm really sorry—'

A shrill meow cut through his words. Jess perked up. 'Did you hear that?'

51

Mac grimaced. Any doubt drifted away; it was clear Rufus was loved, and Jess, no matter how irritating she was, didn't deserve to be kept from her own cat a moment longer. Maybe she'd understand. Maybe he could explain and—

'I don't suppose the three-legged cat I'm looking for is the one you're currently holding, is it?'

Shite. He'd moved his arm without realising it, and Rufus was on full display. He gulped down a deep breath, heart thumping forcefully. 'I can explain.'

Jess narrowed her eyes as she opened the gate. With it still swinging on its hinges behind her, she marched up the garden path and snatched the carrier from Mac's hands before opening the cage's door to free him. 'Oh, look. He even wears a tweed collar with his name on it. Do you think this Rufus might be the same one you claim not to have seen?'

He scraped a hand across his face. 'I'm so sorry, Jess. I was about to take him to the vet and find out if he's microchipped.'

'Then why would you lie to me?' Jess bundled Rufus in her arms protectively, and the cat purred, nuzzling his head into the crook of her neck. 'You *stole* my cat.'

'"Stole" is a strong word. Cats are quite independent creatures. You can't *really* own them in the first place, can you?' An awkward laugh.

'You *stole* my cat,' she insisted.

He slumped, defeated. 'I didn't *mean* to steal your cat. It's complicated. I . . .' He didn't even know where to start. Not really. He tugged at the roots of his hair, trying to find an explanation that would sound good enough. It probably didn't exist. There was no denying that he *had* accidentally, unknowingly, stolen her cat.

'You know, I was willing to give you the benefit of the doubt, but you really are a first-class prat,' Jess spat. 'Fine, we were teasing one another and it was annoying and a little bit funny, but you've crossed a line.'

'I didn't *know* it was your cat!' he said desperately. 'I

swear, I didn't. Maybe if you just come inside, we can talk about this properly. Please?'

Jess's gaze darted between the cottage door and Mac, hesitant. He wouldn't blame her if she said no.

But she pursed her lips, her features opening just slightly. 'Fine. It better be a bloody good apology, though.'

'I'll grovel on my hands and knees if that's what it takes,' he replied softly. He unlocked the cottage door again and held it open. Jess carried Rufus into the hallway as Mac tipped his face to the sky. He wasn't a religious man, but if there was ever a time to start praying, he suspected it might be now.

Rufus hopped out of Jessamine's arms as soon as she stepped into the kitchen. She was so distracted by her new surroundings that she let him, watching as he cosied up on a striped scarf slung over a kitchen chair.

The cottage wasn't what she'd expected. It was rustic and warm and full of rich, autumnal colours, but it was also wildly untidy. Coats were strewn across tables, dishes piled in the sink, and she'd almost tripped over a pair of muddy wellies on her way in. When she saw the fridge, mostly hidden by drawings and school certificates addressed to someone named Arran, she began to understand why. A child lived here, too.

Arran. She'd heard that name only yesterday. The boy she'd met by the loch. *He* was Mac's child?

The understanding caused a kernel of guilt to sink in her stomach, but she tried to ignore it. Rufus was her cat, her only friend, and not having him around for the last couple of days had left her even more unsettled and lonely than usual.

Mac cracked his knuckles uncomfortably after placing the pet carrier – which definitely was not big enough for poor Rufus – down on the dining table. 'Would you like a drink?'

'No.' She couldn't help the bluntness that flattened the word, made even firmer by the fact that Rufus seemed calm, peaceful, where he'd curled up, as though he'd already made himself at home. *Traitor*.

'OK. Would you like to sit down?'

'No.' She tilted her chin up and crossed her arms stubbornly. 'Let's get it over with.'

Mac's shoulders rose and fell with a deep sigh. He leaned against the kitchen counter, his fingers turning white where he clenched the surface. His nose was bracketed by a splotch of green going on purple: the sweeping brush's doing.

'It was my kid who found him,' he said finally.

Something swelled in her; something she didn't want to acknowledge. 'Right . . .'

He scratched his red-brown stubble, the sunlight pouring through the window and illuminating half of his face. He didn't look the way he had yesterday anymore, all smirks and youth. She noticed now the dark crescents beneath his eyes, the square tension in his broad frame, the muscle ticking like a pulse in his jaw.

'My foster kid, I should say,' he answered finally. 'Arran is twelve, and much as I love him, he's a wee sneaky sod. Turns out he hid Rufus's collar to make me think he was a stray. I'll be having words with him when he gets home. You have to understand, though, that he only did it because he took a real liking to him. There wasn't any ill intent. He's just . . . he's had a difficult upbringing. We're working on it.'

Jessamine could no longer grip on to her anger; it was slipping like sand through her clenched fingers. 'I actually ran into him on the banks of the loch yesterday. Of course, I didn't know he was yours.'

His brows rose in surprise. 'Aye. That's where he goes to cool down. We argued because I told him he couldn't keep the cat. He's still not talking to me, mind.'

She wanted to tell him to stop; stop making her feel bad for wanting her bloody cat back. God, she'd preferred it when he'd just been an arrogant, sarcastic arsehole with a charming smile.

His gaze was too heavy, too stifling. She turned away, pretending to be interested in the old, yellowing wallpaper and the glass cupboards stuffed with mismatched belongings: mugs, medicines, empty fruit bowls, paints.

'I am sorry, Jess,' he said again, and she winced because she loved hearing him say her name, shortened down to one soft syllable rather than a clipped mouthful of harsh consonants and vowels. She liked being just Jess. She'd never been just Jess before. 'I only tried to hide it just now because I was hoping Arran would get a goodbye first. He'll be home from school this afternoon, and I don't know how he'll react without Rufus there.'

When he put it that way, it was a little bit easier to understand why he'd blatantly lied to her about Rufus's whereabouts. Defeated, she perched on the edge of the kitchen chair beside Rufus. 'I see.'

'But I'm glad I found his owner.' Mac's voice was light, but it sounded strained, forced. 'I was worried I'd have to run all over Fort Aileen. How did he get in the gardens, anyway? Has he followed you to work?'

'I . . .' She bit down on her lip, debating whether to tell him. He'd been so honest with her, after all. More honest than she'd expected. But wouldn't it just make him feel worse if she told him she was living in Rosemire? While he was managing a foster child in a tiny little cottage, she was roaming a grand castle with only dust motes and Rufus to keep her company. It didn't feel right. She didn't want it to define her here, the way it did everywhere else. She wanted to keep being Jess for a little longer. And then there were the things Robert had said. She couldn't bear another person to see her that way. Taking a cat from a foster kid would surely not do much to disprove Robert's *selfish and hates kids* claim.

'Perhaps,' she agreed finally.

His lips curled in a slow smile. 'You mustn't live too far away, then.'

'No.' Uncomfortable, she cleared her throat. 'I'm sure Rufus will still be around, anyway. Perhaps Arran will run into him and have the chance to say a real goodbye. Just as long as he doesn't abduct him again, that is.'

Mac snorted. 'I'll let him know. I do mean it, though. I'll talk to him about this and make sure it doesn't happen again. Are we forgiven?'

'I wouldn't say that.' Still, the corner of her lip twitched as she stood up, taking Rufus with her. 'I suppose I should be glad he was taken care of.' He *looked* taken care of, anyway, and there was a stack of empty tuna tins on the side. Rufus's favourite, aside from the gourmet food pouches Jessamine bought for him.

'That he was. You needn't worry there.'

Jessamine shifted uncomfortably, tickling Rufus's chin and taking a final glance round. It *was* cosy in here. She felt tucked away, safe, never to be found by Petra or her other responsibilities. A tiny pocket of tranquillity where even her cat had come to hide. She almost didn't want to leave, but she'd run out of things to say and anger to burn. 'I should probably go.'

'Aye, of course. Sorry again.' Mac rushed to guide her to the front door, the bristles of a worn welcome mat rustling beneath his soil-caked boots. He opened the door, the epitome of chivalry. Definitely not the man who had come at her with a pair of shears last week. 'Bye, Rufus.'

Rufus blinked, oblivious, his tail curling around Jessamine's shoulder.

She almost felt like saying sorry, though she'd done nothing wrong. Still, as she bid Mac goodbye and retreated down the garden path, she grew heavy with confusion. If possible, there were even more flowers here than the rest of the castle grounds, some of them – powdery bluebells, bright pink coneflowers, red tulips – only just beginning to bloom. Others – buttery daffodils and rich purple hyacinths – were wilting with the spring.

As much as she wanted to dislike Mac, she couldn't deny that he had a way of making things beautiful. Whether he was trustworthy or not, on the other hand, remained to be seen. Either way, she would be keeping a closer eye on Rufus from now on.

Chapter Six

Jessamine tapped her chewed nails against the glossy wooden desk, anxiety bubbling in her gut as she waited for the video call to connect. One perk of staying in the Highlands was the terribly unpredictable internet connection. With any luck, it would be just as useless now as it had been all week, and she could shut her laptop without talking to her mother at all.

Of course, that's not what happened. A pixelated image of Philippa Byron appeared on the screen, with Jessamine confined to a small box in the corner, where she glanced quickly to check her fringe was straight and blouse uncreased.

'Ah, there we are,' her mother said, smoothing down her grey-blonde bob and straightening her narrow shoulders. 'Can you see me, Jessamine? *Yoo-hoo*.' She gave a wave, clearly having not quite grasped the concept of a video call yet.

'Yes, Mother, I can see you.' Jessamine forced a smile.

'Wonderful. How's Scotland?' Ebbing daylight streamed through the open windows behind Mother, highlighting the blue skies and green grass of the well-mowed but otherwise unexplored lawn. Their Kent home, where Mother usually stayed alone if her schedule wasn't too busy. Though beautiful, Jessamine had never quite taken to it. She missed Cheshire, missed the manor she'd grown up in. The fact it was barely visited now felt like they'd turned their back on the memory of Dad. She understood that losing him must have been painful for Mother and she didn't want to be reminded of it, but it was all Jessamine had left of him:

Christopher Byron, Earl of Cheshire. He'd died when she was just six, but Jessamine remembered how warm he could be. He doted on her, calling her his little turnip. She couldn't remember Mother ever loving her like that.

She nodded stiffly now. 'The castle is quite lovely, and the scenery is beautiful. Thank you for suggesting the visit.'

'Well, I do hope you're doing more than just enjoying the view,' Mother retorted, her features a smooth marble mask that Jessamine had never learned how to read. As a teenager, she'd convinced herself that Mother's heart had been replaced by a hollow piece of metal like the Tin Man's in *The Wizard of Oz*. Now, she only had to try not to turn out the same way. She couldn't quite remember if Mother had been just as cold before Dad's passing, or if it had come with the grief. 'There's work to be done and a gala to arrange, you know. While you've been holidaying with your feet up, I've been doing an awful lot of damage control.'

Pain lanced through Jessamine. Pain and humiliation. 'Mother—'

Jessamine was swiftly cut off. 'You'll be glad to know that I've invited plenty of potential suitors to visit the castle. Now the ink has dried on your divorce papers' – Mother said the word "divorce" as though it was some awful, contagious, flesh-eating strain of bacteria – 'it's time to find somebody to settle down with. Somebody who might look past your . . . reputation, and prove you are not all those awful things Robert suggested you were.'

Jessamine fought not to roll her eyes, instead taking her frustrations out on the bottom button of her blouse, the thread slowly coming loose as she twisted and tugged. 'I've been hoping to talk to you about that. The gala in particular.' She shifted in her seat. 'You didn't tell me you were arranging it. It came as quite a surprise.'

'Well, somebody must fix this awful mess, and it's quite clear *you're* incapable of it after that little champagne fiasco. I've not heard the end of it since, I'll have you know. People are saying all sorts of things about you, and I shan't sit by and watch the Byron family name be tarnished. I mean, I've had to tell them you're on a yoga retreat learning mindfulness and self-improvement, for heaven's sake. Can you imagine?' Mother patted her already pristine hair down dramatically.

The horror. 'But I thought I was supposed to be taking a break from it all. A gala seems the complete opposite.'

She tutted. 'Yes, but not *too* long a break. We need everybody to forgive, not forget. We need to find you a new husband, too – or at least an escort for the night. Somebody nice like the Viscount Ashbury. It will do away with these silly rumours, not to mention I'd like grandchildren this century.'

Jessamine was an only child, and so she was Mother's one chance when it came to grandchildren. Her parents had hoped for more, assuming they'd have plenty of time to create an entire army of Byrons. Only they hadn't, and now all of the traditional, outdated expectations of marriage and babies and maintaining their family's wealth and status fell to Jessamine. That the default was 'husband' at all left her nauseated, angry. She'd come out as pansexual years ago, explaining to her rather clueless mother – who'd thought the word was kitchen lingo for a fondness of pots and pans – that it meant she experienced attraction to anyone of any gender. She had even dated a female influencer before Robert, and yet Mother seemed to think she could ignore it until it went away. Just like everything else.

Every conversation was like this. Jessamine despised being made to feel bad because she didn't fit the mould created within the peerage system hundreds of years ago. It felt like a betrayal to herself each time she gave into her mother's expectations. It felt like a betrayal to herself just to sit here and discuss things with a woman who didn't see the world through her eyes.

'You have a grandchild,' Jessamine said finally, attempting to lighten the mood by picking Rufus up from the armchair behind her and holding him up to the camera.

Mother shuddered, disgust twisting across her features. 'Do get that thing away from the camera. It's ghastly to look at. Can't a vet fit it with a prosthetic?'

Jessamine put Rufus down, Mother's earlier words still ringing in her ears. She couldn't help but wonder what life would be like if people *did* forget. If she could just get on with her work without anybody else having an opinion on who she was. Better to be irrelevant than what she was now. A pariah in hiding.

'Mother, I really am not in the mood to plan a gala. All of this . . .' Tears thickened her voice, refusing to be swallowed back down. 'It's been difficult, and I just want some time to figure things out for myself. Please . . .'

'Oh, heavens, Jessamine.' Mother batted her away. 'You'll ruin your make-up weeping that way. Grow up and handle this like a lady. Like a *countess*. You will host the gala and you will show everybody you can be a desirable, civilised woman of nobility. It isn't all that complicated.'

For once, Jessamine just wanted her mother to comfort her. An ache settled in her chest, her throat growing scratchy as sandpaper. Wasn't she allowed a moment away from it all? A moment to figure out who she was outside of her loveless marriage? A moment to decide what she wanted next?

Wasn't she allowed to just be understood?

'I just need time.'

She sniffled, dabbing her nose with a tissue in the careful don't-wipe-off-your-foundation way Mother had taught her long ago. 'I've been focusing on my work, and—'

Mother pressed her lips together in a thin line – lipstick bleeding into wrinkles that defied the Botox, thousands of pounds' worth of facial treatments, and God only knew what else she'd tried. 'And I am asking you now to focus your energy elsewhere.'

Like throwing extravagant galas to redeem herself for crimes she hadn't committed. As though sitting and looking pretty in a room full of high-brow, influential, rich people was Jessamine's only job.

'My charities are important to me. Surely that's a good thing for my reputation. What would people think if I stopped putting in the work now?'

It was the only way to get through to her mother: to bring up other people's opinions. Mother could live with anything but people saying bad things. It was another reason she despised Jessamine's divorce so much, even before the article. A failed marriage was another imperfection, and one their so-called friends would revel in, especially since they'd all worshipped Robert. Jessamine was already the outcast: she took up more space than her diet-obsessed Size-6 friends; she didn't go to polo at the weekends just to flaunt her newest designer handbag; she was always the first to leave a dinner party because bubbly drinks made her woozy and too many conversations even woozier. The only way she'd ever fit in was with her bland, charming baron of a husband, who had elevated her reputation as a respectable woman and looked lovely on her arm.

But the marriage hadn't worked. Jessamine would rather be alone. And now she was.

Mother sniffed haughtily, the tendons in her neck visible beneath papery skin, still tanned from a trip to the South of France last month. 'And what would they think if your biggest investor stopped her donations?'

Jessamine's blood went cold, and for a moment she was desperate to believe she'd misheard. Mother brought up money plenty, always throwing how much she'd 'done' – *bought* – for Jessamine back in her face whenever they disagreed. But using the charities both women had invested in . . . charities that Jessamine had spent countless time and energy on . . . That was just cruel. Selfish. Proof that Mother really did have a tin heart.

And if she stopped investing in Jessamine's charities, other people might, too. Huge chunks of regular donations would come to a halt, if they hadn't already. Everybody would wonder why Philippa Byron had stopped aiding her daughter's charities. It would confirm Robert's lies, but worse, it would harm everything Jessamine had ever cared about: Shimmer, an LGBTQ+ charity that she'd been building awareness of alongside its founders for years. Mental-health charities that needed support in an underfunded, under-resourced system.

'The gala will go ahead,' Mother repeated.

Numbly, Jessamine tipped her head. What other option did she have? 'All right. Let me know what needs preparing.'

'And what is the plan until then? I certainly hope you're not spending your days lazing around while I fix the messes you've made.'

'Of course not. I'm contributing to the planning of a spring fete on the castle grounds, to raise money for local charities.'

'Good. Let them see you're getting involved in the community. They'll adore you for it and hopefully begin to question Robert's words. I shall invite a few journalists to snap some candid photographs, so make sure to do your make-up properly.'

Jessamine held her breath, wondering if Mother had ever done something without the performance; without the intention of bolstering her social status. Jessamine had gotten lost in the same habits for a couple of years in her late teens and early twenties, still naïve enough to see the good in everything, but after getting married with such innocent hope, it had all come crashing down. Marital problems aside, she was so exhausted with the constant pretending, the socialising and travelling that her reputation became an afterthought. Until the article, that was. Now, it haunted her. And when she'd been at her most popular in the public eye, she'd been miserable behind closed doors, with a husband who didn't understand her and a life that wasn't hers. There was no winning.

She couldn't take much more, and judging from the way

Rufus scurried – well, hobbled – out of the study, neither could he. 'I must get going, anyway. Busy busy.'

Mother batted her away with a lazy hand. 'I shall see you in June, then. Oh, and do remember—'

'Yes, yes, I remember, goodbye!' Jessamine ended the call, cutting her mother off mid-sentence. In the new silence, she massaged her temples. A headache was beginning to form.

Sometimes, she truly didn't know what her purpose was. Everybody had so many different opinions about it, and in the end, she seemed to please no one.

She stood up and closed her laptop before leaving the study, locking the door behind her just in case any visitors decided to sneak around the residential wing. The hallways outside were empty, though the echoes of children playing in the gardens drifted up the spiral staircase. Afternoon sunlight painted everything a fiery orange, the prisms of the chandelier casting rainbows onto smoothly papered walls. In desperate need of fresh air, Jessamine trudged downstairs and stealthily ducked under the red rope cordoning off her rooms from the rest of the castle. Luckily, the only tour upstairs was in the grand library, and nobody noticed her slip away.

The entrance on the ground floor, on the other hand, was brimming with people. She tried to weave her way through them, but her name being called thwarted her.

'Lady Byron?'

She spun round, flashing a warning look at the young receptionist who had said her name behind the information desk. If anybody had heard, though, they didn't show it.

'Sorry, ma'am. It's just that somebody left flowers for you earlier. Well, they said they were for Jess, but there aren't any Jesses here.' The receptionist – Hayley, Jessamine recalled her name was – plonked a bunch of dusty-blue and lilac hydrangeas on the desk, the stems tied together with twine.

Jessamine frowned. Only one person called her Jess, but he wouldn't . . .

She took the flowers and muttered her thanks, finding

a small, handwritten note folded and tucked between the delicate petals. *Jess* had been scrawled in looped handwriting across the front. She stepped outside for a bit of privacy, glancing curiously at the small gardener's cottage. It was nothing more than a brown fleck across the grounds, and she couldn't see any sign of Mac tending to the gardens the way he usually was.

Anticipation finally got the better of her, and she opened the note. It read:

Jess,

Sorry again about earlier. Would love to buy you a drink to make up for unintentionally stealing your cat if you're around tonight. Fresh start?

Find me at the Hairy Coo if you fancy it. No hard feelings if not.

Mac.

It was the last thing she'd been expecting – but then, she never seemed to be right about anything when it came to Mac. She pressed her back to the wall, reading the words until the ink blurred. She couldn't go, obviously. If anybody recognised her as they had in the tea room the other day, she'd never know peace again – and Mac certainly wouldn't call her Jess anymore or joke around with her.

Then again, the alternative was sitting in bed with a bottle of wine and a book. When was the last time she'd been asked to do something normal like go to a pub? Probably not since university, and even then, she'd spent more time in cocktail lounges than the Student Union bar. And it wasn't as though it was a date, even if he had given her some flowers. It was just an apology. If she didn't go, he'd assume she was still angry, which she wasn't. That would be rude of her.

Maybe she could just pop in for one drink. She doubted nobility fanatics like Margaret would be in a pub named the Hairy Coo on a Friday night.

Yes, she decided. *Just one drink*. What harm could that do?

'Maybe I shouldn't go.' Mac sank his head onto his mother's kitchen countertop while she whizzed around him, pulling out mugs, fruit and barley squash, and biscuits for when Arran decided to stop sulking in Mac's old bedroom upstairs – which had now technically become *his* room.

'Nonsense.' His mum gave Mac a light slap on the back of his neck before flicking on the kettle. 'You must take time for yourself sometimes, Mac.'

'I know. But Arran's upset with me. It doesn't feel right to leave him here tonight.'

Arran hadn't spoken a word to him since he'd come home from school to find Gherkin-slash-Rufus gone, claimed by his owner. After the dreaded lecture about lying, Mac had assured him over and over that Rufus would still be around like Jess had said, but the kid was good at holding a grudge. On the way here, he'd glared at the same small scratch on the front window of Mac's truck until Mac had swiped his hand in front of his face to make sure his fury hadn't left him completely catatonic. And then he'd stomped straight upstairs without so much as a hello for Mac's mum and dad, who he usually adored spending time with. It was all a big mess, and worse, confirmation that Linda was right. Mac was failing.

'Will you give over? He probably needs a bit of time out, and so do you.' Mum tutted, her short, silver hair swishing at her chin as though it had a life of its own. That was what Mac loved about her. She was all life. Visiting her usually left him feeling warm, peaceful, loved. Today, it just seemed like an admittance of his defeat.

Mac rarely left Arran with his parents to go to the pub, but he'd planned this outing for weeks to celebrate his best mate's birthday. It just so happened that 'cat-gate' had struck this week, too, and all the internal pep talks he'd given himself to go out and have fun for a change had quickly unravelled.

He straightened now, scratching the back of his neck and choking on his aftershave in the process. Perhaps he'd gone a bit overboard on Hugo Boss tonight, but that definitely had nothing to do with the fact he'd invited Jess to come along, too, and now his stomach was in knots in case she showed up. Definitely not.

The sound of floorboards creaking upstairs drew him out of that train of thought, and he glanced up at the ceiling as though he could feel Arran's daggers piercing through the plaster from upstairs. 'Mum . . .'

'Hmm?' As she poured water from the kettle, her glasses fogged with steam and she pushed them onto her head.

A lump formed in Mac's throat. He tried desperately to swallow it down, but it was lodged there like a brick. 'I'm worried he hates me,' he forced himself to admit finally, quietly.

The countertop pressed into his rear as he turned to face her, half-perching awkwardly. This house was once the biggest thing in his universe; now, he felt like a giant in the cosy little kitchen. He always knocked his head on the doorframe when he came in; always managed to bang his shoulder on a cupboard or trip over a chair leg. Like his body hadn't realised it had grown. Like he was still just a boy inside, a little bit lost and a little bit found. How the hell could he take care of another child if that was the truth?

Mum stopped stirring her tea, her delicate, wrinkled features softening. 'Mac . . .'

'I thought we were going all right for a while,' he continued, sniffing in an effort to disguise his cracking voice, to gather his composure. 'But this cat thing has just set him off again. Linda said he might be better off in a bigger family. Like I'm not enough for him. Now I'm wondering if she was right.'

She closed the distance between them, her hand falling on top of his on the counter. He used to crane his neck to look up at her; now it was the other way around. Still, she'd never stopped treating him like her wee boy. She still brought homemade soup when he caught the flu, and gifted him fleecy pyjamas for Christmas. Mac had tried so hard to be like her and Dad when he'd fostered Arran. He'd covered the kitchen in syrup once trying to make fresh strawberry jam, only to find out Arran was allergic; had spent a bomb on cosy bunny-patterned bedding he washed every week with extra lemon-scented detergent just so Arran had a reminder of home to cling on to if – *when* – he left. Shit, he'd even let a bloody vicious rabbit into his house, making sure Arran cleaned out the hut every week so it didn't smell too much of wee-soaked sawdust, of course. He'd taken him to Pride festivals and painted his nails when he asked. Had done his best to raise him with nothing but openness and understanding and love. But none of it felt like enough. Maybe it was time to come to terms with the fact that nobody would ever come close to his parents and their ability to make a home out of splinters and cracked stone. Maybe Mac just wasn't cut out for it, after all.

'You know, when you came home with us, I thought the same as you,' his mum said gently, squeezing his fingers. Her dark eyes glittered. 'You wouldn't look at me at first. You were such a skittish wee thing. And then the next morning, you threw a bloody paddy because I cut the crust off your toast and didn't speak to me for a good few days. Took weeks for you to open up. Months. *Years*, even. And every time something went wrong – I didn't let you eat chocolate before bed, or I wouldn't let you keep a goldfish we won at the fair, or you wanted a book that was for adults – I worried we'd go back to square one and you'd never let me in properly. I worried you'd never let me be your mother at all. But you did, Mac, despite all that.'

His chin wobbled with the threat of tears, and he bowed his head to avoid her seeing. 'I don't remember that. The toast thing, I mean.' He didn't remember any of the things, except perhaps the brief teen rebellion phase and giving the goldfish to his best friend, Gem, because he hadn't had a fish tank. He knew he'd been wary at first, perhaps scared. Adults hadn't been trustworthy then. But when he looked back now, he only saw all the love he was given. All the ways he was saved from a life of instability and loneliness in the system. To him, his parents had been perfect.

'Exactly. You don't remember.' Her lips thinned with a wise, bright smile. 'Things always feel like the end of the world . . . until they're not. And then they're just blips. This is all it is with Arran: a blip. When he's older, he'll only remember everything you *did* do for him. Not the few things you didn't.'

The words set him at ease. He hadn't known how badly he'd needed somebody to understand. He hadn't known Mum had been through the same things with him. He must have been a bloody pain in the arse.

'God, I hope so.' His breath whooshed out of him, all relief and gratitude. 'Thank you, Mum.'

The corners of her eyes crinkled, and she patted Mac on the cheek with warm hands. 'You're a good father, darling. Arran knows that, deep down. He's just at that age. I'll have a word with him, see if that helps. Anyway' – her attention darted to the clock, and then she was ushering him out of the kitchen – 'get gone. You don't want to be late.'

'You can't be late to the pub, Mum,' Mac said, though he had promised to meet Brodie at seven, and it was now ten-to. 'Let me say bye to Arran.'

He climbed the narrow staircase two steps at a time, the spindly banister wobbly beneath his heavy hands. Arran's door was slightly ajar, but a piece of yellow card with black bubble letters reading *DO NOT ENTER IF YOUR NAME IS MAC* with three exclamation points had been tacked over the top of Mac's old Iron Man stickers. Mac stopped, lingering in the shadowed hallway.

The sign was another stab to his fragile heart. He'd never expected fostering to leave him more insecure than both high-school PE classes and dating in his twenties combined, and yet Arran's hostility made him want to shrink. Disappear.

You're a bloody dad, Mac, he scolded himself silently. *Get a grip.*

Then, he knocked.

'Read the sign!' Arran shouted.

Mac rolled his eyes and nudged the door open, anyway, peeking his head through the crack. Arran glowered, sitting cross-legged on the single bed, Mac's old comics splayed out in front of him. It made him feel like the Ghost of Christmas Past, looking back on his younger self. They were so alike. Maybe that was why it was so difficult to know how to manage Arran.

'I'm off now, kiddo,' Mac said, offering a grovelling smile. 'I'll see you tomorrow morning, aye?'

Arran said nothing, his piercing scowl unwavering.

Mac sighed. 'Just be good for Pam and Stewart. No staying up past ten-thirty, and no giving lip.'

'Whatever.' Arran crossed his arms.

Unease swirled around Mac's gut. There was no quick fix for this, no way of getting Arran on his side again. He leaned against the door jamb in one last, futile attempt, fiddling with the wheels of a miniature Volkswagen toy on the pale blue bookshelf. 'I know you're angry at me, and that's OK. I can keep saying sorry, Arran, but I'm not sure what else there is beyond that. When you're ready to talk about it properly, let me know.'

Nothing. Not even a blink.

Defeated, he stepped back into the hall. 'Bye, then.'

Silence followed him like a midday shadow as he shut the door, glaring at the sign a final time before trudging back downstairs. He grabbed his coat from its hook, shouting goodbye to Mum and Dad, who liked to settle down in the front room watching *The One Show* at this time.

They, at least, deigned to bid him farewell. So not everybody hated him.

He wondered if he'd find the same at the pub. Would Jess be there, or was his attempt at an apology just another mistake to add to his list?

Only time could tell. As he stepped into the bitter twilight, his stomach jittered with nerves.

Chapter Seven

The Hairy Coo looked about as glamorous as it sounded from the outside. Jessamine hovered at the door of Fort Aileen's only pub, working up the nerve to go in and scratching her head beneath the itchy hand-knitted hat she'd smuggled from the castle's lost-and-found box – just in case anybody recognised her. As an extra precaution, she'd also nabbed some purple-framed glasses that kept slipping off her nose and were most definitely prescribed for somebody short-sighted, which made it hard for her to walk in a straight line or, well . . . see.

Pushing them onto her forehead, she checked her rose-gold wristwatch for the seventh time in as many minutes, wondering if she was too early, or maybe too late. Mac hadn't given her a time. What if he wasn't there? What if she walked in and had a repeat of the tea room? What if she was recognised despite her last-minute disguise?

'Are you going in or just standing in the doorway?' a gruff voice said behind her.

She lowered her glasses and turned around, finding a plump man with a large red nose and only a few strands of grey hair on his liver-spotted head.

'Oh!' She tried to hop out of his way, but he didn't move, which meant she was trapped between the green-painted arch door and the stranger. It seemed the decision had been made for her.

'Bloody dawdler. Get a shifty on,' he grumbled as she wiped her clammy palms on her tailored trousers and her boots on a worn mat that read *Dram o'Clock*. She didn't even know what that meant.

The sounds of laughter and clinking glasses floated out as she pushed the door open and finally stepped in, the stale, musky smell of beer and old furniture greeting her. The warmth was a welcome reprieve from the mild night, though the number of people crowding around the bar made her shift uncomfortably and tug her hat down to her eyebrows.

'Bleeding tourists,' the man who had followed her in murmured, skirting around her and disappearing.

She felt lost and untethered as she glanced at the sea of blurry, unfamiliar faces. This wasn't where she was supposed to be. She felt as out of place here as she did everywhere else. Why had she come? Why hadn't she stayed at home and—

'Jess!' Relief danced across her skin at the sight of Mac's wide grin. Relief, and something else, something she didn't want to name. He'd weaved his way from the bar and now stood in front of her, a pint of beer in his hand. 'I didn't think you'd come.'

She offered a forced smile, unlooping her thin scarf as heat began to crawl up her neck. 'I didn't think I would either,' she admitted quietly.

'I'm glad you did.' He shifted on his feet. 'Nice hat . . .'

'Oh.' She scanned the pub and found everybody too engrossed in their conversations to even notice her. Maybe she'd been self-absorbed to believe anyone would care about her at all. Gingerly, she pulled off her hat and smoothed down her hair. 'Thanks.'

'Here.' He chuckled and rearranged her no doubt awry fringe, his touch feather-light where she'd expected it rough. But then, she'd seen him handle his flowers with the same care and she couldn't help but imagine herself as one of his roses. His tenderness felt like an honour so special that heat warmed her cheeks.

'Thank you,' she mumbled.

'I didn't know you wore glasses, either.' His hand fell to his side as though lost, without purpose.

'Well . . .' She nudged the glasses up her nose, feeling silly now. For once, she was anonymous. She doubted anyone in this pub even cared about her scandals. They had their own lives, ones not centred around her. 'I forgot to put in my contacts.'

'They're very cool.' She couldn't tell if he was making fun of her or being sincere. With Mac, it always felt like a bit of both. Either way, she didn't mind his teasing. It was harmless; made her feel like she was in on the joke rather than the butt of it. 'Fancy a drink?'

With a wary glance at his frothy beer, she looked around, trying to gauge the quality of the drinks, but there was not one fruity cocktail in sight. Not even a fresh slice of lemon.

'Gin and tonic? What is it Scots call it, a "wee bram"?' She imitated her best Scottish accent, which came out sounding more Irish.

His lips twitched as he led her to the bar and they slipped into the queue together. 'A wee *dram*,' he corrected. That explained the mat outside, then. 'And that's whisky, not gin.'

'I don't suppose a martini is on the menu?' She clasped her hands together in a meek attempt to avoid the drunken customers around her, some of whom were singing along to a song Jessamine had never heard before about somebody named Caroline who was quite sweet.

Mac winced. 'I wouldn't risk the cocktails here. I made that mistake once and woke up in the middle of a field without my trousers.'

She stifled a laugh and tried not to imagine the sight. 'I'll stick with the gin, then. Thank you.'

'Gin it is.' He pushed to the front of the bar, his hand resting on the small of Jessamine's back to keep her from getting lost. Flames sparked from his touch, though his fingers barely grazed her as he ordered her drink. Still, nobody had ever touched her quite like that before. So gentle and unforced, as though he wasn't sure whether he had permission. She found herself pushed closer by the current and wriggled uncomfortably into his side to avoid a glass of what looked like Coke but probably wasn't being tipped all over her by a man attempting to dance.

She saw what he meant by the drinks, too. The woman behind the bar poured almost half a glass of gin before moving onto the tonic, her shadowed eyes flitting between Mac and Jessamine curiously. 'And who is this, Mac? Aren't you going to introduce me?'

Mac rifled through his wallet for a five-pound note. It was the first time Jessamine had seen his hands free of mud or grass stains or gloves, his nails cut just below the tips of his fingers and his skin covered in calluses. 'This is Jess. She works at the castle.'

'Interesting.' Mischief laced the bartender's smirk, the silver hoop in her nose glinting as she moved. 'I'm Gem, a friend of Mac's. I run the place.'

'Pleasure to meet you.' Jessamine nodded politely, feeling stripped bare suddenly – as though Gem could see through her, or perhaps knew something she didn't. 'It's . . . a lovely pub.'

'It's all right.' Gem shrugged and then glanced between them again. 'Are we on a date then?'

'*No*,' Jessamine blurted quickly, her palms growing damp again.

'*Oof*,' Mac puffed out. 'Let me down gently, won't you?'

She narrowed her eyes, glad when the glass of gin and tonic was set in front of her on a sticky beer mat. She tried not to be too disappointed by the lack of ice cubes or fruit. 'This is an apology drink. For stealing my cat.'

Gem let out a shrill chuckle. 'You stole her cat?'

'*Arran* stole her cat,' Mac corrected, handing over the cash. 'And I'm glad to see my attempt at making amends is working.'

'Just let me know if you need any of my *special* cocktails.' Gem winked and pocketed the change rather than giving it back to Mac. Very strange relationship indeed. 'Those'll inspire some forgiveness, I'm sure.'

Mac was already steering Jessamine away. 'No, thank you,' he called over his shoulder.

Jessamine sipped her drink through a black straw, which would do her image no favours if anybody caught her, since she was involved in several environmental charities. She could imagine the headlines now: *Bunny-boiler Byron continues reign of terror by killing the turtles.*

As expected, the gin burned her throat until she felt as though she was breathing fire. Maybe *she'd* be the one waking up with no trousers tomorrow.

Dear lord, don't go there, Jessamine, she told herself, before her brain could conjure images of her and Mac without trousers *together*. Definitely not a good idea, nor a welcome one . . . she didn't think.

Thankfully, a man cheering in their general direction from a booth in the corner distracted her. 'Aye, your lass came!'

Mac stiffened against her back. 'She's no *my* lass, but cheers, Brodie.' Then, he whispered, 'Take no notice of him. He's already pished.'

Either Mac was already pished, too, or he was just whispering strange, non-words. Either way, she fought back a shiver when his breath curled in the shell of her ear. The earthy scent of pepper and citrus wafted over her as he moved to her side. 'Lads, this is Jess. Jess, these are a bunch of numpties nae worth knowing.'

'And Mac here's a wee bawbag! Dinnae go oot with him, Jess.' Brodie grinned lopsidedly. She was beginning to understand what Mac meant by 'already pished'. His two friends behind him just booed as though Mac was a pantomime villain.

'I shan't be going out with him, thank you.' Jessamine flashed Mac a saccharine smile, wriggling out of his personal space until her hip bumped the closest chair.

Mac only placed his pint down on the table and crossed his arms, his eyes glittering with humour. 'I think you already established that at the bar. At this point, you're just kicking me while I'm down.'

'You'll recover, I'm sure.' Jessamine shrugged nonchalantly, though with her clammy palms, she was having trouble gripping her glass. *Did* Mac think this was more? She hoped not. That would only complicate things, and she quite liked teasing him when she was off hiding from Petra. Besides, then she might have to tell him who she really was, and he probably wouldn't want to bring her to pubs anymore – an experience that was quickly, unexpectedly growing on her.

Brodie whistled under his breath. 'Got your work cut out for you there, mate. Thought you said she was into you?'

Mac shook his head impatiently. 'I definitely didnae say that. Shouldn't you be off chatting up that karaoke lady, anyway?'

'Now that you mention it . . .' Brodie slapped Mac on the shoulder before stumbling off, his friends following behind with knowing grins.

Mac watched them leave before collapsing onto the bench at the back of the booth. 'Sorry about them. Clearly they're not used to being around humans.'

She laughed and slumped into the chair opposite, twirling a beer mat around absently. This was all very new and strange for her. Her shoes were sticking to the floor and her back was so sweaty she was afraid to take off her jacket. And it was loud, conversation and music a constant buzz in her ear. She felt almost . . . normal. Nobody was judging her or telling her to straighten her posture and slow down on the drink.

Free. She was free.

At the realisation, her stomach seemed to unfurl, open up, from that hard fist. She could breathe again.

'That's OK,' she said. 'They're harmless.' The opposite of everything she'd ever known.

Mac smiled fondly, leaning on his elbows. His cheeks

were flushed, his face cleanly shaven. She noticed permanent laughter lines sinking around his mouth for the first time and a slight dimple on his chin. His jaw was rounder, cheeks more like apples. He was . . . handsome. Younger than he'd looked this morning, and not quite as rugged. 'Aye. Pains in the arse though. I hope you don't regret showing up.'

Jessamine shook her head. She didn't. It was odd seeing Mac in this new environment, a little bit less uptight without his precious tulips and whatnot to worry about. Nice, maybe. He was funny and his laugh sounded like a low rumble of distant thunder, and he grinned at her without sarcasm or teasing, sometimes biting his bottom lip as though his smile was a wild horse he was trying to rein back in.

'Not yet,' she answered honestly. 'Thank you for the flowers, by the way.'

He tilted his head. 'Not a problem. I didn't know which were your favourites, and they seemed appropriate given how we met.'

'Of course.' She shook her head with a chuckle. 'Very thoughtful.'

'So am I forgiven, then?'

Tapping her chin, she pretended to think about it. Rufus had settled straight back into the castle, and in the end, no harm had been done. On her end, anyway. She couldn't imagine how Arran had reacted to his absence. 'Maybe. How did Arran take it?'

Shadows darkened his face, and his focus fell to his pint glass. 'Arran isn't on speaking terms with me at the moment. I'm sure he'll forget about it in a couple of days, though. Nothing a few pancakes and a bag of Haribos won't fix.'

She pulled her chair closer to the table, to him. The noise around her became muffled and distant, and guilt left her tense as she remembered the sad child on the banks of the loch. 'I could talk to him; tell him Rufus will be around plenty.'

Mac shook his head. 'That's really not necessary. You, shouldnae have to do that.'

'I wouldn't mind.' She frowned. She wanted his smile back, or at least wanted him to look at her. For the first time, she saw how his shoulders sank beneath an invisible weight, how there was a permanent line etched between his brows, how his throat bobbed as though something was stuck there. It must be hard work, being a foster parent. 'Is it just you and him, then?'

She hadn't thought of it before: that Mac might have a partner. She'd seen no evidence in the cottage, but then, she'd been too busy worrying about her stolen cat.

He pursed his lips and nodded. 'Aye. Just me and him.'

She ignored the rush of relief, thinking instead of how difficult it must be to raise a child alone. How rarely she met a man who was dedicated to being a full-time single parent. And Mac had chosen it. 'Must be tough sometimes. What made you want to do it?'

'Well . . .' His chest rose and fell with a sigh. 'I was in and out of foster care as a kid myself. Until I was adopted when I was six. My parents were amazing. I can't even imagine what my life would have been like without them. I wanted to be to a child, what they were to me. To change a kid's life for the better. It's lonely, growing up in care homes. I suppose some people are just meant to be parents, and I thought I was one of them.'

'"Thought"?' Jessamine said. 'Past tense?'

His cheeks puffed out as he leaned back in his chair. 'Don't get me wrong, I'm trying my bloody best, but . . . Arran and I aren't always on the same page. It makes you doubt yourself. You feel guilty for everything you can't give them.'

'I'd imagine it's hard, even given your similar upbringing. When I met him, he seemed very . . .' she considered her words carefully before settling on, 'stuck in his own head, I suppose. That doesn't mean you're not a good parent. We all just need different things. It seems like you've already given him a lot.'

And she knew that well because she'd never got those

things as a child. She might have grown up on a beautiful estate and had all of the material objects she needed – pretty clothes, lots of space, financial security that kids like Arran could only dream of – but it didn't change the emptiness inside her when her mother refused to read her a bedtime story or shouted at her for singing too loudly or resented the fact Jessamine didn't fit into the right dress-size for her age. She'd never felt wanted. Not the way Mac clearly wanted Arran.

'I suppose. We'll see how it goes.' He scratched his jaw, sipped his beer. 'What about you? Any bairns?'

'Any what?'

His lips twitched. 'Any kids?'

'*Oh*.' She shook her head. 'Nope, only Rufus.' Another reason she'd needed the divorce. Robert had been desperate to fill their house with mini barons. Jess couldn't think of anything worse. She fidgeted as she thought of the article: of how Robert had implied that she hated kids and was too selfish to care about anyone but herself. Mac would never look at her the same if he saw it. He was the complete opposite of *Splendour*'s version of Jessamine.

As though sensing her discomfort, he changed the subject. 'How'd you come to be a tour guide?'

She gulped down her sharp drink to distract herself from the flicker of guilt. She didn't have to lie about everything, at least, when she replied, 'I just fell into it, really. I was . . . travelling for a little while. For work. The castle is sort of my break from that.'

'What sort of work do you usually do?'

He was looking at her too intently. She wanted to crawl out of her skin and slither out the door. 'I work with charities, mostly.'

'That must be very rewarding.'

She swirled her straw around her glass. 'It is. Especially . . .' She paused. She didn't have to tell him if she didn't want to. It wasn't something she usually dropped into conversation – but then, that was because most of her conversations were with closed-minded elitists who saw the world in black and white. Mac wasn't like that, was he? He was a single father and a gardener, for heaven's sake. With newfound confidence, she tilted her chin higher and continued, 'I like to focus on LGBTQ+ charities.'

'Oh.' He nodded enthusiastically, brightening. 'That's brilliant! I've been meaning to start getting more involved with local charities myself. Fort Aileen does a lot of stuff for Pride but . . . it doesn't always feel enough. I want to make sure kids Arran's age feel safe and accepted, no matter who they are.'

'That's all we can hope for,' she agreed. 'It's not easy to figure out who you are if people don't give you the safe space to let you.'

'Aye. It took me a while to come to terms with my bisexuality, what with the lack of discussions around it growing up. I thought I was straight for a long time, and then people acted like me liking men instantly made me gay. I don't want Arran to have to grow up not knowing who he is, too, y'know? It can be confusing, and it needn't be.'

His words were a relief and this time her smile wasn't forced. It was so rare that people she knew talked about sexuality so openly. It was the second time in a matter of days that she'd finally felt . . . seen. She felt the way she hoped her charities made others feel, the way she'd never been allowed to feel growing up. 'Exactly. I didn't think I'd ever find a label that fitted right until I finally learned about pansexuality, and that wasn't so long ago.'

'It can be hard, even now. They think adults have it all figured out, but we don't. It's brilliant you're trying to use your experience to help other people, though.' His features seemed to soften – *all of him* seemed to soften – as he brushed a hand through his tousled hair. One strand of grey streaked through it, curly and incongruous. That's what Mac was. A grey streak. Different. Different to what she'd thought, and different to anybody else she'd ever met. And he might not have known the truth about her, but he knew more than most. The thought made the seat beneath her more comfortable, and she melted into it finally.

'If you know of any local charities, artists, or businesses, I'd love to work with them,' she offered.

'I can make up a list and give it to you next time I see you.'

'That would be great. Thank you, Mac.'

He rested his hand on the table, and their fingers almost touched. Almost. She could so easily brush against him if she wanted.

Which she didn't. Couldn't. Instead, she said, 'I was a little bit wrong about you, I think.'

'You mean, you don't think I'm a cat-stealing, garden shears-armed – what was it you called me? "Tosser"?'

She flinched with regret. 'No. You're just a regular old tosser now.'

He laughed, straight from his throat, and it made her laugh, too. 'That's an improvement, then.'

An improvement, indeed.

'Your friend has lost a shoe,' Jessamine observed. She was on her second – and last, she promised herself – G&T, and her already blurred vision was getting a little bit hazier around the edges of her borrowed glasses, but she was absolutely certain that Brodie was dancing by the bar without a shoe.

'He's not my friend anymore.' Mac shook his head in despair, sipped the last dregs of his second pint, then stood. 'I'd better go and . . . sort that out.'

Jessamine had a feeling Mac often had to go and sort things out, and she wondered whether he got tired of it, the way she did. Then again, her responsibilities felt superficial compared to his.

She rose and followed him to the bar, the least she could do should he need her help. He placed his empty glass down and shot Gem a withering glance. She only raised her brows, intimidatingly unimpressed. 'I'll kick him out if he carries on.'

'It's your fault, with your bloody cocktails. They wipe out grown men.'

Gem only shrugged. 'Not my problem if you lot can't handle your booze, is it? Now kindly collect your friend from that armchair before he breaks it, otherwise he'll be paying for a new one.'

Jessamine followed Gem's stony gaze and found Brodie had, in fact, taken to performing the robot on the armchair by an old, unlit fireplace. Her heart stopped when she saw his audience comprised one face she'd never expect to find here. No matter how much Jessamine ran, she always seemed to find her.

Petra.

Her assistant's eyes were glassy as she cheered Brodie on, her face beetroot-red and her hair matted to her sweaty cheeks. *Drunk?* Surely not. Petra was more likely to sip champagne at soirées than get tipsy in a local pub. Besides, it was Friday night. She usually interrupted Jessamine's Saturday mornings bright and early to run through next week's schedule. She'd never once appeared hungover.

Jessamine stepped back until her spine collided with the bar. Petra would tell everyone who she was. She would ruin this strange new normality. No, not normality. *Fun.* Easy, unexpected fun. With Mac. Mac, who had already shared his past with Jessamine. Mac, who she had lied to in return because her own truth had been manipulated by people who despised her.

'Brodie, mate.' Mac shouted to be heard over the music and roaring laughter as he marched over to his friend and tugged on his arm. 'Get down, you daftie, before you break your neck.'

From the bar, Jessamine couldn't hear Brodie's mumbled reply, but Mac managed to drag him off the armchair, instead propping him onto a stool. It was the only opportunity she would get, so as nonchalantly as she could, she wandered over to Petra and pinched the sleeve of her blazer, veering them both towards the windows, where they were shielded by the crowds.

Petra's brows furrowed, recognition only flickering across her features once they'd stopped by the door.

'What on earth are you doing here?' Jessamine hissed. 'Did you follow me?'

'What?' Petra swayed on her feet, the rasped word reeking of sharp, acrid vodka. '*Pardon*?' She corrected herself mid-way through a hiccup. 'No, I mean. Miss Jessamine Townsend . . . Your Ma'am, I didn't expect to see you here.'

It seemed unlikely that Petra hadn't followed her. She always caught up to Jessamine. It was a wonder Jessamine could even go to the bathroom in peace sometimes. 'Then why are you here?'

'Why are *you* here? I didn't know you wore glasses.' Petra poked the lens, leaving a smudged fingerprint behind. 'Are they vintage Chanel?'

Jessamine huffed impatiently, glancing over her shoulder to ensure nobody could hear. Mac was still preoccupied with Brodie, trying to force him to gulp down water, which Brodie just spurted back out again like a fountain come to life. 'I just wanted a drink. Is that all right with you?'

'There is a-plenty of nice wine in the castle's cellar, Mrs Towns-Byron,' Petra slurred.

'Yes, I am aware,' Jessamine ground out through her teeth. Frustration kept building in her. She'd just wanted one night to herself. One night. Well, actually, she'd wanted more than a night, which was why she'd come to Scotland in the first place, but that wasn't working out either. 'Are you *sure* you didn't follow me? Because I must say, I'm growing quite tired of you always hovering around. Quite frankly, I've reached my boiling point. Perhaps on Monday, it's time to enforce some boundaries, but—'

'I didn't follow you, Ms Byron,' Petra interrupted.

Jessamine's fire quickly ebbed when she noticed tears had gathered in Petra's brown eyes. 'Honestly, I had no idea you'd be here at all. It's . . . I'm . . .'

'You're . . . what?'

'Well, I just wanted a drink, too. It's all a dreadful mess.' Another violent hiccup as Petra collapsed into a booth – almost sitting on a middle-aged woman's lap in the process. Jessamine shot her an apologetic smile, glad when she shuffled down and left them alone. 'I think my boyfriend is breaking up with me, and my sister hates me, and I'm in a bar with a disgusting name, and it smells like a men's urinal in here, and that man just hit me with his shoe!' She pointed hysterically across the pub, where Brodie was now gobbling up a bowl of dry-roasted peanuts. Mac looked as though he was on the verge of committing murder, and Jessamine couldn't blame him.

She massaged her temples, even more puzzled than before. 'Why does your sister hate you?'

'Because!' Petra stretched her arms out dramatically and almost hit the woman she'd just lap-danced with in the process. 'I'm here! I'm never home! My sister had a baby last week, and I missed it. I'm terrible. A terrible, terrible aunt.'

Guilt coiled in Jessamine's stomach, heavy as lead. She'd had no idea. In fact, she'd never spared Petra's personal life a thought. She'd just assumed she didn't have one, what with the fact she was always trailing after Jessamine.

But perhaps she'd been wrong.

'Petra,' Jessamine whispered softly, placing her hand over Petra's as she sniffled. 'Why didn't you tell me?'

'Because you need me, and I love my work. I do. I wouldn't want you to think I'm complaining, Ms Byron.'

'I don't *need* you. Not when you should be with your family. You're a wonderful help, but there is nothing here that's worth sacrificing time with your loved ones for.' If she had a close family like Petra's, a town to go home to, a real family, nothing in the world would stand in Jessamine's way. A pinch of cold jealousy ran through her. Even Petra had better places to be. She had a real home, real loved ones. Jessamine couldn't remember how that felt. She couldn't remember anything beyond that gaping hole of loneliness that seemed to swallow everything around her.

She let out a breath and shook her head before continuing. 'I'm on holiday, Petra. My only responsibility for the next three weeks is to organise the fete. Now is an opportune time to take a break. When you're back, we'll look at your schedule and see what we can change to suit you.'

'Really? You wouldn't mind?' Petra wiped her nose with a napkin that had previously been soaking up condensation from someone's drink, all damp-faced and splotchy. Jessamine felt terrible for not noticing sooner. It was something her mother would do: get so wrapped up in her own problems that she didn't notice how it affected her staff. Was she so self-absorbed?

'Of course not.' She pressed her lips into a watery smile, determined to make things right. 'Despite what my mother thinks, I *am* capable of managing on my own, you know.'

A small laugh. 'Thank you, Ms—'

'Call me Jessamine,' she begged, squeezing her hand. 'That's an order.'

'Jess?' a gruff voice questioned from behind. Dread stabbed through her as she turned around, finding Mac standing behind them. 'Everything all right over here?'

'Oh, yes. My friend has just had too much to drink, so I was going to call for a car.'

'Hang on.' His eyes narrowed on Petra, and Jessamine stopped breathing. 'Don't you work at the castle?'

'Yes. I'm Jessam—'

'She's my colleague. Petra.' The lie was out before Jessamine had time to think about it, and it didn't do her guilt any favours.

'Another tour guide?'

Petra looked befuddled. 'No—'

'—Yes, exactly. Anyway, I should be getting her home.' Jessamine stood and yanked Petra up by the arm, trying not to stumble against her dead weight.

'I'll find my coat and help—'

'No, no,' Jessamine assured. 'I should be going, too, anyway. It's getting late and all that gin has gone to my head.'

'If you just wait, we can—'

'Honestly, Mac. I'm fine.'

Mac watched hesitantly, his mouth already open in protest. Desperate to avoid the danger of Petra spilling everything about who she really was, Jessamine guided her to the door. 'Goodnight!'

Her shoulder snagged painfully in the doorway, the threshold too narrow to walk through side by side with Petra. With a sharp 'Ow!' Jessamine manoeuvred Petra and they hobbled like drunken crabs down the cobbled path, the door swinging shut behind them. Now she just had to find a car. There was no chance she'd be able to drag a slumped, clumsy Petra up the hill and across the castle bridge in the dark. She had no idea whether cabs bothered to pass through such a small village, either.

Her shoulder and neck aching against Petra, she puffed out a breath. 'Sit there a minute, will you?'

'Was that the *gardener?*' Petra asked as she obeyed, sagging onto the kerb.

'Yes.' Jessamine pulled her phone from the inside pocket of her blazer and opened Google to search for cabs in the area.

Petra frowned, stretching out her toned, bare legs indecently. 'Why does he think you're a tour guide?'

'You can't tell him I'm not,' Jessamine demanded. 'He just . . . he assumed, and I'd prefer to keep it that way. I'm trying to keep a low profile until all the drama from the article blows over.'

'But if he knew—'

'He can't,' Jessamine snapped, not angry, but desperate.

'Please, Petra. You mustn't tell him the truth. We're friends and I'd like to keep it that way.'

Petra's damp eyes glistened in the moonlight as she looked up at Jessamine. Witnessing her uptight assistant making herself comfortable on the ground in a Ralph Lauren dress was perhaps the strangest thing to have happened tonight. 'All right. Do you . . . do you not truly enjoy being the Countess of Cheshire?' Petra asked.

'It isn't about enjoying it.' Exhausted suddenly, Jessamine sighed and collapsed beside Petra. 'It's been a long year, that's all.'

'It's only April.'

'I don't mean that. I mean, since the divorce and everything. It's made me realise that perhaps I'm not as happy as I thought I was. And now everyone thinks these awful things about me . . .' A lump stuck in her throat, heavy and pressing into her vocal cords. 'And Mac . . . He treats me like I'm normal. He calls me "Jess".' She smiled softly despite herself. 'He isn't a suitor handpicked by my mother. He isn't trying to use me for the sake of gaining a title. He has bigger things to worry about than a silly scandal, and he doesn't judge me the way everyone else does. He just talks to me, and I talk back, and it's easy and nice. Nobody who sees me as Jessamine Byron likes me very much. Is it wrong to want one thing that isn't touched by that life? By wealth and status and lies? Is it wrong to want someone to look at me like perhaps I'm a real person?'

'No.' Petra, who had already sobered up a little, shook her head, her shoulder-length hair ruffling in the breeze and curling at the ends. 'No, Jessamine. It isn't wrong. And for the record, I like you. Robert is an utter arse for making up all those lies and treating you how he did.'

Relief seeped through Jessamine, as though she'd sunken into a hot bubble bath – something she could do with when she got home. It occurred to her that it was the first time anyone had said that to her. That anyone had taken her side. That anyone had held Robert accountable instead of blaming her. 'Thank you, Petra.'

'Jess!' a voice called, followed by the sound of a door slamming shut.

'Speak of the gardener and he shall appear,' Petra mumbled.

Jessamine sucked in a deep breath and stood, dusting her knees. Mac was running towards them, holding her scarf, hat, and shoulder bag. She'd forgotten all about them.

'Here you go,' he offered. Meeting her eye, his own twinkled, his cheeks still rosy from the warmth of the pub and his lips a bit pinker than they usually looked.

'Thank you, Mac. I'd forget my own head if it wasn't attached to my neck.' Her terrible attempt at a joke. Still, he was polite enough to laugh as she took her belongings and tucked them over her arm.

'Did you manage to find a cab?'

'No, actually. I, er . . .' She shifted awkwardly, out of her depth. 'Do you know any?'

'How about I go and get Brodie, and we can share one?'

The thought of being squished into a car with two drunks was less than appealing, but she couldn't think of a polite way of saying no, especially not since she was asking for his help. Still, how would she explain why she was going back to the castle?

'I don't know . . .' she began.

'You live near the castle, don't you? It'll save you a cab fare. I'll pay.'

She couldn't find a way out of this that didn't make her sound ungrateful, but it would mean lying. Again. 'OK,' she agreed finally, stiffly. 'Sounds good.'

'You can't put me in here, Jessaaaa— Jess. It smells like beef,' Jess's friend, Petra, whined as Jess tried to put her in the front seat. To be fair, it *did* smell like beef, on account of Craig the Cabbie's open pack of Hula Hoops, which he'd taken to munching off his fingers one by one while waiting for them to get in.

'My patience is wearing thin, Petra,' Jess warned. She sounded like a primary-school teacher scolding one of her students, and Mac tried not to acknowledge the fact he quite liked it.

Finally, Petra slackened and Jess fastened her seatbelt. Meanwhile, Brodie had already collapsed head-first in the backseat and was spread out across all three chairs. Mac scowled and pushed his legs off to make room for him and Jess.

'Dinnae boak in my cab, ye' wee group of Jakeys,' Craig ordered.

'Was that English?' Jess asked as she climbed into the backseat beside Mac. Perhaps he hadn't thought this through. She was so close he could smell the gin she'd been drinking, the perfume on her neck that reminded him of lilacs. He clenched his jaw and yanked his seatbelt. As he clipped it into place, his fingers brushed Jess's thigh and she tensed just slightly.

'Sorry,' he apologised quickly, pulling away.

'It's OK. Here.' She took his seatbelt and clipped it in herself, shifting so she wasn't sitting on the buckle. Unfortunately, they faced the same problem when Jess had to put hers on. Who the hell had put in these bloody things, anyway? People with arses the width of pencils, perhaps.

'Are ye goin' tae tell me where ye' going, or just fancying a drive roond?' Craig said.

Mac cleared his throat, conscious now that Jess's thigh pressed against him, warm and soft and slightly wider than his. 'Just head for Rosemire, Craig. Cheers.'

'The castle?'

'No, the bloody country. Aye, the castle.'

Craig huffed through a mouthful of crisps, causing Petra to recoil in the front seat. 'No need to get yer knickers in a twist.'

Finally, they set off, the lights of the village blurring past them. Brodie snored on Mac's shoulder, and Mac had never been so embarrassed by another human being before. Then again, he noticed that Petra, who was also asleep, had left a trail of saliva against the window.

'This isnae how I planned the end of the night to go.' He chuckled nervously.

Jess's lips curled with a smile that left dimples below her mouth, just above her cleft chin. In the darkness, she shimmered, her eyes a rich, powdery blue like the colour of forget-me-nots, and he couldn't stop thinking about the fact that they were touching – had been touching like this for most of the night. And he'd liked it.

'I didn't think you'd be the sanest one in the pub,' Jess said, her voice hushed against the whirring car engine as the passing amber streetlights dappled her face.

'I hope it hasn't put you off. I don't go to the pub often, mind, but . . . I had fun tonight.'

Her throat bobbed as she leaned in just slightly. 'I did, too.'

'I didn't,' Petra, waking up with a start, put in. 'Your friend hit me with his shoe.'

'Actually, you walked in front of me while I was kicking it off, so *you* hit my shoe with your heid,' Brodie, also now awake again, muttered.

'Maybe shoes are not something that should be flying around pubs,' Jess commented. She received only a '*Booo*' from Brodie in reply, and then more snores.

'Can't take 'em anywhere,' Mac said.

Jess only shifted her gaze to the window. They were crossing the bridge, the blackness of Loch Leannan encroaching upon them until the golden lights dotting Rosemire chased the shadows away.

'Haven't we gone past your gaff?' Mac had assumed she lived on the other side of the bridge, by the loch banks.

'It's OK. We can just walk from the castle.'

'Craig wouldn't mind—'

'Yes, he would,' Craig said.

The car wheels chafed against gravel, and then the brakes screeched as they pulled up outside the closed visitor's entrance, where the portcullis cast grid-patterned shadows on the floor. It seemed as though Mac was walking to his cottage, too.

'Oot ye get. Who's paying me?'

'Brodie is,' Mac decided, swiping Brodie's wallet from where it had been poking out of his jacket pocket. He barely stirred.

After paying Craig – and not offering to let him keep the change due to poor customer service – they scrambled out in varying levels of intoxication. Petra just about managed to stagger to her feet, her heels getting stuck in the stones. Jess and Mac were the designated crutches. And Brodie, of course, fell face-first out of the cab.

'Jesus Christ.' Mac helped him up, winding his arm under Brodie's shoulder. 'Will you be all right getting home, Jess?' It didn't sit right, letting her walk back across the loch with only a drunk friend for company. It was dark and not safe.

'We'll be fine. Thanks again, Mac.'

'At least let me give you my number so you can text me when you're back?'

She hesitated before unlocking her phone and handing it to him. As Mac punched his number in as a new contact, Brodie decided to start wandering the gardens, almost getting himself run over as Craig reversed. *Numpty*.

'Let me know,' he said again firmly as he handed Jess her phone back. 'I mean it. Otherwise, I'll have to grab my baseball bat and come looking.'

She laughed, her white teeth flashing in the darkness. 'I'll let you know, Mac. Promise.'

'All right.' Reluctantly, he thrust his hands into his pockets and backed away, though it was the last thing he wanted. In fact, he'd been dreading the night's end since it had begun.

Usually, he hated being out past six – the day was exhausting enough, and he quite liked his soft flannel pyjamas and watching *The Great British Bake Off* with Arran, who claimed to hate it while never tearing his gaze from the screen. But he hadn't thought of going home early or wishing he was tucked up in bed at all tonight, too busy learning things about Jess. His skin felt brand new, his stomach a warm, fuzzy tangle of questions he still wanted to ask her, just so he could hear her talk again. 'See you, then.'

'Bye.'

'Goodbye, Old MacDonald.' Petra waved and then snorted at her own joke. That was Mac's cue to leave. He grabbed Brodie roughly and began the walk through the gardens, the fresh smell of the earth a comfort to his stuffy nose. He could still hear Petra singing 'E-I-E-I-O' in the distance.

'You're sleeping on the couch, by the way,' he informed his friend.

'*Pfft*,' Brodie scoffed. 'I'll keep Pickle company in the wee lad's room.'

Mac agreed absently, still distracted; still tingling. He looked back over his shoulder, but there was no sign of Jess and Petra.

'Look at ye, all smitten. Is love finally in the air?' Brodie teased, pinching Mac's hot cheeks.

Mac smacked him away, scowling. 'Get off me, daftie. You know I don't have time for all that.'

'I'm sure Arran wouldnae mind a step-mum. Bit posh for you, though. You're punching, Mac.'

Arran *would* mind, actually. Mac was sure of it. And he himself couldn't afford to be distracted now, not when he was thinking about adopting Arran. So, whatever spark he felt for Jess would have to be snuffed out quickly.

Still, when he kicked off his shoes later and collapsed onto his bed, after having fed, watered, and tucked Brodie in Arran's room, his belly fizzed at the text he found on his phone from an unknown number.

Both home, safe and sound. I hope you got back
OK, too. Thank you again (and sorry about Petra).
Jess x

Mac bit back a smile and then bid her goodnight.

Chapter Eight

After a week without Petra, Jessamine was beginning to realise just how difficult it was to keep to her schedule on her own. She'd spent the days between Fort Aileen, beginning plans for the upcoming spring fete, and Fort William and Inverness, where with Mac's list she had found branches of the LGBTQ+ charity Shimmer, and the mental-health charity the Every Effort Fund, to support – discreetly. Somehow her re-emergence into reality hadn't drawn much attention yet, and Fort Aileen remained a place away from her everyday life; peaceful and quaint and surprisingly summery for the north of Britain.

She tugged at her blazer as she waited for Fort Aileen's planning committee to arrive, trying to protect her nose from the warm, pollinated breeze as best she could using her clipboard of notes. Despite her incessant hay fever, she could only hope the sun would stay for the fete in two weekends' time, otherwise it would be a miserable day – and her mother would truly love that. To see Jessamine fail. Again.

'We couldn't have had this meeting in the bloody village?' The familiar grumble caused Jessamine to turn, and her heart sank with dread at who she found. Hamish, the grumpy man from the tea room who had practically bared his teeth at her. Red-faced and breathless, he led the other organisers across the grass. Under a daisy-printed head scarf, she was certain she recognised Lauren's mother, Elsie. Next to her . . . Was that Gem, the bartender at the Hairy Coo?

Gem, who also happened to be Mac's friend.

Jessamine was done for. Her secret would be out by the

time the fete began. She could say goodbye to the random bunches of flowers she'd found throughout the week, left on the castle's steps with her name on the note. Mac was still trying to figure out what her favourite was with a bit of trial and error. Each time she'd tell him, 'Nope, not these ones,' another hand-picked bouquet would appear hours later. A little game she was enjoying too much, one that left her giggling like a child.

The idea of that all being over shouldn't have left her feeling so empty, but it did.

'Oh, stop your whinging, Hamish.' Elsie tutted, flashing Jessamine a warm smile as the group reached her. 'It's no problem at all, Lady Byron. We just usually meet in the village – but then, we don't usually have royalty in our midst.'

Jessamine clenched her jaw, forcing her features to remain polite and welcoming. She purposely avoided meeting Gem's gaze, though she could feel that dark gaze searing her face all the same. 'I'm sorry. I hadn't realised. Still, I'm not a royal, Elsie. Call me Jessamine.'

'Hang on, hang on. What's this about Byrons and royals?' Gem asked, crossing her arms over her chest.

'Oh, don't you know, dear?' Elsie asked. 'Ms Byron is a c—'

'—Let's get started, shall we?' Jessamine cut her off, clicking her pen ready as anxiety crept under her skin. She was so tired of it, and this time, she had nobody to blame but herself for lying in the first place. She'd never be able to outrun reality. 'I have a lot of ideas for the fete. I've asked Naomi, the castle's archery instructor, whether she would offer sessions throughout the day. And of course, Lauren will be there with the birds of prey.'

'She's ever so good with the owls,' Elsie added proudly.

Jessamine nodded in agreement. 'There are plenty of local and national charities who have been invited to set up stalls, too, but I was under the impression that the town organisers would be booking the fairground attractions beyond that. Is that right?'

Hamish, of course, snickered, his wispy grey hair plastered to his temples with sweat. 'Oh, aye? You do the easy part and we do the heavy lifting, then? Typical Byron.'

Jessamine pursed her lips, refusing to let the fact that she was intimidated show. She was tired of Hamish's rudeness, especially when they were all working on the same side. In a way, he reminded her of her mother, always nitpicking to belittle her. 'That's not at all what I'm suggesting, Hamish. I'm at your disposal if there are any more responsibilities you'd like me to shoulder. I'd just like to gauge where you're at in terms of planning.'

'Well, we've hired one of those bouncy castle thingies,' Elsie answered. 'That can go somewhere around here, can't it?'

Oh, good. They only had another few acres to fill.

'I can assure you, Miss Countess, we've done quite all right without you,' Hamish continued scathingly. 'The fairground attractions have all been hired. I assume you'll be covering the cost.'

'Absolutely. I'll email over the payment details at the end of the meeting.'

'We wondered about an old car show,' Gem added. 'My dad has a few bangers, and my uncle offered to drive his fire truck down from Dingwall.'

Jessamine didn't know what a Dingwall was, but she nodded enthusiastically all the same. 'That would be wonderful. Thank you, Gem.'

Gem blinked, her face blank as ever. It made Jessamine more uneasy. It seemed only Elsie could stand her.

'Well . . .' She cleared her throat and skimmed over the list she'd made earlier. 'Other than that, we only need volunteers for stalls and such. I . . . have these flyers.' She juggled the leaflets tucked between her notes, then gave them to Hamish, who snatched them roughly and looked down his nose at them. 'Perhaps you can hand them out. Make sure local businesses know they're welcome to sell their goods – we've hired more than enough stalls.'

More conversation ensued, and Jessamine nodded along, though she couldn't hear much over the thunder in her chest. Gem knew. Mac would know soon, too. What would he think, after all he'd done for her? All the trouble she gave him with the garden and Rufus? All the flowers and the help he'd offered with finding new LGBTQ+ charities?

He'd think she was a liar, just as Robert had accused her of being. He'd agree with all those awful things people were saying about her. Fort Aileen would end up being just another place Jessamine would have to run from.

'Will that be all, Your Highness?' Hamish shoved the flyers into his jacket and sniffed.

Jessamine tried to dispel the lump in her throat. 'If there are any other questions, you have my email. Thank you, everyone.'

'Thank you, my dear.' Elsie grinned. She tucked her arm through Hamish's and tugged him away. 'Come on, you old fandan. Let's go and get some lunch. You and I are going to have words.'

Jessamine had a feeling Elsie's words would do nothing when it came to Hamish, but she smiled appreciatively all the same and waved her off. The rest of the group dispersed, too – all except for Gem, who remained still as a statue and just as stone-faced. *Here it comes.*

'Mac didn't tell me you were a countess.'

Jessamine glanced around warily, searching for Mac. She hadn't seen anything of him today, and the gardens were quiet, except for the tulips dancing in the breeze. Despite the warm sun, she shivered. 'Perhaps this is a conversation we should have inside.'

'Inside your castle, Ms Byron?' Gem raised a thick, dark, pierced brow. 'The secret countess living in Rosemire. Everyone in town's been gossiping about you. Well, Elsie's book club. Elsie said she was sworn to secrecy and couldn't mention your name, but everyone knows the Byrons own the castle. Your family has quite the reputation.'

Jessamine hadn't known rumours were spreading, nor was she aware of her family's reputation, which Gem didn't make sound good. She'd barely been into town, and nobody on the grounds had mentioned it. As far as she knew, her family hadn't visited this castle since her father inherited it. She supposed it explained Hamish's hostility that day in the tea room – how bitter he had been about her surname and title.

'You're in a book club?' It was the wrong thing to focus on, but she still couldn't figure Gem out. In her experience, frosty thirty-somethings wearing Metallica T-shirts over tattoos and under leather jackets didn't join town committees or book clubs. Then again, they didn't befriend kind gardeners like Mac, either. It seemed Jessamine didn't know much about people at all.

'The meetings are at the pub, and Elsie brings biscuits.' Gem shrugged. 'Are you, then?'

She couldn't lie. It was too late for that. 'Yes. I am. But . . .'

'Mac doesn't know, does he?' If Gem was surprised, she didn't show it.

'Why do you assume that?'

She smirked. 'He probably wouldn't have brought you to the pub if he did. That, and like the rest of us, he despises the Byrons.'

Fiery shame prickled through Jessamine's blood like red ants. 'Why?'

Gem gave a mirthless, sharp laugh. 'Right, OK,' she said. 'Play it clueless, then.'

Jessamine knew Mac hated tourists, but she hadn't known he hated her family. Surely it wasn't because of the scandal attached to her? He would have recognised her already if it was. Wouldn't he?

'I really don't know, Gem.' Her voice wavered. It seemed as though everywhere she went, people found a reason to hate her, and this time she didn't even know why.

Gem narrowed her eyes. 'I don't know much about it, but when your family took over the castle, I believe it wasn't exactly a welcome change for the rest of Fort Aileen. They hired their own staff from London to take over the maintenance. A lot of locals lost their jobs, Mac's grandfather included. He was groundskeeper of Rosemire.'

She hadn't known that. She hadn't even been alive when Rosemire had been bought by the Byrons. When she was little, her father had told her about the grand castle that might one day be hers, her very own fairy tale. After her grandfather had passed it down to Dad, she'd had one or two holidays here, but that was it. She'd inherited it when she was too young to understand, leaving it forgotten. She knew nothing of the history behind it all, but for what she'd learned from the exhibits.

She certainly hadn't known Mac's family was linked to it. If he'd been annoyed by her standing on his tulips, how would he feel to find out that she was descended from a man who had angered an entire village and lost his grandfather his job? What would he say about the hideous *gala* her mother wished to throw just to shove their wealth and status into people's faces?

'I didn't know that,' she said quietly. 'I'm not here to cause any grief. I only want to help out where I can.'

'That's very good of you. Helping the peasants.' Gem toed the flattened grass, scuffs covering her burgundy Doc Marten boots.

This was just another reason why Mac couldn't know who Jessamine was. Her title, her family, stripped everything else away from her. It pushed her into a glass box, giving her a view of a world she would never be part of. But she *had* been part of it for a moment with him, and she had liked it. She was clutching on to it now with two hands, waiting for the inevitable shatter. Waiting for him to hate her, say things about her, the way Robert had. The way Hamish did. Because she was a Byron. Because she was a countess.

She bowed her head, her cheeks stinging as though Gem's words were a slap. 'Are you going to tell him?'

Gem let out a long sigh, tucking her hands into the pockets of her jacket. 'It's not my place, is it? Mac has a complicated life. With Arran, I mean. Friday was the first time I'd seen him having fun in months. The last thing he needs is someone who's lying to him, especially someone who doesn't really care about the consequences.'

She knew that. She did. But this thing with Mac felt simple and easy and right, and it wasn't as though they'd kissed or declared their undying love for one another. Fine, maybe her heart did stutter a bit at the sight of him, and maybe he made her laugh in a way no one else ever had, but nothing had happened. Nothing *would* happen. They were just friends. Friends with chemistry. And friends didn't always tell each other everything. 'It isn't like that. We're not dating.'

'It doesn't matter what you are. Just don't get into the habit of lying to him. He deserves better than that.'

The words clanged through her like a church bell on the hour. He deserved better. Of course he did. Nobody deserved to be kept in the dark.

Jessamine chewed on her lip. Maybe it was best if she stayed away. She was in hiding, after all. 'I suppose I'll keep my distance, then.'

Gem cocked her head. 'Why not just tell him?' she said more softly. 'Why hide it at all – especially if you didn't know about the family history? Mac has a bit of a grudge, but he's an understanding bloke.'

'Some awful things are going around about me at the moment. Things that aren't true. I needed a break from it all, and this would just . . . It's complicated.'

'Like I said. He doesn't *do* complicated.' Under Gem's scrutiny, Jessamine realised just how much Mac was cared about. *That's* what he deserved. Friends who would protect him. Jessamine might have had a castle to hide away in, but she didn't have anybody fighting for her like this. Everybody had turned their backs on her the moment Robert had painted her as his evil ex-wife.

'For the record, he likes you,' Gem continued, already backing away. 'He doesn't form his impressions based on other people's opinions.'

Mac liked her. In another world, this would have been good news, but now, it only drove guilt deeper into Jessamine's gut.

She'd have to keep her promise and put some distance between them. It was the only way.

Two weeks later, Mac glowered at the trucks rolling onto the castle grounds, the sharp, wooden spike of his garden fence digging into his spine as he leant against it with crossed arms. He hadn't known there'd be this many fairground attractions, and he certainly hadn't known he'd have to watch the thick, colossal tyres flatten all the hard work he'd put in since the weather had turned milder for the sixth year in a row. Always the second week of May, of course, when many of his flowers finally bloomed, only to be trampled by feet and wheels. He needn't have bothered spending two hours mowing the grass this week. At least the grounds were dry. Most years, wellies were needed to navigate the sloppy, rainy fairground.

He ground his teeth, imagining all the visitors that would come tomorrow, picking leaves off his shrubs and treading on his flowers, dropping empty crisp packets and candy floss sticks all over the place. *Bastard tourists.*

A splodge of colour in the corner of his eye distracted him – Jess, wandering up the path by his cottage, her brows knitted together as she scanned the bushes. Mac pushed off the fence, ignoring the lick of heat that seeing her always brought.

'Haven't lost an owl again, have you?' he drawled, allowing himself a smirk.

Jess's intent gaze fell to him, her body straightening in surprise. 'Mac. I didn't see you there.'

He shrugged. 'Just watching my gardens get ruined. What are you doing?'

'Oh . . .' She smoothed down her dress, and only then did he notice she was carrying a wicker basket. 'Well, Elsie asked for contributions for her pastry stall tomorrow. I was hoping to find some blackberries for a few pies.'

Mac's jaw clenched instinctively. Fine, maybe he was a little bit fond of the tour guide, but she was still part of the problem. Everyone was at the moment. And perhaps he was being silly and grumpy because these were, after all, not really his gardens, and it would all grow back anyway, but he put a lot of love and care into his plants. More than he should, maybe. More than he was paid to. Sometimes, he wished he could set up his own gardening business. Tend to smaller gardens in Fort Aileen, ones that would be admired rather than ruined. But then he wouldn't feel close to his grandfather, and the idea left a sad ache.

'Oh, no.' Jess gnawed on her bottom lip, her eyes widening. If only she wasn't so bloody pretty. 'Aren't I allowed to pick your blackberries?'

'You'll have a hard time finding any. They're not in season.'

'There goes that idea, then.' Her shoulders slumped, the wicker basket dangling aimlessly at her side as she trudged closer. He only noticed then that her mouth tugged down, as though something more than just the blackberries was bothering her.

Hesitantly, Jess lingered by the fence, watching the trucks grumble around as people milled about, setting up funhouses and stalls and gazebos. Hamish, the town's self-elected event organiser, was among them with a clipboard, ordering people about with stiff jabs of his finger here and there. She began to glower.

'Grumpy old sod is Hamish,' Mac remarked, recalling the time Hamish had asked him to stop mowing the grass because it was 'disrupting his customers'.

'I'm trying to avoid him,' she admitted. 'Hence the pies.' When he raised a questioning eyebrow, she winced and shrank away. 'I helped to organise the fete.'

Mac couldn't hide his surprise. He hadn't known Jess was an organiser, too, especially not since she was so new to Fort Aileen. Hamish probably wasn't best pleased. He hated non-locals even more than Mac, which often meant castle visitors were scared away before they made it across the bridge. No wonder she'd wanted to bake instead.

'Right.' He scratched at his stubble irritably. 'Interesting.'

She blinked as though expecting him to say more, but what *could* he say? The damage was done, and he'd made the mistake of being too blunt with her once before. Maybe it was just exhausting that he was the only one who seemed to care about the gardens. When he'd first started working here, after plenty of hesitance, they had been just fine. The bushes were just bushes and the grass was trimmed regularly enough, but there was no colour, no life, nothing to look at between the fountains and statues. Everybody thrust their energy into the upkeep of the castle and exhibitions, yet the gardens spanned twice as many acres. Granddad was always devastated to see it go neglected, and Mac had been given the chance to fix it for him after he was gone.

'I hadn't thought about the damage it would do.' A crinkle formed between Jess's brows. 'I should have spoken to you about it first.'

'You said it yourself.' Mac ran his fingers along the rough, painted wood of the fence, feigning nonchalance. 'They're not really my gardens. It's all about getting more visitors in, aye? Besides. Happens every year. Nothing you could do about it.'

'Yes, but . . .' She fiddled anxiously with her bracelet. 'Why *do* you care so much about the gardens? I've never known anybody so passionate about their job.'

'I suppose I just like helping things grow. Bit like you and your charities.' He thought of Arran, who was – hopefully – doing his homework in the cottage behind him. Arran still wasn't happy with Mac after the Rufus situation, but they were getting there, slowly. Mac had always known it would take time. Caring for things, people, plants, always did. Maybe his need to pour love into everything and watch it grow was just something he'd inherited from his parents, part of the gratitude he felt for them.

'My granddad used to be the groundskeeper here. He always talked about how the gardens were the best part about Rosemire. He loved them.' He shrugged finally, decisively. 'But the grass'll grow back. Besides, Arran will enjoy the fair.'

'You'll be here, then?' Her voice lightened – was it hope, gladness, or just Mac's wishful thinking?

'Always am, aren't I?' He smiled wryly, noticing her features were still lined faintly with disappointment. And perhaps it was just his need to fix things, to make things better, or perhaps it was because he wanted more time with Jess, but he offered, 'How about a strawberry pie?'

She frowned. 'Pardon?'

Mac motioned to the garden with his head. 'I've got a few strawberries ready to harvest in my greenhouse. Will they do for your pies?'

'I don't know. I've never made a strawberry pie. Wouldn't you want to use them for something, though?'

'Nah. Arran's allergic, so I've been sending them all to my mum, anyway. You're welcome to them.'

'Really?' She brightened, the low afternoon sun streaming through her hair until he couldn't tell where it ended and the light began.

He couldn't help but smile back, shoving his suddenly clammy hands in his pockets. 'Aye. Why not?'

'Thank you, Mac.' She squeezed the soft flesh of his upper arm, and he hoped she couldn't feel his feverishly hot skin.

'Arran's in there if you need a helper. I'm still trying to cheer him up after the whole Rufus situation.'

She bit her lip. 'Oh, I wouldn't want to intrude on your home . . .'

'Well, it wouldn't be right to leave you out here. It's not safe.' He motioned to Hamish, who threw his hands in the air before shouting at another truck driver. His face had turned a dangerous shade of crimson and the vein in his forehead throbbed as though about to explode. They were too far away to hear the conversation, but Mac could imagine the colourful words being used. 'Hamish is on a warpath.'

Mac didn't know why he was pushing it, especially when Jess was acting so reluctant around him today, as though scared to get too close. After weeks of leaving flowers around the castle for her, it made him anxious. Had he come on too strong? Had she had enough of him?

She buried her chin in her thin chiffon scarf bashfully. 'All right. If you're sure.'

Relief filled him as he led her into the back garden through a rusty old gate.

'To be honest,' she said, 'I might need your help. I don't cook very often.'

He chuckled. 'With three pairs of hands, I'm sure we'll get by.'

Chapter Nine

Jessamine knew she shouldn't be here. She hesitated by the gate, debating whether to make up an emergency so that she wouldn't spend more time with him. More time lying to him. She'd told Gem she'd keep her distance, after all. But Mac motioned her forward as he stepped into the small greenhouse and her legs followed without permission.

It was suffocatingly warm inside and smelled like earthy herbs and soil. 'You want the biggest, reddest ones,' he instructed, motioning to the leafy potted plants on the middle shelf.

There were plenty to choose from. Jess plucked a few from the vines carefully and placed them in her wicker basket, her fingers trembling. She didn't know why. 'How many?'

'However many you need to make a pie.' He smirked as though he knew she had no idea what she was doing.

The idea to bake had come from Elsie's request for contributions this morning. Though she could have just nipped to the nearest grocery store and picked up shop-bought pastries for the stall, she craved something familiar, something comforting. Avoiding Hamish – and Gem – was a bonus. It didn't help that she'd accidentally opened her text messages for the first time in weeks and found somebody had sent her links to a fresh story about Robert. He'd been spotted out and about with a new woman: younger and slimmer and prettier than Jessamine – but it wasn't any of those things that hurt. It was the fact that his world continued to turn while he'd tried to make sure hers couldn't. It had made her feel as lonely as ever, and a slice of homemade blackberry pie with a scoop of vanilla ice cream always made things better, didn't it? She needed a reminder that not everything good could be taken from her. Blackberry pie had always provided that, often made by her old home tutor to cheer her up after her father's death. Mother was never home. Miss Hampstead was the only one with time for her, so she let her help with the pastry. She missed belonging somewhere, having somebody to bake with between lessons. But it had been so long ago, and Miss Hampstead had always done the heavy lifting when they'd made pies. Jessamine didn't even have a recipe.

Gently, Mac offered, 'As many as you like. All of them if you want.'

She wasn't used to such understanding. It was as though Mac could see the hollowness lying beneath her confusion. As though he knew just how utterly lost she was.

'This one looks juicy.' He reached over her, wafting a wave of musky deodorant and the smell of freshly cut grass with him. The back of her head hit his soft chest and she was unable to lift her gaze from his fingers as he found a particularly large strawberry amid the leaves.

It was selfish, but she couldn't bring herself to go home now. This was all it took to break her resolve: his smile and his smell and his bloody strawberries. *Weak, weak woman.*

But was she? Or was she just experiencing something new, something she might actually deserve to enjoy? All of her relationships had been watched closely by journalists and friends and her mother before. The dates had been awkward, usually sitting around plates that were too small to satisfy Jessamine's appetite. She'd never met a person like Mac. With him, it was easy. Natural. He was kind and warm and attractive without seeming to know it. A magnet. One that held her hostage with its pull.

She resisted the urge to turn around and press her lips to his.

Instead, she went back to finding fruit, pulling away and

hoping her face wasn't too pink. 'Have you always wanted to be a gardener?'

He shrugged. 'I threw a lot of ideas around when I was a teenager. I started a biology degree at one point, but sitting in lecture halls and scribbling down notes wasn't for me. I always ended up looking out of the window and daydreaming. Would rather be outdoors.'

'So what got you into it?'

'My granddad. He taught me everything when I was young. Nothing quite beat the feeling of watching his sunflowers grow a little bit every day. I liked being responsible for something, maybe. Taking care of plants is a lot more work than people think. I didn't know making it a career was a possibility until a few other locals asked me to help them with odd jobs, too. Eventually, one of the people I worked for told me a job was going on the castle grounds, and . . .' He lifted his arms and then slapped them back down to his sides. 'Here I am.'

Jessamine couldn't imagine ever being that free. Having so many options and choices. Her life had been mapped out for her: a human, social, and political science degree at Cambridge. A good husband. Kids. Only it hadn't turned out that way. She loved her work too much and the idea of bearing children was not enough – not yet, anyway. Certainly hadn't been with Robert.

'What about you?' Mac asked. 'Did you dabble in anything else before charity work?'

'I was taught a lot of skills as a child, but nothing that ever stuck. I wanted to be a ballerina at one point.' She bit back a dry smirk. 'My mother said I was too heavy-footed and refused to let me have the lessons. It took me a while to figure myself out, I suppose, but my family planned a lot of fundraising events when I was younger and I liked the creativity that came with organising them – as well as the helping part, obviously.'

He stopped picking strawberries to look at her, his eyes

twinkling; a constellation of stars she couldn't quite read. 'I must admit, you're not what I expected when you shouted at me for holding my garden shears.'

She laughed at that, and it echoed around the greenhouse. 'No?'

His gaze lingered just a little bit too long as he replied, 'No.'

They picked the strawberries quietly after that. Mac's voice remained a low hum as he told her about the type of soil he used and how he had to make sure the greenhouse was a certain temperature all year round, until suddenly, she didn't need a pie to feel at home.

When they'd filled two small baskets, they went inside to wash the berries. Arran watched them both warily.

'Hello, Arran,' Jessamine greeted happily.

His response was a mumbled, 'Hi,' before he went back to jotting something down in a school workbook.

'Are you going to help us bake?' Mac asked. 'Jess needs an assistant.'

Arran's brows remained furrowed. 'No, thanks.' And then: 'Mac?'

Mac was already pulling out flour, eggs, butter, and sugar. Distractedly, he questioned, 'Hmm?'

'What is "iambic pentameter"?'

'Eh?' Mac stopped, scratching his head. 'What's what?'

'*I-am-bic pent-a-meter*,' Arran said slowly, syllable by syllable, this time.

Mac's eyes widened as they met Jessamine's. 'Er. It's that thingy. Something to do with Shakespeare, isn't it?' he said.

Jessamine trapped a laugh. She remembered her English lessons with Miss Hampstead well, so she hunched over Arran's workbook to see the task herself: to identify which verses from different poets used pentameter.

'It's a type of line in poetry that measures the rhythm. So, "pentameter" means that there must be five feet, which is basically five pairs of stressed and unstressed syllables.'

Arran's brow furrowed, but he listened carefully. Jessamine

demonstrated on her fingers with the first line of the first poem: *My Last Duchess* by Robert Browning. When Arran's features remained crumpled with confusion, she took his pencil and drew underscores and slashes over the syllables. 'When you read it, your voice naturally adds stress to certain syllables. These ones' – she pointed to the underscores – 'these are unstressed, and these are stressed. There are five pairs of them, see?' She read the first line again, following the stressed and unstressed syllables with her pencil and making sure to emphasise each one.

Something in Arran's face clicked. 'Oh, I think I get it!' He scanned the line again. 'So the line would have to have ten syllables to be iambic pentameter?'

'Exactly!' She grinned, lifting her attention back to Mac. The world seemed to freeze when she found him looking back, features lit softly by both the afternoon sun and his surprise.

'Thank you,' he mouthed, face drawn with sincerity.

Jessamine's stomach fluttered, and she felt unsteady, as though she was teetering on the edge of a cliff – but on purpose. She wasn't afraid, didn't feel as though she was falling to her death, like the day she'd walked down the aisle in front of a sea of smug faces. More like she wore a harness, ready to abseil, and the adrenaline had just kicked in.

'I think I can do it on my own. Will you check it after, though?' Arran asked her.

'Of course.' Jessamine returned his pencil and then joined Mac at the sink. 'So. Pie?'

'Aye. Pie,' he agreed. He'd already washed the strawberries, and now they dripped in the colander over the sink. She stared at them, and then at the bag of flour and tub of butter. She had no idea what she was doing.

'I don't suppose you know a recipe?' Jessamine asked, grimacing at her own uselessness. What sort of person baked a pie without the ingredients or the recipe? Especially when she was supposed to be helping Hamish set up the fete, no less. But she'd grown tired of him and his sour words after another rotten meeting yesterday, and she couldn't face him anymore. Not without wanting to slip off her loafer and hit him on the head with it, anyway. He brought out the aggressive side of her. Besides, he couldn't shout at her for doing as Elsie had asked, could he?

A disbelieving chuckle fell from Mac as he leaned against the countertop. 'When you said you wanted to bake a pie, how, exactly, did you imagine it going?'

'Not like this,' she admitted. 'In my head, I was a chef extraordinaire, with one of those flowery aprons and a perfectly thin pastry. I was sort of focusing on the blackberries before I thought about the rest.'

'Well, I'm not sure about my pastry skills, but I do have an apron somewhere . . .' He searched through the cupboards above their head, pulling out a white, poppy-patterned apron. It even had a pocket for . . . Jessamine didn't really know what a baker would need pockets for. Softening their butter somewhere warm, maybe?

She clapped gleefully. At least something had gone right. If nothing else, the apron would save her the trouble of trying to get the flour off her clothes later. She was too busy celebrating to notice that Mac had looped the neck hole over her head. It fell over her torso, smelling like freshly baked cakes and lemon curd. She lifted her arms and he shuffled behind her, tying the strings around her waist. Her skin tingled when his fingers fumbled against the knots of her spine, heat stirring within her. They were slow, gentle, as though teasing her. As though he knew. She pursed her lips and hoped he hadn't noticed her breath hitch.

Jesus, Jessamine. Pull yourself together.

'There we go,' he said finally. 'At least you look the part now.'

She brushed her hair off her sweaty neck and turned to him. 'Dare I ask why you're in possession of a flowery apron? Not that I'm judging. I'm sure you look lovely in it.'

He snorted. 'It's my mum's. Then again, I'd probably buy one just as flowery. Men's aprons usually have misogynistic jokes or naked bodies on them, I've found.'

'Good point. Either way, your mum is a lady of taste.' She smoothed down the creases to hide her smile. There was something about imagining Mac wearing this same apron that made her feel as though she was floating in a warm ocean somewhere. She'd never met a man who didn't strut around like a peacock, trying to prove his masculinity wherever he went – her ex-husband included. But Mac was just Mac, and he didn't seem to care about much beyond that. He had nothing to prove.

Her glance fell to Arran, still scribbling in his homework book at the kitchen table. His hair was long, curly, and today he wore pink corduroy dungarees. She wondered if he knew how lucky he was to be loved by someone like Mac.

'I think I'm finished,' Arran finally said with a sigh. 'Can you check them, Jess?'

Jessamine sidled back over to him, scanning over the texts he'd highlighted as being in iambic pentameter. He'd gotten them all right as far as she could tell. 'Looks good to me. Well done!'

He brightened. 'Can I go outside now?'

'You could go and find Rufus if you want,' Jessamine offered. 'I'm sure he misses you. He was hovering around here earlier.'

Arran lit up. 'Can I?'

Mac nodded. 'Just don't leave the gardens. Dinner is in two hours. Make sure to be back by then.'

Arran stood and tucked his chair under the table, the legs screeching against the kitchen tiles. He ran off without another word, disappearing out of the back door.

'Thank you,' said Mac, more softly than Jessamine had expected. It caused her to do a double-take, and she swallowed down the fluttering wings trying to rise from her stomach. 'I'm useless with homework duties.'

'Of course.'

'He might just forgive me for not letting him keep Rufus now, too.'

Jessamine pretended to look interested in the strawberries, hoping the heat in her face hadn't turned her cheeks the same colour as the fruit. 'He's a good kid, really. A great kid. Very bright.'

'Aye, when he reins in his attitude a bit.' Mac sighed, setting the strawberries aside and washing his hands. 'Anyway, shall we get started on these pies?'

'Sounds good to me.' Jessamine followed his lead, the smell of milk-and-honey hand soap wrapping around her as she lathered it between her fingers. The blue sky streamed through the window, into the kitchen, into her, and though she didn't know why, she was certain she'd remember this moment for a while. A small, teal-painted kitchen, fresh strawberries on the counter, an apron tied around her waist. It was the most normal thing in the world.

So normal that she could almost forget that none of it was real.

'Mac . . ?'

'Hmm?' He was too busy concentrating on hulling the strawberries to look up, though Jess's apprehensive tone didn't fill him with much confidence. At present, the kitchen was covered in failed batches of pastry, with an extra dusting of flour that had somehow also made it into his hair. It turned out that Jess didn't have much culinary prowess when it came to pies, which was probably why she was making a mess of his kitchen instead of her own.

'Is pastry supposed to be gloopy?'

He frowned and finally straightened from the chopping board. Jess stood by the kettle, slightly cross-eyed as she watched a strange, grey-beige concoction drop off her wooden spoon. 'Er . . . I've seen healthier pastries, I reckon. Another batch, maybe?'

She pushed the bowl away, swiping her fringe out of her face and leaving a smudge of the gloop behind. 'This is going terribly.'

'I don't suppose we could just buy the pies from the shop and pretend you baked them?'

'That feels like giving up.' She sank onto a kitchen chair, flour-coated and defeated. 'I didn't think it would be this hard.' Her tongue swiped along her bottom lip. 'Miss Hampstead always made it look so easy.'

'Who?' Mac couldn't help but peer into the mixing bowl, sprinkling another lot of flour in for good measure. The problem was that the eggs had curdled with the milk somehow – and also that he didn't think there was supposed to *be* milk in the pastry recipe he'd found online.

'Oh, just my old . . .' she hesitated. 'Just an old family friend. She used to take care of me sometimes and we'd bake blackberry pies together. It was so simple, so easy, and they were always tasty. I just wanted to remember how that felt. That probably doesn't make sense, does it?'

Mac softened, turning around. He visited his mum so often because he felt the same. Every time he sipped English Breakfast tea from the old cup he'd got in an Easter-egg box one year, or helped himself to the Bourbon biscuits from the tin, he knew he was home. Sometimes, adulthood was just chasing that nostalgia until things didn't feel so heavy.

'It makes plenty of sense, Jess.' Her eyes glittered and he fought the urge to look away. 'You put milk in the pastry?'

Her brows furrowed. 'Was I not supposed to? It was in the ingredients.'

'I think it's for the glaze afterwards.' He pulled his phone out of his pocket again and opened the recipe. 'C'mon. Let's start again. Seventh time lucky, isn't that what they say?'

A small giggle fell from her as she joined him at the counter again. He towel-dried a bowl from the sink, one that had already been used in an earlier failed attempt, and then measured out the ingredients on the scales.

They were on the wrong setting.

'Have you been measuring in ounces instead of grams the whole time?' He couldn't hide his amusement, a small smirk tugging at his lips.

'What?' Jess's face turned pink as realisation dawned. 'Oh, dear lord. I'm absolutely useless, aren't I?'

He chuckled softly – with her rather than at her – as she put her head in her hands, causing her fringe to stick in the gloop she'd smeared across her forehead earlier. He could have politely ignored it, yet his fingers danced at his sides and he couldn't help himself.

'You've got curdled eggs on your face.' His voice came out quiet, shy, as though making room for his racketing heart. God, what was he doing?

'Oh . . .' Her hands rose to her face, missing the gloop completely.

'C'mere.' He dampened a clean cloth and wrung it out over the sink before returning. 'Shall I . . ?'

She nodded, her lids fluttering shut, lashes fanning the crests of her cheeks. Mac held his breath as though he was diving underwater, and it felt like he was. He felt as though he was somewhere else, somewhere new, somewhere he could float and laugh and nothing could drag him down. She tilted her face to him expectantly, all soft curves, as though she'd stepped out of a Pre-Raphaelite painting, like he'd seen in an Inverness art gallery a few months ago, after Arran had begged and begged to go.

He swiped the gloop as gently as he could, smoothing away her frown at the same time. Her lips parted – maybe the cloth was cold, or maybe he'd surprised her. He quite liked surprising her.

'There.' He gulped. Cleared his throat. Stepped away.

She opened her eyes, and then her mouth, but whatever she was going to say was cut off by Arran stepping back into the kitchen.

'Rufus told me he wants to stay with me,' he said. Rufus

was cradled in his arms, happy as Larry. If cats could talk, Mac might have believed it.

Jess laughed again, her cheeks swelling. 'Is that right?'

'Can I take him up to my room? He also said he misses Pickle.'

'Don't you want to help us with the pies?' Mac asked. As awful as it was, using his foster child as some sort of buffer, he needed something to stop the pounding in his chest. He needed to remember why he didn't get involved with people; needed to remember that he and Jess were just friends.

But Arran said, 'No,' and trudged out without another word, so he would just have to do his best. Even if Jess's smile, golden in the setting sun, drew his attention to her lips.

He couldn't go there. They were just friends. He repeated it in his head until he almost believed it. Almost.

'Well . . . it's definitely cooked,' Mac said.

Jessamine groaned. That was a massive understatement. *Burnt* would have been more accurate. The charred lattice pastry steamed over caramelised strawberries. She had well and truly failed, and had ruined Mac's kitchen in the process.

A shrill alarm rent through Jess's attempt at an apology. Mac cursed under his breath and grabbed the tea towel she was clutching. 'The last pie's burning!'

'Oh, crumbs!' Jess had forgotten about the third monstrosity, and now smoke was curling out of the oven. She turned it off before the heat could disintegrate them all entirely, opening the oven door and—

She was choked by plumes of smoke, the stench engulfing her until she could no longer see.

'Stand back,' she heard Mac command from somewhere close. His hands, heavy and steady, found her shoulders and nudged her away gently. She stumbled into the kitchen table, catching her hip on the corner and wincing, but her main concern was Mac in the grey smog, flapping the tea towel fruitlessly.

Sense returned too slowly, but finally Jess opened the kitchen door wide to let in the fresh air. Arran appeared in the corridor a moment later with Rufus still in his arms.

'Is there a fire?' he said.

'No, just a bit of smoke.' She hoped it was the truth. 'Why don't you wait in the garden until the—' A knock echoed down the hallway, just loud enough to be heard over the alarm. The three of them turned towards it. 'Was that the door?'

'Jesus Christ,' Mac muttered, still flapping the tea towel. The smoke was at least dissipating slightly. She knew because she could see him again. He'd worked up a sweat, his face red, and dark patches dampening the grey T-shirt sticking to his hips and broad shoulders and all sorts of places Jessamine shouldn't have been thinking about amid the chaos.

'I'll get it.' She brushed past Arran and opened the door.

A middle-aged woman stood on the other side, her hair tied in a scraggly bun. Jessamine frowned. Mac hadn't mentioned that he was expecting visitors. For a moment she worried it was his mum, but she looked slightly too young to have a thirty-something-year-old son and not the type to own the flowery apron Jessamine currently wore. She was dressed in grey and black instead, pencil skirt curling slightly at the hem. The sign of a long day.

'Hello. May I help you?'

'I'm Linda, Arran's social worker. Who might you be?'

Jessamine glanced helplessly back to the kitchen. The smoke was travelling towards them now. Linda must have noticed, because she shimmied over to avoid being engulfed before looking past Jessamine, her thin brows rising. 'Oh, dear. Not a good time?'

'It was my fault.' Jessamine winced. 'I tried to bake a pie.'

'Right. Well . . . Sorry to turn up unannounced, but

I'm here to talk to Mac and Arran. Perhaps I should have brought a fire extinguisher?'

'I . . .' Jessamine was lost for words, even more so when Linda swept past her without invitation, leaving her gormless on the threshold. She closed the door, panic rising in her. What if her terrible cooking would cause problems for Mac and Arran? Should she even be here? Should she leave?

Helplessly, she followed Linda into the kitchen, her nostrils stinging from the last dregs of smoke. The fire alarm was still blaring, only now Arran stood on the kitchen table and was hitting it with a tea towel while Mac continued to fan the oven with his back to Jessamine and Linda.

'Mac . . .'

'Bloody hellfire, Jess. This is the last time I let you use my oven.'

'Mac, you have a visitor.'

He straightened up, and the colour leached from his face when he turned around.

'Linda.'

'Hello, Mr Douglas.' She tipped her chin to Arran, who was still taking his rage out on the smoke alarm, and smiled. 'Hello, Arran.'

'Arran. Get down off there.' Mac had to shout to be heard above the alarm. 'Mrs Murphy's here—'

The alarm came to an abrupt halt midway through Mac's sentence, leaving his shout to float through the air uncomfortably. Jessamine's ears rang in the new silence, and she bit the inside of her cheek.

Arran didn't seem too concerned about Linda's presence. He climbed down slowly and found Rufus at his feet.

'Hello, Arran,' Linda said again. 'I'm sorry to have caught you at such a busy time. I was hoping we could have a wee talk about how you're doing. It's been a while, hasn't it?'

Arran's wary eyes fell instinctively to Mac's. Mac flashed

him a reassuring smile and urged him forward. 'Why don't I put the kettle on while you two have a chat in the living room?'

Wordlessly, Arran led Linda out. Jessamine frowned, wondering why Arran was so timid all of a sudden. He was always quiet, but she'd never seen him *shy* before.

Mac blew out a breath and flicked the kettle switch on.

'Mac . . . I'm so sorry. I didn't know who she was. You had no idea she was coming?'

'No.' He scrubbed a grimy hand over his face. 'They do this from time to time. Just drop by unannounced, like they're trying to catch you out.'

'I hope I haven't caused you any problems.' She glanced at one of her blackened pies sizzling in a pastry tin on the counter.

With a wave, he dismissed her words. 'No. It's just a burnt pie. Look, I'm sorry I wasn't better help with the baking, and I hate to make you feel unwelcome, but . . .'

'But you need me out of your hair,' she finished for him. 'No, of course. But I should at least clean up. The mess is mine, after all, and—'

'I'll sort it out. I just . . .' He pinched the bridge of his nose between his fingers, and looked so anxious it made her stomach ache. Was it her fault? She wanted to comfort him, but no words would come. Only guilt, a stone in her throat. 'I'll see you at the fete tomorrow,' he said.

His words punctured through her, sharper in her mind than she knew they'd sounded. Despite the kitchen catastrophe, she'd been having a nice time. The best time, perhaps. She'd laughed and made a mess and she could still feel the ghost of his touch on her forehead, just above where her now-greasy hair met her brows.

But this wasn't about her. This was about Arran. Of course Mac wanted her gone; she'd messed it up enough.

'Yes,' she said finally. 'Yes, I'll see you then.' She wondered what would happen if that were true. People would know who she was at the fete, even if she ransacked lost-and-found for a disguise again. There would be newspaper reporters and photographers hired by Mother to document the event. This might be the last normal thing in her life. Tomorrow, it could be gone.

Mac turned his back to her, all hard lines as he pulled mugs out of the cupboard.

Jessamine opened her mouth to apologise again, but it probably wouldn't do much good. So, she collected Rufus from the hallway, where he'd crept from the living room, and left without another word.

'New girlfriend?' Linda enquired casually, bringing her chipped mug of tea to her lips as Mac sat down.

'Just a friend.' He wondered why the word tasted wrong in his mouth. His gaze flitted between the social worker and Arran, trying to gauge what had been said when he was in the kitchen – but Arran was too interested in a loose thread on the couch to look up. Linda always made Arran nervous, even though she made plenty of effort to be patient, kind.

'She shares her cat with me,' he mumbled quietly.

'Aye.' Mac grinned, fidgeting when Linda raised an eyebrow. 'Jess's cat wanders around the gardens, so she and Arran have come to a little custody agreement.'

'Ah, I see.' She crossed her legs, clasping her hands over her knee. 'And how are things between you both? Are you still getting along? Arran, do you like living with Mac?'

Arran nodded. 'Most of the time.'

'Not all of the time?'

A shrug. 'He didn't let me keep the cat. And sometimes he makes shepherd's pie for tea, even though he knows I don't like mince.'

Mac gulped, nerves jittering in his belly, though he attempted to laugh them off. 'I only made it once. Learned my lesson there.'

'The thing is, Arran,' Linda leaned forward, her glasses slipping down her nose, 'you've been here for over a year now, and we wanted to know if you're happy to continue on as you are. If you wanted, we could help you find a bigger family. Would you like that? Some brothers and sisters?'

The thought made Mac feel sick. He wouldn't know what to do with himself without Arran – but maybe that was the problem. Arran was supposed to rely on him; not the other way round.

Arran only shrugged again, tugging on his brown curls. 'I like the bed I have here. Mac bought me a pink quilt, even though the person at the till said it was for girls.'

It wasn't the most solid argument Mac had heard for his parenting skills, but he melted all the same, resisting the urge to ruffle Arran's hair. Arran didn't define himself by the 'girls' and boys' sections', whether they were shopping for clothes, furniture, toys, books, or anything else there might be. He never had. Mac had been trying to help Arran grow as comfortably as possible into whoever he might become, making sure to find books and movies with queer protagonists his own age that he could enjoy so he didn't think there was anything wrong with not conforming. Making sure Arran knew that if he didn't fit the mould most people expected, that was OK. Nobody should be confined by outdated constructs, and Mac had sensed almost immediately that Arran didn't see himself through a black-and-white, traditional gender-centred lens – much like Mac didn't – nor was his attraction to someone tied to their gender. And if he was wrong, if Arran just happened to be a boy who sometimes liked girls' things, that was fine. At least he'd had the freedom, the education, the acceptance, to figure out his place on the vast spectrum of identities. He'd never have to fit into a box. When it came down to it, if Arran wanted a pink bloody quilt, he'd get one. The rest didn't matter.

'Well, that's nonsense. Pink is for everybody who likes it.' Linda's thin smile put Mac at ease. 'Tell me about school. How's that?'

'OK.' It was only when Arran started biting his green-painted nails that Mac realised he was doing the same, and he thrust his hands in his pockets before he was accused of being a bad influence. 'I don't like PE.'

'Not many people do,' said Linda. 'Have you settled into high school well? Do you have lots of friends?'

'Yes. Liv and Callum. They're in my English class.'

'That sounds lovely.'

'I don't want to move away from them.' A frown crinkled Arran's face, making him look older than he was. 'I'm tired of moving. Mac said I can stay as long as I want to.'

'You don't have to go anywhere you don't want to, Arran.' It was a lie, and Mac hated her for telling it, no matter her intentions. He knew the foster system as well as anyone. Arran could be yanked away at any moment and put somewhere else, somewhere where the walls weren't decorated with flowers like his were, and Arran wouldn't be allowed to choose the colour of his bedding. He deserved better than that, and he deserved better than to be lied to about it.

Linda stood up and brushed invisible crumbs from her skirt. 'Well, it's been lovely to see you, Arran. You have my number if there's anything else you'd like to talk about, and I'll come and visit you again soon.'

'Does that mean I'm going to have to go somewhere else again?' asked Arran.

Pain stabbed through Mac. There was nothing worse than not having that stability as a child; never knowing what might be next, who might be next, who to trust. He just wanted to chase those insecurities away. Make sure Arran knew he was safe. But how could he, when Linda was just waiting to yank him into another family, another home, another wave of chaos? He couldn't stop her if that was what she wanted. He could only make sure Arran was loved while he was here.

'Not yet, no. Not unless you want to.' Linda's voice softened just slightly. 'You needn't worry, Arran. We'll tell you if that happens.'

Arran sank back into the cushions, his expression unconvinced.

She pursed her lips, motioning to the hall with her head. Mac's turn.

He followed her out, shutting the living-room door to block out the conversation. The hallway still reeked of smoke, made syrupy by the charred strawberries.

Linda stopped by the coat hooks and tugged on her cardigan. 'Does the smoke alarm often go off in this house, Mac?'

He cringed. 'No. I'm usually decent at cooking, actually.'

'Might I suggest that next time it does, you don't have Arran on the table, wafting the smoke?'

'I think that's fair, aye.' He'd been so flustered that he hadn't known what he was thinking.

'And I trust' – Linda stepped closer, lowering her voice – 'that your personal life won't affect your responsibilities as a foster parent. A child like Arran might find it difficult to adjust to more change, as much as he gets on with your *friend* now. You'll be careful, won't you?'

Mac shook his head. 'Jess and I aren't together, and if we were, I'd never do anything to risk Arran's security. Never. He comes first. You know that, Linda.' Or she should have known that.

Then again, there always seemed to be something to make him look more incompetent than he was when she was around. Running late, burnt pies, a messy house. He couldn't blame her for seeing the worst.

Linda finally gave him room to breathe again. 'Good. I just thought I'd remind you. I'll schedule a follow-up with you via email.'

'Can't wait,' Mac muttered under his breath, glad when she opened the door and let herself out.

'Nice azaleas, by the way,' she commented halfway down the garden path. 'Mine never seem to bloom.'

'Probably pruning them too much.' He flashed her a gracious smile and wave before shutting the door.

In the silence of the cottage, wrapped in the haze of burnt pies, Mac couldn't help but let out a breath. He loved being a foster father. He just wished it was easier.

Chapter Ten

Jessamine was on edge, and the only way to distract herself was to shovel handfuls of candy floss into her mouth, focusing on the way the sugar dissolved on her tongue as she walked around the castle grounds. She was on her third bag, but it didn't matter. She'd seen the same child get a 99p flake from the ice-cream van four times now, and if they could do it, she could, too.

Of course, she did have to avoid the photographers. God help her if Mother saw pictures of Jessamine with a blue-and-pink stained mouth. *Splendour* would have a field day with that. *Lady Byron turns to comfort eating after divorce scandal* or maybe something wilder like, *Countess cravings: secret baby on the way?* – not an uncommon conclusion to jump to when journalists were running out of interesting stories.

The fete, at least, was proving successful, so she could brag about that if nothing else. The gardens teemed with families enjoying the attractions, with pop songs blaring from the Twist ride, which made her feel sick just to watch, and children laughing as they jumped around the bouncy castle. The Waltzers looked a bit rickety, mind, so she'd stayed clear of those.

She'd also managed to stay clear of Mac – whether he was here or not, she didn't know, but she'd made sure to avoid the cottage just in case. Still, every time she saw a spark of red hair or a scrawny, hunched over child, something fluttered in her. She was floating around alone while the rest of the world lived, just as she always did, and she wondered how long it would be before she found her place, her people.

'Ms Byron!'

'Shh!' Jessamine scolded, glancing around nervously. But other than the organisers and charities she'd been planning with all week, nobody had approached her yet. Nobody who treated her differently, anyway.

Surprise stopped her in her tracks when she found the source of the voice. Petra was rushing towards her, ice cream balancing precariously on its cone in her hand. 'I'm back!'

Jessamine blew out a sigh of relief. As much as she'd enjoyed the peace, she enjoyed the helping hand more. 'Petra! I wasn't expecting you today!'

'Well, I was going a bit stir-crazy in London.' She stopped in front of Jessamine, breathless, her ice cream melting over her fingers. 'Turns out that babies cry all the time. They never stop, Jessamine. I shan't ever have one of my own.'

Jessamine bit back a laugh. She was on the same page there. 'What about your boyfriend?'

Petra sobered, taking a solemn bite of her chocolate flake. It left a smudge of ice cream on her nose. 'He broke up with me. He'd been cheating while I was away.'

'Oh, Petra.' With a sympathetic sigh, Jessamine patted Petra's shoulder. She might have hugged her, were it not for the dripping ice cream. 'I'm so sorry.'

'Anyway,' Petra gave a watery smile, 'I'm back now, and that's that. I think I'm better off in Scotland. There are no men. Except for that one over there.' Jessamine followed Petra's point – only to find Brodie, Mac's friend, significantly more sober than the last time she'd seen him. He was with a teenage girl dressed in black who looked as though she'd rather be anywhere else while they queued for the dodgems. 'And he's an imbecile. He doesn't count. Ooh, but what about your gardener?'

Jessamine shielded her eyes from the overcast sunlight, hoping the shadow hid her blush. 'He's not *my* gardener. We're just friends.'

'God, you two are annoying.'

Jessamine jumped at the new voice, lower and gravelly. She whipped around, finding Gem leaning out of the hook-a-duck stall with a long pole in her hand. Great.

'Who's this?' she continued, eyeing up Petra. 'Your lady-in-waiting?'

'She's my assistant,' answered Jessamine carefully, and then frowned at the set-up. Plastic ducks bobbed behind Gem, stuffed orangutans gripping onto the pillars with long, Velcro-joined arms. She would have preferred to win the Eeyore toys on the other side of the stall. 'Do you work everywhere?'

Gem smirked. 'Maybe. Hamish roped me into it last minute. Something about the stall owner breaking a hip.' She waved her words away as though unconcerned. 'I proposed he rename it *Fuck-a-duck* but it didn't go down well.'

'I can't imagine why not,' Jessamine retorted, though she would have liked to see Hamish's face.

'Still staying away from Mac?' Gem asked.

Jessamine pursed her lips and stuffed another mouthful of candy floss into her mouth to muffle the screaming guilt inside her. 'Trying to, but it's harder than it seems.'

Every time she tried, he pulled her back in. Not that she put up much of a fight.

'So you're going to tell him, then.' Gem made it sound like an order.

Petra glanced between them. 'The gardener still doesn't know you're a countess?' she blurted.

Jessamine gritted her teeth. 'Please, say it louder, Petra. I don't think that man over there heard you.'

'Sorry,' she whispered with a wince. 'It's just . . . why haven't you told him?'

'She's a scaredy-cat.' Gem shrugged and began playing her own game with the hooks and the ducks, fishing out an orange-beaked one and then letting it plop back into the water.

'I'm *not* a scaredy-cat . . .' – she was – '. . . and I'm not having this conversation today.' Jessamine straightened out her dress and scrunched her bag of candy floss. 'I'll sort it out, all right? Just give me more time.'

'The more you lie, the harder it'll be,' Gem warned. 'For both of you.'

As though she didn't know that already. The closer they got, the viler she felt for keeping her secret hidden – but also the more desperate she was to keep it that way. To keep things as they were. To keep Mac. It was even worse now that she knew about Mac's grandfather and their family history.

Frustrated, Jessamine blew her fringe out of her eyes. 'I need to go and check up on the charity stalls.' In other words, she needed another sugar fix before her anxiety could build.

She marched off in the direction of Shimmer's table of treats, where George and Sammy, the charity's Inverness representatives, shone brightly beneath the pale sun. But they weren't the only ones. Mac and Arran were testing George's homemade cakes.

She made to leave, but then Sammy's face lit up and she called, 'Hello, Jess!' before waving her over. Thankfully, everybody at Shimmer treated Jessamine like she was one of them, part of the reason why she felt so strongly about expanding and pushing the charity forward. They were accepting of her, friendly with her, and not just because she invested money into them. Besides, she was getting used to her new nickname, and it had just slipped out when Sammy had first introduced herself.

Mac spun around, breaking into a soul-crushing grin. Pink frosting dusted his lips. 'Hello, you.'

That was it, then. No running away now. She sucked in a breath and made her way to the stall, smiling at each of them in turn. 'Hello. You found the cakes, I see.'

George chuckled, their white-framed glasses slipping on the bridge of their nose. 'They're going down a treat.'

'What are these?' Arran gestured to the selection of

badges displayed at the front of the stall, a mouthful of cake thickening his words. The badges had been designed by George, some of them with different flags for the queer community, and others with pronouns to avoid misgendering and make it known this was a safe space. Jessamine had purchased one this morning that read, *she/her*, with the pink, blue, and yellow flag – a symbol that she was proud of her pansexuality. There was nowhere Jess had felt more comfortable than here, now. George wore their *they/them* badge, coloured with the yellow, white, purple, and black of the non-binary flag, and Sammy the blue, pink, and white stripes of the trans flag, also with *she/her*. On the other side, a lesbian flag coloured rainbow.

'These are badges to celebrate our community,' George explained. 'If you'd like, you can choose the one that fits you best and pin it to your cool shirt.'

Arran's shirt was, in fact, cool, with rainbow stitching along the neckline and cropped sleeve cuffs. He deliberated George's words for a moment, running his finger along the badges. They stopped on the same one as George's. *They/them*. 'I think I like yours.' Their gaze fell warily to Mac. 'Is that OK?'

Jessamine hadn't known. She wasn't sure Mac had, either, though she supposed it wasn't her business either way.

'Does it feel OK, kiddo? You tell me how to refer to you, and that's what we'll do.'

'*They/them* feels . . . right,' Arran admitted. 'Like Adira from *Star Trek: Discovery*.'

Mac ruffled Arran's hair, the picture of fatherly pride. 'We'll take that one, and I'll have the bi flag with *he/him* too, please. Oof' – he licked his lips – 'and a box of those cupcakes. You've tempted me.'

George grinned, while Sammy used a calculator to total the order.

'Would you like me to help you with the pin?' offered Jessamine. Arran considered her for a moment and then nodded, handing the badge to her. She held Arran's T-shirt as delicately as possible, weaving the pin through the fabric and then patting the badge down. Her chest swelled with warmth. 'There we go.'

'Thanks.' Arran glanced proudly at their new pin, their cheeks rosier than Jessamine had ever seen them. Pride spread through her. This was why these charities mattered to her, now more than ever. Because finding the right community, a place to belong, meant a difference to people everywhere. Everybody deserved to understand themselves and wear a colourful badge just to show how proud they were of it.

Mac put on his own badge, bright and wonderful on the breast pocket of his pale yellow button-down. His eyes locked on Jessamine's for a moment. She couldn't help but grin, and he returned it with a misty, appreciative gaze before paying and grabbing the cupcakes. With the sun streaming down on them, Jessamine was certain she'd never seen anything as beautiful as this. A father with his child, making a home for them.

And maybe she was a little bit envious that she couldn't be a part of it. She often wondered what Dad would think of her now. Whether he'd still be as playful and loving as she remembered. Or, if like Mother, he'd be disappointed in Jessamine's choices.

She wondered if, in another life, she'd have felt loved the way Arran was.

Pushing away the unexpected grief, she smiled, admiring the warmth and support that Shimmer had created today. The gardens were filled with people wearing their Pride badges. Her world was far from black-and-white here, and that had to be enough. It *was* enough.

When Mac asked if she wanted to join them, she agreed, because she could never quite say no to him.

Mac couldn't pretend to be happy about all the litter he'd already found scattered around the gardens. Luckily the day had stayed dry, so his grass wasn't yet the mudslide he'd dreaded. Still, he glared at a toddler picking one of his poppies as he walked by the stalls with Jess. Arran had fallen in front, interested in the second-hand books Margaret sold and the wooden figures whittled by Pete, Fort Aileen's milkman. It was nice to see them enjoying themself, sporting their new badge happily. Mac had suspected Arran was non-binary for a long while, and Arran had always had plenty of questions whenever they watched or read something with queer characters. The first time Mac had taken them shopping, Arran had gone to the girls' section of Primark and straight to a colourful, rainbow-patterned cardigan. 'Do you want this one, then?' Mac had asked.

'No,' Arran had said, defensive. But they'd touched the knitted pink sleeves again and whispered, 'It's for girls.'

Mac had shrugged. 'It's for anyone who wants to wear it. I think it's cool. You'd suit it.'

So Arran had picked it up, and just to make sure they knew it was OK, Mac had also chosen something from the women's section: a lilac shirt with white daisies that he'd worn to Fort Aileen's little Pride parade not long after.

That was what ballooned in Mac now: pride. That they felt comfortable enough to be themself, unapologetically . . . Mac couldn't have hoped for anything more.

'Did you know?' Jess asked, her shoulder brushing his arm as they fell into step. The corners of her mouth were stained candy-floss-blue.

Mac shrugged. 'I thought maybe it was a possibility. We've talked about it before. I guess seeing other people like them made it easier to pick that badge. And . . .' he nudged her lightly, 'I suppose I have you to thank for that, for bringing the charities here today.'

'I'm glad they could help. Thank you again for that list. I've found so many wonderful charities to work with.'

She stopped, and Mac did, too, keeping a careful eye on Arran, who had found Elsie's pastry stall. Elsie had already started talking their ear off, rising from a collapsible chair and pointing to a doughnut that had been shaped and decorated to resemble Jodie Whittaker's Doctor Who. Another thing Mac would be paying for, no doubt. Not that he minded.

'I owe you an apology for yesterday.' Jess bit her lip, concern wrinkling her forehead.

Mac waved her off, the box of cupcakes he'd bought rustling in the paper bag in his hand. 'No, honestly, you don't. Linda likes to show up at the worst of times is all. I'm sorry you had to leave so abruptly.'

'No, I understand.' She softened, and something in Mac's stomach swooped, as though he were a wooden birdhouse filled with restless sparrows. He wished it was easier to not like her that way. Wished he could stand in front of her and feel steady. He was usually good at keeping his composure – had to be for Arran – but with Jess, it felt impossible. As though she'd cracked him open like an egg and his feelings were dripping all over. It had never been like this before. Not with anyone. He didn't like it. Or maybe he did. Too much. 'I hope the burnt pies didn't cause any problems,' Jess added.

'Actually, she was more concerned about us.' The words slipped from him before he could stop them, and his heart stuttered. He hadn't meant to say that. Why on earth had he said that? 'I mean . . . not that there's an "us".' He scratched his neck, his cheeks blazing. 'She just assumed. And obviously she was worried that if I was seeing someone, which I'm not, it would impact Arran. Not that I'm not allowed to date, just . . . you know.'

Her brows flicked up as though she didn't know at all, and she fidgeted with a button on her blazer. 'Oh.'

He'd expected more. He wasn't sure what; it wasn't as though she liked him the way he liked her, was it? And besides, even if she did, the way he'd shut her down was sure to ruin it. Still, the birds in his stomach were sinking, wings tucking back in, and he regretted it all. He shouldn't. He was doing the right thing, making it clear nothing could happen . . . but it felt like closing a door that he wanted to remain open.

He opened his mouth – to say what, he wasn't sure – but a shrill call interrupted him. 'Mac!'

Sara Willis waved at him and made her way over, tugging her daughter, Olivia, along with her. Olivia had a small glittery pink and blue butterfly painted on her cheekbone.

'Arran!' Olivia called happily, pulling out of Sara's grip to join Arran by the stall. 'Cool badge!'

Arran lit up – they'd been best friends since their first day of high school last September, when Arran (all right, Mac) had forgotten to pack their pencil case and she had lent them a pen. Of course, that meant Mac was sometimes subjected to Sara's rants about single parenthood and how difficult it was, and not-so-subtle hints about how much easier it might be if she had a man like Mac in her life. Mac usually shrugged it off as harmless flirting, but he tensed now with the knowledge that Jess still stood beside him.

'Hi, Sara.' He forced a smile as she met them, her heeled ankle boots sinking into the soil and her jeans already grass-stained. 'Good to see you.'

'And you. I haven't seen much of you recently.' Her eyes slid across to Jess. 'Who's this?'

'I'm Jess.' Jess offered her hand and Sara shook it hesitantly, as though Jess was hiding a mousetrap in her palm. 'I'm, er, one of the fete organisers.'

Sara didn't bother to hide her scrutiny. 'You look familiar. Do you have a child at Fort Aileen High School, too?'

'Oh, no.' Jess tucked her hair behind her ears and gulped as though nervous. To be fair, Sara often made Mac nervous, too, and not in a good way. She could be very . . . intense. 'Nosy', some might have whispered in the schoolyard now and again. 'You've probably just seen me wandering around. I work here.'

'Oh.' Sara nodded, though suspicion still sharpened her dark features. 'Just a friend of Mac's, then?'

'Apparently so.'

Mac frowned. What the hell did that mean? He tried to meet Jess's eye, to figure it out, but her attention remained fixed on Sara.

'Mum, can I go in the funhouse with Arran?' Olivia asked, clasping her hands together as though praying.

'If that's OK with Mac?' Sara raised a brow, rooting around her shoulder bag and pulling out her purse.

'Mac, can I get my face painted too?' Arran asked.

Mac sighed, overwhelmed with whatever had just happened with Jess. Had he messed up somehow?

'Yes. Of course.' He dug his wallet out of the pocket of his jeans and rattled the loose change into his palm. There wasn't much of it, but he dropped it into Arran's hand anyway. 'That's all I have in coins. Here—' A crumpled five-pound note, and then another. 'In case you run out. Just don't go spending it all on sweets. And don't go too far.'

Arran grinned as though Mac had given them a bar of gold. 'Thanks.'

The kids ran off together hand in hand, and it warmed Mac more than the spring sunlight could. Despite his doubts, Arran really had built a life here.

'Maybe we could have a go in the funhouse, too,' Sara suggested with a coy grin.

Mac couldn't think of anything worse. The spinning tunnel always made him dizzy.

Jess shifted beside them, then said, 'I should go.'

Disappointment sank in him. 'I thought—'

'I just remembered, I said I'd help Naomi out with the archery sessions. I'll see you later?' Jess was already dashing away, as though Mac's answer didn't matter. He couldn't help but curse himself inwardly: *numpty*. He shouldn't have said anything about Linda. About them.

Her absence left him chilly, his gut unsettled with the knowledge that he'd just torn something between them, something he wanted to mend. He crossed his arms, clearing his throat when he realised Sara's attention still pierced him.

'She seems very nice,' she said.

'Aye.' Mac sent a final glance over his shoulder before searching for Arran again. 'She is.'

'Suppose we should catch up to the kids, then.' Sara tilted her head, still all smouldering brown eyes, but Mac wasn't interested in being smouldered. Not by Sara, anyway, pretty as she was. He could think only of ash-blonde hair, pink lips, and round, rosy cheeks.

Politely, if not a little distractedly, he agreed, and they followed Arran and Olivia's path to the face painters. Arran asked, 'Where's Jess?' and Mac tried not to wonder what that meant – about what Linda had said, and about what he felt whenever her name was mentioned; and about whether she could be somebody important – not just to him, but to Arran, who noticed her absence just like Mac.

He tried not to think about anything at all, because thinking only seemed to make it worse.

Chapter Eleven

Jessamine already knew how to use a bow and arrow, and when Naomi saw her first shot hit the centre of the target, Jess was despatched to spend the rest of her afternoon helping to teach families. It was at least quieter at the back of the castle, with no photographers or journalists about, though a group of children had just flooded past after watching Lauren's birds-of-prey demonstration. Bartholomew remained on his lead, no longer trusted.

'I didn't know countesses had to learn archery,' Lauren shouted over the fence separating the archery space from the birds of prey, putting the falcon back into its outdoor cage and removing her glove to unwrap a sandwich from tin foil. Jess's own stomach grumbled at the sight. The smell of fried onions and hot, sugary doughnuts had been following her for hours from the food trucks stationed at the front of the castle, but she hadn't had a chance to grab anything since the candy floss this morning.

She swallowed her hunger and nocked her next arrow, though her arm ached and hitting the target had lost its novelty now. Thankfully, nobody she knew was around, with only a few families picnicking on the grass. It was nice, actually. She and Lauren had bonded since the runaway-owl incident – mostly over Elsie – and other than Mac, she was the first person Jessamine had felt *semi*-comfortable with in a while. It would be even better if Lauren stopped bringing up her title, mind, but Jessamine usually managed to steer the conversation away from countess-talk, asking how the birds were or whether she'd been busy that day.

'We don't have to learn archery,' she said. 'But I read *The Hunger Games* when I was fifteen and wanted to be like Katniss. Begged my mum for lessons until she gave in.'

Lauren's mouth tipped with a smirk. She kissed her middle three fingers and saluted them in the air, closing her eyes dramatically just as the characters did in the franchise. 'I understand, my friend. I kept my hair in a plait until there was a permanent kink. In my hair, that is. I don't have a Katniss kink. Well, I do fancy Jennifer Lawrence a bit but . . . you know what I mean.'

Jessamine smiled, and then sighed when another ache shivered through her. She couldn't stop thinking of Mac and she hated herself for it. It was silly to get upset over his words – what had she expected? Mac was a single foster father and she was a divorced countess in hiding. Still, when he'd said they were just friends, it had been a kick to the gut she hadn't been prepared for. And then perky, beautiful Sara had shown up, a single mother who *clearly* had a thing for Mac. And it made sense. A woman like Sara was what he needed. Somebody who knew what it meant to be a parent, somebody who was an open book with an uncomplicated life. Somebody a little bit older and more mature. He didn't need Jessamine and her burnt pies, lies, and baggage. He didn't.

'Are you OK?' Lauren asked.

Jessamine frowned, realising she'd pulled her arrow back so tightly that the bowstring quivered and her arm ached. She released it, and it struck the inner ring of the wooden target. 'Yes. I'm fine. Why?'

'You looked like you were imagining the target as someone's head – and you've been hiding from your own fete for hours.'

'I'm not hiding,' she lied, wandering over to the target and pulling out the arrow carefully. 'And it's not *my* fete. I just helped to plan it this year.'

Lauren shot her a doubtful look.

Jessamine sighed, biting her bottom lip as she placed the

arrows back into their holder. 'I'm . . . confused. Men are confusing.'

'Ah, yes. They are,' Lauren agreed knowingly. 'I try to stay clear of them. Wouldn't happen to be about our friend, Mac, would it?'

Jessamine wanted to scream. Was it so obvious? Did everybody know everything about her? Maybe she was less complicated than she thought. Maybe she was too transparent to ever keep secrets from anyone. Still, she gave it a final go. 'What makes you think that?'

Lauren shrugged, then made a start on the second half of her sandwich, a piece of egg mayonnaise dropping onto her chin. 'I've seen you two together a lot recently. You seem to smile more when he's around.'

Heat flooded Jessamine. She was absolutely sure her face had turned the same shade as a cherry tomato.

Did she smile more around Mac? Probably. He made her laugh, with his silly quips and his crooked smile and . . . Oh, dear. This was worse than she thought.

'I can't blame you,' Lauren continued, voice muffled through her chews. 'He's got that rugged dad thing going on. Tall, too. Course, his mind's always elsewhere. Can't have a straightforward conversation without him drifting off or remembering he's left the oven on at home or something. That must be frustrating.' Her expression was all innocence, but Jessamine narrowed her eyes at the subtle probing.

'He's a busy man.'

'I'm sure nobody's too busy for a countess.'

Jessamine sighed, wringing her fingers nervously and leaning across the fence so she wouldn't have to talk too loudly. 'He doesn't know about that. He . . . thinks I'm a tour guide.'

Lauren choked until she had to thump her chest. She managed to rasp out, '*What?*'

Jessamine grimaced, putting her head in her hands. She didn't know why she was telling Lauren. Lauren, who already knew who she was. Soon, only Mac would be left in the dark, and that wasn't fair to him. 'I know. I'm terrible.'

'I don't understand. Why wouldn't you tell him?'

'*Because,*' she huffed, unfastening her leather armguard with more force than necessary, 'everybody treats me differently, and I'm supposed to be on holiday, and I just got divorced from an awful man, and I didn't think we'd . . .'

What? She and Mac weren't anything. He'd made that clear. Still, when he'd approached her with garden shears and scolded her for stepping on his tulips a month ago, she hadn't imagined they'd end up here. Wherever 'here' was.

'I didn't think it would matter,' she went on. 'We didn't even really get along. But then . . .'

'But then he threw you a little smirk and you were smitten,' Lauren completed.

'*No!*'

Lauren rolled her eyes. Perhaps she was *too* comfortable around Jessamine these days. Or perhaps just too blunt. 'You should tell him. He's going to find out eventually. I mean, you live in the bloody castle. Besides, I'm sure his interest would be piqued if he knew the woman he fancies is a countess.'

'He doesn't *fancy* me,' Jessamine protested, though her stomach fluttered at the very idea.

'Oh, he does. He's always looking around the gardens for you, even if he doesn't admit it. He . . . Oh, shit. He's coming.'

She frowned. 'Pardon?'

Lauren pointed and whispered, 'Behind you,' while spraying mayonnaise and cress all over the grass.

Jessamine whipped around, nerves spiking when she found Mac's broad figure approaching. Only he looked . . . orange. As he entered the archery pen, she realised he'd had his face painted to look like a tiger, with black stripes and whiskers. Arran had a colourful rainbow spanning from the side of their temple to their cheek, just like the ones on their shirt. Sara was the only one who hadn't been made up, looking perfect as ever as she laughed at something Arran and their friend said.

Mac stopped when he caught sight of her, and he shifted closer to the fence, behind the painted lines in the grass that marked the safety zone. 'Wondered where you'd got to.'

Jessamine forced a smile. 'You make a very lovely tiger, Mac.'

A surprised chuckle emerged from him and he touched his cheek as though he'd forgotten about the paint. His fingertips came away orange. 'Arran's idea.'

'Can I use a bow and arrow, Mac?' Arran shouted, already inspecting the bows.

Mac grimaced. 'That's an accident waiting to happen.' Still, he turned around and replied, 'Only if Naomi says it's OK.'

Naomi flashed him a thumbs-up and then handed both Arran and their friend a bow and their armguards. Mac turned back to Jessamine, the sun rolling over the castle top and into his pale eyes.

He bowed his head, squinting, all bronze lashes that matched the colour of his face paint. 'Look, can we talk? I feel like something went wrong earlier, and I don't . . .' He sighed as though he couldn't find the words, brushing his wavy hair off his forehead. He glanced at Sara, who was staring at them, and then nudged Jess further away as though wanting privacy.

'You don't what?' Jessamine asked, her mind beginning to race. For once, she wanted them to acknowledge what was between them. No more hiding. Hypocritical, since that's what she'd done all day – well, all month – but it felt different now. Lauren was right; she liked having Mac around, and she didn't like seeing him with Sara, and the idea of him having his face painted for Arran's benefit made her want to melt into a sad little puddle, because it was lovely and wonderful, and the whiskers were adorable. *He* was adorable.

'I don't know,' he murmured. 'I like your company. I wouldn't want to do anything to upset you.'

And then there was the guilt, back with a vengeance. Mac was working hard, talking to her, always so open and real, and she hadn't offered him the same. She couldn't hide it anymore. Not if they were going to have this conversation. She put her hand on his elbow and then pulled him further away – this time from Lauren, who was attempting to catch their conversation, despite the fact a group of children were congregating around the bird cages. The painted lines in the grass were forgotten. Everything was forgotten but the lies weighing heavily in Jessamine's gut.

'There's something I need to tell you, Mac.' Her hands shook, and she folded them into her dress.

Mac's brows wrinkled. 'OK. You can tell me anything—'

'—Hold!' Naomi shouted, but Jessamine was barely listening. She took a deep breath.

'Well . . . I'm . . .' Oh, God. This was it. She tried to force the words out of her throat, onto her tongue—

'—Oi!' shouted Lauren, as a flurry of feathered wings flapped behind the fence. At the same time, on this side of the fence, something whistled through the air. Mac roared as though he'd embodied the painted tiger, straightening to twice his usual height. Arran stood behind him, bow pointed at Mac's back, with a mouth shaped like an 'o'. Naomi covered her mouth with her hands, paling in shock.

Jessamine didn't know whether to laugh or cry.

Cry, she realised as Mac crumpled in on himself, hopping around as though he was stepping on hot coals.

Definitely cry.

The arrow dropped to the grass, but the rubber end had torn a hole in the back pocket of Mac's jeans, displaying some interestingly patterned boxers – were they Christmas trees? In May?

Not the time, Jessamine. She gasped as the realisation finally hit, gripping Mac's arm as he grumbled and clutched his rear end. 'I've been shot. I've been shot, Jess.'

'It hasn't gone through your . . . underwear,' she reassured, taking another look just to be sure. She certainly wanted to be sure, after all.

She was vaguely aware of Lauren ranting about not setting the birds free, and peered over the fence to find her with the falcon perched on her arm, her face filled with thunder, while the four young teens displayed varying degrees of guilt. One was crying. Another was arguing back in a deep Scottish brogue. They must have opened the cages while Lauren was eavesdropping – which would have been a disaster if not for the extra safety precautions Lauren had taken since Bartholomew's escape.

Dear lord. Jessamine didn't know where to look, which tragedy to focus on first.

'"Be a foster father", they said,' Mac muttered, still hopping. '"It'll be so rewarding". *Arran!*'

'It was an accident!' Arran replied.

Cringing, Naomi gently eased the bow from their grip: a wise decision.

'The target is over there!' Mac jabbed a finger to the wooden targets, which were most definitely nowhere near his bottom.

'Are you all right, Mac?' asked Sara, running over.

Mac hissed through his teeth, and Jessamine's brows knitted together.

'Maybe we should take you to a hospital, just to be sure your . . . bum is all right?'

'No. No,' he whispered, using Jess's shoulder to prop himself up. 'If Linda hears about this . . . Fuck . . .'

He didn't need to complete the sentence. It wouldn't reflect well on either of them.

'Then we should get inside. Get some ice on it,' she suggested, eyeing the castle's conservatory warily. Lauren was asking where the kids' parents were as she put the falcon back in its cage. Oblivious, Mac was pulling in the other direction, limping across the grass.

'Come on, Arran,' he said. 'We're going home.'

Arran at least had the good sense to follow, head bowed and steps dragging.

'Mac . . .' Sara had shock written all over her features.

Mac's face creased with a strained smile. 'Sorry, Sara. Thanks for a lovely afternoon. I'll see you next week, aye?'

Flustered, Jessamine didn't know what to do. She couldn't just leave him, not without knowing how bad the damage was. She trod over to the discarded arrow and shot a wary glance between Lauren, Naomi, and Sara in turn. 'I'll make sure he's OK.'

They nodded, faces full of concern.

'The arrowheads are rubber,' Naomi provided. 'Should just be a bad bruise. I tried to stop them, but the birds and . . .'

'Too much happening at once,' Jess replied, understanding. She was just glad Lauren hadn't lost another bird. They were truly adding a new meaning to the term 'flight risk'. Lauren was marching off in the other direction, the children leading the way. Someone's parents were about to get an earful. At least Bartholomew's escape had been an accident. She wouldn't have liked to be on the receiving end of that. She could practically see the steam billowing from Lauren's ears.

After waving goodbye, Jessamine rushed to Mac, slowing when she reached his side. 'Are you all right?'

'Have you ever seen a grown man cry, Jess? Because I think you're about to.' It looked that way, too; his features were taut as though he was just barely holding it together.

'I didn't mean to,' Arran said again.

'It's OK,' Jessamine said, squeezing Arran's shoulder in reassurance and then huddling into Mac's side so he could drape his arm across her shoulders. His breaths were laboured, body heavy, as they staggered their way down the gardens, to his cottage. 'At least you're in disguise,' she whispered, noticing the face paint smudging where sweat emerged from his hairline. 'Cry it out. I wouldn't judge.'

But he didn't, and they walked in silence, him biting his

knuckle as he waited for the sting to subside and her just trying to hold them both together.

Mac soon found out that he wasn't ready to sit down. He took to pacing the kitchen while Jess rooted through his freezer. 'Will a bag of Lawson's sausages do? I can't find anything else.'

Mac nodded, tight-lipped, and was glad when she passed the pack of frozen sausages to him. He pressed them against his left bum cheek where Arran had shot the arrow. He knew he'd be fine once the pain eased, but at the moment the shock was still making him dizzy.

Arran stood in the doorway, pale and lost. Mac tried desperately not to be angry, but it had bloody well hurt – the type of well-placed pain that had dragged a lump of tears straight to his throat, like the time he'd thought he could do a seat drop without a trampoline and bruised his coccyx. 'Arran, why don't you go and watch TV upstairs?'

They wandered off, the sound of their footsteps thudding up the stairs a moment later. Mac let out a breath of relief.

'You should sit down,' Jess suggested.

'Not sure I can.' He leaned against the countertop instead, using it to wedge the sausages against his wound. His dignity whirled down the sink's plughole with last night's murky dishwater, and he couldn't meet her eye. What an embarrassment he was, getting shot in the arse with an arrow by his own foster child while wearing tiger-themed face paint. He didn't even know how it had happened: whether Arran had aimed on purpose or whether it had been a result of the children next to them messing with the birds. He was just glad it had hit him rather than an innocent bystander like Jess.

'Maybe . . .' She shifted uncomfortably. 'Maybe I should take a look, just to make sure it's not bleeding.'

'I'm not . . .' He coughed, and then regretted it with the new wave of pain. 'You really don't want to look at my bruised bum, but thank you.'

'I wouldn't mind,' she whispered, colour smattering her cheeks.

He wanted to disappear. 'I would.'

'Maybe you really should see someone.'

'No.' His answer was too firm, too sharp, but he couldn't help the defensiveness that ignited in him at the thought. He raked a hand through his hair. 'I'll be fine. The sausages are already numbing it – a sentence I never thought I'd say.'

Her lips quivered with a suppressed laugh. 'At least let me make you a cup of tea, then.'

He hesitated, about to reject the offer out of pride alone – but then she'd leave. He wasn't ready for that yet. He pursed his lips. 'All right. Cheers.'

Exhaustion weighed on him as Jess flicked the kettle's switch. He helped her find the mugs, feeling as though he might collapse at any moment. Not from the arrow. His stomach was wrenching, and those tears he'd kept at bay all the way home were on their way. He was hurt. By Arran, by the way it never seemed to get easier. Sometimes, he felt like he was getting somewhere, but it was always ripped away before he could feel that joy. Before either of them could. And if Linda found out . . .

'On second thoughts, I'm going to try to sit down,' he mumbled, trudging unsteadily into the living room. He had to sit on the frozen sausages and use the arm to keep his weight off the bruise. It had been going so well today. Too well.

His throat ached. He squeezed his eyes closed to try to staunch the tears, but it made no difference. They came anyway. All he could do was try to breathe while he listened to Jess hum an unrecognisable tune in the kitchen, voice soft and soothing as honey. He never wanted her to leave. Wanted to hear her milling about his cottage as though she belonged here forever.

'You didn't have any milk – my fault, with the pies and all. I made the tea black, but I'll get you a fresh carton later,' she said. 'Nothing beats a good strong tea, does it?' Her feet inched closer, but he couldn't bring himself to open his eyes, though he wiped the dampness from his cheeks.

She paused in front of him, two steaming mugs in her hands. 'Mac?'

'Cheers, Jess.' He forced a wobbly smile, his vision blurred. 'I actually think I'm all right now. You don't have to stay. Go back to the fete; you planned it, after all.'

She contemplated him for a moment before putting the mugs down on the coffee table. And then she sank beside him, lacing her fingers through his, and it only made him want to cry more.

'I'm sure it was an accident,' she whispered. 'A lot happened. They could have been distracted by the kids letting out the birds. Maybe they were even trying to stop them.'

He only hummed. Maybe his lack of confidence in Arran was wrong, but after all the overwhelming mistakes Mac had made recently, he couldn't be sure. Besides, wasn't it worse if Arran was aiming for someone else?

'You're OK, Mac. You're both going to be OK.' She shuffled closer. Her breath smelled like sherbet, her perfume like honeysuckle after the rain. He could smell the outdoors on her, grass and fried food from the trucks. It grounded him. Made him feel less like he was floating alone on a deserted island and more like he was here, with Jess. OK. 'You're a good father. A really good father. Arran knows that.'

'I wonder sometimes,' he admitted. 'I wonder if Arran would be better off somewhere else.'

'You know that's not true.' Jess shook her head. 'I've never seen any parent love a child the way you do Arran. You must know that.' She squeezed his hand delicately, and he wanted her to hold him that tightly always.

Don't let go. Please, don't let me go.

A slither of him knew it was true. He was doing his best with Arran. He had an infinite amount of love and patience to offer, and he was doing his best. But . . .

'It never feels like enough,' he admitted, bottom lip wobbling. 'Feels like they see right through me sometimes. Like they know that, really, I have no idea what I'm doing.'

'You know what you're doing,' she said. 'You're loving them. You're supporting them. You're giving them a good home. That's what you're doing. What more is there?'

Her finger twirled through a kink in his hair, and his lids fluttered shut involuntarily. She was so gentle, so delicate, so solid against him.

'It's enough, Mac,' she promised. It was all he'd needed to hear. For the past year, it was all he'd *wanted* to hear. And maybe it wasn't coming from Arran or Linda or anybody else, but it meant just as much to hear Jess say it. Because everything Jess said meant something to him, and he couldn't keep fooling himself into thinking otherwise.

So, he leaned against her. Her fingers stroked his hair, along his striped-painted cheek, and they stayed like that for minutes, hours, years, with the sound of Arran's blaring television drifting down the stairs.

He promised himself tomorrow would be better. With Arran, with Jess, with everything. He'd keep trying. He wasn't giving up. Arran would know it, too, sooner or later.

'I'm going to say goodbye to Arran, if that's OK,' Jessamine said, squeezing Mac's shoulder gently before getting up from the couch. They'd been sitting for almost an hour, and she really did have to chat to the charity workers before they began packing up for the day. While the fairground didn't shut until dark, the stalls were due to close soon. It was nearing five o'clock, the sun sinking lower, and she could no longer put it off, no matter how much she wanted to stay, to make sure Mac knew he wasn't alone. 'I'll come back later.'

'No, no.' Mac shook his head, tiredness fraying his features. His hair was a disorganised nest of curls and his five o'clock shadow darkened his chin and jaw below the smudged paint. He stood up, disappearing into the kitchen with his thawed sausages as he said, 'I need to talk to Arran. Fix things. But first, I need to get this shite off my face.'

She knew better than to force it any other way. This was between Mac and Arran now.

Following him down the corridor, she was glad to see him moving easier. After turning on the tap and cupping his hands beneath the running water, he splashed his face, scrubbing off the orange and black paint. Jessamine could only watch his hunched shoulders roll beneath his shirt for a moment, mouth falling open involuntarily as he lathered his hands with a bar of soap and dragged off the last stubborn dregs. The man's skincare methods were poor, but even now, she couldn't ignore the tug of attraction in her belly.

'Let me know how it goes?' she managed to get out in the hopes he didn't catch her speechless and staring.

He nodded, drying his damp face before turning around. Streaks still lingered here and there, but at least now it was easier to decipher his expression. 'Thank you, Jess. For everything.'

'Of course,' she whispered, and meant it. Somehow, somewhere, Mac had become important to her. His well-being, his family. She found herself thinking about him when she was pottering around the castle, sipping tea or in a meeting or drawing a bath. He was always lingering in the corners of her mind, waiting, and . . . she just wanted to be around him. She just wanted to see him smile, hear him laugh. She wasn't sure what that meant; she'd never felt it before.

'And of course you can say goodbye to Arran,' he added softly.

Jessamine offered him a final smile before heading back to the entryway. She placed her unsteady hand on the paint-chipped banister and went upstairs, taking slow steps in case she alarmed Arran. She assumed their door was the one painted red, a Minecraft poster pinned to it. The others were coated in the same sage green as the kitchen cupboards downstairs, two doors clustered on a tiny landing with a tall snake plant potted atop a side table by the window, basking in the amber light and casting spiked shadows on the carpet. It was so small and homely, and so Mac. She could easily sink to the floor and just exist here peacefully, letting her worries drift past with the clouds.

Instead, she tapped on Arran's door.

No response.

'Arran?' she called. 'It's Jess. May I come in?'

Only silence rang across the landing. She didn't want to invade their privacy, not when it wasn't her place, but worry fizzled in her all the same. Her hand hovered on the doorknob. 'I just want to pop my head in and say goodbye. Is that OK?'

Nothing.

'I'm coming in.' She sighed and pushed the door open, peeking through the small opening warily. Arran's room was covered in comics and books, and a row of small succulents lined their windowsill. The window was wide open, and the bed was unmade, empty.

They weren't here. She stepped in just to be sure, avoiding a crumpled drawing as she did. A wooden hutch sat beside a desk, and a grey rabbit stared accusingly at her from its wired cage. The curtains rippled in the slight breeze. It wouldn't have been difficult for a skinny twelve-year-old to climb out of the window, especially not in such a small cottage. There wouldn't be too big a drop into the back garden.

Dread surged through her. If it hadn't already, Mac's heart was going to break – and she would have to be the one to break it.

'Mac!' She hopped down the stairs two at a time, breathless as the panic began to set in. 'Mac!'

'What's wrong?' Mac met her in the corridor, alarmed.

'Arran isn't in their room. The window was open . . .'

'For Christ's sake.' He scrunched his eyes shut, exhaling slowly through his nose. She'd never known how, even now, he could find that patience, though he was no longer making it look easy. He pulled out his phone from the front pocket of his jeans and dialled quickly. A moment later, a generic ringtone vibrated from upstairs. Mac swore. 'I keep telling Arran to have their bloody phone with them at all times. I have to go and find them.'

'I'll help.' She pulled on the jacket she'd left draped across the armchair in the living room, and together they left the cottage. 'Maybe they'll be by the loch. Doesn't Arran go there a lot?'

'Aye, to cool down.' Mac spoke through gritted teeth – pain or stress, she didn't know. Once he'd opened the gate for her and they strode back into the jam-packed gardens, it was instinct to slot her hand into his, if not to comfort him, then to catch up with him as he frantically weaved through the fete-goers. His palms were rough, but his grip tightened around hers as though he didn't want to lose her. As though he wanted her here beside him.

'Everything all right, Mac?' Gem called as they passed the hook-a-duck stall. Jessamine tried not to blush at Gem's raised brows when she glanced pointedly at their interlocked hands.

He stopped, but still didn't let go. 'Have you seen Arran?'

'About fifteen minutes ago, maybe. Tried to ask about their new badge, but they looked like they were on a mission. I thought they were looking for you. Oh—' her attention landed on Jessamine, '. . . and that assistant of yours was looking for you, Jess. She needed help. Brodie caught her, and she wasn't too impressed.' A smirk.

'Assistant?' Mac asked.

Jessamine swallowed, trying desperately to come up with an answer. Gem, too, seemed to realise her mistake, and they locked eyes warily.

'Petra, she means,' Jessamine answered finally.

'Aye. Just poking fun. She's always trailing after Jess like a little lap dog, isn't she?' Gem shrugged it off, the lesbian flag pinned to her shirt bouncing with the movement. Even

151

she had supported Shimmer today, and the thought might have left Jess warm if she wasn't so wary of the woman.

Mac frowned but tipped his head sharply, scanning the crowds a final time. 'Just text me if you see Arran, will you?'

Her brows knitted together. 'Of course.'

They plunged back into the throng of people, Jessamine's heels sinking into the trampled grass as they paced towards the bridge. 'We'll find Arran,' she reminded him gently when his grip grew too tight, his jaw too clenched.

'They wander off a lot, but never without telling me. Never like this.'

The waters of Loch Leannan lapped against stone beneath them as they began the walk across the bridge. Cars were parked on every inch of the road, visitors standing around and devouring ice cream, taking selfies, enjoying themselves. She should have been happy to see it, happy to know the fete had been successful and one less thing her mother could criticise her for, but none of it meant anything if they didn't find Arran.

Finally, past the brimming tea room where Hamish begrudgingly cleaned down outdoor tables, they reached the grassy banks where Jessamine had first met Arran. She let out a relieved breath at the sight of a hunched figure in exactly the same spot, their arms crossed to keep warm and their hood pulled over their head. Even with their back turned, she knew it was them.

'Is it better if I stay or go?' she asked as Mac came to a stop.

His gaze lowered to her, as soft and gentle as Leannan's waters. 'Stay.' It came out cracked, the same way Jessamine's aching chest felt.

She drew across his callused knuckles with the pad of her thumb, glad he wanted her here if only for now.

Then Mac pulled her forward, and they approached Arran together, as a team.

He stiffened behind them as though not sure what came next. Jessamine didn't know either, but she knew how it had felt to sit beside them once before and thought it best to start the same way. She patted Mac's shoulder in reassurance and then took her place where she'd sat last time, a couple of steps away from Arran so they didn't feel cornered.

Arran only glanced at her before throwing a stone in the loch, cross-legged and blank-faced. The water plopped and rippled through the reflection of the clouds above.

'You come here when you're angry?' she asked gently, finally.

They shrugged, chucking another stone. 'Not just when I'm angry.'

Mac's boots crunched as he took his place at Arran's other side, keeping just as far away. 'Can we talk about it, kiddo?'

Arran only glowered, their lashes casting shadows on their scrunched, rosy cheeks.

'I remember I broke my mother's window when I first took up archery lessons,' Jessamine said, feeling the heat of two sets of eyes on her neck. She kept looking into the lake, just as she had last time she'd talked with Arran. She needed them to know that this wasn't an attack. They could talk. 'Shot an arrow straight through the glass. She grounded me for a month. I did it on purpose, too.'

'Why?' Arran asked.

'Because I was angry.' She tugged a dandelion from the cracks in the rocks, twirling the stem until the seeds dispersed across her dress and floated into the breeze. 'She didn't . . . see me, I don't think. I wanted her to pay attention to me, even if it was to shout at me, because otherwise . . . I felt like perhaps I didn't exist.'

'*Did* she shout at you?'

She shook her head. 'No. Not really. She lectured me and threatened to cancel the lessons, but she didn't shout. My mother never shouts, really. She doesn't care enough to react a lot of the time. Not unless I've embarrassed her in front of her friends.'

A beat of silence passed between them, and then Arran said, 'I didn't do it on purpose.'

'Arran . . .' Mac's shoulders slumped, and he leaned back on his palms, half hovering on the side that was injured. 'Do you *want* to be here with me? Because it's OK if you don't. We can tell Linda you'd rather be taken in by someone else, and—'

'*No*,' Arran interrupted sharply. 'I don't want to go back or move away.'

'You're not in trouble, y'know. If you say it was an accident, then I believe you. I just . . . I don't know what's best for you. I thought I did, and I'm really trying, but it seems like I'm not what you want. And it's OK if I'm not. It's really OK. Just tell me how to help you.'

Arran sniffed. Jessamine's own eyes began to tear, both from Mac's words and the fact her allergy tablets were wearing off for the day. There was nothing in the world worse than feeling unworthy, like nothing you did was enough. Nothing. She'd faced it her whole life, and it still left a hole festering inside her whenever Mother criticised her.

'I don't know why I do things sometimes,' Arran admitted. 'I just do. I don't want to leave. Will you make me leave?'

Jessamine thought she understood, then. It had been a test. Arran had done it because they expected Mac to send them away, probably having lived a life where every mistake led to a new home, a new bunch of adults to be surrounded by. Arran was trying to see if Mac was just another temporary father, another person who would get sick of them too quickly if they pushed hard enough. Just as Jess had tested her mother to see if acting out would get her the attention she'd been craving. It wasn't the same, not by a longshot, but their motivations weren't so different. Arran needed stability, and they didn't know how else to find out if they had it.

Mac softened. 'No, kiddo. I wouldn't *make* you do anything. But I need you to work with me at least a little bit. The thing is . . . Linda isn't sure you should be here, and I can't convince her otherwise if I'm getting silent treatments and arrows to the buttocks.'

'She wants to take me away,' Arran said. It wasn't a question.

'She wants what's best for you. We all do.' Mac dared sidle closer. 'But you need to tell us what you think that might be. You need to tell me what I can do to give you the best – and before you ask, no, we can't get a cat.'

'I want a cat, though,' Arran said, bowing their head. 'But . . . I want to stay. With you. I like it here.'

Mac's lips curled with a smile, and Jessamine couldn't help but match it as warmth finally returned. She sank with a relief of her own. She never wanted to see him in pain again.

'OK, good. Because I want you to stay.' He ruffled Arran's curls and threw his arm around their shoulders. Resting his chin on the top of their head, he mouthed, 'Thank you' in Jessamine's direction, just like the day before.

She only grinned, though a twinge of sadness shot through her, for the little girl who had never been shown that love she'd longed for. She found herself wondering again if things might have been different were her father still alive. Or maybe it would have been twice as bad, because he could have been just as absent as her mother. She averted her gaze, tearing up the dandelion stem in her hands until her fingertips were stained green. She dabbed her runny nose with the flared sleeve of her dress.

'You're going to wee the bed tonight,' Arran pointed out.

Jessamine laughed. She remembered her father had always had the same superstition about dandelions, calling them piss-the-beds, much to the disgust of Mother. Particularly when a five-year-old Jessamine had passed on the information to a handful of friends at a dinner party. *Yes*, she thought. *Things would have been different if he was still alive.*

'Let's hope not,' she said aloud.

'C'mon,' Mac said. 'Who fancies a ride on the carousel before the fair closes?'

Arran hopped up excitedly, already running back towards

the bridge. Jessamine only slapped her hands together, not sure whether the offer extended to her.

But Mac stood and dusted down his jeans before holding out his hand. 'Are you coming?'

She couldn't find it in her to say no, so she let him pull her up off the ground, and together, they walked back to the castle.

Chapter Twelve

Jessamine had never been on a Ferris wheel before, and her hands shook as she gave the engineer a handful of pound coins – Mac had insisting on paying for the carousel, so it was only right. Gem had joined them, after sneaking away from the hook-a-duck stall early, and Arran had decided they wanted to ride with Gem, leaving Jessamine and Mac to trail behind.

'Are you all right? You look a bit pale,' Mac asked now, keeping a careful eye on Arran, who skipped over to their carriage with Gem in tow. They sat down, the engineer pulled the safety bar down, and then the wheel took them, giggling, upwards and it was Jessamine and Mac's turn.

'Just a bit queasy from the carousel.' Not a lie. All that spinning had made her so dizzy that she'd been clutching on to the unicorn's purple horn for dear life.

'Oh, really?' Mac scratched his neck, a little grey himself. 'Because we don't have to get on. We can just watch.'

Jessamine narrowed her eyes, noticing Mac's tense shoulders. 'Oh my goodness.' She laughed. 'You're scared. You're a scaredy-cat.'

His features sharpened. 'No, I'm not. I just . . .' He sighed. 'All right, I might be a wee bit scared of heights.'

Jessamine shouldn't have taken so much joy from it, but she couldn't help it. He kept surprising her with new quirks. 'It's OK. We don't have to go on.'

Still, the idea made her heart sink. She'd been looking forward to trying the ride for the first time, especially as the sun set over the castle. She wanted to touch the sky, and she wanted to do it with Mac. Maybe she just wanted to be a child for a night.

His brows furrowed, but before he could reply, the engineer butted in through a bubble of pink gum, 'Are you two gettin' on or wit?'

'No,' Jessamine said, making to step out of the queue – but Mac dragged her back gently, his fingers looping around her wrist.

'Aye, we are. Sorry.'

'Mac—'

Ignoring her protests, he led her towards the blue Cinderella-painted carriage and motioned in invitation. 'Ladies first.'

Guilt twisted through her. She didn't want him to do something he clearly didn't want to on her behalf. 'Are you sure?'

'For you, I am.'

A lick of fire sparked from the crown of her head to the tip of her toes, but she tried not to read into the words as she climbed into the carriage and sat on the bench. Mac sidled beside her inelegantly, careful to lower slowly onto his injury. He was a little too long-legged and broad to appear comfortable in the small space. His thigh pressed against hers, warm and denim-clad, and his elbow poked lightly into her ribs. She gave a jittery smile. They were so close. There would be no escaping that when they were up in the air.

The safety bars were brought down, sealing their fate, and then the carriage gate was shut and they were hauled up for the next riders to take their place.

'I've never been on one of these before,' she admitted, laughing when she caught sight of Arran waving above them. She waved back until Gem peeked over the bench, her face as sternly curious and accusatory as ever. *You didn't keep your promise*, it seemed to say. *This isn't staying away*. Jessamine's stomach turned again, this time not so pleasantly.

'You didn't go to fairgrounds as a kid?' Mac asked.

'No. I . . .' She bit her lip. 'I suppose my mother just didn't have time for that sort of stuff.'

They rocked up again, the umbrella that sheltered their carriage flapping in the wind. Jessamine's insides swooped with the movement and she clutched the bar. Mac did the same. Their pinkie fingers brushed accidentally, sending another wave of heat through her, but also comfort. He made her feel safe. Steady. Even when they were suspended in mid-air.

'What you said to Arran earlier . . . Thank you, Jess.'

'It was nothing.' She shrugged, cheeks blazing.

'No,' he murmured quietly. His pinkie crossed hers, and then his hands were curled around her own, clammy and cool from the metal bar. 'No, it wasn't nothing. I hadn't even realised that Arran probably acts out to test my limits. How clueless does that make me?'

She shook her head. 'Not clueless at all. In fact, you're probably one of the most understanding, empathetic people I've ever met. And I think . . .' She clamped her lips, unsure if it was her place.

'Go on,' he nudged carefully. 'What?'

'It's just that . . . from an outside perspective, it seems as though when Arran pushes your boundaries, your instinct is to question what *you* can do better rather than punish them. If more parents were as patient and mindful as you, the world would have a lot less unhappy children, I think.' Even now, Jessamine still wished for something she'd never get: an apology, or at least an acknowledgement of the ways that Mother's distant, cold nature hurt Jessamine. As long as Arran had Mac, they'd never feel that unfixable crack in their soul.

Mac's lips curled with a shy smile, gaze lowering and features softening. 'Thank you, Jess. Honestly.'

'Of course.'

He straightened, glancing out of the carriage and down to the grass for a moment before paling again as though he'd forgotten where he was. Jess suppressed a smile.

'Tell me about you, anyway.' It was almost a plea. 'I feel like you know far more about me, and you can consider me interested.'

She tucked her wind-knotted hair behind her ear, anxiety surging through her. 'There's not much to know.'

'It doesn't seem like you were close with your mum. And you never mention anything about a dad. Were you . . . were *you* an unhappy child?'

She shrugged. 'In some ways, maybe. My dad died when I was six and my mother was difficult to be close to. She had a lot of expectations. I never felt like I could meet them.'

The confession seemed to linger like smoke between them. She wondered how she'd done so well at hiding from Mac and yet somehow managed to reveal every bit of her soul. She might have been keeping a secret or two, but the rest of her . . . she'd laid herself bare today. Maybe being a countess, a Byron, didn't matter. Maybe these conversations were all that mattered.

Or maybe she was trying to convince herself of that, because it was easier than risking whatever was growing between them. Because she wasn't ready to let it go and have Mac see her the way everyone else did. Have him judge her.

'I'm sorry. It must have been hard. No kid deserves to feel like they're not enough, especially not after a loss like that.' He squeezed her hand – tighter still when the wheel juddered to life and they began their ascent to the top. The wind left the carriage rickety, and Mac's throat bobbed. She couldn't help but giggle, sliding closer until there was no space left between them. They drifted into the pink sky as though they were falling into a painting, Loch Leannan, a vast blue pool hugging the castle walls below.

It was beautiful up here. Far less lonely than the turret that pierced a lone wispy cloud; the one she would have to go back to tonight. Alone.

Tears pricked her eyes, her breath hitching.

But Mac was still tense and pale, staring at the bars rather than the view. As they reached the peak, Jessamine tilted his chin up in an attempt to distract him. He met her eyes reluctantly.

'I've been meaning to give you something.'

'Is it a paper bag to boak in? Because I could do with one.'

She shook her head, rooting through the inside pocket of her jacket. Her fingers curled around the cool metal that had been weighing her down all day. She pulled it out, displaying the black-iron key in the palm of her hand. She'd found it yesterday evening, and this seemed as good a moment as any to give it to Mac.

He wasn't looking. His gaze darted everywhere but at her, panicked.

'Mac.' They began to descend again, sinking back to the ground with the breeze carrying them. 'We can ask to stop the ride if you can't—'

'No,' he answered, defiance burning in his gaze. 'No, I'm fine.'

It was a good job, because the ride continued its loop and they were sent to the sky again. He looked down at her palm finally – and stilled. 'Is that . . ?'

'The key to your secret garden,' she confirmed. 'It took some searching, but it was found in the castle cellar with all sorts of old rubbish.' She covered her mouth, remembering the glare of Bill, the castle's groundskeeper, when she'd said the same thing during their search. In her defence, though, there had been cobwebs everywhere. 'Sorry, "antiques".' His lips twitched with a smirk, his hair both copper and silver against the low sun. He took the key, tracing its jagged teeth and round bow. Awe spread across his features as though it was made of magic and not just metal. 'I can't believe you. Do you know how long I've been asking for this?'

She tucked her chin into her chest bashfully, pretending to be interested in a passing plane overhead. 'You can take it as my apology for ruining your gardens on several occasions.'

He shook his head as though dazed, gaze flitting between her and the key. It seems he'd forgotten about his fear of heights, and pride spread through her. 'I don't know how to thank you. I really don't.'

'Plant something for me,' she suggested dryly. 'My favourites are hydrangeas.'

They hadn't been her favourites before he'd sent her the bouquet weeks ago as a peace offering, his scrawled apology tied to the bunch. She hadn't even *had* a favourite, and nobody had cared enough to ask.

He smiled as though he knew. She found herself hoping he did.

'Deal.' He slipped the key into the breast pocket of his shirt, causing his bisexual-flag badge to ripple, and she couldn't keep pretending as though everything about him didn't feel like a blessing. She wanted to explore every part of him, wanted to know what books he'd pick up if he went to a library and what *his* favourite flowers were; why. She wanted to soak him up like soil did rain, like flowers did sun. She wanted all of him.

Their knees brushed again, and his focus fell to her lips. She licked them involuntarily, every atom seeming to halt within her. Nothing had ever felt like this. Nothing.

The ride groaned to a stop halfway down, and the people in other carriages began stepping out. She looked away, both hot and shivering at once and still clutching the safety bar for dear life.

'Will you come with me to see it?' he asked. 'The garden, I mean.'

'Now?'

He pursed his lips as though deliberating, focus skimming over Arran. 'Aye, now. Arran'll be right with Gem for a while.'

She should have said no. Should have kept to her already broken promise.

But her will was weak and she wanted to see him happy,

so she agreed. And when he smiled again, she couldn't find it in her to regret it. Not even when Gem threw her daggers.

Mac had to fight not to skip his way to the gated garden, the key heavy and warm in his palm. They'd left Arran to enjoy the fete with Gem, the lights twinkling behind them in the lavender dusk. Screams still drifted towards them from the fairground rides, muted and scattered by the wind along with the smell of freshly cut grass and sweet fuchsias. One of the best evenings he'd had in a long time, even if his left bum cheek still throbbed from the earlier incident.

He felt like a flame in the dimming light, burning brightly every time Jess brushed his hand or laughed.

She cast him a sidelong glance now, smirking. Her nose was pink and shiny, her eyes gleaming. 'I've never seen somebody so excited about a garden before.'

'I've been dying to know what's behind that gate since the day I found it. It's been torturing me.'

'Didn't your grandfather ever tell you?'

'Never. I wonder if it was locked even when he worked here.' He was so restless that he couldn't wait a moment longer. 'Let's find out, shall we?' He threaded his fingers through hers and pulled her forward. Together, they set off into a run.

A laugh tumbled from her as they scampered along the grass, almost tripping over each other's feet when they turned the corner.

And there it was. The wrought-iron bars rusted into a stone archway, crawling with ivy and long-dead vines. Breathless, Mac grinned and slowly made his way to the gate. He wanted to savour every moment of it.

'Here we go, then,' he murmured, slotting the key into the padlock. It resisted at first, the metal old and slow to wake. But then it turned and clicked, coming loose.

He chuckled, half believing it was too good to be true. When he pushed the gate, though, it gave way on creaking hinges, burying itself into the thorns and brambles. All his for the taking. All *theirs*.

He stepped aside to let Jess through. 'After you.'

She brushed past him, her heeled boots clicking against uneven flagstones. Mac followed, shutting the gate behind them – shutting out everything. It was just the two of them, spilling into a pocket of the earth both new and ancient as the world continued turning a few miles away.

Jess turned around expectantly, her ash-blonde hair whipping across her face. 'Well?'

'Well . . .' It sounded like an agreement. Mac wasn't sure what else he could say. The garden was bigger than it had seemed through the bars, though most of it was covered in lifeless foliage. A fruitless cherry tree drooped over an old stone birdbath, filled with grimy rainwater and moss. He could already imagine it blossoming pink next spring, scattering confetti while birds and bees flitted around the currently shrivelled bluebells.

'There's so much we could do here,' he breathed. 'Maybe a vegetable patch. Kids can harvest their own carrots and tomatoes and take them home. And' – he kicked his toe into the grass, finding that the soil was soft – hopefully still fertile – 'we could grow flowers. Ones people can pick if they want to. A greenhouse, even.'

Jess's smile was so wide that her nose wrinkled. 'It sounds perfect, Mac. Really.'

'We'd need more benches.' He wandered over to the only one, an old, rotting wooden seat. A glint of gold caught his attention, and he swiped away the overhanging leaves to find a rusty plaque. Words were etched into it, faded but still readable.

For Bearnard,
As long as your flowers bloom here,
so will our love.
Yours, G.J.R.

Mac's breath hitched, trembling fingers tracing over the indented metal. 'The last Lord Rosemire. What was his first name again?'

Jess hummed, her warmth pressing against him. 'Lord Gaven John Rosemire, wasn't it? Why?'

Mac had known the initials were familiar. He shivered, feeling suddenly as though he was on sacred ground. He pointed to the plaque and stepped aside so she had a better view.

As she read, she narrowed her eyes until the corners creased endearingly. 'Lord Gaven never married. He had no heir.'

'No.' Locals had wondered for nigh on two hundred years why Clan Rosemire had ended with Lord Gaven, the only child in the fifth generation of Rosemires. It was part of the mystery of the castle, and part of the fascination for visitors. The family had built the castle themselves and, as far as Mac understood, had a hand in making Fort Aileen the village it later became. Their history began with them, hence why, long after Lord Gaven's death, the castle was still preserved by the Scottish Castles Association as a historical site. Not even the Byrons were allowed to touch or remove exhibitions or artefacts, nor were they allowed to demolish or rebuild the oldest parts of the castle. The residential areas were theirs, but the rest would always be Clan Rosemire's. As it should be.

'Because he was in love with Bearnard, maybe,' Jess surmised, her cheeks turning rosy. 'It sounds like this garden was his. Theirs.'

Mac looked around, imagining a man not too unlike himself tending to this garden. How devastating that while bronze statues of Clan Rosemire stood in every corner of both the castle and the village, another history had been lost to the weeds somewhere along the way. No love story deserved that.

He would make the flowers bloom again.

'All along, it's been here and nobody even knew. It's sad.'

'Romantic, though,' she replied, and only then did he realise that they were centimetres away from touching. She tilted her chin up to look at him, her eyes glossy and swirling with something. He didn't dare let himself wonder what. 'It feels special to stand in the place where two people once fell in love.'

'Aye,' he said quietly. 'It does.'

Her throat bobbed, tongue wetting her lips so he had no choice but to let himself look at them. He couldn't. He knew he couldn't. But why not? She'd been sturdy as a rock today where she could have just run and left Mac to face the chaos of being a foster father alone, like he usually did. Having someone by his side, someone who seemed to understand Arran, too – care about them, even – had made Mac realise how lonely he'd been until now.

His concern had been Arran all along, but did he need to worry? Jess was good for them. *Both* of them.

He could no longer remember the reasons he'd tried to suppress his feelings for her, not when they were this close.

Before he leaned in, she closed the distance, perching on her tiptoes and catching his lips with hers. They were soft, balmy from the spring breeze, which seemed to still now as though something had clicked into place. As though the universe couldn't stand to disturb them. He let out a breath as he pulled her close, one hand around her waist and the other slipping beneath her hair, to the warm nape of her neck. Goosebumps peppered her skin and spread through his palms, along his arms, covering him, too.

Heat stirred in him when her tongue ran across the seam of his lips. He let her in, dizzy and unable to stop. He wanted to taste every bit of her, wanted to feel her everywhere, and their pace quickened with desperation. They were moving backwards, stumbling over their own feet as they kissed harder, more passionately, all the desire Mac had been working hard to bury finally rising to the surface like wildfire. He burned, suffocated in the smoke, but he couldn't pull away. All he knew was her. All he wanted—

'*Ow!*' Jess yelped. Her head jerked suddenly, her forehead knocking against his nose.

'Shite!' he cried out, his eyes tearing immediately. 'My bloody nose.'

'Sorry! I'm . . .' She sighed and twisted awkwardly. 'I'm stuck in the thorns.'

'Oh.' He took a step back and chuckled. In his daze, he'd walked her right into a tangle of thorns, leaving criss-cross ladders in her tights. Beneath those, the pale skin of her thigh was exposed and dotted with pink scratches. 'Fuck. Sorry. Let me . . .'

He crouched down to get a better look, déjà vu coursing through him when he found her dress knotted in the branches, just like the day they'd met. Only he hadn't been that close to her thighs then. He gripped her hips, desire coursing through him as he looked up at her over her softly curved stomach. 'This is becoming a bit of a habit.'

'Gardens don't like me.' Her breath felt uneven as she imagined his head between her thighs. His lips all over her body. But then her face contorted and she took a sharp intake of breath . . .

And let out an almighty sneeze.

'Bless you,' he whispered, plucking a folded napkin he'd stolen from a cake stall earlier from his breast pocket and handing it to her.

'I'm sorry. This is becoming less romantic by the minute.'

She sniffled and then blew her nose, and he couldn't help but chuckle at the trumpet-like sound. It might not have been the way it happened in movies, but he wouldn't have changed it. It felt more real this way. It felt more *them*. 'Bloody hay fever. Sorry.'

'I'm not,' he murmured, looking up at her. Tearing away the napkin, she met his gaze and softened.

He snapped out of it before he got too carried away,

returning his dazed focus to the dress. The thorn was well and truly embedded this time. 'I don't think I can get it out without ripping the dress.' He tried anyway, to no avail. His clumsy, trembling fingers were no use to him when all he could think about was the heat stirring within him, the way his lips still tasted like candy floss after kissing her; how cold his skin felt when her hands weren't pressed against it.

'Oh, forget it.' She yanked it without care and pulled him back to his feet with only a firm finger beneath his chin. Then she kissed him again. He smiled through it this time, giddiness bubbling inside him. It had been a long time since he'd felt this way, this safe, this at ease, and all of the other kisses he'd had before felt like no more than practice runs now. He'd never been sure with anyone else. Not like this.

She pulled away, finally, pressing her forehead against his cheek as her chest rose and fell with trembling breaths. 'Is this a good idea?' Her wispy hair tickled his nose, lashes damp and face splotchy.

Mac's stomach sank. 'Probably not,' he admitted. The words seared like acid on his tongue, dissolving the light happiness he'd felt only a moment ago. 'But I'm finding it difficult tae care.'

'Mac . . . I . . .' Her brows knitted together as though she'd said something he hadn't heard. Maybe she had. His pulse pounded so erratically in his ears that it was hard to tell.

'You what?' he whispered.

'I haven't . . . I haven't kissed anybody since . . .'

Oh, God. She was going to tell him she was in love with someone else. Dread filled him, and he instinctively took a step back as though the distance might protect him from the impending pain. 'Since what?'

'Since my divorce.' Her eyes brimmed with tears, ones he didn't think were allergy-related this time, and she fidgeted with her torn dress nervously.

It wasn't what he'd expected. In fact, he hadn't known *what* to expect. He didn't know Jess, not really. He didn't know where she was from or how long she was here for. He didn't know about her past, her dreams and ambitions, or how much she liked him. Jess knew so much about him . . . he'd unravelled himself to let her in – not just into his life, but Arran's, too.

Idiot. Despite how cautious he'd tried to be, he'd dived in head-first. *Selfish, selfish idiot.*

'I didn't know you were married.' He sank onto the bench, the leaves rustling behind him. Somehow, he wagered, Rosemire's meetings with Bearnard here had been a little smoother.

'I was.' She spoke softly, her skirt fanning out as she collapsed beside him, wiping her nose again. 'It ended less than a year ago. Not on the best of terms.'

He imagined this person, this stranger, who Jess would have kissed and laughed with and fought with. His stomach tightened. 'How long were you together?'

'Four years. It was . . . Well, it wasn't right. *He* wasn't right for me.'

'Then why . . ?'

'I was young and naïve. He swept me off my feet. I thought I loved him. I was lonely as a child. It felt like I'd been waiting for this fairy tale all my life, and suddenly there he was, taking me out on dates and buying me gifts, making me feel special, like he really was Prince Charming. And he could have chosen anyone, but he chose me. Everyone told us how wonderful we looked together. I think it was the first time my mother had ever been proud of me. I was so focused on the fantasy of it all that I pushed away my doubts. We had nothing in common, below the surface, but I wanted it to work.'

She sighed, eyes as cool and hazy as a foggy winter morning. 'Anyway, his charm disappeared soon after our wedding. He just wanted a housewife, someone to have his babies and put dinner on the table and take out his frustrations on when things didn't go his way. He was impatient, and I was *too* patient for a while. Until I wasn't.' She looked at him, and her expression broke him. Pain, doubt, fear. He curled his fingers into his palms, wishing more than anything he could chase it all away.

'You weren't happy,' he concluded.

She laughed humourlessly. 'Not even a little bit. But everybody made me feel like I was wrong to leave him. Like it was a miracle he liked me at all, and I should have been content with him, no matter how he treated me, because he was wealthy and charismatic and he fooled them the way he fooled me at first. When he was angry at me for being independent or made his silly little remarks he could pass off as jokes, that was *my* fault, and I should have laughed it off. I was too "picky". Too "sensitive". And he was perfect. That's how it felt. So, I thought maybe I'm just not . . .' She shook her head, staring down at her restless fingers.

'You can say it.' He spoke softly. 'You've seen my life and you haven't judged me even a little bit. Let me do the same.'

'I thought, what with the way my mother was and how tragic my marriage turned out to be, that maybe I'm just not made to be loved.' A tear dripped down her cheek. 'And I was trying to be all right with that. With not ever feeling wanted or connected to somebody. Until . . .'

He ached for her. She deserved better than that. Anybody did, but Jess . . . She was a good person. A person who felt like sunlight. He wanted her every time he saw her, each time with more intensity, and the connection building between them felt like an unbreakable tether between them. And it hurt. It hurt to know she had ever felt alone. Unwanted. It hurt to imagine her married to someone cold, someone who wasn't able to love her the way she deserved: in the most intense, passionate way possible.

'Until?'

She looked at him and didn't have to say it. He knew. *Until him. Until them.* Whatever this was, it wasn't just a bit of flirting anymore. It was something real, visceral. Something he wanted to keep.

'I didn't mean to make it weird. Sorry. I just wasn't expecting . . . Well, I wasn't expecting *you*, Mac. And I'm not used to feeling things like this.' She tore her gaze away, instead staring off into the shadows. The sun no longer reached over the walls, leaving them in darkness save for the slatted amber pouring between the gate's iron bars.

'Neither am I.'

It was true. He'd had a few short-term relationships, but not in years, and never like this. He liked to keep things separate: his work, his family, his friends. Everything in neat little boxes because it was easier to handle that way. He'd done it since he was a child, keeping his scant belongings organised under his single bed in whatever foster home he found himself in. His way of reminding himself that he could still maintain a grasp on things, even when his world was slipping beneath him and he was forced to move again, again, again. Sometimes, he'd even crawled into the boxes in the hopes that hiding might mean no more change. One of his earliest memories was sitting in a foster home. By the time he was old enough to understand anything about life, his biological mother was long gone, and Mac had only Walter the teddy bear left from that strange, shadowy life of neglect that he couldn't remember living. Like Arran, he'd been forced to learn how to cope with instability long before he'd been offered love and care. And though he'd found the stability he'd needed in the end, his coping mechanisms had carried on, until now.

But he felt like he wanted Jess in every box rather than carefully folded in just one. He wanted her in his kitchen, helping Arran with their homework. He wanted her laughing in the Hairy Coo with Brodie and Gem. He wanted her here, in this tiny, leafy corner where Rosemire had once sat with his lover. He wanted her everywhere as long as she was with him. As long as she was happy.

'I know you said there's no "us" because that wouldn't

be right for Arran.' Jess worried at her lip, but then let out a mirthless laugh. 'Actually, I have no idea why that just happened, why we . . .'

She shook her head and stood up, smoothing down her dress as though she wished the wrinkles were the last five minutes. But their kiss couldn't be swiped away that easily, and Mac's heart wrenched at the idea she wanted it to be. He caught her wrist, his touch gentle enough she could have pulled away – but she didn't.

'We both did it,' he murmured. 'We both wanted to, didn't we?'

She tilted her head. 'But you said—'

'You know that I have to put Arran first, always.'

'Of course.' She sat back down, a line creasing between her brows.

'I have no idea if this is right or not – for me, for Arran, for anyone. But I also know it doesn't feel wrong and I'd like the chance to find out properly. I'm running out of reasons not to, Jess. Arran likes you. *I* like you. Does it have to be any more complicated than that?'

She softened, sidling closer and brushing a wind-ruffled curl off his brow. Her touch sent another explosion of sparks through him, and he clenched his jaw to resist the urge to kiss her again. He wasn't sure how he could ever sit beside her now and not want to kiss her.

'Problem is' – he lowered his voice, swallowing hard – 'I don't know where we go from here. Where *you* want to go from here. If you're not ready for this . . . it's OK. I get it. I just hope you know that you deserve better than to feel as though you're not made to be loved. You deserved better than an idiot who let you think it was true. And I'm glad you told me. I just want to know you, Jess. And I want to maybe kiss you from time to time, too, if that's OK.'

Her breath was ragged, uneven, the smell of sugar clinging to it as she giggled. His spirits lifted finally with the sound. 'I have no objections to that,' she said.

'Good. Shall we give it a practice, then?' He nudged her nose with his own, asking. She answered with another kiss, this one calm and steady and familiar. Not a practice, but something that gave him enough hope to finally just enjoy it.

The fairground was slowly beginning to close when they returned, shutters being pulled down on burger vans and the carousel still and empty in darkness. Mac found Gem and Arran scarfing down a tray of chips and ketchup not far from where they'd left them by the Ferris wheel.

It was instinct to drop Jess's hand as they wandered over. This was all new, after all, and it was better to keep Arran out of it until things got serious. *If* they got serious. Still, Gem's gaze snagged on his movement, and her brow arched suspiciously. He blushed and wiped his clammy palms on his jeans, feeling like a child who'd been caught sneaking out after dark.

'I hope you saved some for me,' he said, forcing a grin as he nicked a chip from Arran's tray.

'Oi!' Arran scolded, snatching the tray back. 'Get your own.'

Mac stuck his tongue out before ruffling Arran's hair.

'Have fun?' Gem questioned, her tone laced with something Mac couldn't decipher. They'd been friends since school, so he was used to her changing attitudes and occasional hostility, usually only teasing her about it, but this felt different. He shifted his focus to Jess, who was rubbing her arms to warm herself, rocking back on her heels awkwardly and avoiding Gem's gaze just as well.

'Aye, we did. Thanks for watching Arran,' he replied.

Jess twirled a bracelet around her wrist and said, 'I should go and say goodbye to everyone, actually. I'll see you all later.'

'Right. See you later.' He gave her a soft smile, but it soon fell when Jess turned without so much as looking at him. She disappeared into the falling darkness, a silhouette against the red and blue lights of the funhouse.

Fear snaked through his gut, cold and slippery. Had he already done something to fuck it up? That was a record even for him.

He tried not to dwell for Arran's sake, pinching another chip that ended up dripping red sauce onto his chin. He dabbed his beard with a napkin. 'What've you two been up to, then?'

'We went on the dodgems,' Arran said, stabbing a wooden fork into the polystyrene tray absently. 'I've had fun today.'

The words surprised him. It wasn't like Arran to be so upfront about how they felt, not unless they were angry about something. It warmed Mac, leaving him wrapped in a bubble of relief. He'd done one thing right. That was better than nothing, which he usually felt was the case. 'Good. I'm glad, kiddo. I've had fun, too.'

'I still have two pounds left. Could I go on the ghost train again?'

Mac tried to hide his cringe. He'd suffered through the ghost train twice already, when Arran and Olivia had begged for a second go pre-archery fiasco. He'd been squished into a seat not made for six-foot adults who lived on a steady diet of pasta and pizza, made worse because Sara had been beside him.

Arran must have sensed his reluctance, because they added, 'I don't mind going on my own.'

Mac debated. The ghost train was in sight from where they sat on a picnic bench, and a couple of people still queued for the final rides. 'Go on, then. Just don't go running off.'

'I won't!' Arran grinned and skipped off, tagging along behind a teenage couple by the ticket station.

Mac shook his head, unable to hide his smile as he sidled closer to Gem and finished Arran's chips off. 'I hope they haven't been too much of a pain.'

'What are you doing Mac?' Her question was sharp and unexpected, her dark eyes boring into him with . . . judgement?

He frowned. 'I'm eating chips.'

'I mean with Jess. You've had the opportunity to date before, but you've always said it wouldn't be fair to Arran. Why are you running off like some smitten teenager now?'

His appetite disappeared, and he pushed the tray away, leaning back to look at her properly. 'I didn't know you had a problem with it. You usually like spending time with Arran. I'm sorry if it felt like I was shoving them on you so I could have fun. It's just, Jess wanted to show me something and—'

She silenced him with a heavily ringed hand, tattoos snaking from the cuffs of her sleeves. 'That's not what I meant. I never have a problem with watching Arran. I wasn't . . .' She sighed and scraped her dark hair back as though struggling for words. 'I wasn't having a dig at *you*, Mac. I just don't think you know what you're getting yourself into.'

'Meaning what, exactly? You don't like Jess?' Defensiveness prickled through him, though he tried to keep his tone steady.

'I'm sure she's lovely.' She chewed on her lipstick-coated bottom lip. 'I just worry she isn't right for you.'

He tried to make sense of what Gem was saying, but couldn't. She didn't know Jess well enough to decide if she was right for Mac. As far as he knew, they'd only spoken once or twice, at the pub and possibly in the planning meetings. In his unease, he tried to make a joke out of it:

'Is this your way of saying she's too pretty for me?'

She didn't laugh. Didn't do anything but clench her jaw until a muscle ticked there.

'Where is this coming from, Gem? You're going to have to help me out a little bit.'

'I'm just saying that you should be careful,' she responded, burying her hands into her pockets. 'There's a reason why you've avoided dating since fostering Arran. I know it can be easy to forget that when a pretty woman rocks up and pays attention to you.'

The words set Mac's teeth on edge. As though Mac was only entertaining Jess because she was beautiful and satisfied some non-existent craving. It was the furthest thing from the truth. He'd tried not to have these feelings for her, but she was warm and clumsy and not afraid to laugh at herself, and more than that, she genuinely cared. She'd held him together today. She hadn't judged him or let him deal with it alone.

She was *good* – for him and Arran.

'That's not fair,' he muttered gruffly, anger simmering in him. 'That's not what this is.'

'Then what is it?' Gem snapped.

'I don't know yet,' he ground out slowly. 'Don't I deserve the chance to find out?'

Her steely gaze drifted back to the ghost train. Arran was passing through the front of the ride, beaming. He wanted them to always be this happy, to have their fill of the things they'd never had growing up. And why couldn't somebody else, somebody he was beginning to trust, be a part of that if he chose? Why had everyone, including himself, decided that he had to do this alone?

They weren't thoughts he'd had before now. He knew that most people he might have dated in another life wouldn't give their time to a single father of a troubled foster child, and he didn't particularly blame them. It wasn't for everyone. He'd chosen it for himself, not because he thought it would earn him brownie points when it came to looking for love. But something had changed. And he'd seen the way Jess interacted with Arran. Was it so wrong to chase more than one form of love at a time? With the right person, there was no reason why he couldn't.

'I'm only worried that you don't know her as well as you think you do,' Gem said finally.

He didn't have to know all of her yet, did he? They had time, and she'd been honest with him about the divorce. It wasn't as though he was asking her to move in and be Arran's foster mother. As long as he knew she cared and was comfortable, as long as she knew where he stood and that Arran would always be his priority, things could still progress as naturally as they would under any other circumstances.

He huffed, scraping a hand through his hair. The fact that he was already thinking of a future was terrifying, but he couldn't help it. He wanted her around.

'I'm *getting* to know her. Look, I appreciate you looking out for me,' he decided finally. 'I do. But at the moment, there's nothing to worry about. We're just seeing where it goes.'

'And what if where it goes leaves you heartbroken?' Gem's hair rustled in the wind, but her features remained hard as stone. 'Worse, what if it leaves Arran heartbroken? It might be early days, but I've seen them with her. They like her, Mac, and soon enough they'll get attached. What then?'

'You're like a scarier version of Linda,' Mac groused, scraping his hand over his face in stress. Maybe Gem was right. Arran was fond of Jess, or at least comfortable enough to share her cat and talk to her in a place where they used to want to venture alone. If they broke it off now, Arran would probably be fine, but in a month's, two months' time . . . Who knew?

'I want you to be happy.' Gem spoke softly, a rarity for her. Her hand found his wrist. 'I just want you to be careful, too. She's not from here. She might not stick around forever. You need to decide if she's worth the potential pain.'

'I'll be careful,' he promised, but he didn't know if it was the truth. He wasn't ready to end whatever this was with Jess. He wanted to kiss her again, and she hadn't given him a reason not to.

So he'd heed Gem's warnings as best he could, but he wouldn't give up on Jess yet, either. He could be careful. At least that's what he told himself. The kiss earlier hadn't felt careful. It felt like he was being tugged away by the current.

Mac caught sight of Brodie, then, and . . . he squinted. Was that *Petra* eating a burger with her pinkie fingers poking up into the air on the other side of the fairground?

'Surely Brodie isn't cracking on with Jess's friend,' he said, motioning his head towards them. Petra was far too sophisticated for a man like Brodie. Then again, the same might be said about Jess and him. But still. Brodie was . . . *Brodie*.

Gem guffawed at the sight, leaning her elbows back as though taking in a movie. 'Of course he is. He's Brodie. Charming the ladies is all he's good at.'

'There's no way he can pull someone like Petra, though. I mean . . . look at him.'

Brodie was currently inelegantly swiping his tongue across his top lip in an attempt to lick some mustard off his nose.

'Bet you thirty quid she gives in eventually. He'll annoy her until she has no choice.'

'All right.' Mac smirked. He was just glad to dissolve the tension between them. 'Deal.'

'*And* if they end up snogging, you have to do something for me.' She clicked her fingers. 'You have to wear a kilt for a day. Full Scotsman.'

He rolled his eyes. Mac had once lost a far worse bet against Gem, one where he had to endure a full body wax because he didn't think Gem would be able to get the number of the prettiest woman in town. Needless to say, he'd underestimated her flirting abilities and ended up losing at least fifty per cent of his skin cells in the process. A kilt was nothing.

'Fine. But if they haven't hooked up by . . .' He pondered his terms, deciding on, 'August, you have to give me that thirty quid *and* wear one of Joss's One Direction T-shirts. *All* day.' Joss was Brodie's teenage daughter, and she went through obsessions faster than Brodie had gone through his first marriage. Last year, it had been One Direction, which Mac had said was a little delayed considering they were no longer a band. A mistake. Joss was very sensitive about it and insisted they were just on 'a hiatus'. Then, there had been Chris Evans – Captain America, not the British radio producer. Last Mac had checked, she was stuck on Winona Ryder's character from *Beetlejuice*, hence her recent penchant for black clothes.

Gem glowered but shook his hand. 'You won't win. Look at them.'

He did. Petra was laughing, while Brodie did some form of a half-dead chicken dance. There was nothing attractive about it, so Mac smirked confidently. 'Pfft. We'll see.'

As long as he and Gem were still OK, he didn't mind either way.

Chapter Thirteen

The following Thursday, Jessamine studied the oil painting of Lord Gaven John Rosemire – the fifth and last Lord Rosemire – hanging in the hallway. Her phone was pressed to her ear as her mother wittered on about her wonderful weekend at the polo. Jessamine certainly didn't miss attending events she had absolutely no interest in. She didn't miss much of her old life at all.

She wondered if Rosemire had felt the same once. In the portrait, he had fiery red hair and a curly beard that reached his chest, sporting a kilt, a puffy shirt – unlike the half-naked statue, thank goodness – and knee-high socks as he posed proudly by a fireplace. His was at the end of a line of paintings, each one a different generation of broad, warrior-like Rosemire men spanning back to the eighteenth century. He'd always looked so regal and untouchable before.

After finding the plaque in the gardens, Jess had been searching for signs of his secret love affair. She'd even asked one of the tour guides if they knew anything about Bearnard, the man to whom the bench had been dedicated, and she'd confirmed from old records that he had been the castle's gardener for the last twenty-five years of Rosemire's life – up until his death three years after Rosemire's in 1856. She wondered if the next clan to own the castle, Clan Macintosh, had been the one to shut the gates on Bearnard's garden, or if it had happened much later. If the gate was already closed when Mac's grandfather worked here, it couldn't have been the Byrons, but beyond that, everything was speculation.

Even the relationship she was certain had existed between Lord Gaven and his gardener.

Everybody saw Lord Gaven as a perpetual bachelor, admired for his role in the Battle of Kilmore, where he'd fought beside Highlanders against Parliament's restrictive laws concerning farming and land-owning in an attempt to change the rural way of life. But Rosemire had been more than a heroic, solitary figure in an old tale. He'd been in love for, Jessamine could only assume, a long, long time. More than that, she'd learned, he'd been part of the community. It had made her realise that she could have that, too. The castle wasn't a barrier, nor was her title a decider of her fate. She didn't want the suitors her mother picked out for her, didn't want to keep feeling so tethered to tradition when her heart followed another path. And she didn't want to be how she'd always thought Rosemire was before, alone in a castle. She wanted . . .

Well, she wanted Mac. She wanted his laughter and his kindness and his passion. She wanted to watch him spend his days caring for everything around him – the flowers, Arran, his friends. She couldn't stop thinking about the way his lips had felt, a little bit rough and a little bit soft, just like him, and the way his hands had crawled up and down her body so tentatively, as though he was expecting her to pull away at any moment. She wondered if Rosemire had felt that, too, here: that innate sense of belonging, not because of the castle, the luxury, the scenic views, but because of Bearnard. If he had, it deserved to be known about.

'Jessamine. Are you listening to me?' Mother questioned, her voice clipped, as ever. Jessamine imagined her pursed lips, the clucking of her tongue, and knew she didn't miss her, either. Terrible, perhaps, but true.

'Yes, of course.' Jessamine sighed and pressed her spine into the gilded banister, her voice echoing around the tall walls and ceilings. The rain hammered on the windows, the dark clouds casting the hallway a dull grey. Scotland was making up for its few weeks of warm sunshine with miserable weather;

April showers postponed until May. It had barely stopped raining since Sunday, despite the temperatures warming with the promise of summer. 'I was wondering if you had time to talk about the gala in June,' she added. 'I have some ideas on how to make it more beneficial for charities.'

'Quite the event organiser now, aren't you, dear?' Condescension seeped into Mother's voice, as though she was humouring a child. As though organising charity events hadn't been Jessamine's job for a very long time. As though the fete hadn't been a complete success.

'I'd like to give everybody the opportunity to attend, not just . . .' Jessamine searched for the right word, '*acquaintances* from London. Fort Aileen is a lovely community – well, minus a man named Hamish – and I think it would be nice to welcome everybody into the castle properly. It was made to be enjoyed, after all, and there's more than enough space.'

A scoff crackled down the line. 'I'm sorry. I don't quite understand. You wish to invite the . . . villagers?' She might as well have said *commoners*. Jessamine knew that's what Mother was thinking, and the vitriol certainly proved it.

'I don't see why not.'

'Because, darling' – a humourless chuckle – 'this is a gala. You've had your fun with the fete and the tacky food trucks and whatnot. Now it's time for a bit of class and elegance. Remind people who you are and perhaps turn a few gentlemen's heads in the process.'

She rolled her eyes. 'I'm not interested in proving my class and elegance—'

'And you've certainly been making that clear—'

'—nor am I interested in turning heads. I think I've turned enough recently as it is, and not for the right reasons.'

'And whose fault is that?' Mother gulped, most likely sipping her eleven o'clock tea, though it was rare she did so without company. 'I understand you're trying to be more – what do the young people call it? "Inclusive" – but you simply can't have people named Bob parading around in dusty tweed suits when our family is already under so much scrutiny.'

Restless and growing increasingly irritable, Jessamine began pacing the hallways, letting the heavy patter of the rain on the arched windows soothe her. 'Why not? Why does it matter what other people think?'

'Because . . .' Mother sputtered, 'it does! It was important to your father to raise you with as much respectability as had the Byrons who came before.'

'And including my community *wouldn't* be respectable?' Jessamine couldn't help but erupt. She was tired of being taught that only superficial things mattered. She liked the community of Fort Aileen. She liked seeing people enjoy themselves. What she didn't like was parading around in a dress her mother had picked out, spending the night talking about the quality of hors d'oeuvres and whether she would be going to so-and-so's wedding, all the while pretending she didn't know she was being judged by everyone in the room for not looking or acting the way they wanted her to. It was tiring and pointless and it wasn't who she was anymore. She'd divorced Robert to escape it, for goodness' sake. She'd come *here* to escape it, and she no longer wished to go back. Not to mention the Byrons clearly had loose ideas about respectability anyway. Unlike Rosemire, they'd left the villagers to fend for themselves when they'd bought the castle. They'd brought more poverty to Fort Aileen. Even now, enjoying their retirement in Tuscany, they barely kept in touch with Jessamine despite them being her only living grandparents, usually sending her a cheque at Christmas while declining Mother's party invitations.

If that was being respectable, Jessamine wasn't interested in living up to the family name. She didn't want to imagine that her father wouldn't share the same ideals if he was still here.

'Oh dear,' Mother sighed finally. 'You're becoming a country bumpkin. It was those archery lessons, wasn't it?

You came home so very muddy and smelly, as though you'd been rolling around in manure all day, and now look.'

'Mother,' Jessamine said through gritted teeth, 'I am not a country bumpkin. I just think it's time for change. Aren't you bored?'

'Bored of what?'

'I don't know. Caring about silly things. Weekly hair and nail appointments. Wearing uncomfortable suits just to sit on your sofa all day with people you don't even like. Afternoon tea. You could just eat cake whenever you wish, you know. You needn't wait until the afternoon.'

Silence followed Jessamine's words, and her phone trembled against her ear as she awaited the reply. Finally, it came.

'I think you should come home at once, Jessamine. I don't like this new attitude and I cannot imagine where it's come from. You are a countess, for goodness' sake. Please act like one, otherwise I cannot support this lifestyle of yours a moment longer.'

'I'm too busy here to come home, unfortunately.' Jessamine sank down onto the top step, feeling suddenly numb. There was nothing she could do to change her mother's mind, and perhaps she was done trying. Perhaps it was time to make her own decisions regardless of what her mother said. Even if it meant losing her investments. Who could stop her from inviting the town, anyway? Mother had never paid an interest in the castle. It was Dad who'd loved Rosemire. It belonged to Jessamine now.

'You know, I sometimes wonder if you say such absurd things just to cause me stress. Do you have any idea how silly you sound? Honestly. You'll be the death of—'

Jessamine did something she never had before. She hung up on her mother mid-sentence, letting the silence embrace her with warm arms as she breathed deeply and counted to ten. She wouldn't keep doing this. If she did, there would be no end to it.

Her phone rang in her hand again a moment later, but she

left it unanswered, putting it on silent as she took the steps down to the ground level of the castle. No guests filled the foyer today, staved off by the torrential rain outside.

Petra stood by the noticeboard, though, scanning the pamphlets as though she was engrossed by them.

'Petra?' Jessamine asked.

'Hmm?' Petra hummed, then animated herself back to life again. 'Oh, Jessamine! Sorry. I was just daydreaming.'

Jessamine moved to stand beside her. 'Is everything OK?'

Petra nodded without conviction. 'Of course. I was just going to pick up some of your clothes from the dry cleaner.'

'Do you have a moment first? I was just wondering . . .' Jessamine felt suddenly timid. Somehow, Petra's opinion mattered far more than her mother's. She clasped her hands in front of her. 'What would you think if I proposed that we made the gala an open event for the people of Fort Aileen?'

Petra's brows furrowed. 'For everyone?' she asked. 'Even . . . normal people?'

Jessamine blinked, patience fraying. 'Yes, Petra. For *everyone*. Even *people*. Even ones who live *here*. The fete had such a wonderful turnout, and the community is very warm and welcoming. It would be nice to have some friendly faces fill the castle for a change, wouldn't it?'

Tilting her head, Petra considered this. 'Well . . . I suppose you're right. But does that mean' – she lowered her voice, putting her hand beside her mouth as though it made a difference in the echoey foyer – 'the gardener knows about you?'

Jessamine's stomach twisted. She'd been going back and forth about telling Mac all week. After that kiss . . . she just wanted things to remain as they were. She wanted him to keep calling her Jess. She wanted to be selfish, and perhaps she wanted to be like Rosemire: in love without the worry of titles. Could she have that if Mac knew the truth?

'No. Not yet,' she admitted. 'But I'll have to tell him sooner or later. I can't keep it a secret for much longer.'

'You really like him, don't you?' Petra's brown eyes gleamed knowingly.

Reluctantly, Jessamine said, 'I do.'

An ear-piercing squeal ripped from Petra, and she jiggled on the spot like a toddler. 'How wonderful! The countess and the gardener . . . Sounds like the title of one of those raunchy books my sister reads.'

'All right, let's not get too ahead of ourselves.' Jessamine winced, heat filling her cheeks. 'He might not like me when he finds out the truth.' The thought left her cold.

'Nonsense,' Petra tutted. 'You two are meant to be.'

'Whew!' A loud exclamation interrupted their conversation. A draught followed as Mac trudged in, looking sodden. His hair had flattened to dull red waves across his forehead, and his raincoat dripped, leaving puddles of water on the floor that the receptionist at the desk looked none too happy about. 'It's raining cows and sheep out there. Not sure we can take much more of it. The grass is saturated.'

Jessamine shot Petra a warning look, and Petra imitated zipping her lips shut before slipping into the castle's gift shop down the painting-lined corridor.

'Not a good day to be a gardener?' Jessamine teased, feeling slightly awkward. She hadn't seen him since the night of the kiss, what with the rain tormenting them all week, and she wasn't sure where it left them. What if he regretted it or didn't feel the way she did?

But his face brightened. 'I was hoping to find you in here.'

'Really?'

He nodded. 'Was after a tour.'

She fumbled with a loose thread on her cardigan, her heart racketing in her chest. 'Oh?'

'Nah. Just wanted to see you. And get out of the rain.' He broke into a lopsided grin, closing the distance between them. 'We haven't really talked since . . .'

'I know. I wasn't sure if maybe you'd changed your mind.'

'Why would I?' Still, he frowned, gaze slipping to his boots as though something was on his mind.

'How's your . . . backside?' she asked carefully.

'Not a pretty sight. Very bruised.' He chuckled. 'But better. Arran's been in high spirits the past few days, too. It's all looking up.'

'That's great. I'm glad.' She tucked her hair behind her ear and hoped he didn't notice her fingers trembling. 'I've actually been hoping to run into you. I've been thinking a lot about the garden. About Bearnard and Rosemire.'

'Yeah?'

'It just feels wrong that nobody knows. Like it was kept hidden.'

He crossed his arms, brow furrowing in thought. 'Yeah. I suppose it would have been a bit taboo for a long time.'

'But it shouldn't be now. We should celebrate their love. Bearnard was clearly a huge part of Rosemire's life. Why should this castle display his statue and his swords and his silverware, but not the person he loved?' It had been bothering her since discovering the bench. Every exhibition room brimmed with old belongings on show for all to see. With paragraphs of who Lord Gaven was in the eyes of local historians – a perpetual bachelor with too much money and a hero complex. But that wasn't right. Somebody had shut the gate on Bearnard's garden all these years for a reason. They'd locked away the truth because it didn't match up with what they thought they knew. How many other queer historical figures had suffered the same fate? How many more children would go on believing that heterosexuality had always been the norm because they were never told about all the people who were different?

Jessamine had imagined what she would have felt if she'd learned about more LGBTQ+ people as a child. If she'd gone on school trips to castles like these and found out that the men who owned them weren't just a cheap stereotype immortalised by their wealth and wars. That queerness was for everyone. It would have made all the difference. Maybe let her know that her pansexuality was OK and she could love anybody she wanted to long before her early twenties.

'I agree,' Mac said, softening. 'But how can we change it now, other than opening up the gardens?'

'I'm sure there's somebody I could contact.' Absently, Jessamine's focus wandered across the walls. 'The people who maintain the exhibitions, historians, researchers. I want them to know about Bearnard. I want it to be part of the castle's history like everything else.'

'Do you think Rosemire would want that?'

'He probably hid because he had to. But I've never met anybody truly in love who hasn't wanted to scream about it from the rooftops. Have you?'

'No.' His voice was gentle, now. A soft murmur only for her. 'I haven't. You're right.'

'I just . . . I couldn't bear to think of that bench rotting away again behind a locked gate. We've come too far for that. People need to know that queerness has always been here. That love is love, not something defined or bound by gender or social standing. It's woven into our history whether people like it or not.'

Mac's finger twirled through her hair. 'I think that's a really beautiful way of putting it and I'm with you completely.'

It was all the encouragement she needed. She laced her fingers through his and squeezed. 'Thank you, Mac.'

He glanced at the receptionist warily. Hayley made no attempt to disguise the fact that she was listening, which didn't help Jessamine's nerves. Everyone in the castle knew who she was. Everyone but Mac.

'*Do* you fancy giving me a tour?' he asked again. 'I've never been in the castle properly, to be honest. Not the good parts, anyway.'

Of course, Jessamine had. Apart from the fact it was currently her home, she'd snuck around with a group of visitors on the first day, before anybody at all knew she was here. Whether she'd give a convincing tour, on the other hand, was another matter entirely. But they *did* need some alone time to figure out what came next.

She let out a deep, quivering breath. 'Yes. Of course. I'd love to.'

Mac's wellies squelched noisily as he followed Jess down a wide painting-lined corridor, trailing mud along the glossy, hardwood floors and gold-patterned rugs. The cleaner wouldn't be best pleased with him, but it wasn't his fault he'd been caught in another vicious downpour while he'd been pruning his soggy yellow roses, was it?

Jess had already shown him a grand parlour and a room exhibiting old jewels and diamond-encrusted brooches, Clan Rosemire's tartan and preserved letters. None of them to Bearnard, but perhaps that would soon change. He couldn't really pretend to be impressed by anything else. While the castle was beautiful, he knew too well what it felt like to live outside of it and couldn't help but wonder if the people of Fort Aileen had resented the nobles and aristocrats who had lived here over the centuries, looming over their modest village with pretty chandeliers and silver spoons. The fifth Lord Rosemire might have stood up for the Highlanders when it mattered, but he still went home to a castle at the end of the battle while the villagers worked hard just to scrape by.

Even so, Mac hung on to Jess's words just for the way they rose and fell like small strokes of piano keys. He asked silly questions just to hear her laugh, and knew he was in trouble for it. Because he liked her too much, and maybe that meant Gem was right.

But he couldn't stop.

'This would have been the banqueting hall,' she said now as they emerged through a tall archway. Her words echoed against the dark-wood panelled walls and across the high painted ceilings. In the centre, cordoned off by red rope, was a long dining table, set with gilded plates and flagons.

'Fancy,' he commented, burying his hands in his pockets

so he wouldn't be tempted to reach over the rope barrier and touch the centuries-old dining ware.

'Clan Rosemire's crest sits in the middle of the room.' She gestured to a coat of arms, decorated with roses, swords, and eagles painted within the shield. 'And next to it, the crest of Clan Macintosh, who became the castle's next inhabitants after Rosemire's passing, under his own instruction in the mid-eighteen-fifties. One of the first Macintosh sons ended up marrying a royal duchess, making them a duke.'

Mac smirked. 'My mum's maiden name was Macintosh. Maybe I'm royalty, too, eh?'

She shrugged, shuffling closer to him until her elbow brushed his middle. His body prickled, pulse quickening, but he did his best to remain calm, even if all he could think about was how much he wanted to kiss her again.

'Maybe,' she said, with an impish smile. 'You're certainly a royal pain in the arse sometimes.'

He feigned shock, pinching her waist playfully. 'Are we pretending we don't like each other again now?'

She batted him away, cheeks bright red. '"Pretending". Is that what we're calling it?'

With a crooked smirk, he pulled her back.

'When you say "mum". . .' she said.

'I mean my adopted mum.' He tucked his hands into his pockets meekly. 'I don't know much about my biological side. I was put into care when I was just a wee bairn.' He gave a weak smile in an attempt to lighten the mood. It was rare he talked about his life before adoption. Not because he was ashamed, but because it no longer felt like his. Abandonment and struggle hadn't defined him. The love his mum and dad had shown him had. 'I found my clan, anyway. Clan Douglas. What about you?'

'We don't have clans where I'm from.'

'A clan just means family.'

'I didn't have much of that, either.' Her voice lacked mirth, leaving something to wilt in Mac. Sometimes, the people who were born with a family weren't always the happiest. Mac felt chosen, wanted, by Mum and Dad, but Jess . . . she never talked about her parents as though she'd been chosen. It seemed as if she hadn't been loved much. She deserved better than that.

'My family was big,' Jess said. 'But after my dad passed, the house was usually empty. I didn't really feel part of a clan.'

'That sounds lonely. I'm sorry, Jess.'

Mac wondered if that was why she'd sought out the fairy tale in her ex-husband. Wondered if she'd dreamed of being saved and loved, the same way he had in care. Before he'd really understood his mother's abandonment, he'd held on to the hope that one day she'd come back for him. That one day he'd be rescued. He had been rescued, of course. Just not by her. Was Jess still waiting for that?

She only shrugged, and he didn't dare pry. Not if she didn't want to talk about it. 'You'll find your clan,' he whispered instead. 'We all do. Some just later than others.'

Her voice was shaky as she replied, 'I hope you're right.'

Quietly, Mac scanned the coats of arms hung side by side. Clan Macintosh must have lived in Rosemire for a long time, because there was only one more after theirs: Clan Ferguson, whom his grandfather had worked for before the Byrons bought them out. 'What about now, anyway? The fancy Byrons don't have a coat of arms?'

Jess seemed to stiffen as she followed his gaze beyond the slanted light pooling from the ruins of Venetian windows. 'I'm not sure,' she said.

'Isn't it your job to know?' He jabbed her playfully in the soft cushion around her ribs, then wandered over to examine the dining table and large fireplace on the other side of the room. 'Then again, I suppose they're not here often enough to bother. They just fired the locals, enjoyed a few years of castle life, and then buggered off when it suited them. What's the point of having a castle if you're not going to enjoy it? Why did my granddad lose a job he loved for a family we never see?'

'Mac . . .' Her wavery voice brought him back, and he waited expectantly until she shook her head. 'Yes . . . I don't know. It isn't right.'

'No, it isn't.' It still made him angry to think about.

'Why *do* you work here if you hate the owners so much?' Jessamine said, her back turned, her head bowed as she inspected the exhibits.

Mac shrugged. 'My granddad loved the gardens more than any other part of the castle, and he always used to say it went neglected when the Byrons took over. I suppose I feel close to him here. Like I'm finishing what he started. Making him proud. I'm just glad the Scottish Castles Association takes care of things now, otherwise I'd probably never have got the chance.'

'Did your granddad struggle after he was let go?'

'Everyone did. The castle gave plenty of locals jobs, until the Byrons stepped in. Granddad already had his first kid by that point – my uncle Ross – so he ended up working on a farm to feed his family. He hated it. All the dust and injuries from the machinery left him in bad shape. But he got by. It was just different back then.'

'Of course.' She spoke quietly. 'It must have been awful.'

'Everyone recovered in the end, I suppose. "Rich folk will never ruin Fort Aileen," he used to say.'

She spun around, a small smile on her lips. 'He sounds like a good man.'

'The best.' Mac beamed, despite the heavy ache in his chest. He'd been twenty-five when his granddad, well into his nineties, had passed, and it hadn't been nearly enough time. Like Mum and Dad, he'd never once treated Mac like anything but his own.

The scuffling of approaching footsteps interrupted them, and Jess straightened stiffly. A moment later, there was the sound of one of the other tour guides leading somebody along, reciting the same information he'd just heard from Jess.

Before he understood what was happening, Jess had taken Mac's hand and was pulling him towards the back of the room. 'Quick!' she hissed.

He followed clumsily, his hand clammy in hers as she pushed on an alcove in the wall. But it wasn't an alcove at all, he soon realised. The wall gave under her fingers and swung open. It was a hidden door.

'Thought they only had these in films,' he muttered.

She shushed him aggressively and yanked him into the dark, foisty space. The door clicked closed behind them, just as he heard the guide's words echo into the banqueting hall.

Mac's back pressed into the damp stone walls as he looked around, bewildered. Dim, electric lights flickered in sconces down a long, narrow corridor, imitating flames. A distant dripping sound somewhere in the blackness kept time with his pulse.

'Is this part of the tour?' he whispered, examining the slimy cobbles beneath his feet.

'Lord Gaven was the one to have these passages put in. Nobody knows why, but . . . I like to imagine him meeting here with Bearnard,' Jess whispered back. 'One of the corridors leads outside, beside the conservatory.' She was pressed opposite him, the corridor just big enough for their bodies. Still, they were close. Maybe even closer than they'd been on the Ferris wheel. He pushed off the wall, half to stop the damp from seeping into his already soaking shirt and half so he had the excuse to be even closer.

'Jess . . ?'

'Hmm?' She was breathless, and his lips tingled with the awareness of being watched, his bones aching with the need to close the last slither of distance between them.

'Why are we hiding?'

She blinked in surprise, as though it wasn't what she'd been expecting. 'I . . . er . . . I'm giving you a free tour. I'm probably supposed to be downstairs, waiting for visitors. I wouldn't want to get either of us in trouble.'

'Right.' As long as it wasn't another reason. As long as she wasn't embarrassed to be seen with him.

'We should keep moving.' She laced her fingers through his again and took careful steps down the passage. Spider webs and trickling water followed them, until they came to a fork of two paths. She led him down the first one, where they reached a set of spiral steps going upwards.

'Rosemire was a shady character,' he noted, his calves straining as they ascended the tall staircase. Dull daylight bled through a small window, and he peered out of it to find that they were at the front of the castle by the bridge, looking out on the gardens. In the front tower, he realised. It still rained outside, the black clouds hanging low over the trees and hills.

A thrill hopped down his spine. Nobody knew they were here. Completely alone, completely hidden, with no flying arrows or stolen cats to disrupt them. It was rare Mac got these moments. He wanted to make the most of this one.

Heat stirred in him as they reached the top of the steps, his decision made. He pulled Jess back before she could open the door leading to the real world.

'What?' she asked, her forehead wrinkling.

He said nothing, afraid that if he did, it would be the wrong thing – or his voice would wobble with everything he felt. Instead, he pulled her closer, bending down slightly to twine his fingers through her silky hair before kissing her.

Her breath seemed to hitch a little, but she didn't hesitate before returning it. Her fingers brushed along his jaw, through his stubble, and when his hands fell to the small of her back, he was certain she whimpered. It almost drew a moan out of him, too, especially when she nibbled his lip delicately. Still, it wasn't enough. His entire body was on fire, and he wanted to feel her everywhere.

Through broken kisses, she backed into the door, and it fell open beneath their combined weight. Still, they didn't stop. Mac didn't even know where he was until she pushed him into a shelf, the papery, dusty scent of old leather-bound books wrapping around them. The library.

'We're going to get caught,' she whispered.

'I don't care.' His hands found the curves below the base of her spine, her thighs, and he urged her up desperately.

She wrapped her legs around his waist, her kisses falling onto his earlobe, his jawline, peppering his nose and his chin, while he nuzzled into her neck. He breathed in her perfume, the smell of her lavender shampoo. He felt as though he was in a garden, where he was always most at peace, always most himself. As though she was just an extension of everything he already loved.

He stumbled as they writhed desperately for more. She held her hands out, using the shelves behind them to steady them both. 'These are centuries-old, Mac.' A giggle tinkled from her like bells. 'Be careful.'

'I'm sure Rosemire would approve,' he replied, grinning. He levered off the shelves and lowered her onto an old, leather love seat. Jess's hair cascaded around her like sunlight onto the burgundy cushion, her eyes glistening with unbridled fire. Nobody had ever looked at him that way. It made his knees weak. He kissed her neck, her shoulder, before drawing back to admire her again.

Her face scrunched as a drop of water fell between her brows and dribbled into her lashes. 'What on earth—'

He looked up to find a patch of damp spreading across the ceiling and bubbling beneath the wallpaper, causing it to sag. Another fat drop of water plopped down, and then another, until it was drizzling onto them both.

'Shite,' he cursed, dragging her off the couch quickly. 'I think there's a leak—'

And then the ceiling exploded.

Chapter Fourteen

Half of the castle's staff had gathered in the library in an attempt to evacuate the most valuable books and protect the old furniture. Jessamine was soaked as the water continued to pour through the broken ceiling, leaving plaster to crumble onto the floor. She was also very aware that her white blouse had become see-through, but there was not much to be done about that.

The castle caretaker was on his way. In the meantime, everybody scrambled to help, though it felt like fighting a losing battle. The leak had burst so quickly that there was no preventing the damage, and everything Mac and one of the tour guides, Adam, worked to shift into the hallway was already sopping.

Jessamine's job was to place and swap buckets, catching the water as they filled, though there were so many cracks in the ceiling now that she would have been better off using bathtubs. Petra had rushed into the commotion, too, her brown hair plastered to her cheeks and her expression a permanent grimace. 'Dare I ask what you two were doing up here?' she asked.

Unable to hide her blush, Jessamine could only pretend to be interested in the splashing water. 'I think I should keep that to myself.'

Petra gasped. 'You surely weren't doing the deed with the gardener in the library! That's like a saucy version of Cluedo!'

'*Shush*!' Jessamine commanded, glancing around to make sure nobody had overheard. 'No deed was done, thank you very much.'

'So why is your button is undone?'

Jessamine snapped her head down to her blouse, sighing when she found her buttons all fastened, though the material had creased and ridden out of the waistband of her trousers. She tucked it in again quickly.

'Ha. Made you look,' Petra teased.

Jessamine rolled her eyes and went to help Hayley, who was offering out tea towels and newspapers to soak up the puddles on the floor. She took a stack of each and began spreading them along the floorboards.

Mac's gruff voice echoed around the library as he returned. 'That couch was bloody heavy. Are you all right in here?'

'Oh, she's dandy, I bet,' Petra answered for her, sending him a knowing smirk.

Jessamine was positive that she looked like a tomato as she shot Petra a scolding glare.

Mac looked questioningly at Jessamine, asking slowly, 'Need help?'

'Er, OK.' She pulled another newspaper apart – and froze. Her face was plastered on the second page of the *Highland Gazette* with the headline: *A Fete Fit for a Countess*. Underneath was a photograph of Jessamine enjoying a cake sample with Sammy and George. The ink was already smudging against her damp fingers, and she turned the paper over quickly as her stomach twisted. There were more photos on the back: an old one of her at the races with Robert – with a caption detailing their divorce – and another of her mother.

'Actually, why don't you help Hayley?' she said quickly.

'You sure?' Mac hovered above her, a frown fraying his features.

She nodded. 'Yes. Petra and I are managing here.'

Confusion flashed briefly in his eyes, but he joined Hayley all the same. Jessamine didn't feel any relief. She looked at the newspapers again, sweeping her wet fringe off her forehead as nausea gripped her. She couldn't keep doing this. Lying to Mac. She'd lain awake last night full of guilt. It was eating her up.

She couldn't even look at her smeared image in the newspaper. She covered it up with another page, and then another, wishing she could bury the truth the same way, at least for a little while longer. It was so easy to forget when he was near her. In the library, before the leak, she'd been so engulfed in him that nothing else had mattered. It was blissful and dangerous and whether she let the lies continue or not, it was all going to shatter.

Tears pricked her eyes, blurring her vision.

'Jessamine?' Petra murmured, kneeling beside her.

Jessamine could only shake her head, sniffling as she distracted herself with the towels. 'I'm fine. Really.'

Petra's brows furrowed. She glanced at Mac, who chatted with Hayley obliviously. 'Did he say something?'

'No.' That was the problem. He was perfect, to her at least. He was generous and witty and honest. And she had to give him up. 'No, it's me. I'm . . . going to see if the caretaker is here yet.'

She never got that far. Lauren appeared at the door, her features pale and pinched with worry. Her gaze slipped right past Jessamine. 'Er, Mac?'

'Aye?' Mac turned around, resting his hands on his hips, his skin glistening with a sheen of sweat.

Lauren's throat bobbed. Another bout of dread left Jess's knees weak.

'It's the loch's banks. They've burst, and your cottage . . .'

Mac paled, wobbling slightly as he stepped closer and scraped a hand over his stubble.

'How bad?'

'I don't know, but the water is already gushing downhill. Everywhere is flooding again,' Lauren said. 'I had to call my mum and tell her to go and stay with my brother, just in case it reaches the village.'

A damp library suddenly seemed nothing in comparison. These bricks had stood for thousands of years, through all sorts of unpredictable Scottish weather, but Fort Aileen was all peaks and troughs, the walk out of town exhausting with its steep inclines. The water was bound to run and gather on lower land, especially after the dry weather over the last few weeks. The earth hadn't had time to absorb so much water so quickly.

'Again?' Jessamine asked, frowning.

'We usually suffer with floods closer to winter,' Lauren explained. 'It's been a nightmare the last few autumns, but never like this. Never so early in the year.'

'We should go, Mac,' Jessamine suggested gently, putting a hand on his arm and squeezing. He seemed not to notice at all, his muscles like stone.

Rufus. Guilt gnawed at her for how long she'd gone without worrying about her cat, too. If it was flooding outside, she needed to find him, make sure he was warm and safe.

Petra appeared next to them, worry crinkling her features as well. 'Go, Jess. We can handle things here.'

'*Mac . . .*' Jessamine pleaded.

His gaze sharpened. 'Right. Come on, then.'

She followed him out of the library, with a final appreciative glance at both Petra and Lauren. It was an effort to keep up with Mac. He strode down the stairs two at a time, his footfalls echoing in the eerily empty foyer. The sound of the rain still ricocheted through the castle, making her feel hollow, useless.

Until she heard a gentle meow.

Rufus had curled up on the information desk without a care in the world, his tail wafting as he noticed them. Jessamine sighed in relief. 'Oh, thank goodness, Rufus,' she breathed, scratching his head lovingly. He purred, brushing against her palm. 'You're a good boy, staying out of the rain.'

'Maybe you should, too,' Mac said by the door. 'It's torrential out there, and the water is getting deep.'

'No,' she replied without missing a beat. She couldn't let Mac face whatever damage awaited him at the cottage alone. So, she laced her fingers through his and, together, they braved the storm.

Mac felt as though he might collapse as he waded into the cottage. His hallway, like the rest of the gardens, was now a river that reached above his ankles. Their shoe rack had already drowned in it and the first few steps of the staircase were submerged. He almost didn't want to continue.

Jess squeezed his hand, the water splashing around her feet as she stepped closer. An hour ago, he'd been happier than perhaps ever before, running around the castle like a teenager with her. Now, he was numb. Her touch was the only thing tethering him to reality at all.

'I'm so sorry, Mac,' she whispered.

He closed his eyes for a moment, counting to five in his head to steel himself for what came next. And then, together, they went into the living room.

The murky water covered everything. The legs of the couch and armchair were underwater, the cushions were soaked, the coffee table wonky and sinking. Mac's crooked bookshelf . . . his favourite spider plant . . . Arran's colouring table . . . All of it was ruined.

He could smell all that dingy damp spreading along the walls. This cottage was his home. Arran's home. It was supposed to be their future, the place where he would raise them for as long as Linda allowed it. They'd painted the walls yellow together one rainy Saturday. Arran collapsed onto that couch every afternoon to watch TV after school, while Mac complained it was rubbish.

And now it was ruined, gone, and he couldn't imagine any of it anymore.

He blinked back tears, shaking his head in despair. 'I don't know what I'm going to tell Arran.'

'Do you have somewhere else to stay?' she asked softly.

'My parents.' But their house was only a two-bedroom. Mac would have to sleep on the couch. He needed to call them, make sure they weren't caught in the floods, either. But he couldn't move, couldn't breathe. And then there was Arran at school . . . but their teachers would have called by now, he reasoned, and the building was on higher ground on the opposite end of Fort Aileen.

The image of Pickle in his hutch upstairs jolted through his mind. 'Shit. The bloody rabbit,' he muttered, splashing back into the corridor. He didn't dare put his weight on the sagging banister as he climbed up the stairs, glad when he reached dry carpet a few steps up. Jess's footsteps followed him into Arran's room, where everything remained untouched by water. For now.

In his wire cage, Pickle chewed one of his carrot-shaped toys, nose and whiskers twitching happily. Mac sighed in relief.

'We should pack some of Arran's things. And yours,' Jess suggested.

He nodded. He knew he was supposed to move, pull his finger out of his arse and do something, but he couldn't force his brain into rationality. He could only look around, overwhelmed. Arran had decorated every inch of their room themself, Mac letting them choose the furniture. They'd even taken a mini road trip to IKEA, the closest one all the way in Glasgow, though Mac could have just ordered online. But he'd wanted that time with Arran, and had wanted Arran to feel . . . wanted. Chosen. Finally at home.

Somehow, it felt like all that hard work was collapsing with the shelves and wearing down with the carpets.

'Mac,' Jess said delicately, her hands resting on his jaw and bringing him back to the present. 'It's going to be OK. It's fixable.'

The cottage might be eventually, but he didn't know about the rest.

He sighed, brushing his nose against Jess's lightly just to breathe her in. Her warmth gave him the strength to spring back into action. Reluctantly, he then pulled away and yanked out the two duffel bags from under Arran's bed, both pale blue. The ones Arran had arrived with when Linda had dropped them off the first time. Arran had been lost and meek, then. Not the fierce twelve-year-old they were now.

He opened Arran's wardrobe, drawing clothes off hangers and piling them on the bed. Jess folded them carefully and packed them up. It was as though she instinctively knew what Arran needed, and the fact was almost enough to thaw Mac's shock. Almost.

He paused at the rainbow cardigan Arran had chosen the first time Mac had taken them shopping, when he'd told them it was OK to wear any clothes they wanted, regardless of which section they were in. The wool was full of pulls and bobbles in the thread now. Mac's throat clogged, and as though there was no longer enough room for them inside, the words he'd been stewing on for days leaked out. 'I was going to ask Arran if they wanted me to adopt them this week.'

Jess stilled, pressing one of Arran's stripy shirts to her chest as she looked at Mac sadly. It made him want to burst into tears.

'That doesn't have to change. You still can.'

He clenched his jaw, distracting himself with the last of the clothes, and then the few shoes that hadn't been left to drown by the welcome mat downstairs. 'I don't even have a home for them now. I'm a single, working-class foster father who doesn't even have a fucking home for their kid.'

'You do have a home. It's just a bit . . . soggy at the moment.' She put the shirt down and cupped his face again. His breath came out ragged and strained as he desperately tried not to fall apart in front of her. It felt like he was always trying not to fall apart in front of her. 'This isn't the end, Mac. It isn't. I can lend you the money to speed the repairs up here. We can figure it out.'

Mac made a mangled sound of disbelief. 'No. Don't be silly, Jess. I wouldn't let you do that.'

'You're not on your own,' she said. 'A lot of people are here, and they want to help you and Arran.'

He knew it was wrong to rely on her – on anyone. He couldn't. Wouldn't. But in another life, he could see it. She and Arran, like they'd been at the fete, by the loch. He could so easily imagine that being their reality. Jess being Arran's . . .

No. He couldn't think like that. Jess was offering money and support, not a bloody life with him. She hadn't signed up for this. He couldn't be like her ex-husband, the one who had expected nothing from her but motherhood and domesticity. The one who hadn't known how to make her feel loved.

In the end, he could only say, 'Thank you. For being here.'

'Of course,' she murmured, placing a careful kiss on the tip of his nose. His eyes fluttered closed as he sank into her, her arms looping around his neck and his around her waist. And he held on for all it was worth, because she was the only steady thing he knew. 'Anything I can do, Mac,' she repeated. 'You're not on your own.'

Though he knew it was dangerous, he was starting to believe it was true.

Mac felt lost as he stood at the school gates among the rest of the parents. Luckily, flooding in the village wasn't nearly as bad as it was in the cottage, though a few people on lower land had evacuated their homes. The rain had at least shown mercy now, only a drizzle spitting across Mac's skin as he clutched the duffle bags and Pickle in his cage, muscles aching with tension.

The kids were already pouring out of school, indistinguishable in their uniforms. Mac searched for Arran's yellow raincoat, but it looked like the older teens had been dismissed first today.

'Everything all right, pal?' Brodie appeared beside him, motioning to the bags with his head as his brows furrowed. Brodie was picking up his daughter, Joss, no doubt. He took her straight from school to her dance lessons in Inverness each week. It was the only time Mac saw Brodie at the school gates, now that Joss was old enough to walk herself home.

'Cottage has flooded,' Mac murmured quietly, swiftly avoiding Sara's attempted eye contact on the other side of the gate. He didn't have the energy for her chit-chat today. 'We're going to have to stay with my parents until it's all sorted.'

'Oh, shite.' Brodie's eyes widened as he rubbed his bearded chin. 'I knew the loch's banks had burst, but I had no idea it had reached the cottage. I'm sorry, Mac. Is there anything I can do?'

Mac shrugged. 'Might need your help with the refurbishments once the house is all dried out, but at the moment, there's not much to be done.'

Brodie squeezed his shoulder sympathetically. 'Just give us a call if there's anything, will you? Even if you just need a wee pint and a chat. I'm here for you – *and* Arran.'

'Aye. Cheers, Brodie.' Mac forced a smile so tight it felt like his cheeks were cracking. 'I'll let you know.'

Joss emerged from the crowd, then, drawing Brodie's attention. Since her parents' split, Joss shared none of her father's perpetual cheeriness; she was all broody teenage indifference.

'Hi, Joss,' Mac greeted her. 'Had a good day?'

Joss only grunted, pulling out her phone. Brodie rolled his eyes. 'I'll catch up with you properly soon, aye?'

'Aye. See you later.' Mac waved Brodie away, relieved when he saw Arran finally wandering out of the school gates, their pin-badge-covered backpack a size too big for their lanky frame. They still wore their non-binary badge everywhere they went, and so far everybody had been nothing but supportive, including their teachers and friends.

Arran's face turned bone-white when they lifted their head to find Mac, as though they already knew.

A ringing in Mac's ears echoed above the din of chatter,

and he waited patiently as Arran, at a torturously slow pace, made their way over.

'Hello, kiddo.' Mac did his best to keep his voice steady as he ruffled Arran's hair with his free hand.

But Arran wasn't paying attention. They were staring at the bags as though they were about to detonate. 'You said I could stay with you. You promised.'

Mac frowned, glancing between Arran and the bags. It took him a few seconds to work it out, considering the conversation they'd had just this weekend. But Arran thought it was time to leave; that it was time for another move.

And the anguish crumpling their features . . . it broke Mac's heart.

He lowered to one knee so that Arran had to look down at him, placing the bags and cage down on the pavement. 'I meant what I said. You're not going anywhere, Arran. Not until you want to.'

'Then why do you have my bags?'

Mac wondered how many times this had happened before. How many times had Arran emerged from school to find a social worker waiting, ready to move them to a new home? Enough times that Arran expected it, now. That they saw bags and assumed the worst.

'Look at me,' Mac ordered gently, tilting Arran's chin to meet his gaze. 'You'll stay with me for as long as you want to. For as long as you'll have me. Don't ever think I'd let anyone take you away from me. Do you understand?'

Arran nodded, their chin wobbling.

Mac sighed, unable to let go yet. He needed Arran to feel safe. To know they could trust Mac, if no one else in the world. 'There has been . . .' He didn't even know how to say it. How to tell Arran that their home was sinking, that they couldn't go back. 'There was a flood,' he confessed finally. 'With the rain, Leannan's banks burst and the cottage is a wee bit damaged.'

'We heard about it in school,' said Arran. Their brows knitted together. 'So where will we live?'

'We're going to stay with my mum and dad for a while. They'll look after us until everything's fixed. It's not forever, though. It might only be a matter of a few months.'

'What about Pickle?'

'You don't think I'd forget Pickle, do you?' Mac's smile was muted as he shifted the duffel bags to display the rabbit carrier between them, in which Pickle lay content on a bed of sawdust.

Arran's shoulders relaxed with relief. They picked up the carrier, poking their finger through the cage and muttering, 'Hello.'

And for the first time that day, a flicker of hope sparked in Mac. Arran was still here. They were safe. They still had a roof over their heads, even if it wasn't their own.

It would be all right. It had to be – and it was Mac's job to keep it that way.

Chapter Fifteen

Jessamine took a deep breath before walking into the Hairy Coo two days later. Travelling through Fort Aileen had been bittersweet as she took in the aftermath of the rain. Apparently, flash floods had happened all over the Highlands, the relentless downpour unable to be absorbed quickly enough after such unusually dry weather. Fort Aileen had been one of the luckier places, but it was still terrible, especially with the loch's banks bursting, too. Thankfully, nowhere was as badly damaged as Mac's cottage, but the community milled about with sandbags and cups of tea for the unlucky ones all the same. The May sun shone on them smugly, and she sent it a glare as she closed the door on it, almost catching Petra's nose in the process. She'd forgotten she was back to being followed.

'Oh, here she is,' prattled an irritating voice from the bar. 'Late. Her Majesty mustn't own a watch.'

Sighing, Jess glanced first at her wristwatch and then at her phone, just to be certain. 'Actually, Hamish, I'm right on time. Perhaps it's *your* watch that's faulty.'

She met his eye sharply, though inside she jittered with nerves. She didn't have the patience for snide remarks today. Not knowing that Mac needed her help, as well as the rest of the village. She'd got up this morning deciding that she couldn't go on as she was. She couldn't just sit back and watch everybody struggle. She had to do something.

Which was why, after making donations all morning, she'd called a meeting among Fort Aileen's event-planning committee. The rest of them – minus Elsie, who Lauren had said was still staying with family outside of town – were perched on bar stools, staring at her. Gem stood behind the bar, for once not smirking at her.

'Thank you all for coming,' Jessamine began. 'I know it's a difficult time for us all—'

'*Us?*' Hamish interrupted. 'I'd imagine *you're* quite all right in your grand castle.'

She couldn't do it anymore. She couldn't stand by and be bullied by a man old enough to know better. 'I beg your pardon, Hamish, but the castle is damaged, too – not to mention I have watched people I care about dearly suffer from these floods. I suggest that if you're only here to bicker with me again, you leave now. I didn't call this meeting to be demeaned. I called it to help the village.'

His wispy brows rose above the round frames of his glasses and his mouth finally clamped shut. Splotches of red blossomed on his wrinkled cheeks. Jess caught Gem's eye as she took a deep breath and was surprised to find the bartender's chin tipped up with . . . *respect*? It was difficult to read her when she wasn't glowering.

Jess smoothed down her blazer and laid her file on the nearest table. 'I'd like to introduce my friend, Petra.'

'Hello.' Petra gave a timid wave. 'Lovely to meet you all.'

'Apologies for calling you all here today on such short notice,' Jess continued, 'but, as you know, a few properties around Fort Aileen have been damaged in the floods, including the castle's east wing, the gardener's cottage, and a few local homes and businesses.'

Hamish crossed his arms and muttered something about 'ulterior motives', but Jess ignored him.

'Now, I know people's spirits may be low in the coming weeks – which is why I'd like to host a grand re-opening for the entire village. A celebration of sorts. Proof that we're a community that always bounces back. It would bring new people into the village and uplift everybody again, and would allow our local businesses to reach farther and wider. I want to make this the biggest festival we've ever seen.' Jess was making it up as she went along, but judging by the intent gazes, it seemed to be working. 'If people aren't ready to join in, that's OK, too. But we have to try, and I can think of no better way than to bring excitement and life back to the village after such an awful incident.'

A moment of silence followed. She cleared her throat, pretending to look interested in her notepad.

'I had an idea for the theme, if you'd like to hear it.'

'Please enlighten us.' Hamish couldn't help himself.

Jess clenched her jaw. 'Well, I thought about how much people love to dress up, and how wonderfully historic Fort Aileen is. We could go with a medieval theme. Knights and princesses, jousting, entertainers for the children, food stalls, music. It could be quite magical, really, and lots of fun.'

Hamish tutted as the rest considered.

It was Gem who broke the silence, expression unreadable. 'It isn't the worst idea I've ever heard. It's something different, I suppose, and the pub's been a bit quiet of late. Not that I'd dress up.'

'You wouldn't have to. People wouldn't even have to stay all day. They can just pop in and see what's happening.'

'And how shall we afford this whimsical little party?' asked Hamish.

'You needn't worry about that. I'll handle the finances.'

'With taxpayers' money, no doubt,' he muttered.

'Not at all. If you have a better idea, Hamish, we're all listening,' Jessamine said patiently.

She tapped her foot in the silence that followed, quite enjoying the way his furious blush spread to the top of his ears. Rendering Hamish speechless twice in less than an hour was quite the accomplishment.

'Well, you can count the Hairy Coo in,' Gem said. 'God knows we all need a good drink.'

Jess nodded slowly, excitement bubbling in her. 'Thank you, Gem. Thank you ever so much.'

'Calm down, love. Doesn't make us friends.' Still, Gem winked at her.

'I suppose I'll start preparing the bakery,' Wendy, who made the most delicious blueberry muffins Jess had ever tasted, agreed. 'When will this be?'

'Three weeks away. The second weekend of June,' Jess suggested. 'I know it's short notice, but I talked to the local contractors, and they think the main repairs will be done by then. Plus, it would help our businesses pick themselves up and look forward to something. And if you could spread the word to the others . . .'

'Of course.' Wendy gave her a soft smile. 'I think it's a wonderful thing you're doing, love. I'm not that keen on the royals, but they could all take a leaf out of your book.'

Jess opened her mouth to tell her she wasn't a royal at all, but Hamish was already adding, 'Well, I can't help. The tea room's flooded, too.'

'I'm aware, and I was sorry to see it closed.' Jess frowned, remembering the empty café she'd driven past this morning at the opposite end of the bridge. The water of Leannan had puddled across the banks to where the tea room was located. She already planned to distribute her money there, too, but it was the disruption to business that would hurt the village more. The summer holidays were on their way, and she had no doubt they would be the busiest period of the year for Fort Aileen, with even more visitors and tourists than they'd had all spring. If the businesses weren't up and running again by then, it would surely be a struggle to bring back customers when they eventually re-opened. Hosting an entire day to uplift and revive the community would ensure they weren't forgotten by people outside of the village. At least, that's what she hoped. While she would pay for the refurbishments and losses herself, she knew it wouldn't be enough if there were no longer customers to support them in the long run.

Hamish hummed as though unconvinced. 'As you can

imagine, there's plenty of work to do and I've wasted enough time this morning. We done?'

'Yes. Thank you for coming.' She'd rather he hadn't, though she still shot a sympathetic glance his way. No matter his temperament, nobody deserved to lose their business. 'Thank you all,' she said. 'And if there's anything else I can help with, or you have any ideas, do feel free to email me.'

They all stood, pulling on coats and beginning to chatter among themselves. Jessamine slumped, glad it was over, and looked at Petra, who flashed a reassuring thumbs-up.

'Gem,' Jess said, 'I think I need a drink.'

Jessamine's phone rang before she could take so much as a sip of her midday G&T. She pulled it out in the hopes it was Mac – and then groaned to find her mother's caller ID on the screen instead.

'Excuse me,' she muttered, slipping off the stool and relocating in front of the unlit fire, where Petra and Gem wouldn't hear above their own chatter. Well, *Petra's* chatter. Gem was still not very talkative around either of them, unless the conversation was about Mac. Not that her aloofness stopped Petra from blathering on.

'Hello?' Jessamine said upon answering the call, sinking into the dusty armchair. She focused on the old, uneven brickwork, always so desperate to detach herself as much as possible from her mother.

'I received your email.' Mother's voice was stony enough to make Jessamine shiver.

'And?' Jessamine had sent the email this morning, telling Mother that the gala would be cancelled in light of the floods. She hadn't mentioned that she was replacing the event with another, one for the town rather than the snooty people she had no interest in entertaining. The charities had still been invited, should they wish to attend, and she had already promised to collaborate with them on more fundraisers once her work in Fort Aileen was complete. Beyond that, she had no desire to host a fancy gala while the rest of the town struggled. It wouldn't be right. Jessamine was determined not to be another Byron who ostracised the village from her castle.

Cancelling the gala was the best thing she could think to do, and also perhaps a realisation that she had far too much on her plate already. She could not be an ambassador for every charity in the country, no matter how badly she wanted to make the world better. It was why she'd been so focused on the Inverness branches of Shimmer and the Every Effort Fund these past weeks. Before, she'd cut ribbons and posed with charity founders next to plaques with her name on them, but she'd never seen the difference she could make first-hand. She was always too far removed from the people she was supposed to be helping.

But ever since she'd seen Arran pick out that non-binary badge at the fete, and the hundreds of people walking around wearing their own flags and pronouns proudly – and ever since she'd begun working with Sammy and George to expand the charity further and offer more support to the community – Jess's true vocation had become clear to her. She'd even shared her story for the Shimmer website, and it had made her realise just how valid her pansexuality was, even when she'd been married to a man and was currently smitten by another. Who she was in a relationship with didn't change who she was. Sammy and George had welcomed her with open arms. Accepted her. Just like Mac had when she'd told him. Of course, it also made her realise just how wrong her mother had been to ignore who she was. How badly she had needed a place to belong, where she didn't have to justify any of it or feel different.

Passing that along to others was what mattered now. That, and helping Mac and the people of Fort Aileen with the village's recovery. She couldn't save the world, no matter how much money she donated, but she could do this. She could do her best.

'*And?*' Mother repeated, pitch rising to a disbelieving squeak. '*And?* And you cannot just cancel a gala, Jessamine. Everybody has already received their invites. They have been excited for weeks.'

'I've already informed everybody on the guest list of the cancellation.'

'This is ridiculous,' Mother ranted through her sputters. 'I always knew you would turn out like this: away with the fairies, impulsive, unable to stop and think like a rational human being. You are selfish, Jessamine. And ungrateful! I have been preparing new prospects for you. Nice young men who are willing to overlook your scandal and give you a chance. And this is what I get in return, is it? An email. A cancellation. I was wrong. That place is no good for you. Living in a castle has clearly gone to your head. I don't know *who* you think you are.'

Jessamine pinched the bridge of her nose, her sinuses stinging with the promise of tears. All of her life, she had never been enough. She would never have Philippa Byron's approval. She would never be the countess she had hoped for. Maybe she *was* a fool – for ever believing that enough charity events and galas and marriages would earn her love and respect. They hadn't. They never would.

'I'm doing what I believe is right,' she stated finally. 'The town is struggling with the consequences of flash floods and I've decided to help them. They don't need an extravagant gala. They need community. I have to help the people I care about.'

'*What* people?' She could hear the click of Mother's heels against the tiles of their grand town-house foyer. 'Heavens, don't tell me you've taken a liking to one of the *villagers*. Have you forgotten who you are? Have all those cows and haggis and God-knows-what given you some rare case of amnesia? You are a *countess*—'

'I *know* who I am!' Jessamine roared, forgetting that Gem and Petra were there. Forgetting everything but the painful knot in her gut, the one she'd lived with for far too long. 'I know who I am and what I want, and I'm sorry it doesn't match up with what you hoped, but I am doing my best. I have *always* done my best.'

Silence crackled down the line for a moment, causing Jess to pace restlessly. She clutched one of the tattered, beer-stained Highland cow-patterned cushions and tried to blink back her tears.

'If you choose to disobey me, embarrass me, Jessamine, then that is fine. I cannot force you to see sense.' Mother's voice was eerily calm and searingly bitter. 'But I shall not be involved in it. I'm withdrawing my investments into your charities. If you wish to drag the Byron name through the dirt, I shan't have anything to do with it. It is clear that assistant of yours is doing nothing to stop this, either, and I will be informing her that she's fired.'

Jessamine's stomach dropped. She whirled around, wide-eyed as she looked at Petra. Mother's withdrawal of money, she had expected, but she hadn't spared a thought for Petra's job.

Both Petra and Gem were watching intently from the bar, as though they could hear every word.

'Petra has done nothing wr—'

'When you decide to grow up, you may return to London and make amends. Until then, I bid you goodbye.'

The line went dead, and Jess clamped down on her wobbling lower lip as she slipped her phone back into her pocket. Her ears rang in the new quiet.

'How much of that did you hear?'

'Nothing. Nothing at all,' Petra answered innocently.

'Enough,' said Gem.

Jessamine swallowed thickly and slumped back into the armchair, where they could not see her fall apart. She still felt their gazes burning through the back of the chair, though. A moment later, stool legs squeaked across lacquered wood and Petra came to sit on the couch adjacent. Her phone began to ring, an upbeat tinkling tone that did not match the ID she flashed at Jessamine.

'Calling to fire me, I presume.'

'I'm so sorry, Petra.'

Petra declined the call and placed the phone on the coffee table. 'I'm not. I couldn't stand that woman. She always called me Petal. At first, I thought she was just being kind, and then I realised she didn't actually know my name.'

That sounded like Mother. She'd called their maid Barbara for twenty years, only to find out her name was Alice.

'Well, then, I suppose you're free now. Of all of us.' Jessamine smiled sadly, realising perhaps too late that she didn't want to lose Petra. She hadn't understood her before, but these last few weeks, she'd been a good friend, had kept Jess's secrets and supported her through her work. Even Rufus liked having her around.

Petra smirked. 'I quite like Fort Aileen. Perhaps I might stay a little bit longer. Lady Byron might have been my employer, but you are the one I've been working for, Jessamine. And I would like to keep working for you, if only as someone who wants to help you.'

Jessamine sighed with relief, leaning forward and placing her hand atop Petra's. 'Really?'

Petra nodded. 'You do more good than your mother will ever know. I've been proud to watch you do it.'

'Then you won't work for me,' she whispered. 'You'll work *with* me. As my friend. And I'll give you a raise. And more holidays.'

Petra's brown eyes warmed, and she squeezed Jessamine's hand tightly.

'Cute,' Gem commented dryly from the bar. 'Is this the part where we group-hug?'

'Ooh, yes, good idea!' Petra missed Gem's sarcasm and piled on Jessamine immediately, her grip tight and unrelenting. But Jessamine could only giggle and sink into the comfort. It had been a long time since she'd felt supported, accepted, for who she was. A long time since she'd had a real friend. 'Come on, Gem!' Petra urged.

'No thanks.'

'She thinks she's too tough for hugs,' Petra whispered.

'Her loss,' Jessamine replied, finally freed. 'We should get going, anyway. Lots to do.'

'Yes, including eating cake for lunch. I think we deserve it.' Petra slung her handbag over her shoulder. 'Bye, Gem.'

'Yep.' Gem tipped her head, focusing on cleaning down the bar with a damp cloth. Still, when Jessamine went to follow, the bartender called her back. 'Jess?'

'Yes?' The draught wafted through her hair as the door opened, then shut, behind Petra, leaving the two of them alone. Jess already had a feeling she knew what was coming.

'He'll understand, you know,' she said – and Jess had been wrong, because she hadn't expected that at all. 'Mac is a good man. He'll understand if you tell him. If he heard what I just did . . .'

'I'm worried he won't,' Jessamine admitted, the tears finally springing to her eyes. She could handle being belittled by her mother, but the thought of Mac and all of the ways she was ruining things with him before they'd ever truly begun . . . that was more difficult to bear. 'I'm worried I've dug my hole a little too deep.'

'You care about him. I see that now. And what you're doing for the town, the floods . . .' Gem pulled at the thread of her cloth, her brows furrowed. 'That's not me giving my approval, by the way. I'm just saying that maybe I get it. A little bit.'

'Well, thank you.' To know that fiercely protective Gem didn't believe Jessamine was a terrible person was a slight relief, another weight off her shoulders.

'And I won't tell him,' Gem said. 'He has bigger things going on. He doesn't deserve to have his heart broken, too.'

Jessamine nodded, understanding. 'I never wanted to hurt him. I only want to help him, now more than ever.'

'Yeah, well . . . I'll still kick your arse if you fuck it up,' Gem warned.

Jessamine didn't doubt her. Still, she mustered a small smile before walking out of the pub. Though unsettled by her mother's phone call, she felt . . . hopeful. Stronger. There was plenty to do, plenty to fix, but it no longer felt impossible. She would tell Mac about who she was when the time was right. And until then, she would organise the biggest, brightest festival the Highlands had ever seen.

Chapter Sixteen

Mac was at the end of his tether when his parents' doorbell rang. It had been a hectic morning, trying to settle into a two-bedroom house, knowing all the while he was disrupting Mum and Dad's peace, and now Arran had somehow disappeared. Right on time, too, because the caller at the door was no doubt Linda, who had sounded quite alarmed on the phone after Mac had told her what had happened. He only wished he had Arran's talent of vanishing whenever the social worker showed up.

'Doorbell's ringing, love!' Mum shouted from the living room as though Mac had not heard.

He sighed, shoved one of Arran's half-unpacked duffel bags in the pantry to project some sense of organisation, and went to answer the door.

Linda somehow looked more concerned than ever. After the last strawberry-pie-related fiasco, he hadn't believed that possible. 'Hello, Linda.'

'Hello, Mr Douglas.' She raised her eyebrows expectantly, and he stepped aside to let her in. With her briefcase swinging in her hands, she examined the hallway, from the school photographs of a very ginger, very snaggle-toothed Mac, to Mum's random Winnie the Pooh cross-stitches. 'Lovely home your parents have.'

She never said that about the cottage, he thought bitterly, closing the door and smoothing down the crumpled flannel shirt he'd pulled straight from a bag this morning. 'Cheers. It's a bit small for four, mind, but we're making it work.'

She followed him as he guided her into the kitchen and gestured to a stool. 'Can I get you—'

'Where is Arran? Upstairs?'

'Er . . . yes,' he lied, shifting. This was why he'd got caught shoplifting a tub of hair gel at age fifteen. Couldn't lie to save his life.

'Good. Can you call him down, then?'

'Arran goes by "they/them" now. And they're having a shower.'

Linda softened, much to Mac's surprise. 'Well . . . that's a development. I must admit, Mac. Arran really does seem to be coming out of their shell with you.'

'Thank you. I'm doing my best.' And because she was being so nice, Mac caved like the weak man he was, putting his head in his hands. 'Actually . . . Arran's not here. They must have gone for a walk.'

'Right.' Linda opened her file on the table and began scribbling something. Mac hated it. He hated that Arran was reduced to a pile of papers in a brown folder. He hated that everything he did, said, was a reflection of Arran and their relationship, though no one would ever know just how hard they were both trying. 'Does Arran often go for walks alone?' she said.

He grimaced, using the breakfast bar for support. 'Not far. They like sitting by the loch when they're . . . taking a time out.'

'The loch whose banks just burst,' she acknowledged. 'And you let them? Is that safe?'

As though Mac ever had any say in what Arran did or didn't do. 'They don't need mollycoddling. They're used to being independent, and I don't think it would be productive to take that away now. They have their phone with them.' He hoped, anyway.

'Most of our foster parents are a bit more . . . hands-on,' she said.

'Most of them aren't taking care of Arran,' Mac retorted,

clenching his jaw impatiently. He was tired of feeling as though he was in an interrogation room every time he opened his door to Linda. It wasn't that she was unkind; more that Mac was just terrified of how he might be perceived. He hadn't been sure before, but after the fete, the arrow, the conversation at the loch, he understood Arran better than ever and knew exactly what they needed. He knew he was the right father for them.

Linda scribbled again then clicked her pen and set it down. 'All right. Well, I came to make sure you're still capable of fostering Arran here. Do they have their own bedroom?'

'Yes.'

'Do you?'

He could only blink guiltily at that. His back already ached from a night spent on the tiny living-room couch, but he'd do it all again every day for Arran. To keep them here, safe and loved.

'Obviously we vetted your parents back when you started fostering, so there's no concern there, but are they all right with this new arrangement?'

'Absolutely we are!' Mum's voice drifted through the kitchen like a spring breeze as she entered, her fingers still tangled in a purple ball of wool. She was currently knitting Arran a cardigan with the colours of the non-binary flag, though Mac had had to explain what non-binary meant, and how, no, it was not related to computers. She'd shown the same solidarity when Mac, a nervous nineteen-year-old, had come out as bisexual just over a decade before, and had taken him to his first Pride in Glasgow the following summer. The best woman he knew. Even now, as an adult, he was relieved just to have her here.

Everybody needed their mum. He only wanted to be that for Arran. Men could be mums, couldn't they?

'Arran and Mac are a joy to have around. I always say I don't see them enough,' said his mum. She saw them most evenings and weekends, but Mac smiled all the same. 'Having them here is no bother at all.'

'Thank you, Mrs Douglas,' Linda said, watching the knitting needle she was brandishing quite threateningly – well, threateningly for Mum, anyway. 'That's good to hear.'

'Besides, this is the place where we raised Mac,' Mum continued, narrowing her eyes. 'I hope Arran will be just as at home here.'

'I'm sure.' Linda gave an encouraging smile.

'Arran told me the other day that they wanted to stay,' Mac added, just for good measure. 'After the floods, when I picked them up from school with their bags packed, they were devastated. They thought they were leaving me, and they didn't want to. They'll stay with me. We'll make it work.'

'Of course. As long as Arran is safe and happy, there's no reason to disrupt them. But what we discussed still stands. If they *do* feel they might want a change, now might be the right time to consider it, what with the damage to the cottage—'

'Houses can be refurbished,' he cut in, as steadily as possible. 'The cottage will be fixed. But Arran's fear, their insecurities, their sense of abandonment . . . That can't be fixed so easily. They're just settling down. Just learning to trust me. They can't go through another change. Our house is ruined, but they still have a home with me.'

'And we know that. We do.' Linda's words were so sincere that Mac found himself believing her. 'You're doing a good job, Mac, all things considered.'

Mac nodded, trying to gather his composure as relief rushed through him. His mother soothed him, rubbing his back softly, knowingly. She loved Arran as much as Mac did. They were her grandchild, perhaps the only one she'd ever get. And Arran loved her. They loved watching movies with her on a Saturday night, loved listening to Dad's old records on a Sunday morning. They didn't deserve to lose that. None of them did. Finally hearing Linda acknowledge that was more than he'd ever expected.

Linda sighed. 'But, I can't pretend I'm not still a little bit concerned, Mac. You say you want things to be steady for

Arran, but you've been all over the place each time I've met with you. A flooded cottage, a new girlfriend, burnt pies, running late. Are you really as stable as you think you are?'

He knew the answer. Defiantly, he met Linda's gaze, his face, body, burning. '*Yes*.'

'Girlfriend?' Mum questioned excitedly. 'You kept that a secret. You must have her over for dinner some time . . .'

'Thanks, Mum,' he murmured, and then, as an afterthought: 'And she's not my girlfriend. But even if she was, that wouldn't matter. Arran loves her. They get along like a house on fire. And Arran loves my friends. They love their school friends. They love Fort Aileen. They've built a life here.' His voice cracked.

Linda clamped her lips together, weighing Mac up carefully. 'I'm going to schedule another meeting for three weeks' time. See how we get on. How's that?'

'OK.' Relief left him in a huge gust of breath, scattering the pages of Mum's Nigella Lawson cookbook on the side. 'Thank you. Let me show you where Arran's staying?'

She nodded, and together, they went upstairs.

Jessamine couldn't help herself. No matter her personal dislike for Hamish, she had to stop outside of the tea room on her way back to the castle to see the damage. She'd already sent Petra away with a long, long list of tasks they'd need to get done if they wanted to have the fundraiser ready in time.

The fifteen-minute walk back to the castle was the first time in a long time she'd felt at peace, even with so much uncertainty. The village was beautiful. The hills were . . . difficult to walk up, but still quite pretty, and her leg muscles were slowly adjusting. The locals were becoming friends. She'd never been anywhere like it before. She'd never felt this comfortable, this at home, anywhere else.

Perhaps she wanted to stay.

It was why she worried about the tea room. It was popular with castle visitors and locals alike, and despite the poor customer service, Jess quite liked being able to pop in for a midday cake whenever she wished. Now, it sat in darkness.

She peered through the window and saw the chairs piled onto the tables, the cake stands empty, and the tiles covered in water. The damage was sure to halt business for at least a couple of weeks, not to mention the harm it must have done to the kitchen appliances.

She sighed and pulled away, wishing she could do more than just throw her money everywhere. She felt a sense of responsibility for the damage, as though she'd brought down the rain herself. Probably because Hamish was right. She'd never struggled the way the locals did. The way Mac did. Money wasn't an issue. It wasn't something she even thought about, because it had always been there. But these things took time and her wealth was no longer enough. She'd never lost anything that mattered this way. She just wanted to use her privilege for something better. She didn't want to be a countess by heritage. She wasn't sure she wanted to be a countess at all, but if she had to be, she only wanted to take advantage of the power it gave her to make a change. She wanted to bring meaning to the title again.

The phone call with Mother earlier had left her feeling heavy. She sighed and began to wander across the bridge, avoiding the puddles where she could, though she was already covered in muck. The loch was still swollen, but the water level was receding again, the gardens having finally soaked up a lot of the flood. To think only two days ago, it was running through the streets, destroying homes.

A figure across the bridge drew her attention, small and hunched. She recognised the curls carrying in the wind immediately. Arran.

She looked both ways before crossing the road.

Below, their usual spot on the banks had become a mudslide. Arran gave her a sidelong glance, leaning on the wall and squinting against the watery overcast light.

'Mac didn't tell you to come, did he?'

Jessamine smiled. 'No, he didn't. I was just visiting the tea room.'

Gaze downcast, Arran scratched their pastel-painted nails along the stone.

'Is everything all right?' she asked carefully.

A shrug. 'I'm avoiding my social worker. She's going to make me live somewhere else, probably.'

She froze, fear gripping her. 'I'm certain Mac wouldn't let that happen.'

'He keeps saying that, but it's how it always happens.'

'Well, not this time,' she replied softly. 'Mac cares about you more than anything else in the world. He'd sooner jump into Loch Leannan than let anybody take you somewhere you didn't want to go. You don't have to worry about that.'

Arran's attention remained fixed on their untied shoelaces. 'But I'm getting older. And I'm not always good. I hurt Mac last weekend.'

'You apologised for that.' She wanted so badly to reach out and comfort them, but she had no idea whether they'd want that or not. After all, she was little more than a stranger to them, even if they felt like so much more to her. 'Mac forgives you. There's no use in worrying about it now. You can only try to be better next time.'

'Is that what you did after you broke your mum's window?'

Jess sighed, tucking her hair out of her face as the wind picked up. 'Yes. I tried everything. I'm still trying. But I didn't have anybody like Mac to take care of me when I was your age. I didn't have anybody to tell me that I was good enough just as I was, even when I did silly things. You do. And Mac . . . Mac will put up with just about anything as long as it makes you happy. As long as he can still be your father.' It wasn't her place. She knew that. But her stomach ached and twisted at the thought of Arran not knowing just how much they were loved. 'You're allowed to make mistakes. They don't affect his love for you.'

'Are you his girlfriend?' Arran said.

She almost choked, her face flaming with embarrassment. 'Er . . . No, I don't think so.'

Their brows furrowed. 'Why not? You like each other.'

She would sooner dive into Loch Leannan herself than discuss her love life with Mac's twelve-year-old child. She averted her gaze awkwardly, contemplating it for just a second – but she didn't really want to dirty her new blouse. 'Well, it's all just boring adult stuff. Besides, Mac is focused on you.'

'He can focus on both of us.' They raised a stubborn brow. 'I mean, I take care of Pickle *and* Rufus.'

'Well, humans are a bit harder to take care of than furry friends.' She grimaced, trying to search for a way out of this conversation, but her mind was completely, uncomfortably blank. And then she wondered why Arran was asking her so many questions, what it meant. It seemed as though they wanted Jessamine's answer to be different. 'Do you . . . Do you *want* Mac to focus on both of us?'

Arran nodded slowly. 'He's less boring when he's with you.'

She couldn't help but giggle at that, her insides warming. 'Is that right?'

'Not saying I want you to be my mum or anything,' they murmured as though it was an afterthought.

'I didn't think you were,' she replied lightly, and then couldn't help herself. She ruffled their curls the way Mac always did.

Arran batted her hand away, though they begrudgingly sidled closer all the same. 'Gem is coming for dinner tonight. Mac said I should invite you, too.'

'Did he?'

She tilted her head, unconvinced. If Mac wanted her to come for dinner, he would surely ask himself. Then again, there was a lot on his plate. Perhaps he'd forgotten. Still, she didn't fancy being stared down by Gem all night. It wouldn't be fair to put her in that position, not when she was already keeping Jessamine's secret.

'I'm not sure about that. Mac's parents probably have enough people to cook for already.'

'Mac is cooking,' Arran said. 'Please? He wants you to come.'

She watched them hesitantly, but those big hazel eyes were enough to make anyone cave. 'I'll see if I can make it, but I'm very busy. Want to know why?'

They nodded.

'I'm planning something special for Mac – and the rest of the town.'

'Are you going to propose?'

She snorted. 'No! I'm planning a huge festival to help everybody who's struggling after the floods, and it's going to be medieval-themed. The castle and all of Fort Aileen will be decorated. Would you like to help me?'

'Does that mean we'll be able to get the cottage back?' Arran's eyes danced with a light brighter than she'd ever seen before – hope, she realised. Arran desperately wanted to be able to stay. This was their home, too. Their life.

'Well, it will take a few months still, but Mac won't have to worry about the refurbishments and repairs. I've already made sure it will all be fixed for him.'

Arran grinned, all gappy teeth and beauty spots, acne and dimples, and Jessamine couldn't help but beam back, floating on their joy.

'I'll help . . . if you come for tea tonight,' they said.

'That's bribery,' she said.

'Please?' Arran begged.

Sighing, she held her hand out. She wasn't going to win this one. Not when Arran was pouting at her like that. 'All right, fine. Deal. You'll have to give me the address, though.'

'Deal.' Arran sealed their bargain with a firm shake, and Jess knew she would have agreed to anything as long as that smile remained. It might have been cloudy, but here on the bridge, it felt like the sun had finally come out.

Chapter Seventeen

'Look, Arran.' Mac sprinkled a handful of grated mozzarella on top of his head and grinned. 'I'm Mac 'n' cheese.'

'Not funny.' Arran gave Mac a deadpan expression before continuing to chop the mushrooms into uneven chunks. As dangerous as it might be to trust them with sharp objects after the archery fiasco, Arran seemed to enjoy helping with dinner. Since the school had started offering catering lessons to their students, Arran had been coming home with all sorts of cold, sloppy food in Tupperware containers that Mac had to pretend was delicious. He would never discourage Arran from learning new hobbies. As long as they were happy and not doing any damage, Mac was, too. It was brilliant to watch them discover new things to love. New possibilities of who they might one day become. It gave Mac hope that even though they weren't going to be here forever, Arran would be OK. They'd find themself all on their own.

Mac brushed off the cheese and returned to his pan of simmering pasta sauce.

'No, you're right, Arran. It's not funny,' Mum chimed in, slapping him with a tea towel as she hovered around the kitchen like a fly. Mac had decided to make his parents a nice meal to say thank you for letting him and Arran stay, but so far, he had only been allowed to stir. Mum did not like people cooking in her kitchen. She was like a territorial wolf, one step away from baring her teeth at Mac if he dared use her fancy pots and pans or scrape the ladle against the pristine stainless steel.

'I'm wasted in this house,' he murmured.

'Mac.' Mum tutted, peering over the boiling pot of pasta. 'Your spaghetti is going soggy.'

'It's supposed to go soft, Mum. Unless you'd like to eat it raw.' He brandished a spoonful of uncooked spaghetti and shooed her off with it, which caused her to tut and try to snatch the wooden spoon off him. She loved an excuse to take over. She was given one a moment later when the doorbell rang.

'I'll get that, then,' he grumbled, surrendering the spoon. 'See if someone else finds me funny.'

'Unlikely!' she called as he padded down the corridor, peeking his head into the living room on the way past to find Gem and Dad playing a game of Rummy. Sometimes, he wondered if she preferred him to Mac; they got on like a house on fire. Probably because somewhere inside that thirty-two-year-old woman was a grumpy old man.

He opened the door . . . and froze. Jess stood on Mum's welcome mat, which read 'Go *away unless you brought beer*', courtesy of Dad's trip to B&Q last month.

'Hello.' She wiggled a wine bottle with a smile. 'No beer, I'm afraid. But I brought wine. And . . .' With a flourish, Jess revealed a leafy, colourful bouquet of flowers she'd been hiding behind her back, her cheeks the same shade of pink as the dahlias. 'I brought you some flowers.'

Mac was very aware that he was staring, but he couldn't seem to stop. How on earth had Jess found out where his parents lived? And why was she standing on their doorstep with a bunch of flowers? 'Er . . .'

She frowned. 'You have something in your hair.'

He swiped through his waves again, grated cheese falling around his feet like snow. 'It's cheese. Promise I don't have a bad dandruff problem.'

Her lopsided smirk, half-hidden behind the foliage, made him feel clammy and faint. It had only been two days since he'd seen her last, kissed her in the library, and still he'd missed her. Even if he didn't know why she was here.

'Well . . . you look like you weren't expecting me, so I can only assume Arran didn't tell you they invited me,' she said, one eyebrow raised.

'*Arran* invited you?' he repeated. 'When?'

'I found them by the loch earlier.' She tucked the wine bottle under her arm so she could hold the bouquet with both hands, shifting from foot to foot and causing the flowers to rustle. Her expression became doubtful. 'Actually, I should just go. I wouldn't want to intrude, and—'

'No, no.' He pulled her in before she could leave, unable to keep from smiling now, as he looked down at the flowers. They were beautiful: as well as the dahlias, there were yellow chrysanthemums and white roses, lilacs and sunset-coloured alstroemeria. Nobody had ever bought him flowers before. His entire life was dedicated to growing them, yet nobody had ever thought he might like a bouquet of his own. He was always the one giving, never the one receiving. Until now. Until her.

'I'm glad to see you. Just wasn't expecting you . . . or flowers. What are they for?'

She grinned as he wound his fingers through her hair, pulling her closer. The musky, sweet pollen engulfed him, the baby's breath tickling his nose. He couldn't get enough of her. Couldn't stop loving how soft she was when she was pressed against him, how warm.

'I just wanted to make you smile,' she said. 'I realised in the florists that I don't even know what your favourite flowers are.'

But it was as though she knew him inside and out, knew things he hadn't even known about himself until she pulled his heart from his ribcage and showed him the different parts.

'Thank you, Jess,' he said.

She poked him gently. 'But really. I want to know what your favourites are.'

He hummed in thought. 'That's like asking me to pick a favourite child. But—'

He found the answer when he looked into her eyes. 'I like forget-me-nots.'

A line sank between her brows. 'Aren't those wildflowers?'

A nod. 'I always think there's something a bit magical about things that grow without permission. Just because they can.'

It was the same with whatever was between them, he thought. He'd never intended for it, never watered it or meant to shed sunlight on it, but it had grown anyway. All on its own.

Jess's gaze was heavy with intensity. And then the sound of Mum humming a Lizzo song, of all things, drifted down the hallway and he tensed. 'You do know that I'm going to have to introduce you to my parents now.'

'Well, yes. I hadn't really thought that far ahead.' She chewed on her bottom lip. 'I hope you don't feel bombarded or rushed into anything. I know you're going through so much at the moment, and I wasn't trying to pressure you. I mean, we've only kissed a few times. I'm not . . .'

He kissed her again before she could get any more flustered, but it seemed to have the opposite effect. Her breath caught with a ragged tremble, her tongue running along her bottom lip as she gazed up at him. And he knew then. There was something here, something he'd never experienced before. She made him feel more himself; made him feel important and special and alive.

He was done for. Falling headfirst.

It didn't scare him at all.

'I don't feel pressured,' he murmured, because he couldn't yet tell her just how weightless and fluttery and pathetic she made him feel. 'Believe it or not, I really like having you around.'

'Good. I like being around.' She left a final kiss on the tip of his nose. 'How was the meeting with Linda?'

He bit his lip at that, the dread encroaching again as he remembered. 'Fine, all things considered. I'm thinking it's time to ask Arran about the adoption. Whether they'd like to try.'

'Arran wants to stay with you, Mac. How could they not? They'll be made up. Really.'

'I hope so.' Mac still wasn't sure, but he couldn't keep putting it off either.

'Are you going to invite your girlfriend in, Mac, or are you going to canoodle on my front doorstep all night?' Mum's voice echoed from the kitchen.

He turned and glowered at her. Innocently, she raised her brows from behind the kitchen counter, sauce-covered spoon in hand.

'Nobody is *canoodling*, thank you. This isn't the fifties.' And then, in Jess's ear: 'Don't say I didn't warn you.'

She laughed at that.

Squeezing her hand, he led her inside and shut the front door. 'Mum, this is Jess.'

'It's lovely to meet you, Mrs Douglas,' Jess said.

'Pam is fine.' Mum put down the spoon, wiped her hands on her apron, then joined them in the corridor, her warm, curious eyes dancing up and down Jess's frame. 'You look familiar, you know. You look like thingy . . .'

Jess seemed to tense beside him while Mum wiggled her finger towards Mac as though he might know what on earth she was talking about. He shook his head slowly.

'Thingy? Who's that?'

'You know, Thingamajiggy Whatsherface,' she continued.

'Ah, yes. Her. I see the resemblance now.' Mac shot Jess an amused look, but she wasn't focused on him. Her face seemed pale as she waited for his mum to finally spit it out.

Finally, she did. 'That woman who was killed by a sheep in *Emmerdale*!'

Mac rolled his eyes. He'd been forced to watch his mother's favourite soap last night, thought he hadn't noticed any murderous sheep. 'OK, now that's all resolved, can we—?'

'What's going on out here?' Dad emerged from the living room, his glasses halfway down his beaky nose and his cards still clutched in his hands. 'Me and Gem cannae focus on our game.'

Gem poked her head out behind Dad, her gaze snagging on Jess. 'Oh. I didn't realise you were coming tonight.'

'Arran invited me,' Jess said meekly.

'*Arran* did?' Mum repeated. 'Arran doesn't usually like adults. It took months for them to warm to us, didn't it, Stewart?'

'Yes, darling,' he murmured, which was Dad code for: *I'm not actually listening*. He returned to the living room as though no longer part of the conversation.

'Well, Arran gets on well with Jess. They have joint custody of Jess's cat, actually.' Mac scratched his stubble. 'Long story,' he said when Mum frowned. 'Anyway. Isn't dinner ready yet?'

'Oh . . .' Mum's eyes twinkled as she looked at Jess a final time. 'Yes, it is. I hope you like pasta and garlic bread, Jess.'

'Who doesn't?' Jess smiled.

'You must get those flowers in some water, Mac!' Mum called as Mac watched her wander back to the kitchen. He smiled. Jess fitted in so easily, it was as though she'd always been here.

He beamed down at the flowers like a kid with a new toy on Christmas Day. 'Aye,' he replied. 'Will do.'

They hovered in the hallway a moment longer as though savouring every bit of it. Jess's gaze snagged on the photographs hanging on the wall. Mac as a chubby kid, Mum and Dad beaming on their wedding day . . .

She stopped in front of one. 'Is that your grandfather?'

'Yeah. Not long before he passed, actually.' It had been taken on Mac's twenty-fifth birthday. He was blowing out the candles while Granddad grinned in his wheelchair next to him, his mouth half open in song. The loss and grief still throbbed through Mac. He missed him.

'He looks happy.'

'Always was. They said even when he lost his job at the

castle, he still walked around Fort Aileen with a smile on his face.'

Jess's lips thinned with a strange expression – unease disguised as a smile. Maybe she'd lost her own grandparents. He made to ask, but then Mum was shouting at them to hurry up and the moment seemed to snap like an elastic band pulled too tight.

'I'm starving,' Jess said, slipping her hand back into his. 'After you, then.'

'Are they a woman?' Pam asked as she stuck a yellow Post-it note on her forehead, going slightly cross-eyed for a moment. 'Freddie Mercury' had been scrawled across it by Gem, who had organised all of the cards for the game, but it was upside down so it took a moment to decipher.

Jess didn't really understand the game yet. According to Mac, the person with the sticky note had to guess who or what their card was based on the clues they asked for. When Arran had suggested playing a game, she'd assumed they'd meant Scrabble or Cluedo, something she'd at least heard of before. But this was chaos. Mac was red in the face from his last intense round, where he'd taken a good ten minutes to guess Indiana Jones, and only after Pam had claimed that Mac used to wander around using the hose pipe as his whip in an attempt to imitate him.

'I dinnae ken, Pamela,' Stewart grumbled in his armchair, squinting. 'You've got it on bloody upside down, you numpty.'

'Oh!' Pam turned it around with a flourish, and Stewart nodded.

'Oh, aye. I know who he is now.'

'Dad!' Mac complained. 'You'll give it away.'

'So I'm a man!' Pam surmised. 'Am I an actor?'

They all shook their heads.

'Singer?'

'Yep,' said Gem.

'Ooh!' Pam stood up and pointed eagerly. 'Am I that bloke from Two Directions? Whatshisname? Larry Miles?'

'Harry Styles,' Arran corrected. 'No, you're not him.'

'Erm . . .'

Stewart began playing air piano, humming the opening verse of 'Bohemian Rhapsody' slightly off-key.

'What are you doing, Stewart?' Pam frowned. 'Oh! Am I in The Beatles?'

'Nope.' Mac shimmied closer to Jess on the couch. 'Are you all right?' he asked quietly.

She'd never been more all right in her life. Her belly was full of homemade food, the taste of red wine lingered on her tongue, and her cheeks ached from laughing. Though she wasn't the best at the game, she didn't feel excluded. They'd spent dinner chatting away, Pam asking Jessamine plenty of questions that she'd had to answer carefully. Photographs of Mac hung across every wall, from him as a timid six-year-old to awkward stages of adolescence to now. His smile hadn't changed, she'd noticed. Still slightly crooked and bracketed with dimples of that charming, unbridled joy not everybody was lucky enough to see.

It was a home. And only now that she sat here, watching Mac's family laugh and talk and just be, did she realise that she'd never had one. All of the photographs in her childhood estate were posed and tensed, Jess with her hands clasped and her shoulders back as Mother had instructed, smiling without teeth because she hadn't yet got her braces to fix their crookedness. They'd never played games after dinner, never filled the house with life.

It was as though she'd been trapped in a glass casserole dish her entire life, told this was where she belonged, this was who she must be. And now the glass had shattered and she realised it had all been wrong. She'd missed out on so much.

'I'm perfect,' she answered honestly, brushing her fingers lightly across the back of his hand. His fine vellus hairs stood on end, bare arms freckled and peppered in goosebumps that disappeared into his cropped shirtsleeves.

It was him at the centre of it all. At the centre of this family. There was not a person in this room who didn't adore Mac, and it had been so clear – in the way Pam talked about his childhood, the way Stewart called him 'son,' the way Gem was protectively watching them both now. And Arran, who twirled their spaghetti around their fork in the same way Mac did and only picked up their garlic bread after he had, as though teaching themself how to be part of the family, too, with Mac their guide.

In a summer bouquet, Mac would be the sunflower, bright and tall and difficult to ignore. He laughed louder and made everything into a silly joke just to make Arran laugh, too. He paid attention when other people talked. He appreciated every moment.

And when Pam's questioning had grown incessant, Mac had held Jess's hand under the dinner table just to show her she wasn't alone. He'd changed the subject when needed, had offered her the last slice of garlic bread, even taking the wispy rocket leaves she didn't like, and when she'd complimented the spaghetti, he'd slipped more onto her plate in exchange. Nobody had been so attentive and caring to her before. Robert used to order her food for her, even if he knew she wouldn't enjoy it. He'd made sure she never got the chocolate dessert, always something light that didn't fill her up too much. He'd ignore her while he topped up his friends' wine glasses, and she'd sit on the edge of their conversations. But Mac had even explained the stories behind Stewart's anecdotes just so that she felt included.

All this time, she hadn't known there was anything this important, this comforting, this wonderful. Now, she wasn't sure how she'd ever let it go.

Mac's lips twitched with a soft smile. His hand found the small of her back and traced circles along her vertebrae while they watched Pam finally guess her card. That, of course, led to a re-enactment of the 'I Want to Break Free' music video, which involved the hoover and the TV remote as a microphone.

'Your go, Jess.' As Pam finally sat back down, slightly out of breath, Gem got up and stuck a note to Jess's forehead.

Jess winced as her fringe fell in the way, and she tutted and moved the note to her nose instead, earning a laugh from everyone. She fidgeted, feeling suddenly clammy from so much attention, especially when they squinted to read the note. When she caught Gem's smirk, panic tightened in Jess's gut. What if Gem had written something that would give away her true identity? What if she'd written 'The Countess of Cheshire' or, worse, Robert's name?

It was a silly thought, and a conceited one, but . . . Gem wanted Jess to tell Mac the truth, and instead Jess had barged in on their dinner plans and lied to his family, too.

She dried her palms on her dress and pushed the thought away, though paranoia still niggled under the surface.

'You have to ask us questions, love,' Mac nudged gently.

'Right. Of course. Am . . . am I a singer?' she started nervously.

'No,' Arran answered. Mac had to lean over her to read the note, and his lips puckered with suppressed amusement. 'She does sing in one episode though.'

Jess breathed a sigh of relief. It wasn't her. She almost wanted to laugh at herself for believing Gem might do that to her. 'So I'm female . . . and a television character?'

They all nodded.

'And films!' Arran added. 'And comic books.'

'All right. Am I a superhero?'

'Not technically,' said Gem. 'Although she is *my* hero. And my gay awakening, I might add.'

'I dinnae even want to know what that means,' Stewart mumbled.

Mac choked on his sip of water. 'It's what I felt when I watched *Indiana Jones*, Dad.'

'Oh, you mean a "crush".' Stewart nodded his head. 'That's what the kids call it these days, isn't it?'

'Yes, Stewart. A crush,' Pam confirmed. 'Like what Mac has now for Je—'

'*Anyway*,' Mac interrupted, cheeks flushing. 'You're a woman in a TV show, Jess. Any guesses?'

'Erm . . .' She drew the word out, pretending as though she had the foggiest idea of any fictional characters. She rarely watched TV unless she was trying to relax with *Masterchef*. There was something comforting about watching red-faced reality stars have a bit of a breakdown over undercooked chocolate pudding. 'Rachel from *Friends*?'

'No!' they all answered.

'The show isn't a comedy,' Gem supplied. 'It's more . . . supernatural.'

'Oh, is it someone from *Twilight*?' She'd been introduced to that one by a university friend after a drunken night where she'd been adamant that they'd bumped into the British actor who played the brooding vampire. Turned out it was just somebody from their rugby team.

'No,' Gem sighed in exasperation. 'A TV show, not a film!'

'I don't know.' Jess cringed. '*Doctor Who*?'

'She's American,' Mac offered helpfully. 'You were close, though . . . with the vampires.'

She didn't *know* any more vampires. 'I give up. Who am I?'

'Buffy, from *Buffy the Vampire Slayer*!' Arran said, as though that was supposed to mean anything.

She frowned and tore off the Post-it note, reading the scribbled writing. 'Who?'

'Oh my God.' Gem gave a withering look. 'Where did you find this woman, Mac?'

'I don't know who this Buffy is, either,' Stewart said, which

237

wasn't that reassuring to Jess, considering he was probably forty years older than her.

'Buffy is my favourite show ever,' Arran gushed, standing up from their cross-legged seat on the floor and grabbing Jessamine's hand. 'You have to at least watch the best clip. I have all the episodes on my tablet.'

'Oh—' It didn't seem Jess had much of a say. Arran was already pulling her along, out of the room. 'Bye, then.' She waved to everyone, catching Mac's smirk on the way out. Still, his eyes danced with joy.

If it meant he and Arran were happy, she'd follow them anywhere.

Mac needed a breather, otherwise he thought he might explode. It felt like Christmas. The family playing games, having fun, only now it was even better because Arran and Jess were here. Now, it felt complete. Yesterday had felt like the end of his world. Today felt like the beginning.

He leaned on the fence of the decking in the backyard, the dusk-bathed garden all shadows and dancing midges and the smell of the baked earth after a day of warm sun, and he couldn't believe he was here, alive. OK. There was nothing that could take his happiness away tonight. No matter what happened to the cottage. Everything had aligned for him to be here, now.

Footsteps creaked along the wood behind him. He glanced over his shoulder to find his mum, rosy-cheeked and misty-eyed as she came to stand beside him. Soapy suds still covered her wrists from washing the dishes, and he could smell the lemony liquid on her.

'You look very happy tonight,' she said.

He only shrugged, afraid to betray too much of what he really felt. He didn't need anybody else to tell him to be careful, the way Gem had the night of the fete. He knew he was a fool for Jess, tonight more than ever, but reality could wait until tomorrow.

Mum nudged him lightly. 'She's very pretty, Mac. I hope you don't pick your nose in front of her.'

He scoffed. 'No, Mum. I don't. Thanks.'

'Arran adores her.'

'Yeah, they do.' He fidgeted with the wooden rail, plucking a splinter before it caught him.

'I do, too. She's a lovely girl. Much too lovely for you.' She jabbed him again just to show she was joking.

'Oh, I'm well aware of that.' He scratched his neck, feeling the heat creep into his hair. 'I'm glad you like her. Gem wasn't too sure.'

Mum rolled her eyes. 'Gem's never too sure about anyone. But what's important is how you feel.'

'I think Arran is most important,' he pointed out. 'I'm trying to take it slow while I figure everything out.'

'Yes. It looks like you're taking it *very* slowly,' she teased, her brows wiggling. 'You know, I knew the day I met your dad that I would marry him. There's no shame in jumping in headfirst.'

'You didn't have me then.' Still, his stomach knotted. Of course, the thought of marriage was ridiculous, and not even something he was sure he wanted, but . . . he had known the moment he met Jess that there would be *something*. Something worth dropping his shears for to help her out of that hydrangea bush. He'd let her in without thought after going years without any relationship, or even dating, at all.

'It doesn't matter.' Mum smiled wistfully. 'Sometimes, you just know.'

'You act like it's easy.'

'Oh, it's not. Your dad drives me up the wall most days. But I love him anyway.'

'That's not what I mean.' He sighed in frustration, thrusting his hands in his pockets. 'I mean with Arran. I feel like I'm finally getting somewhere with them. I can't afford to ruin it with my romantic life.'

'You can't afford to spend your life on your own, either.'

Mum turned and patted his cheek. 'I know you, Mac. You have too much love to give. More than enough for Arran *and* Jess. It doesn't have to be one or the other.'

He met her gaze reluctantly. It was strange to look at her sometimes. She had none of his fair features, none of his blood or genes, and yet it had never stopped her from understanding him on some unspoken, fundamental level. And maybe she was right. If Jess was the right person, it would never have to be one or the other. He could have both of them in his life without sacrifice. 'I suppose we'll have to see what the future holds.'

'Only good things, my dear.' Her eyes crinkled as she smiled. 'I'm certain of it.'

A roar startled him. A moment later, Arran zoomed past them, Gem following on their heels. She wiggled her fingers in an attempt to tickle them, and Arran laughed right from their belly.

Jess stepped onto the decking after them, grinning.

'Enjoy your *Buffy* education?' Mac asked.

'Very much.' She filled the space between him and Mum and said, 'I have learned a lot about the magic of Sarah Michelle Gellar. That Spike man is quite dishy, too.'

'You do know Arran'll force you to watch it with them over and over now? I've seen all seven seasons at least three times,' said Mac.

Jess laughed, her warmth meeting his chest as she sidled closer. 'I'm OK with that.'

'Oh, Arran, don't run all over my marigolds!' Mum shouted, moving away to guard her flowerbed.

'See. Now you know where I get my green fingers,' Mac commented, unable to keep from wrapping his hand around Jess's waist in their moment of privacy. He wanted to be as close to her as he could get, always. Felt uneasy when he couldn't.

She giggled again, craning her neck to look up at him. 'Yup. It all makes sense now.'

He rested his forehead against hers and they swayed slightly as though dancing to a silent song.

'Thank you for tonight,' she said finally. 'It think it was probably the best night I've ever had.'

'I doubt that.'

'No.' She looped her arms around his neck. 'I mean it. My family was never like this. There wasn't fun or even much love thrown around our house. I never had nights like this one. It was ... it was really special, Mac. Your family is really special.'

'Well . . .' He took a deep breath, grazing his knuckle against her warm cheek. The more he learned about her family, the angrier he felt for her. He might have spent his first six years without much love, but the following twenty-seven had more than made up for it. He needed her to know it would never be like that with the two of them. That she'd never have to feel alone with him. 'So are you. Special, I mean. Especially to me.'

Her lips curled into a strange smile as she patted him and lowered from her tiptoes. 'Stop it,' she brushed off. As though he was teasing. As though he was just throwing words around.

He clasped her wrist, desperate for her to know, to feel it. 'I mean it, Jess. You never have to go without fun or l—' He stuttered over the word he'd almost said: *love*. Quickly corrected it with, 'Or family. There's one for you here. You've won us all over.'

Mac followed Jess's gaze – to Mum, who was now running around in her slippers with one of Arran's old water guns left out from last summer. To Gem, forming a shield for both her and Arran with a plank of wood that Dad had supposedly been saving for the last three years so he could make a tiki bar like the one he'd seen on 'the interweb.' And then there was Arran, laughing, for once, like a child who didn't have the weight of the world on their shoulders. Who was just having fun in their back garden, because that was what it was supposed to be like.

Jess gave a sleepy smile, shivering against a mild breeze, and Mac peeled off his thick flannel overshirt and draped it across her shoulders before she could protest, leaving him in only a grey T-shirt. She slipped her arms into the sleeves. It drowned her, sagging off the shoulders and falling over her hands so she had to roll the cuffs. She was the best thing he'd ever seen.

He wished he knew what Jess was thinking. Wished he knew whether she felt this as fiercely as he did, from the crown of his head to the tips of his toes. Like he was full up, brimming, with electricity. Like he was fireworks.

But she said nothing, only nestled into his chest. He curled his arms around her, resting his chin on her head. Her hair smelled like lavender and reminded him of the garden he'd left behind outside his cottage. The one where the strawberry bushes had drowned on the bottom shelf of the greenhouse and the wilting forget-me-nots were probably a much paler blue than the colour of her eyes now. But it didn't matter. Home was here, and the flowers would grow back.

'I should get going,' she whispered.

'I'll give you a lift.' He'd stopped drinking after dinner just to make sure he could. *To make sure she could get home safe*, he'd told himself. *To spend more time with her*, the rest of his brain had niggled.

'No. No, it's OK—'

'I insist,' he said, pulling his keys from the pocket of his jeans and jingling them. 'No arguing.'

She pursed her lips before finally caving. 'Fine.'

'You can just drop me off here.' Jess jiggled her knee nervously as the row of houses by the loch came into view, lit dimly by a lamppost that was just flickering to life.

'Which one's yours?' Mac slowed, gaze searching the painted doors and large front yards. She didn't miss the spark of curiosity there, and it only made her feel worse.

Of all her lies, this would be the biggest. The one she

purposely, actively chose to tell. She glanced at the castle spiking across the loch in the distance. She could be honest with him now.

But she didn't want to. She didn't want him to know that while he was living at his mother's house, trying to hold on to his entire life for all it was worth because his cottage had flooded, she had been protected, stable, in the castle the entire time, just as her grandfather had been, when Mac's family and their community, lost their jobs all those years ago. While Mac struggled and fought, she'd never had to do that for anything. It was . . . awful. Objectionable. Disgusting. It made her want to crawl out of her skin and into someone else's.

And if she felt that way about herself, God only knew what Mac would think. *'Impossible to love'*, the article had said. *'Selfish. Manipulative'*. Maybe Mac would agree.

'The end one,' she said finally, her voice crackling just slightly. Mac didn't seem to notice. He pulled in, the engine rumbling to a stop and leaving them in suffocating silence.

Jess sucked in a deep breath, her stomach in knots as she glanced at the house they'd parked in front of. The house that wasn't hers. The walls were covered in red ivy so the bricks were barely visible, and in the front yard, all sorts were strewn about. An abandoned trowel among overgrown weeds. Faded gnomes. A white, wooden gate with a sign that read *Welcome* in swirling calligraphy. Scattered garden chairs and a rusted barbecue. Fairy lights tangled around the shrubs.

She'd never lived in a house like this: one that *looked* lived in. One that was overflowing with evidence of life. Where you could leave your tools in the yard and come back for them the next day. Where you could sit outside just because the weather was nice.

The closest she'd ever felt to belonging had been tonight, with Mac and his family and their silly games that were for enjoyment rather than winning. And telling Mac now meant losing that. It meant going back to the loneliest time in her life. It meant him hating her, maybe even saying things about her the way Robert had in that article. She couldn't stand the thought of it. She wanted this house, this life. She wanted to be 'Jess' not Jessamine. And if she just held on for a little bit longer, figured it all out, maybe she could be. Maybe it wouldn't have to be a matter of choosing anymore. Maybe she could have Mac, and Fort Aileen, and happiness. Move out of the castle and live a normal life. She wouldn't have to sacrifice her work, and she had no friends to miss back in London.

For the first time, it felt like a real possibility.

'You all right?' Mac asked, breaking her out of her daydreams. 'You're quiet.'

Jessamine forced a smile, pressing her fidgeting fingers into her lap. She still wore Mac's flannel shirt over her own clothes. She didn't want to take it off. It smelled like his aftershave and the outdoors. 'Just tired. But happy. You . . . you make me happy, Mac.'

His features softened, and Jessamine's fears with them. He was so beautiful, so easy to adore, inside as well as out, and she didn't know how to stand it. How to feel so much for someone she hadn't prepared for, hadn't expected. Her life, her marriage, had been made of grey blades and barbs, but Mac was all colourful petals and warm, gentle arms.

'You make me happy too,' he whispered. Carefully, he leaned back in his seat and tucked her hair behind her ear, his featherlight touch tingling along the arched cartilage right down to the lobe. 'I feel like a bloody teenager again.'

She laughed lightly, looking down at her trembling hands. 'Me too.' Another lie. She'd never felt like this as a teenager. Never sat in a parked car with someone she trusted, her heart drumming a song against her ribs.

When she glanced up again, he was there, his breath tickling her forehead and his lips inches away. She closed the distance willingly, desperately, hoping that maybe if she kissed him hard enough, held on to his T-shirt tightly enough, she might get to keep him forever. His fingers curled around hers, warm and protective and a little bit rough. He smelled earthy, like his garden after the rain, and his growing stubble bristled against Jessamine's skin, her mouth.

'We never got to finish what we started in the library,' he murmured.

His husky words seemed to scuttle across her skin now, igniting her with desire. Her breath hitched, that heat coiling in her stomach again as she remembered how it had felt to be so lost in him that she hadn't cared where they were anymore. The bookshelves digging into her back, the smell of leather and old paper, her legs around his waist.

She couldn't help but kiss him harder, deeper, so desperate to be as close to him as possible.

He groaned into her mouth when she slipped her tongue beyond the seam of his lips. 'Jess . . .'

She pulled away, catching her breath. His cheeks were flushed, eyes sparkling as though he'd never seen anything like her. It made her feel like somebody new. Somebody she wanted to be. Somebody she was proud of.

'As much as I want to carry on,' he licked his bottom lip hungrily, 'I was hoping for something slightly more romantic than my truck.'

She shook her head and giggled as reality emerged from the haze.

But then she noticed how his eyes flitted to the house, hinting. He wanted her. And he wanted to go inside a house that wasn't hers.

'I . . . think we should wait,' she said shakily. 'For now. In fact, I should probably go inside. Rufus will want feeding and—'

He kissed her again, swallowing her words. The pad of his thumb ran across her cheekbone and then her bottom lip when he pulled away. 'Another time, then.'

'Another time,' she agreed – and hoped it was true. She couldn't even imagine how it would feel, wondered whether that sharp bite he only seemed to let loose when he kissed her would be allowed to show its teeth completely, or if he'd be slow, gentle. She hoped both: wanted the roses and the thorns. She hoped for it all.

But not tonight.

'Goodnight, Mac.' She kissed his forehead before gathering her purse.

'Night.' His cheeks crinkled with a wry smile, and as she made to leave, he pulled her back for one final, silent goodbye. If she hadn't already been sitting, she might have collapsed, her knees turning to jelly and her stomach swooping as though gravity had suddenly stopped holding them in place.

'Night,' she mumbled, dizzy as she pulled away a final time before getting out of the car. On shaky legs, she turned to the castle – until remembering. She glanced back over her shoulder, into the headlights, and found Mac had not made to move yet. Gentleman that he was, he was watching her. Making sure she got inside safely.

She couldn't think of a way out of this one.

Her only option was to head towards the house. With every step, she waited to hear his car whir to life, to hear him pull away, but he didn't. Holding her breath, she unbolted the gate and searched the house for anyone watching. The windows were in darkness. She was safe for now.

Only when she reached the door did Mac pull the car away. She shot him a wave on the doorstep and then, when he began to disappear, hid behind the shrubs until the coast was clear.

Ridiculous, an awful voice in her head said. She didn't need it to tell her. She knew.

Time was running out. She needed to find a way to tell him that wouldn't end in him hating her. She just didn't know how yet.

So, Jess made the solitary trek across the bridge, back to the castle, half floating and half sinking – just as she always seemed to be.

*

Mac set down his car keys on the coffee table and collapsed onto the couch with a yawn. His lips – and other parts of him he was trying to ignore – still tingled with the ghost of Jess's kiss, the weight of her body against his. The house was quiet, with Mum knitting beside him and Dad watching the news on the telly in his armchair. Gem must have left just after he had.

'Is Arran already in bed?' he asked, doing his best at feigning innocence as he smoothed down his Jess-tousled hair. If anyone knew what he'd been up to, he'd never hear the end of it. He just hoped his burning blush wasn't as visible as it felt.

Mum nodded, a wary expression tightening her features. 'Arran seemed a bit down after you left. I asked them what was wrong, but they wouldn't tell me. Think you should talk to them if they're still awake.'

Mac frowned. Arran had been laughing and messing around all night – in fact, they'd been the happiest he'd ever seen them. What could have gone wrong already?

'Right. I'll see what's going on.' Cold dread doused the fire in his gut as he stood up and left the living room, treading up the stairs lightly. On the landing, Arran's blaring TV drifted through the bedroom door, and Mac took a deep breath before rapping on it three times.

Arran didn't respond. For a moment, fear sliced through him. What if they'd run off again? Mac remembered crawling down the trellis from this very bedroom more than a few times during his rebellious phase, and Arran was practically already a teenager in most ways.

'Arran? Can I please come in?'

An inaudible murmur followed Mac's question, and he slumped in relief, pressing his sweaty forehead to the cool wood before he opened the door. Arran lay in bed, propped up by a pillow and watching *Buffy* while stroking Pickle on their lap.

'Hello.' Mac grinned and stepped in, closing the door behind him. 'Can I join you for a wee bit?'

Arran nodded, blank eyes glued to the intense fight scene on the screen. With a sigh, Mac jumped onto the springy mattress, crossing his legs and letting silence fall for a moment. He was too impatient to wait much longer than that, especially when Pickle kept twitching his nose at him expectantly. 'What's up, kiddo? I thought you had fun tonight.'

Arran didn't reply, instead biting their lip.

'You can talk to me,' Mac whispered, squeezing Arran's protruding knee through the thick duvet. It still smelled like the same cherry blossom detergent Mum used when he'd lived here: like home. 'Whatever it is, it's OK.'

'Nothing's wrong,' Arran murmured.

'Is it about the cottage? Because we'll be back there in no time.'

'No.'

Mac scraped a hand through his hair, guilt twisting through him. He thought Arran liked Jess, but maybe being so outwardly affectionate with her tonight had been too weird, too much. Maybe they'd changed their mind. Maybe he'd been selfish to think he could have both of them.

It was the only thing he could think of; the only reason he'd given Arran to be unhappy.

'Is it about me and Jess?' he asked quietly, afraid to hear the answer. 'Don't you want us to be . . . an item? Because that's really OK. You come first. You know that.' Still, his skin, bones, organs, pricked with a thousand needles at the idea of walking away now. He was falling too quickly, was in too deep, and he couldn't even imagine the conversation. The goodbye. 'I can put an end to it—'

'I like Jess. She makes everybody happy. Even me. That's why I asked her to come for tea.'

'OK . . .' Mac furrowed his brows, at a loss, as glad as he was. He shook Arran's knee as though the truth might fall out of them. 'Then what? Please talk to me. I don't like to see you sad.'

To prove it, he took the tablet out of Arran's hands and paused the show so that they could no longer avoid the conversation or get distracted.

Arran stilled, clamping their lips together. Their throat bobbed. 'Why do you think my parents didn't want me?'

Mac's breath hitched in his throat. It was the last thing he'd been expecting. Arran never talked about their parents, never even asked, as though they didn't exist at all.

'It wasn't that they didn't want you. It's just that they weren't capable of being parents. Sometimes people have kids without really knowing what they're signing up for, and they have things they need to heal from first.' Mac pursed his lips, throat clogging. He didn't know the answer, not really, and he hoped it didn't sound less convincing because of that. He'd always wanted a family. Could never imagine abandoning his child on a bus. But not everybody had the same life he did. 'They thought somebody else might look after you better. They wanted to give you the best life they could.'

Arran's gaze drifted everywhere but towards Mac.

Mac moved closer, finding Arran's hand and holding it. 'Don't ever think it's about you. It's hard, growing up in foster care, having so many different people take care of you for a while and then deciding to put you somewhere else. But you've done nothing wrong. You're a wonderful person and you deserve the home you've always wanted, with a family who will take care of you no matter what.'

'Like yours.' A tear dripped down Arran's cheek, their voice trembling.

'Like *ours*,' Mac replied gently. It made sense now. Having everybody around, enjoying themselves tonight must have made Arran wonder why they'd never had that. Why they'd never been given the life Mac had. But Arran was part of it. Mac wanted so badly for Arran to be part of it. 'We're your family. All of us. For as long as you want us.'

'Until I get taken away again.'

Mac shook his head. 'I told you that won't happen.' He shifted, nervous as his plans weighed on him. He'd wanted to wait for the right moment – the *perfect* moment – to ask, but . . . he couldn't let Arran spend another day not understanding how wanted, how loved, they were. 'Arran . . . Would you like us to be your family?'

Arran contemplated, fiddling with a button on their pyjama shirt. 'Yes.'

'Would you like me to be your dad?' He held his breath, his eyes stinging with the promise of tears.

Arran's chin began to wobble. Silently, they nodded.

'Permanently?' It was as though Mac was the one in need of reassurance now. Because if Arran didn't want this, if they would be happier somewhere else, Mac would let them go. He only wanted Arran to be the happiest they could be, to have a better life now than the one they'd started with – however that may look.

But Arran whispered, 'Yes,' and there was no more room for doubt. No more room for anything but golden, soaring hope. He floated in it like a bubble, even though he knew there was a chance it didn't matter what either of them wanted. It was somebody else's decision, still.

Mac let out a ragged breath. This was it. A moment that might change his life forever. A moment that made him a real dad.

'Good,' he said, 'because I'd really like to try to adopt you. If you'd let me, that is.'

'Really?' Arran's eyes brightened and then burst with tears. They sat up in a desperate jolt, half-tangled in the duvet. Pickle hopped off their lap in alarm.

Mac grinned, tears rolling down his own cheeks. 'Really. I can't guarantee they'll let me, but I want to try. I want to be your dad, Arran – more than anything else in the world.'

A sob fell from Arran, and then they were jumping on Mac, squeezing his neck tightly. Mac laughed and rubbed

Arran's shuddering back, unable to keep from knotting his fingers in their shirt as though they might be ripped from him at any moment.

'I hope they're happy tears,' he croaked in Arran's ear.

Arran nodded furiously, their chin poking into Mac's shoulder. Mac didn't care. He wouldn't trade this moment for anything in the world. And he knew now more than ever that there would be no letting Arran go. They were *his* child, and he would fight to make sure it stayed that way, because that's what dads did, and that's what Mac was.

And there was nothing – not gardening, not being a son, not anything – that he cherished more, felt more right for, than this. He was built for it, built to love Arran the way they deserved. And he would get his chance.

Finally, he would get his chance.

Chapter Eighteen

Jessamine spent the next three weeks planning refurbishments and preparing for the Medieval Festival – she had not been able to think of a much more creative title than that – with Petra and the town's committee. Though Mac was excited about the upcoming weekend, he was occupied with Arran and organising the cottage's repairs, so she'd gone on without him. In a way, she wanted him to be surprised by all the work she'd put in when he came into town on Saturday. It was his celebration too. He deserved to enjoy it.

It was Friday morning, and the town bustled with helpers hanging bunting and setting up stalls. The entire town had come together for the loved ones and businesses still recovering from the floods. Anticipation buzzed like a bee in her stomach as she watched Fort Aileen come back to life.

'How's it going?'

Jess startled, hugging her clipboard closer to her chest and turning around. Gem stood by the pub, her arms crossed. Behind her, the Hairy Coo already had signs in the window advertising *medieval mead and live music*. Jess had to admit that she'd been a huge help the last few days, both inside the pub and outside of it. There was still tension between them that Jess knew wouldn't be resolved until she told Mac the truth, but it seemed Gem could at least tolerate her now.

'Good. I have some loose ends to tie up at the castle. Between you and me . . . I have something planned there for Mac. A surprise. The problem is I'm worried he might find out about it before tomorrow.' She'd been stewing on the idea for weeks, desperate to make Mac's day just a little bit brighter. He loved the castle and the gardens, and she had the power to make the place even better. So, tomorrow, the castle would be part of the festival and Jess could finally show him what she'd been working on when she wasn't focusing on planning everything happening in the village.

'He's not working at the castle today, right?'

She shook her head. 'Arran has just finished school for the summer so he took the last few days off to spend time with them, but he's been nipping in and out of the cottage to check on things.'

Gem shrugged. 'Distract him. Ask him if he wants to go for a hike or something. Or go to the cinema.'

'I can't.' Hesitantly, Jess looked back at the street. There was so much to be done today, not just in town, but around the castle, too. Everything had to be perfect. 'I have to help set everything up, and he probably wants some alone time with Arran anyway.'

Gem rolled her eyes and pushed off the wall, wandering over to her. 'I don't think so. Look, regardless of my issues with you—'

'—Issues? You mean, there's more than one?'

'There is now you've interrupted me.' Gem raised a sharp brow, and Jess mimed locking her lips and throwing away the key. 'I'm only going to be nice to you this once, so you better not take it for granted.'

Desperate not to ruin the moment, Jess shook her head in a silent vow. Gem was intimidating and hostile, but she had every right to be. She cared about Mac. She didn't want him hurt. And anyone who loved Mac must be worth it. Must be as good and as kind as he was. Jess would take anything she could get.

'I see the way Arran dotes on you. They care about you. They like having you around – and so does Mac. That means he doesn't want alone time with Arran. He wants both of you. He wouldn't let you into their life at all if he didn't.'

It took her aback, even with the warning, and she had

to fight back the tears threatening to well in her eyes. That even somebody who didn't like her much saw how important Mac and Arran were to her . . . It meant the world. Made her feel like she truly did belong. Like all along, she had just been wandering until now. She'd slotted herself into a little corner of the puzzle and made it complete.

'Oh, bloody hell. Don't get all weepy on me or I'll walk away,' Gem warned.

'I won't,' Jess promised, sniffling all the same. 'But thank you, Gem. I know I've made mistakes – still making them, actually – but I swear I really do care about Mac and Arran. And I hope one day we might even be friends.'

'That's a step too far,' Gem deadpanned. And then: 'Does that mean you're planning to stick around permanently?'

Wistfully, Jess sucked in a deep breath and twirled in a slow circle. She hadn't been sold on Scotland at first, what with all the hills and the Hamishes – well, just the one Hamish, but that was more than enough. Still, her heart was buried somewhere in this village, or maybe it had been planted with Mac's flowers. She was certain that this was where she would bloom, too.

As long as your flowers bloom here, so will our love. Rosemire's words etched on the bench in the secret garden had stuck with her, and she understood them now, better than ever. She wasn't prepared to uproot herself again. Not when she had found a place where it was easier to breathe. A place that made her eager to get out of bed in the morning. She'd been searching for it for too long to give it up.

This was her home. This was what she wanted.

'It does.' Jess smiled, more confident in her decision than any she'd made before.

Gem contemplated her for a moment and then snatched the clipboard from Jess's arms. 'All right, then. You go and entertain Mac for the day and I'll take over things here.'

'But . . . what if you need me?'

'I'll consult this creepily organised wad of paperwork.

Or I'll use those thingies we all communicate with.' She shook her phone in the air then flipped through the pages of the clipboard, which had, admittedly, been colour-coded and filed in order of priority. Emails, receipts, contracts, to-do lists . . . It was all there, with the time each merchant or entertainer would arrive to set up between today and tomorrow morning. Jess supposed other than greeting them and helping with the decorating, there wasn't much more to do. Nothing Petra couldn't cover for her.

'All right,' she surrendered. 'Petra is over there eating all of Wendy's blueberry muffins. She's helped me with most of the planning and will know the answer to any questions you might have. And she has my number.'

'Yep, OK . . . Ba-bye.' Gem batted her away, still fixed on the notes.

Jess was just grateful for the help, and she stopped on her way towards Mac's parents' across the fields to make sure she knew it. 'Thank you, Gem. I really do mean it.'

'I know.' Gem tilted her head. 'When are you going to tell him, Jess? Really, I mean?'

Jess smoothed down her dress, her palms growing clammy at the thought. But she'd made her decision. She was ready to tell Mac everything, from her title to her divorce scandal. She wouldn't lie to him anymore, and if that meant he didn't want her . . . well, it didn't change her love for Fort Aileen or the friends she'd made. It didn't change her feelings for him, and she'd do everything in her power to fix what she was bound to break. Even if it meant spending the rest of her life here, proving she was more than just a lying countess and a selfish Byron. Proving she was more than the things Robert and the *Splendour* journalist and her mother made her out to be.

'After the festival,' she answered steadily. 'I just . . . I want to do one last thing for him before it's all ruined. Before he knows the truth.'

Jess could have sworn a sliver of sympathy shone in Gem's

eyes. But then she shielded them from the sun. 'For what it's worth, I hope he forgives you.'

She forced an appreciative smile and a wave. In her head, though, she could only think: *so do I*.

Arran had been glowing ever since the adoption process had begun, and that meant Mac glowed too as he sipped his tea and chewed on his slightly burnt toast. Summer was creeping in, the kitchen awash in June sunlight, and even with the cottage still drying out, things finally felt right.

'So. What do you fancy doing today?' he asked. 'We could go to the bookshop or—'

'Oh, no, don't go into the village today,' Mum interrupted as though it was the most absurd thing she'd ever heard. 'You don't want to get under everyone's feet while they set up for the festival.'

'Thanks, Mum,' he deadpanned. 'I was thinking of helping Jess out, actually. She's been pretty busy with it this week and I feel bad I haven't had time to do my part—'

A knock broke his train of thought.

'I'll get it!' Arran sprinted to the door without waiting to be asked, something they'd usually drag their feet about. They'd been different, lighter, ever since Mac had told them he wanted to adopt them. No more running off to the loch or shutting themselves in their room. Like a different child altogether. Like the child they deserved to be – safe and secure and no longer needing to act out as a way of testing Mac's permanence. They knew now that there was nothing they could do to chase him away.

Awed, Mac gazed at their retreating figure and murmured, 'Who is this child and what have they done with Arran?'

Mum smiled, patting Mac's cheek lovingly with soft hands. 'They're happy, Mac. It's wonderful. Enjoy it before the teen tantrums start. Which reminds me . . . have you heard back from Linda about the . . .' she cupped her hands over her mouth and whispered, '. . . adoption, yet?'

'You don't have to whisper, Mum. They already know.'

'Yes but' – she slid her hands into her pockets and shrugged – 'they're probably very nervous. They might not want to talk about it until a decision is made.'

'It could take months,' he muttered. He'd already submitted all the forms to be considered, but now he needed character references; and after those, interviews and background checks, and social services weren't exactly the quickest at processing these things. So far, he hadn't been told no, so he supposed that was a good sign. 'But no. I chatted with Linda over the phone and she sounded surprisingly optimistic.'

'Of course she is,' Mum replied. 'You're the best father there could ever be. None of the other stuff matters.'

'I hope they see it that way.'

Mum nodded. She knew as well as Mac did how tough the adoption process was, of course. She and Dad had tried a handful of times before they were finally considered, and they were the perfect couple on paper.

'It'll happen, love.' She squeezed his shoulder. 'I'm certain. It wouldn't feel so right otherwise.'

'You think?' He needed the reassurance. Needed his mum to tell him it would be OK, even if it might not be true.

'I know.' She smiled, smoothing down his hair the way she used to when he was a kid getting ready for school. He didn't mind, even if he was an adult now. He'd never outgrow the little ways she showed she loved him. 'Arran is your child.' She patted his chest. 'There's no way that big old heart of yours isn't meant for them.'

He put his hand over hers, so full of love he couldn't breathe for a moment. It was all he needed; someone to tell him that he was a father, that he could do this.

'It's Jess!' Arran skipped back into the kitchen, breaking the conversation. Mac turned around, surprised to find Jess following with a timid wave. He felt as giddy as Arran looked at the unexpected visit, palms instantly going clammy.

'Hello, love. Wasn't expecting to see you this morning.

Thought you'd be swamped with festival duties today.' Mac's gaze honed in on her as he blossomed with warmth. He'd missed her. They hadn't had a proper moment to themselves – not since the night he'd dropped her off in the truck – with Mac keeping Arran entertained and Jess organising the festival.

He couldn't think about that night. Not without aching with want. So he thrust his hands into the pockets of his jeans instead, and hoped he wasn't sweating through his shirt in the skinny rays of sunlight pouring into the kitchen.

Jess's cheeks seemed to flame with knowing. 'Actually, my day was just freed up and I thought perhaps you might fancy doing something. I hope that's OK, me just showing up . . .'

'Course it is,' he said softly.

'Can we do something fun?' Arran asked.

Mum clicked her fingers, face brightening. 'I know just the thing!' she exclaimed before dashing into the back garden.

Mac locked eyes with Arran, who shook their head with just as much bewilderment. Reluctantly, Mac followed her outside only to find her struggling to open the cobweb-covered shed.

'What *are* you doing?' He nudged her aside to do it himself, swiping the dust away with his sleeve and giving the door a good shove. The hinges were rusted but soon gave under his weight, meaning he half-stumbled across the step and into the shed.

'There they are.' Mum grinned as though she'd stepped into Aladdin's cave and not a dingy old shed that still smelled of their late guinea pig's urine. She gestured to a set of three bikes propped against the brick wall. Only Arran's orange and white one had seen the sunlight in the last decade. 'You should get your bikes out. I'll do you up some sandwiches and you can take Jess and Arran for a little picnic over the hills. Wouldn't that be nice – *and* romantic?'

Mac narrowed his eyes, inspecting the bike. 'I haven't

ridden this in almost ten years. Think it'll be a bit knackered now. Jess might not want to spend her day off riding a rusty old bike.'

'Nonsense, nonsense, nonsense.' When Mum really wanted to get her point across, she liked to repeat herself three times for good luck. 'Make the most of the glorious weather before it starts raining again. You've been slacking, Mac. It's time to amp up the romance and woo her properly.'

'Please don't say "woo",' Mac begged, scratching his beard and examining the mud-caked chain and pedals. He supposed it *was* something different, and he could probably use the exercise. Then again, he still hadn't forgiven Dad for planning a similar outing when he was a teenager, which had ended in a broken elbow and tears from Mum. Jess deserved nice dinners and pretty gifts, not bike-saddle chafe and squeaky pedals.

But Mum was right. He hadn't had much time to impress her the way he'd hoped, what with everything else going on. And picnics were romantic, weren't they? He knew a few scenic places nearby where they could stop for lunch.

'Arran?' he shouted, poking his head out of the shed.

Arran was still visible from the kitchen table, spreading Nutella across a piece of toast. Their third slice that morning. 'What?'

'Fancy a bike ride?'

He was half hoping Arran would say no, but they brightened and nodded eagerly.

'Jess?' Mac asked hopefully.

She fidgeted for a moment, leaving Arran to plead: 'Please, Jess? It will be fun. We can search for frogs.'

She smiled, the corner of her pretty pink mouth dimpling. 'I don't have a bike.'

'Oh, but we have a spare!' Mum offered, hauling the other bike – her old one – out of the shed and rolling over Mac's toes in the process. He grunted, letting out a deep breath as he waited for the pain to subside.

For once, Jess's fringe had been tucked back, and it made her lighter, younger, freer. Like he could read her better. Still, he wasn't sure what she felt now; she didn't seem too sold on the bikes. 'I don't know . . .'

'Please?' Toast forgotten on the side, Arran clasped their hands together and pouted.

Mac almost wanted to do the same if it meant spending the day with her. With both of them.

One look at Arran and Jess caved. 'All right. I'm not exactly dressed for a bike ride, mind . . .' She looked down warily at her floral summer dress. Perhaps not the most practical gear, but Mac was unable to keep his eyes off her slightly tanned bare legs, remembering his fingers digging into those smooth, wobbly thighs in the truck.

'You look perfect,' he couldn't help but blurt. 'I mean . . .'

'He means you'll be fine,' Mum offered with a kind smile.

Jess's cheeks turned red. 'Good. Shall we get going, then?'

'Hang on, hang on. I need to make you some sandwiches first.' Mum jostled back into the kitchen and began frantically pulling out half the contents of their fridge. Mac rolled his eyes, knowing better than to stop her, and met Jess at the door. He slipped his fingers between hers as discreetly as possible, his thumb rubbing grateful, welcoming circles across her knuckles because he couldn't possibly find any other way to show her just how happy he was to see her.

'Glad you came today.'

'Well . . . I missed you.' She ruffled his hair and then tugged him into the kitchen and did the same to Arran. 'And you.'

Arran glared, but they all knew they secretly loved Jess's attention. Just as Mac did.

He drank in a deep breath, the baking grass and Jess's perfume filling his nostrils. It was going to be a good day. It always was when he had Arran and Jess for company.

*

Jess managed to get away with walking the bike off the street but after that . . . she supposed she was expected to get on it. Mac seated himself and Arran followed as they came to a small overgrown pathway where the sun didn't reach. She hesitated behind them, cringing at her own bad luck.

'Ready, Jess?' Mac asked, fastening his helmet.

'Er . . .' She put her foot on the pedal, imagining it was a stirrup instead, and that the bike was one of her old horses. She wasn't sure what it said about her: that she would be more comfortable riding a live animal than a piece of metal. Carefully, she kicked her other leg over and landed on the uncomfortable seat, which did not seem to accommodate or even cushion certain undercarriages very well. Did people really do this for fun?

Still, she was on. She forced a smile and a thumbs-up, then realised that not clutching the handlebars made her wobble. 'Oops! Yep. I'm ready to go, I think.'

Mac's brows knitted together, humour in his careful gaze.

'You never ridden a bike before?' Arran asked in that blunt, careless way that meant one absolutely had to reply with the truth.

Jess tried to lie anyway, even when her cheeks heated. 'Yes. Of course I have. Everyone has ridden a bike.'

'Not me. Mac had to teach me.'

Well, that did make her feel a little bit better, even if Arran was twelve years old and she was pushing thirty. Faced with Arran's honesty, Jess caved. 'No,' she muttered quietly. 'OK. I've never ridden a bike.'

Sympathy softened Mac as he dismounted again, propping the bike against an old fence. 'You could have told me. I would only have made fun of you a wee bit for it.'

She laughed, though sadness frayed the sound. She wondered what else she had missed out on in a childhood that had given her everything material she could want. There was so much to life she had just never been introduced to because it wasn't considered ladylike or necessary.

'I can teach you,' Mac offered, gripping her handlebars so she wouldn't have to. It meant they were face-to-face and she could no longer avoid looking at him.

'That's silly,' she said, smiling. 'Teaching a twenty-eight-year-old how to ride a bike.'

'Thinking you're too old to learn is sillier,' Arran pointed out wisely, before they rode down the path without a care in the world. They were still in view on the other side, along with miles of green dotted with splodges of yellow buttercups.

'Arran's right.' Mac shrugged. 'But you don't have to ride. There's room on the back of my bike if you'd rather . . .'

But she didn't want to spend the rest of her life not knowing. She was Jess now, and Jess rode Ferris wheels and kissed people in parked cars and, thanks to Arran, watched *Buffy the Vampire Slayer*.

'I want to learn,' she said. 'Will you teach me?'

Mac grinned. 'OK. It's really easy once you get the hang of it. Just make sure to keep your hands on the bars and your feet on the pedals.'

He moved behind her, and then his hand rested near her tailbone as he gripped the back of her seat. She stiffened instinctively, that familiar maelstrom of desire swirling in her again. Mac was the current, and with the way his thumb brushed along her lower back for a moment, she was beginning to think he knew that. Liked it.

'Focus,' he whispered.

'You're making that very hard to do,' she replied.

His chuckle held all of the sharp smugness of the man she had met in the castle gardens. The one who teased her about flattening his tulips. He definitely knew what he was doing to her. She would get him back at some point . . . She smiled to herself.

No time like the present.

She wiggled her hips so her bum met his hand, which also

gave her the advantage of a more visible cleavage. Thanks to the heat of the day, she'd left the top few buttons of her dress undone. Mother would be horrified, but then, she always was horrified by Jessamine. Jess was beginning to shape her life around her own standards and not her mother's, and she'd never been freer.

'I don't like this game,' said Mac.

'Yes, you do.' She shot him a pointed look over her shoulder and whispered, 'Are you going to feel me up, or are you going to teach me how to ride a bike?'

'Both, I hope. Maybe not in that order.' Another wolfish grin before his pressure on the bike seat increased. He kept one hand on the handlebar as she pushed off the fence. 'Pedal your feet forward slowly.'

She did, her stomach swooping when she began to move. 'Oh, crumbs,' she muttered, and then ended up swerving – over Mac's toe.

Mac grunted, his face pained, but he said nothing.

'Sorry!'

'Keep going,' he ordered, holding her upright as she straightened herself out. 'Don't look at the handlebars. Look at Arran.'

From the end of the path, Arran waved at her and she waved back. A bad idea, as taking her hand off the handlebars meant she almost crashed into the fence again.

'Don't take your hands off the bloody handlebars!'

'Sorry!' she repeated, keeping her grip tight this time. 'Am I doing it right?'

'You would be if you were going in a straight line.'

'You're not a very patient teacher,' she remarked.

'I just almost lost a toe for the second time today, so no.'

Still, he kept up with her, until his assistance was barely needed. She shook slightly as she reached the end of the path, but she hadn't crashed yet, and that was a good sign. Arran shifted aside as she approached, and she beamed proudly at them. She was doing it. She was riding a bike. It felt like a much bigger accomplishment than it was, somehow: as though gaining hold of the slightly rusty handlebars was like taking control of her life.

'OK. I'm going to let go when we get to the end and you're going to do it on your own,' Mac said.

Panic dropped like a handful of marbles in her gut, but she concentrated on the view in front of her. Rolling fields, red poppies everywhere, a bridge that crossed a burbling stream. It was like a Monet painting.

'Ready?'

'No,' Jess said, but steeled herself anyway.

'Tough.' Mac let go abruptly as she reached Arran, and then she was off. All on her own. She only swerved into the grass a little bit before righting herself.

'I'm doing it!' she screamed. And then, as she reached the bridge: 'How do I stop?'

She couldn't be sure, but she was certain that Mac mumbled, 'Oh, dear.' Not comforting at all.

'Mac!' The bridge was getting closer, a rickety old thing that would probably collapse and leave her in the stream.

'Squeeze the brakes on the handlebars – but not too hard! Slowly!'

Jess did, but in her panicked state she didn't quite understand the concept of 'slowly'. The brakes screeched and she jolted forward. At the same time, she swerved to avoid the bridge and the tyres skidded across grass and dirt as she tumbled to the floor.

The bike landed across her legs, hitting the sensitive part of her shins, and a cry fell from her. When the world finally stopped spinning, she groaned and realised her name was being called.

'Oh, Jesus. Jess?' Mac rushed towards her in a blur of freckles and red hair, Arran following quickly behind. The weight of the bike was torn away, but the utter humiliation stayed, and that was far worse. 'Are you OK, love? Did you hurt yourself?'

She leaned back with a huff, squeezing her eyes closed against the blindingly bright sun. 'Only my pride and dignity,' she replied dryly.

He snorted, grabbing her hand and yanking her upright again before she could object. He examined her body, from the crown of her helmet to the tip of her loafers, hissing dramatically at the sight of her shins, which were grazed and bloody. But the shock had numbed the sting well enough that Jess didn't care yet. She only cared that she was a sheltered idiot unable to ride a bike, and the man she liked very much now knew this.

'Luckily for you,' Mac said gently, 'my mum always makes sure I carry plasters and bandages. First time I rode a bike, I knocked my two front teeth out. She almost passed out from the amount of blood. Sure you're all right?'

Jessamine nodded, tucking her forehead into his shoulder so she wouldn't have to look at him.

'Please can you go and get my bike and backpack, Arran?' Mac asked, patting Jess's hair. 'They're at the other end of the snicket.'

The sound of their retreating footsteps followed, and then it was just the two of them.

'Look on the bright side,' Mac said optimistically. 'At least you didn't fall in the stream.'

Jess only groaned again, sinking further into his chest.

'It was my fault.' His voice softened with guilt, breath blowing across her head. 'I didn't tell you where the brakes were. That should have been the first thing you learned.'

'I doubt it would have made much difference. I once fell off my horse when it was standing still.'

'You had a horse?'

She stilled, realising her mistake far too late. Slowly, she pulled away, her hair mussed at the corners of her vision as she gauged Mac's expression. He was calm as ever, but a line had appeared between his brows. She hated that line. It was the line of, *do I know you?* The line of *you never told me these things about you before.* And it was only sure to get deeper soon.

'Yes. I did a lot of horse riding as a child,' she explained carefully.

'So you were taught how to ride a horse but you were never taught how to ride a bike?'

She shook her head. Now the shock was gone, she was beginning to feel the sting of her fall – not just on her legs, but her elbows, too. 'My mum didn't have time for the usual kid stuff. Half the time, she let me take all these pointless lessons just to get me out of her way.'

His lips parted, but any response was interrupted by Arran's return. They dropped the backpack beside Mac.

'Cheers, kiddo.' Mac was all smiles again, but Jess could tell there was something more behind them. Questions. Ones she would have to start answering soon. He rooted through the backpack and pulled out a wad of plasters, bandages, and wet wipes.

'Can we have the picnic at the pond over there?' Arran pointed over to where the stream merged into a green pond, and Mac checked his watch. From what she could make out, it was barely eleven-thirty.

'We've only just had breakfast.'

'I'm hungry.'

Mac rolled his eyes as though he'd already predicted the answer. 'All right. You can go and set up if you like. It's all in the bag.'

Overjoyed, Arran leapt across the stream, their head bobbing further away until Jess saw them come to a stop in the grass further down by the pond.

She almost wished Arran hadn't gone again. She needed the buffer, wrong as it was. Needed an excuse not to get too heavy with Mac before she was ready to reveal her secrets.

Mac's gaze remained glued to Jess's leg as he cleaned the graze.

'Ow,' she complained against the sudden sting, almost kicking him in the process.

'Sorry,' he muttered, dabbing more carefully, until it was more of a tickle than anything else. His hands were warm, gentle, against her skin as he held her in place, and she couldn't quite stop watching him tend to her. He was so careful, so caring. Nobody had ever taken care of her like this before. It was just a graze; she could easily continue without a fuss, but he touched her like she was made of glass.

'So.' He gave a sharp intake of breath. 'The more you tell me about your mum, the less I like her.'

'She wasn't the warmest person in the world,' Jessamine admitted. 'Still, we lived in a nice house . . .'

'But she never taught you to ride a bike,' he finished for her.

'No,' she whispered.

'Doesn't really matter how nice the house was or how many horses you had, then, does it? Not if you weren't happy.'

It was the last thing she'd been expecting. Mac had gone through all sorts of hardships in his childhood, and she could only imagine how greatly their experiences differed. Even now, his parents' house was barely the size of the stables and barn they'd had on their Cheshire estate, later transformed into a guest house that was rarely used. She had no right to complain, not to him, and yet . . . he seemed to understand all the same.

Maybe Mac truly wouldn't care about who she was outside of Fort Aileen? Maybe her title would mean as much to him as it did to her: nothing. And maybe he'd base his opinion on her for who she was, not what she owned. It was her only hope, and it would be a first, because her value to others had only ever been based on material and superficial things before now.

'I suppose not.' She couldn't help but straighten a stray strand of his hair that had stuck up in the breeze. His eyes drew back up to meet hers, his expression full of things she couldn't even describe because she'd never seen it before. Nobody looked at her like that. Nobody had reason to.

'Where is she now? Your mum, I mean.'

'London . . . mostly. I grew up in Cheshire, though.'

He picked a sycamore seed out of her hair and flicked it away. 'Do you see her often?'

Not if I can help it.

'She calls now and again,' she said, and sighed. 'It all feels like another life. I feel like I've found something here my family could never give me.'

'I'm glad.' A soft smile; a squeeze of her hand. 'I feel the same. With you, I mean.' He went back to tending to her wounds, and she watched him all the while, content. Perhaps a little bit in love, too, though she wouldn't let herself think about that until after she told him. It wouldn't be fair otherwise. He deserved the whole truth first.

'I put in the forms to adopt Arran,' he said, breaking the silence. 'I need a few character references, but the process has started.'

She squeezed his hand, excitement fizzing through her. 'I'm so happy for you both. I can only imagine how ecstatic Arran must feel.'

'There's definitely been a change in them recently. Though I have to wonder if you're part of it, too. Arran likes you a lot. Trusts you. Thank you, Jess, for being part of their life these last couple of months.'

'Of course. Thank you for letting me.'

He kissed her slowly, tenderly, as though she'd hurt her lips as well as her shins. Goosebumps crawled across her skin, despite the summer heat, as his hand slid to the nape of her neck, pulling her closer. She wanted to stay this way forever, bathed in sunlight while the birds and crickets chirped and the water whispered along the stream and he kept her safe, happy, cared for. She thought of all the lonely nights when she'd been married to Robert. All of the nights they hadn't even been able to stand sharing a bed, but pasted on false smiles and held hands stiffly at parties the next day. There had been no intimacy there. Not behind closed doors. And while she'd tried to love Robert once, she wondered now if any of it had been real or just something she'd built in her head to get her through a marriage she hadn't prepared for, or chosen.

Because this, here, is what it should have been like. It wasn't all fairy tales, and he wasn't a traditional prince, but he made her feel like a princess all the same. And she knew now that Mac would never hurt her like Robert had. He would never use her as an ornament to show off at parties or say terrible things about her that would haunt her forever. She trusted him completely. It was like all this time she'd been falling, and only now had her parachute opened. She was safe.

With him, she was safe.

'All right, we have jam or cheese,' Mac said, digging into his backpack and pulling out a wad of flattened, cling-film-wrapped sandwiches.

'Jam!' Arran and Jess replied at the same time.

Mac threw them a sandwich each and then tucked into his own, feeling like a kid again. Mum made the best picnic sandwiches. Mac hoped one day Arran might say the same about him.

'Can I dip my feet in the pond?' Arran asked after demolishing lunch at record speed, their lips sticky with raspberry jam.

'Go ahead. If you want them to be covered in duck poo.'

Apparently, Arran did, because they wandered off to feed their sandwich crusts to the ducks before sitting on the edge of the small, algae-infested pond. Mac couldn't help but smile. 'How are the legs feeling?'

'Better.' She sidled closer to him on the picnic blanket. 'How are you? We haven't really talked about the cottage.'

'They said it should be dried out and ready to start fixing up in a couple of weeks.' He pursed his lips, missing his beloved home and the plants surrounding it. He'd been trying to revive them in his greenhouse after they'd been drowned, along with half the castle gardens, but going inside the cottage while it was still a mess hurt too much. 'I wonder if I need a bigger place, though. If the adoption is approved, Arran will probably want more space.'

Jess frowned. 'You love the cottage.'

'Yeah, but . . .' He shrugged. 'At the end of the day, it's just bricks and wood.' He leaned back on his hands, losing a deep breath straight from his belly as he realised just how glorious the day was. The sun warmed his skin, the grass tickling his palms, and Arran was more at ease than Mac had ever seen them.

'This,' he said, his eyes locking on Jess's. 'This is home.'

She softened, placing her hand over his and leaning closer. A splodge of pink jam stuck to her chin, and he chuckled. 'You have . . .' He reached out, swiping the jam gently with the pad of his thumb. It pressed into the dimple of her chin as though it belonged there.

The sound of her breath hitching made his own lungs, skin, everything, tighten. Every time he touched her was like the first time, as though he couldn't quite believe he was allowed to. Deserved to. But she glittered like there was nothing in the world she wanted more, and so he slowly drew his thumb onto her lip, leaving behind the excess jam. She licked it off slowly.

'I was . . .' He cleared his throat, his stomach jittering. 'I was thinking . . . Wondering, really. Well, not wondering. More just pondering . . .' He was rambling and he couldn't stop.

Jess giggled. 'What were you thinking-slash-wondering-slash-pondering, Mac?'

'I suppose I just want to make sure we're on the same page. We've kissed a lot and you've met my parents, and I just wanted to know if this is as big for you as it is for me.'

God, he felt as anxious as he'd been as a teenager, asking out the first boy he'd ever liked, but he had to know. He had to be certain before he sank too deep. 'I suppose what I'm asking is . . . is this serious for you? Are we . . ?'

Falling together?

Because he was. Jess lived in his heart, his chest, all day. When he missed her or felt off or overwhelmed, he liked to remember the sound of her laugh. When he wasn't with her, he wondered what she was doing, whether she was thinking about him.

When she was here, he could relax. Enjoy himself. Stop worrying if he was a good dad or how he would fix the cottage. He knew as certainly as he knew how to breathe that she was it for him. That he was hers if she wanted him.

'Are you asking me if we're together?' Jess asked.

He nodded, words failing him.

'I'd like to be.'

She fiddled with the buttons of his shirt distractedly – the same yellow one he'd worn at the fete, because he'd noticed its reflected light made her eyes look brighter, and because it reminded him of being with her on that Ferris wheel, and in the secret garden where they'd shared their first kiss.

'In answer to your first question,' she went on, 'yes. This is big for me. Ginormous, even. *Mahoosive.* I've never . . .' a sigh floated from her as she finally looked up at him, 'I've never felt this way. Nothing has ever felt this . . . right.'

Mac's stomach somersaulted. Even if she hadn't said it, he could see in her expression a mirror of his feelings for her.

'Do you mind me asking how it ended with the ex-husband?' he said. 'It sounds like you were unhappy for a while. What was the last straw?'

Jess's eyes glossed over. 'It didn't end pleasantly. He started throwing little remarks around quite quickly after the wedding. The sort that you could pass off as joking, only I knew they weren't. Things about the way I looked, or my job. Things that festered in me for a long time. Made me doubt myself. Whenever I brought it up, how he made me feel, he said it was ridiculous, that it wasn't his fault I was so sensitive and insecure. In the end, I just got so tired of feeling lonely and rejected whenever he was around . . .

And the final straw was when I found out he'd been sleeping with someone else, while he was supposedly away for work.' She shook her head, probably at what seemed such painful memories. 'When I left, he told me I'd never find somebody like him again.' She gave a short, dry laugh. 'And I . . . I said, "well, thank goodness for that".'

'Jesus. You deserve so much better than that.' Anger shimmered in his words. Mac couldn't imagine anybody marrying Jess only to belittle her, to leave her lonely and bored and discontented. She deserved the world. Deserved to be cherished. He supposed he owed her ex-husband a thank you because now he had his chance to treat her as she deserved. 'Do you ever talk to him? Are you still—?'

'No.'

Her face crumpled, though, and he had a feeling there was more to the story. Still, he didn't want to pry. He waited patiently, wondering if she wanted to talk about it.

'Being in Fort Aileen has made me realise that I don't have to be trapped with the wrong people anymore,' she said. 'I don't have to spend time with anyone who wants to make me feel small. I didn't realise it was even an option a couple of years ago, but now . . .' She laced her fingers through his. 'Now, I never want to go back. This is where I'm supposed to be. So, yes, Mac. I'm serious about us. I'm very, very serious. *Gravely* serious, one might say.'

He smirked, tucking her hair behind her ear so he could look at her. Her fingers crept up his neck, to his jaw, as she pressed a lingering kiss on his lips. But then she pulled away quickly, tilting her head as clouds seemed to approach overhead.

'Mac . . . I think maybe I should tell you someth— Oh my *goodness*!' A scream left her, and Mac released a not-so-manly outburst of his own when a scaly, mottled heap was displayed between them on Arran's hand.

A frog.

'Look what I found!' said Arran proudly. 'Can we keep it?'

'Er . . .' Mac swallowed back shock, shifting away from the frog's eye level all the same. 'I think this one should stay near the pond, bud. Frogs aren't really supposed to be pets.'

Arran pouted but wandered back to the pond and set the frog free. *Thank God.*

Jess still bore a pale, shell-shocked expression as she watched them walk away.

'I think my soul just left my body,' she said.

Mac snorted, though he agreed. He hadn't liked the look of that frog's beady side-eye. He shuddered in an attempt to rid himself of the image, and then put his arm around Jess's shoulder, squeezing her closer.

She sighed, relaxing into him as he rested his chin on her head and watched Arran wade in the murky, lily-pad covered pond. Frogs aside, it was a perfect day.

'What was it you were going to say?' he asked.

But Jess just shook her head, peppering a few kisses along his jaw until he began to ache all over again. 'I can't remember. Mustn't have been too important.'

With his arms around her waist, a goofy grin crossed his face. 'We're in a relationship,' he repeated, as though it might have been a dream. He was just waiting for it to slip from under him – but it didn't. 'I'm your *boyfriend*.'

Jess chuckled and squeezed his arms. 'Yes, you are, my love. It's a good day.'

'Aye. A perfect day.' The best one of his life, maybe.

He never wanted it to end.

Chapter Nineteen

Mac woke to a text from Gem with a photo attached.

Spotted last night. You lost the bet. Time to get the kilt out.

The photograph was of Petra and Brodie kissing in the Hairy Coo with a few locals cheering behind them, beers in hand.

Mac groaned. He'd forgotten all about the bet he'd made the day of the fete. He'd barely seen Brodie and Petra these last few weeks and presumed their strange flirtation had quickly fizzled out. He texted back.

Did you pay them to do this just to see me suffer?

Locking his phone, he got in the shower and washed quickly. When he finished, there was another text waiting, which he read as he wandered into his room with a towel wrapped around his waist.

Nope. Told you Brodie would make his move. Now get your kilt on. Everyone else is dressing up. You have to too.

A bet was a bet, he supposed, and it was true that Mum and Dad had bought outfits for today's festival, so after sending a 'frustrated' emoji to Gem, and then the poo one for good measure, he got dressed – kilt and all. The only one he owned was green and blue tartan from his aunt's wedding three years ago, creased at the bottom of his unpacked bag of clothes. He was surprised he still fitted into it. In an attempt to avoid being mistaken as the bagpiper who hung around the castle every Saturday, he paired it with a black shirt, buttoned only to halfway up, and the same socks and shiny polished shoes he'd worn for the wedding, since he didn't have much choice.

He felt – and looked – like a numpty, and probably not a very medieval one.

Sighing, he texted Gem with a photograph of him pouting in the mirror.

Sure you don't want to change your terms and conditions? He added, *Please?* And a sad face for good measure.

Gem's reply was instant. *Not even a little bit. Besides, Jess probably fancies men in kilts.*

She'd better, he said.

Mac really needed new friends.

The centre of the village was hectic. Bunting hung from every lamppost and eave, and the streets were packed with milling people in fancy dress. At least he wasn't the only daftie in a kilt. Trailing behind him, Arran was dressed as a knight, weighed down by chainmail and a wooden sword. Even Mum wore a fancy bell-sleeved cape, while Dad looked to be some sort of baker, with an apron and floppy hat that bounced on his head like a cloud as they walked.

The wailing drone of bagpipes followed them as they made their way down the main shopping street, weaving through visitors and stalls. Jess had done a bloody good job. Pride swelled in him as he took in all her hard work. Since the floods, the village had been strange and quiet, many shops boarded up while they tried to fix the damage. But today, Fort Aileen was alive again – thanks to her. Even Arran stared, open-mouthed, as though they'd stepped through a portal in one of their fantasy books.

They greeted a few familiar faces as they plunged deeper into the excitement. A Punch and Judy show was being held, and kids surrounded the red pop-up tent to watch the puppets' performances.

As though knowing it would be Mac's first stop, Jess waited along with Petra, Gem, Brodie, and Lauren outside the Hairy Coo. Gem and Brodie cheered and wolf-whistled at the sight of his kilt, causing Mac's face to prickle with fire.

'You made it – *and* you're all dressed up!' Jess beamed at the front. She wore a wide-sleeved, draped white dress with a full-body suede corset that accentuated her curves and turned Mac inside out with desire.

Gem was a stripy-trousered jester with a waistcoat, much to his surprise. When she'd said everyone else was dressing up, he'd assumed she wouldn't. The most effort he'd ever seen Gem put into a costume was a bit of fake blood at the corner of her mouth at the Hairy Coo's Halloween party.

Mac rubbed his eyes as though it was all an apparition, but when he opened them again, everybody was still dressed like performers in a Shakespeare stage production.

'Jesus Christ, Jess. How'd you get Gem in a costume?' he said.

They all laughed, while Gem flashed her middle finger, though she was gracious enough to shield the vulgar gesture from Arran with her other hand. Not that Arran hadn't seen and heard much, much worse.

All eyes fell to Jess as she stepped towards him, her dress floating across the cobbles. He was vaguely aware of Mum, Dad, and Arran having a conversation behind them, glad for the moment of privacy even in such a crowded place. He needed Jess to know how happy he was. How proud.

'You look a bit like a Rosemire lord in that kilt,' she murmured for only him to hear.

The compliment almost made him blush again, but he attempted a charming smirk and kissed his soft biceps, pretending they were more muscular than they were.

'Aye? Does that make you my lady?'

'I hope so.' Her lips curved with a smile as she fiddled with the buttons of his shirt. She glanced down just once. 'Are you a true Scotsman, Mac?'

'You might find out later.' He placed a kiss on her nose, though heat stirred in him at the thought. He would be patient for as long as she needed him to be, but . . . God, he wanted her. Now more than ever. He imagined unfastening the ties of her corset, slowly, teasingly, and then broke himself out of the fantasy before he got carried away.

'Can't believe you did all this,' he whispered. 'It's amazing, Jess. You've put a whole town back on its feet.'

'I had some help,' she said, smiling. 'But, thank you. I'm glad it turned out OK.'

'You two are gross,' Gem deadpanned behind them, taking off her jester's hat to ruffle her hair.

'Oh, be quiet, you scheming fibber. I know Brodie and Petra's kiss was just a ploy to get me into fancy dress,' he shot back at her.

Petra gave an exaggerated shudder. 'Never again, thank you.'

'Aye, if you say so.' Brodie winked and nudged her, causing Petra to slap his elbow away. 'But you didnae take too much convincing.'

'You couldn't just turn up in jeans, could you, Mac?' Gem asked. 'If I have to dress up, so do you. Anyway, Jess asked me to get you in a kilt. Take it up with her.'

'Kilts are sexy,' Jess murmured, quietly enough that only he could hear.

Words danced on the tip of his tongue, three dangerous syllables he knew meant too much so soon. But they were true. He was falling in love with her, his old world tilting to make room for the new. She was kind and silly and gentle and fierce, and he was unravelling in every possible way.

After Mac gave her a gentle peck to show he didn't mind being tricked, Jess wandered over to Arran and tousled their hair. 'And you. You're the bravest looking knight I've ever seen.'

Arran grinned and brandished their sword. 'Liv came as one, too.' They pointed to where Olivia stood on the other side of the street, sipping apple juice with her mum. 'We're going to go and spar now if that's OK.'

'Just don't get too carried away. And stay where I can see you,' Mac said.

Arran skipped off without another word, and Mac's heart warmed, frightened as he was that Arran might impale someone – again.

'You know, by lying, you've forfeited,' Mac pointed out to Gem. 'You have to wear a One Direction T-shirt when I tell you to and there's no way I'm paying up.' Then he dragged her into a hug and added, 'Thanks for joining in with all this for Jess. It means a lot that you're trying for me.'

Something on Gem's face wavered, but it was gone too quickly for Mac to understand. 'Shall we go and get a drink, then?' she asked.

'Aye.' Mac laced his fingers through Jess's, who lingered behind him. 'A drink would be nice.'

As they followed everyone into the pub, Jess squeezed his rear end, mouth twitching with mischief. 'Couldn't help myself. It's the kilt.'

'There's more where that came from.' He chuckled, glad when she pulled his arm across her shoulder so they were closer. He always wanted to be closer.

'I bet there is,' she teased, her cheeks flushing the way he so loved. 'I have a surprise for you later, too.'

Anticipation jittered through him, but not about the surprise. It was his future that excited him now. His future as a father, and his future with Jess.

It had all come together perfectly. Jess admired the teeming stalls and glowing sea of faces as she sat on a bench outside the pub, sipping Gem's mead and sharing a massive slice of Wendy's creamy carrot cake. She'd never seen the village so busy, and she'd never seen Mac's features so bright, either. This was where she was supposed to be. This was what she was supposed to be doing. Her life had been so lonely before. Even her charity work had been impersonal most of the time, either because she worked behind the scenes or the people she collaborated with were intimidated by her title. But now, she was seeing the difference.

Sammy and George had returned with their stall, with a great rainbow flag pinned to their table and even more merchandise to sell. She'd also invited along more businesses that Shimmer collaborated with, including a stall of books by local authors that Arran had already half-cleared out and vintage, gender-neutral clothes that Gem had adored.

The sun was shining too as though it knew. It was perfect, every second of it, and Jess couldn't wait to go to the castle this evening and show Mac the rest.

She propped her head against his shoulder as they watched Arran, Gem, and Mac's parents venture around the stalls.

Arran turned around, cupping their hands around their mouth. 'Mac, can I borrow some money?'

'"Borrow" implies I'll get it back.' Rolling his eyes, Mac turned to Jess. 'Don't eat all my cake.'

'No promises,' she retorted, through a mouthful of vanilla-flavoured cream-cheese frosting. She watched him walk away, his kilt swaying against his calves, and couldn't believe he was hers. She just hoped that would still be true tomorrow when she told him the truth. When she told him everything.

'Ooh, carrot cake. Yum.' Petra plonked down next to her and stole Mac's fork – and then his half of the cake. Of course, she had gone all out in a pretty lilac dress and a grand, conical hat with pink tulle flowing from it: a true princess.

'Thank you for all this, Petra.'

'Of course,' she chirped. 'Is it true, though, that you're going to stay here permanently?'

Jess bit her lip. 'Honestly, I can't imagine ever going back to my old life now. But I wouldn't expect you to stick around. I mean, I'd like you to, but isn't there something else you'd like for yourself?'

Petra hesitated. 'I don't know. You know, the reason I loved working for you so much is that you always inspired me. You're not like your mother or anybody else back in London. And when you left Robert . . . I admired you so deeply for that. I know it wasn't easy. But you had the courage to choose yourself, and you use your title for good, not just a way of enjoying wealth and high society. Seeing you grow here . . . it makes me want to do something meaningful, too. I just don't know what.'

Admiration swelled in Jess. She clutched Petra's hands, their knees knocking on the bench. 'That means a lot. It really does.'

She pondered where Petra might go next. She was bright and bubbly and good at her job. She could be anything.

'You're a wonderful planner. What if you work with me as a charity-events organiser? I'd love to grow the charities we partner with, and you've done such a wonderful job with everything here. You could even expand charities closer to your home so you wouldn't have to be too far away from your family all the time.'

'I *do* like planning,' Petra admitted. 'It means I get to make spreadsheets and use those little pastel highlighters.'

Jess laughed. 'Is that a yes, then?'

A smile broke like sunlight across Petra's face as she pulled Jess into a hug. 'Yes. I'd be delighted, Jess. Really.'

'Good.' Jess squeezed her tightly – and then froze as though a bucket of ice had been tipped over her. Across the road, a familiar blonde woman in a pinstriped suit was wandering around the stalls. Emily Kingsley. The *Splendour* journalist who had tried to ruin Jess's life with that awful interview and article she'd written about her divorce.

Of course. She'd known she couldn't escape her old life forever.

Dread curdled in Jess's stomach. She pulled away from Petra, trying desperately to keep the smile on her face. The old Jessamine would have ignored Emily and just hoped she'd go away, but she couldn't allow her to poison such a wonderful day.

'Excuse me a moment.'

Jess straightened her dress before wandering over, peering

across Emily's shoulder to see what she was writing in that godforsaken notepad. She imagined it on Emily's lap in an interview room as Robert spewed all sorts of lies about their marriage and who Jessamine 'really' was.

'Ms Kingsley,' Jess said, voice clipped.

Emily whipped round. Amusement twinkled in her steel-grey eyes as she scanned Jessamine up and down. 'Ms Byron. What a wonderful pleasure.'

'I wasn't expecting you to be here.'

Emily raised a perfectly plucked brow. 'I imagine not. This event seems to be reserved for tourists and the like. You've come a long way from those lovely dinners and soirées you used to attend with Robert, haven't you?'

'Got sick of the champagne,' Jess said shortly. 'May I help you with something?'

Emily cocked her head, her lip-gloss coated smirk oily and smug. 'I wanted to see where the Countess of Cheshire has been hiding.'

'And how did you find me?' Jessamine's pulse raced, palms sweating. In a moment, she had become that sad, solitary woman again who had to worry about what people thought. This was the life she'd chosen to leave behind. Why wouldn't they let her?

'Well, I was invited to the gala, of course.'

'The gala was cancelled.' Jess's voice shook and she was certain she was going to be sick. Why had Emily been invited to the gala? Why would Mother want Jessamine's worst nightmare in her own home?

She already knew the answer. Her mother would do anything to bolster Jess's standing. Even shaking hands with the woman who had ruined it in the first place.

'Was it?' Emily feigned surprise. 'How bizarre. I mustn't have received the email. Not to worry. I have plenty of other entertainment to busy myself with this weekend.'

No. No, Jess couldn't do this again. Not with Mac and Arran and her new friends not too far away.

'You're not welcome here.'

'Oh, surely you're not still upset with me about that article. The words were all Robert's, you know. I just put them onto the page.'

'I don't care. Unless you're here to spread awareness about the floods and local businesses, you don't belong here. Please leave.'

Emily gave an indecipherable smirk. 'I don't think I will. I think there's a more interesting story somewhere here, and I intend to find it.'

Jess shook her head, but speech evaded her, a lump forming in its place. Emily wouldn't give up until she knew everything. It was what she'd always done. She liked to offer information nobody else had, or be the first to deliver mainstream gossip. There were rumours she'd once camped outside Kensington Palace for three days not long after Prince William's honeymoon, to see if Kate Middleton had a baby bump yet.

What could Jess do? She had no security and this was a public event.

'There's nothing for you here,' Jess mumbled quietly.

'We'll see.'

Thankfully, Petra had already wandered off. Shakily, Jess did the same, Emily's gaze burning into her back as she walked towards where Mac and Arran were.

When Mac pulled her aside to look at a stall of artwork by a local painter, she almost wanted to lurch out of his grip and run as fast as she could, just to make sure Emily didn't catch sight of him.

But she forced a smile, because it was too late to run. Much too late. She would just have to avoid the journalist and pray she got bored soon enough.

Chapter Twenty

'Are you ready for your surprise?'

Mac nodded, covering his eyes, as instructed by Jess. She guided him into the castle by the waist, as voices swam all around him, their footsteps echoing across the foyer. He couldn't help but feel a bit silly.

'You'd better not peek!' Jess ordered, guiding him around a corner. Her warmth radiated through him, clinging to him like an extra layer of clothes. She made him feel safe, despite the uncertainty he was experiencing now.

'I'm not peeking,' he promised, though he was tempted, if only to look at her. Kiss her. He was jittery with anticipation, only intensified by the soft sound of violin music that curled around them.

'All right.' She positioned him, touch featherlight now. 'You can open your eyes.'

He did, slowly, because he wanted to remember every moment of whatever came next. Disoriented, he glanced at her first, a lopsided smile on his face.

'Well?' Jess raised her brows eagerly.

Mac looked around and saw they were in one of the castle's exhibition rooms that focused on the history of Clan Rosemire. Tainted light streamed through the stained-glass window and a few dressed-up visitors were milling about the paintings, artefacts, and information posters.

And in front of him, a laminated photograph of Bearnard's bench had been printed and placed on the wall along with a large paragraph about what the etching might mean – and how LGBTQ+ history was rooted in the castle walls and gardens through a possible romance between the gardener and the fifth Lord Rosemire. An entire wall dedicated to their love affair.

'You did it,' he whispered.

'I did.' Jess's eyes shone with tears. 'I had to. It's the least Bearnard and Rosemire deserved.'

'This is wonderful.' His fingers hovered over the words, all of them a message to visitors that love could be found anywhere, with anyone. 'God, if I'd seen something like this growing up . . .'

'It would have been easier,' she finished for him. 'Less lonely.'

'Yes. Exactly.' Awed, he could only shake his head and wrap his arm around her shoulder, pulling her close. 'It'll never be hidden or locked away again.'

'No. Never.' They stood that way, taking it all in, for a moment longer before she said, 'Are you ready for the next surprise?'

He raised an eyebrow, curiosity piqued. He wondered if the next surprise had something to do with the distant melodies and chatting. The entire day had been one wonderful surprise after the next, and he couldn't comprehend just how much work Jess had put into all of it – not only the entire village, but the castle, too.

Speechless, he nodded and she dragged him back into the corridor. They passed strangers and locals as they wandered towards the back of the castle, a place Mac rarely ventured. It felt older here, the walls turning to uncovered stone that ended with an arched doorway. Daylight poured through, and as he stepped outside, the hot, heavy summer air kissed his face.

They stood in the castle's courtyard in the very heart of Rosemire. Twinkling lights were strung overhead, joining one crumbling wall to the other, and tables and chairs had been set out on the cobbles. The violin music came from a young woman who plucked and stroked out a keening melody, lids low in serene concentration while costumed visitors floated about happily, looking for all the world as though they'd stepped back in time. Ivy and pink clematis cascaded down the stone as though the walls were made of nothing but plants and . . .

Everything sparkled. Mac had never seen something so beautiful, other than the woman at his side, whose smile was now brighter than the lights above.

'You did all this, too?' he asked breathlessly. 'Jess . . . It's beautiful.'

'I thought you'd like it.' She took his hand, gazing up at him. 'Fancy a dance?'

He glanced around. Nobody else was dancing, and he was terrible himself, so the instinct was to say no . . . But he could never deny Jess. He pulled her into the centre of the courtyard, twirling her under his arm and snatching a laugh from her. He loved that sound, and the way she blushed and wrinkled her nose when she realised people were watching.

He didn't care about anyone else. His family were in the gardens, Arran enjoying some sort of re-enactment that involved jousting. It was just the two of them. Just her.

Slowly, they began to sway to the music. He placed his hands on her hips, her curves warm and softly cushioned through the thin material of her dress. His fingers curled, desperate for more. As though sensing it, she looped her arms around his neck so they were chest to chest.

'Every day I've had with you has been perfect,' he whispered. 'Even the one when we burnt the pies and the one when Arran shot me in the arse with an arrow.'

She giggled. 'I'm glad you're happy.'

Still, he was sure shadows danced across her features just for a moment. 'Is something bothering you, love?'

She seemed to deliberate before shaking her head. 'Nothing that can't wait until tomorrow.'

He frowned, but she tucked her head into his chest and they continued to dance. He was certain she must have been able to hear his heart pounding and clanging and crashing by her cheek; hoped she could. He wanted her to know. Even if it was too soon to say it, he wanted her to know.

'I wish this could last forever,' she whispered, words tinged by melancholy.

He tilted her chin up, wondering if she meant the day or them. It didn't matter. He'd make it last forever. He fought for the things he loved, and he loved Jess. He'd make sure she always knew it. 'It can.'

We can.

They turned in a slow circle until Jess pulled away again, fingers curling in the short hair at the nape of his neck. It gave him the chance to kiss her forehead, her slightly too-long fringe sticking to his lips. But when he looked, waiting for that smile he always seemed to draw from her, he noticed her gaze fall past his shoulder and her body stiffen.

It felt as though he was hugging a marble statue and not her; not his warm, lively Jess.

'Excuse me a moment?' she asked.

'Everything all right?' He followed her gaze curiously, but saw nothing to warrant a reaction. Just guests: families, the violinist and a few older couples watching them dance. Hamish was among them, and so was Lauren's mum, Elsie. Back after the floods, finally.

'Fine. I'll just be a second.' She squeezed his hand before leaving, weaving through the throng of guests until he could no longer see her.

Puzzled, he scratched his chin, and after waving at his friends, sat at one of the free tables with rustic wildflower bouquets and candles in the centre. He admired the posies in an attempt to calm his random bout of nerves. Nothing was wrong. It couldn't be. She'd probably just nipped to the bathroom.

But she'd looked . . . shocked. Sad. Distant. And he didn't know why. And her words . . . He'd thought she'd meant she didn't want the day to end, but had there been something deeper in her words? He made to get up, find her and make sure she really was OK, but he didn't get the chance.

'Is this seat taken?' A blonde woman hovered in front of the table, wearing a black blazer rather than a medieval costume like most others. He didn't recognise her, and she didn't look to be with anyone. Still, he couldn't very well say yes.

'No. Please.' He motioned to the empty chair, feeling the woman's gaze on him as she slowly sat.

She wore a strange, calculated expression, tight-lipped and narrow-eyed. It made him antsy. 'I saw you dancing with Lady Jessamine Byron just now. You two make a lovely couple.'

'Who?' The surname stirred something in him. Byron. Jessamine Byron. That wasn't Jess. She would have told him if she was a Byron, just as she would have told him if her full name was Jessamine, and not Jessica as he'd assumed.

But had he ever asked?

'Jessamine Byron. The lady you were just dancing with. Would you mind if I asked you a few questions?'

'That wasn't . . . Sorry, I think you've got that wrong. I've never spoken to a Byron in my life.' Unless . . . he hadn't known he was – he'd seen many new faces today – but nobody had mentioned the Byrons were here. Mac couldn't help but squirm at the thought of the wealthy family finally returning to Fort Aileen. No. This woman had clearly made a mistake. Maybe Jess resembled somebody else. Maybe somebody had given the woman the wrong information.

The woman's brows knitted. 'Is that right?'

'Sorry, who are you again?' Mac tapped the table anxiously.

'I'm Emily Kingsley, a journalist for *Splendour*. I was hoping you might give us an insight into what it's like to be dating the Countess of Cheshire.'

He chuckled, rubbing the back of his neck awkwardly. 'Right, well, my girlfriend's a tour guide, so . . . can't help you there.'

Amusement flitted across her features as though she knew something he didn't.

'Is that what she told you? Oh, dear. What is it *you* do, may I ask?'

'I'm . . .' He needed to stop talking. Needed to understand. But he searched the courtyard for Jess desperately as he said, 'I'm a gardener. Look, what is this? I'm not sure I understand what's going on.'

'And how long have you been romantically involved with Jessamine?'

His palms began to sweat, and the rest of him, too. He couldn't find Jess, couldn't set it straight, but doubt needled through him as though maybe it was true.

No. She *couldn't* be a countess. A Byron. She was *Jess*. She was a tour guide. He'd seen her . . . tour-guiding. Hadn't he?

'I'm not sure it's your business,' he said.

'I'm a journalist. It's my job.' She gave him a condescending smile with a flash of blindingly white teeth. 'Do you stay in the castle with her often?'

'We *work* in the castle.' He frowned, running a hand across his face roughly. 'Sorry, I don't know who you are, but you've got it wrong—'

'I don't think I have, sir.' The woman – Emily – rooted through her expensive black handbag and pulled out an iPad, unlocking it before thrusting it in his face.

Mac stopped breathing.

Jess's face was plastered across a collage of online articles,
Countess of Cheshire gets engaged
Divorce on the countess's cards and
Champagne problems: Lady Byron melts down
The final one, though . . .
Lady Jessamine Byron escapes to ancestral home, Rosemire Castle.

It was true. Jess . . . *Jessamine* . . . was a countess. A Byron. An owner of the castle and the grandchild of the man who had ruined half of Fort Aileen's employment opportunities all those years ago. He desperately wanted to rationalise it, but . . . Had he actually seen her go into that house he'd dropped her off at the night of his family dinner? He couldn't remember. He could only remember all the times he'd offered to take her home and she'd refused. The way she knew the secret passages around the castle. The fact she'd owned horses and spoke with such perfect elocution. How Rufus was always loitering around the gardens, never across the bridge where Jess claimed to live. He'd even been in the foyer the day of the floods.

And she'd mentioned growing up in Cheshire.

He'd tried to ask about her surname in the old banqueting hall. She'd brushed him off so naturally, but . . . He didn't know her full name. Didn't know much at all. Why hadn't he realised how strange that was? It felt strange now. He'd felt so close to her before, so sure he knew enough to love her, but now she was a silhouette. A puzzle. He'd slotted in most of the pieces only to find they were in the wrong place.

Had he even seen her *giving* a tour? No. Not even once, unless the one she'd given him counted.

But how could he have not known? How could he have not *seen*?

No. Denial set in. He knew Jess. This was just some sort of joke. A prank. He scanned the courtyard frantically again but there was no sign of anyone he knew. No laughter or familiar faces or Jess.

'Excuse me,' he muttered, standing on weak knees. He had to find Jess. He had to set it all straight.

He had to be sure the woman he loved hadn't lied to him from the beginning. He wanted so badly to believe she wouldn't, but the dots just wouldn't connect anymore.

Jess should have known it was all too good to be true. Her world hadn't stopped when she'd seen Mother standing on the other side of the courtyard, disdain twisting her features. No, it had started again. She'd been hiding for months, living the fairy tale she'd always dreamed of, and now it was over.

She wended through the crowd slowly and prayed Mac wouldn't follow, the violin music sounding tinny and hollow in her ringing ears. She was distantly aware of people greeting her. Elsie, Lauren, even Hamish. She cast them forced smiles and followed her mother's pale, tailored suit into the corridors.

And there Lady Philippa Byron waited by the windows, her gaze steely and her lips pursed. 'You cancelled the gala, your one chance at redeeming your reputation, for *this*?' she snapped. 'To dance with some farmer and hold a tacky costume party instead?'

Jess clenched her jaw and sucked in a long breath. 'He's not *some* farmer, and this isn't a costume party. It's a celebration for a village I love very much. I do not care about my reputation, Mother. I care about my friends.'

Mother scoffed. 'What *friends*? These are not your friends. This is another one of your silly games of pretend. You like to be the saviour. That's why you work with the charities. And now look. You've taken it too far, Jessamine.'

'No,' Jess whispered. It wasn't a game, nor was she a saviour. She was a woman who had missed out on so much over the years that she never wanted anybody else to feel the emptiness, the isolation, she had. She was a woman who just wanted to use her wealth and title to make the world a little bit easier to bear, because what was the point otherwise? 'I don't expect you to understand, but this is what I've chosen. I deserve that for myself. I don't need your approval.'

'And you certainly don't have it,' Mother hissed through gritted teeth.

Finally, Jess had done something worthy of her attention, her anger. Only she no longer craved it the way she had when she was a child. She no longer needed it. She knew what she wanted, and it wasn't anything close to her mother's life.

'You are dragging our family through the mud every moment you play this silly game,' her mother went on. 'I could barely clear your name after that article, but now . . .

Go and take off that awful dress and meet me downstairs. I've a car waiting to take us back to London.'

Jess looked down at the dress. Maybe she had wanted to be somebody else. For a long, long time. She didn't want to go back to tailored pencil skirts and suits. She didn't want to go back to London.

'No,' she decided. 'I'm not going back.'

'Excuse me?'

'I said no. This is where I belong – and you weren't invited.'

If Mother's glare was deadly before, it was fatal now. 'Don't tell me this is about that scruffy *man*.' The word burned through Jess's skin like poison. 'What can he possibly offer you? A cow? A life on a farm or working in a shop? Will you be driving a tractor next?'

'Everything.' A tear rolled down Jess's cheek. 'He can offer me everything. So much more than you ever have.'

'I beg your pardon!' Mother stepped closer, pointing a bony finger. 'I gave you a comfortable life. A life of luxury. How dare you be so ungrateful.'

'I never wanted any of that!' Jess exclaimed, her voice echoing along the corridor eerily. 'I wanted a *home*. Not a big fancy house with servants. A *home*. A place where I felt loved. And you couldn't give me that, so I found it here. You won't take it away from me now.'

'You are a *countess*! Start behaving like one before you lose it all!'

'I am *Jess*!' she shouted, tears pouring from her now. 'I'm a good friend and a hard worker and you cannot take those things from me anymore. You won't. I don't care about being a countess. I don't care about finding a new husband to clear my reputation. I don't care what your friends think of me, and I don't care about the people who stare at me at dinner parties because they think I need to lose weight or buy a new dress. I don't *care*! I care about this, here. I care about the people in this village. I care about my cat and picnics and Mac. I care about people being free to be who they are and love who they want. I don't care about my *title*, Mother! I don't care about society! I don't even care that you're disappointed in me, because *I'm* disappointed in *you*. I'm disappointed that you treat me like dirt. I'm disappointed that all you expect from me is to sit and look pretty while your friends tear me apart looking for flaws. I'm disappointed that I can't even remember one day where you made me feel like anything but a countess rather than your daughter. I'm disappointed that I grew up completely, utterly, painfully alone.'

Her shoulders heaved with the outburst, and silence followed. There it was, then. All out on the table, never to be taken back. She was glad, relieved. There was nothing left to say, and no illusion left to conform to. She wasn't going to stand by and be bullied into submission. Not ever again.

'I'm not going back to London,' she said finally when Mother didn't respond. 'I'm staying here because it's my home now. I'd like you to leave.'

Mother's lip curled with disgust, and she looked at Jess as though she were a speck of dirt on her cream-coloured blazer. 'I don't even recognise you anymore.'

'Good. That means I'm doing something right,' Jess admitted, biting her lip.

'Your father would be turning in his grave. He gave you this title. He trusted you to follow in his footsteps.'

The words stung, but she tried her best not to show it. 'I was six years old when he died. If he expected that of me, then that was his burden, not mine. I've learned a lot about the Byrons while I've been here. I learned they bought out this castle without recognising how important it is to the village. I learned they were the cause of a lot of pain for people's parents and grandparents. If those are the footsteps I was expected to follow, I'm glad to disappoint you. Both of you.' She sniffled. 'But I remember how Dad would laugh and be silly and play games with me. I have to believe he would want more for me. I have to believe he'd be proud of me now. You're not allowed to speak for him about something he isn't here to witness.'

Mother only checked her watch and neatened her hair as though Jess's words meant nothing. 'I have nothing left to say to you. I cannot stop you from making your own mistakes. Just know I won't be there to pick up the pieces when it all comes crashing down again.'

With that, she turned on her heel, her high pumps clicking against the floor with every step. And then the door slammed shut and she was gone.

Jess gulped, feeling hollowed out, but proud, somehow. Those words had been left unsaid between them for far too long, and now Jess could move on. She could crawl out of her mother's shadow and be a real person.

Half sagging with relief, she turned around – and immediately wished she hadn't.

Mac stood by the open door to the courtyard, pale-faced and . . . Oh, God.

'How much of that did you hear?' she asked, bile rising up her throat and thickening her words.

'It's true, isn't it?' he replied. 'You're . . . you've been lying to me the entire time.'

She shook her head desperately, her voice unsteady with tears. 'I promise it wasn't like that.'

His face crumpled. 'I let you into my life. I let you into *Arran's* life. I let them get attached, and you . . . it was all a lie.'

'Please, Mac,' she begged, choking on a sob. Her head swam as she tried to keep her knees steady. This couldn't be happening. Not like this. 'Please let me explain. It wasn't a lie.'

'You know everything about who I am. *Everything*. I told you about my granddad. About what *your* family did to this village. And you said nothing.' Anger laced his words now, but he still wouldn't raise his voice, and somehow that was worse. 'Was I just some weird way of humbling yourself? Your little charity case? Did you watch me gardening cluelessly from your grand old castle and laugh?'

'*No*, Mac. I would never laugh at you. Never.'

She stepped forward, but he recoiled. Nausea engulfed her, and she couldn't see a way out of this anymore. She couldn't get him to understand, and she couldn't see for all the tears, and she was going to lose him. She knew it. It was over. There was no coming back from the betrayal written all over his face.

And he needed to know. If nothing else, he needed to know what she felt.

'Mac, I'm falling in lo—'

'I can't even look at you. I can't do this,' he croaked. A hive, a flush of rage, was visible on his chest under his unbuttoned shirt, spreading up his neck. 'I can't. I thought I could trust you, but you . . .' Another shake of his head. 'I need to go.'

'No, please,' she pleaded, rushing for him. But when she grabbed his hand, he yanked it away as though her touch burned.

'How could you not tell me?' The scorched whisper was more devastating than any shout, any scorn. It crackled with pain, confusion. Not like the day Jess had told Robert she wanted a divorce. He'd been cold, slamming doors and raising his voice and . . . Even now, Mac would never be that sort of man. He was good, kind, loving.

And she'd broken his heart. Ruined her chance with him.

'I wanted to. I wanted to tell you so many times, but . . . It's not who I am. It's just a title. It means nothing.'

'If that were true, you wouldn't have hidden it so much. And if you care about me the way I . . .' He cleared his throat when his voice broke. 'You would have been honest with me if you meant anything you said about me and my family.'

'It's complicated. It *was* complicated, but it isn't now.' She wiped away her tears because she didn't deserve to be the one to cry. She didn't deserve to be the one in pain. She was the one who had caused it. 'I just didn't know who I was when

I came here, and then I met you and I wanted to be Jess. I wanted to be *your* Jess, Mac, and who I was before . . . she didn't matter anymore. I wanted to leave her behind. She was sad and lonely and divorced and . . . everything I said about my family was true. I'm not like them. I'd never do to you what the Byrons did—'

'You *are* a Byron!' He sniffled, a muscle clenching in his jaw. 'I can't do this. I'm sorry. I can't . . . I just can't.'

I just can't. It was like a blade being thrust into the same wound over and over. Again and again. No matter how hard she clung to him and begged, he kept repeating it. Kept walking away. She couldn't make him stay.

Watching him as he marched down the corridor, she knew there was nothing more to do.

It was broken. Everything was broken. Including her.

She turned around expecting to find herself alone, but she should have known better. Emily Kingsley stood there now, wide-eyed, brows raised, as though she'd just taken in a moving theatre performance.

'I don't care what you write about me.' Jessamine's voice sounded hollow in her own ears. 'But he . . . he doesn't deserve to be thrown into your games. He's a good man.'

Emily tilted her head, expression still unreadable.

'Such a good man that you couldn't tell him who you were?'

'*Please*,' Jess begged. Her lips tasted of salty tears. 'Please don't use him for your article.'

Emily tapped her pen against her notepad. 'I heard what you said to your mother.'

Jess blinked lifelessly. She just wanted to be left alone. Just wanted to process everything that had happened.

'I've also spent my day asking around the village about you. The charities you work with and the friends you've made. You've had quite an impact here. You paid for the flood damage all on your own.'

'They're my community. I wanted to help.'

295

'And the difference you've made for Shimmer. For the local businesses and artists. You certainly go above and beyond in your field of work.'

'Of course. What would be the point otherwise?'

Emily hummed in thought, tapping her pen against her notepad. 'Interesting. A source reached out to me yesterday, as it happens. An old girlfriend of Robert's, but *I* didn't tell you that. They made all sorts of damning claims. Abuse. Embezzlement. Compulsive lying. Robert lied about you, didn't he? *He* was the guilty party.'

Startled, Jess lifted her gaze. 'You must have known that, too.'

She hadn't known about the embezzlement, though she'd never really paid attention to Robert's business affairs. He owned too many companies for her to keep up with. The abuse didn't surprise her, though. He may never have laid a hand on her, but he tore her down in more subtle ways. Taunts and humiliation and, in the end, manipulating their marriage and lying about what sort of person she was. Making sure everybody hated her.

Emily shrugged. 'My job is the story. And stories aren't always true.'

'Then start writing fiction,' Jess threw out, wearily. There was no malice there. Just the wish that people like Emily didn't thrive so much off other people's misery.

Emily smiled stiffly. 'I won't mention his name. Your farmer.'

'He's not a farmer, he's the castle gardener. And why come at all if you're so quick to change your tune? Why not leave me alone?'

'It occurred to me that I never asked for your side of things. Never even looked for it. We always do that, don't we? Ignore the woman's side of things.'

'You might, but I don't,' Jess whispered. 'I hope you never learn what it feels like to be lied about . . .'

She didn't have it in her to carry on with the conversation.

She turned her back and walked away, because it's what everyone else seemed to be doing today, leaving Emily Kingsley and her mother, her old life, in the dust.

But Jess wasn't giving up on Mac. She'd apologise for as long as it took. She would just give him space, until he was ready to listen.

Mac didn't know what to do or where to go. He didn't know anything. Somehow, his feet took him to the secret garden. He expected to find comfort there, but as he pushed the gate open, he only found more heartbreak. A new sign hung on the wrought iron: *Bearnard's Garden*.

Inside, it had been decorated. Like the courtyard, fairy lights and flowers were draped from every wall. Not only that, but the overgrown weeds and brambles he'd never gotten round to taming had been cut down, and a small fence with a wooden plaque named the new green patch of earth *Mac's Flowers*.

Jess. She'd done this for him. Made room for him in a place that was supposed to be Rosemire and Bearnard's. A place of love.

A sob built in his chest as he collapsed onto the bench, putting his head in his hands so he would no longer have to look.

Jess had lied to him. About everything. While he was inviting her into his small cottage and falling in love with her, she was pretending to be someone else. She was living in the castle and lying to him about it, pretending she was a bloody tour guide when she was a Byron.

He didn't know how he hadn't seen it. In fact, he hadn't even known countesses still existed. They seemed some sort of outdated idea of nobility that wasn't needed anymore. What did countesses even *do*?

Pretend to be tour guides to seduce their gardeners, apparently.

Jesus Christ. He couldn't make sense of it. The more he

thought about it, the more humiliated he was for not even wondering. It had been clear Jess came from somewhere far wealthier and classier than him, but it didn't bother him. How could it, when she was always making him laugh and treating Arran . . .

Like they were her own.

Arran would be heartbroken. *Mac* was heartbroken.

It was all a mess, and he'd let himself get here. Gem had warned him. He hadn't wanted to listen.

'Knock, knock.'

He lifted his head to find Gem standing awkwardly in the stone arch.

'You OK?' she asked, inviting herself in and shutting the gate behind her.

Mac didn't have an answer to that, and if he tried to find one, he was certain he might cry. He stared at the wooden plaque with his name on it, the flower garden with no flowers in it. That's what he felt like at the moment. A fenced-off patch of nothing.

'You found out, didn't you?'

He snapped his attention back to her. 'You *knew*?'

The same guilt Jess had worn crossed Gem's features as she sat beside him. 'Aye. I'm sorry, Mac. I just thought it should come from her. She promised me she'd tell you eventually.'

'Eventually.' He scoffed. 'Meaning, when I'm in so deep that my heart'll break good and proper.' And then anger rippled through him as he looked at his best friend. He'd grown up with Gem. She was the Liv to his Arran, really. 'I thought out of all the people in the world, I could trust you to tell me the truth.'

Her brows knitted together. 'I know.'

'Did everyone know?' He licked his dry lips, his throat filling with pain. 'Was everyone just watching me cluelessly fall in love with a fucking countess? A Byron?'

God, imagine that. The entire town knowing. Everyone but him.

She shook her head. 'No. Not everyone. Those who did know found out by accident.'

'Not everyone' still meant enough people knew. And he hadn't been one of them.

'She made you happy, Mac,' Gem whispered. 'How could I be the one to take that away from you? Does a name and a fancy title really matter in the grand scheme of things? I could secretly, unknowingly be related to Margaret Thatcher, but it wouldn't make me a Tory, would it?' She shuddered. 'Fuck no.'

At a loss, he closed his eyes, tears streaming down his cheeks.

'Please don't cry. I never know what to do when people cry.' She patted his back awkwardly, which didn't help him stop crying.

'I just feel like an idiot,' he admitted. 'You warned me. I should have listened. I just thought . . . I thought I knew her in some weird, unspoken way. In here.' He covered his chest with his hand. 'You know when you just know?'

'No,' she deadpanned, ever the commitment-phobe. 'For what it's worth, if I thought Jess was doing it to be malicious or cruel, I would have told you. I kept her secret because when she talked about you . . . she lit up. You deserve someone who cares about you that way, Mac. You really do.'

'Even if they're a liar?' he muttered.

'I think she genuinely believes it doesn't matter. She just wanted you to know *her*.'

'It matters.'

Gem raised a brow. 'Why?'

'Because . . .' He tried to find a solid reason, but struggled. It just . . . mattered. She wasn't who he thought she was. 'Because she lied.'

'Only about the countess part . . .'

'Only?' He bristled with defensiveness. 'She has this life I'll never be part of. She's nobility while I'm just a fucking gardener. She listened to me talk about my granddad, about how much this place meant to him before the Byrons took over. And all the while she was one of them.'

'First of all, you're not *just* anything, Mac. You've never been *just* anything. You have a job that you love and I think that's more than Jess could say about being a countess.'

He had heard Jess scream at the woman, her mother, that it wasn't the life she wanted. But no amount of Gem's reasoning could change the fact Jess had not been honest. If he couldn't trust her to be that, how could he trust her with anything? How could he trust her with *Arran*?

He'd made a fool of himself, day after day, by believing she was like him: just another member of staff at the castle. Not the owner. Not a countess. Not a Byron.

He turned to the bench behind him and went cold as he traced the words etched into the wood. Because he realised now that Jess was Rosemire. And he was Bearnard. Only Bearnard must have known who he was falling in love with, while Mac had been walking around blindly. Maybe the secret garden was actually just a garden of secrets, just like their relationship.

'I just . . .' he faltered, 'I just can't process it all yet.'

'Then take some time.' Gem rubbed his shoulder gently. 'Figure it out. Just don't close the door yet. If she won me over, I'm certain she can help you understand, too.'

At the moment, he didn't want to understand. He just wanted to go home.

So he went to find Arran, and together, they did.

Chapter Twenty-One

Though she'd vowed to give Mac the space he needed, by the following week Jess struggled to keep her distance and occasionally ventured into the castle gardens. But Mac never once even looked her way, sometimes even wandering off as though he couldn't stand her very presence, abandoning his gardening tools for a quick getaway. Jess tried to harden herself. She didn't have a right to be upset.

But it hurt that Mac – the kindest person in Fort Aileen, the man she had been falling in love with – apparently couldn't stand the sight of her. There was no quick fix for the hurt she felt, no painkillers that could cure her.

If she had any dignity, she might have left Fort Aileen by now. But she'd run far enough, from her divorce and the gossips of her social circle. If she carried on running, there wouldn't be a corner of the earth left to hide.

But she had been making plans. Her idea was to move out of the castle and find a permanent home somewhere else here. There was a house for sale that she'd been to view, on the other side of the loch. It was warm and cosy, modest. She could imagine herself in it, but she could also imagine her and Mac curling up by the fire, and Arran doing homework at the dinner table. It had been slightly damaged by the floods, but she'd put in an offer at the viewing so that she would be considered when it was fixed – repairs which, like for the rest of the properties in town, had already been paid for through her donations.

The village was healing quickly from the floods, and tourists had returned in droves to support the local businesses and visit the castle even when it rained. Mac's cottage was still drying out, but Jessamine had already contacted workmen to fix the place up when possible with a pre-payment. She knew if she didn't, Mac wouldn't take her money, even if it was donated, and she couldn't stand the idea of him struggling because of her. Because of what she'd done.

None of it felt like enough, and often Jess felt hopeless. Even just the sight of the hydrangeas outside the castle made her want to curl into a ball somewhere dark and never emerge. At the end of one of the most difficult weeks of her life, she slipped out of the castle on Friday evening for a moment to herself. The tea room was up and running again, the warmer weather meaning that customers could sit outside while it was refurbished, so she ventured in.

It was empty – uncarpeted and midway through getting new wallpaper – but a new counter, fridge, and coffee machine had been installed so the place wouldn't have to remain closed. It was a vast improvement from the sorry state it had been in after the floods.

'Closing now. Come back tomorrow,' Hamish grumbled as he wiped down the counter. He looked up a second later, while Jess was already debating whether she should flee. 'Oh. It's you.'

'Sorry. I didn't realise it was so late.' She made to turn around, leave, but . . . she would be living here now. She wanted to resolve whatever this conflict was with Hamish so she could get a cup of tea without facing his wrath.

So, she grabbed the mop, which was propped against the counter in a soapy bucket of water. Truth be told, she hadn't ever used one before, but there was a first time for everything.

'Didn't think a countess would know how to clean,' Hamish remarked.

She rolled her eyes. 'It's good to see the tea room back on its feet.'

Hamish crossed his arms. 'Hmm. I suppose you expect me to thank you for the donation.'

She shook her head, focusing on the tiles. 'I expect nothing from you, Hamish. I didn't do it for any thanks.'

An unimpressed hum. The tea room fell silent again, Hamish's careful steps over the damp floors echoey and strange. And then she heard the click of switches from behind the counter. 'I'm not turning the coffee machine on, so it's tea or nothing,' he told her.

She was careful not to show her surprise. 'Tea would be perfect. Thank you.'

He set to making it. By the time she had finished cleaning the floor and wrung out the mop head, her tea was sitting on the counter in a to-go cup – along with a large brown paper bag. She peeked into it and found an assortment of cling-film covered cakes and biscuits.

'Might as well eat the leftovers,' grunted Hamish. 'I'll have to bin them otherwise.'

'Thank you.' She rooted for her purse, but when she offered him a ten-pound note, he made no move to accept it.

'Just take them.'

She smiled. 'Thank you, Hamish.'

He nodded, steady gaze for once free of any judgement.

Quietly, she took her things and left the tea room feeling slightly lighter. She might not have gained forgiveness from the person she truly wanted it from, but she'd got a cup of tea without any drama, at least. That was progress.

Her feet knew where to take her next even before her brain did. She crossed the road towards Loch Leannan, pausing for only a moment when she saw a familiar figure sitting there. She hadn't spoken to Arran since the festival. She didn't know if she had a right to; if Mac would want it. But she had to at least try. She didn't just love Mac, after all. She loved Arran, too.

The ground was rocky and uneven, having been disturbed by the flooded banks. She walked over cautiously and maintained a safe distance when she reached them, just like the first time. Arran seemed to know she was there without looking at her, their frame remaining stock-still as they stared out at the water and the rolling Highlands beyond.

'Hello,' she said quietly. 'Is it all right if I sit here?'

Arran shrugged. She took it as permission, warming her hands with her tea and extending the bag of cakes. 'Hungry?'

Arran peered in and gingerly pinched a giant jammy dodger. They unwrapped it carefully, frowning at it as though they were having a silent conversation with the little jam heart in the middle. And then it came, direct as ever.

'Why aren't you and Mac together anymore?'

Mac hadn't told Arran, then. Even when he hated her, when she'd betrayed him, Mac hadn't made Arran feel the same. Sorrow and regret gnawed at her stomach until the tea began to taste sour – or maybe Hamish had slipped her some expired milk.

She opened her mouth to offer some vague answer, but Arran cut her off. 'Don't say "adult stuff". That's all he tells me when I ask and I hate it. I'm not a baby. I'm twelve.'

She sighed, knowing she could never deny Arran honesty. 'I . . . didn't tell him something that I should have. I hurt him very much.'

'He's sad.'

Her chest pinched so painfully she couldn't breathe. 'I know. I'm so sorry for that. I never wanted to make him sad.'

'You're sad, too,' Arran pointed out.

Tears pricked her eyes. 'I'm very sad.'

'Then why can't you just say sorry?'

'I have. But it's complicated, and I think it will take time. When you hurt somebody, you have to be patient. Put their needs before your own.'

Arran's jaw clenched as they picked up a loose rock and threw it into the loch. The water rippled, blurring the reflection of the bridge, hills, sky. That's what Jess's world felt like. Blurred and strange and wrong. She just needed the water to still again.

'I don't want things to change again. I want you to come back,' they said finally.

Jess blinked away her tears, but it only made them fall harder. There was nothing she could say to make it better this time. 'I'm going to do my best to make things right,' she promised.

Arran finally looked at her, all confusion and sadness. Their eyes were pleading, desperate, and she knew there was no letting this go now. Arran was her family. They wanted her around, and she wanted to be around.

She squeezed their hand gently. 'I'll fix it, I promise,' she vowed.

'Jessamine?' The voice came from behind them, more a squeak than anything else. She turned to find Petra hovering at the top of the bank, biting her lip. Her features were full of an urgency that made something in Jess's stomach plummet.

'I have to go, Arran,' she said, lightly touching his shoulder and getting to her feet. 'Make sure you get home to Mac soon, OK?'

Arran watched her get up and go. She cast them a final look of concern over her shoulder before reaching Petra.

'What's wrong?'

'The article's been released.' Petra extended her phone, already lit up on *Splendour*'s website. Jess's picture was at the top, an old one from a gala where she wore a long, rose-pink dress. Her smile was false and dull. She barely recognised that version of her now. That version of her worried about what people thought of her, tried to make people like her. She'd got married because Mother had asked her to, and did most of her charity work from an at-home office.

The headline read: *Behind the castle walls: where has the Countess of Cheshire been hiding?*

Jess shook her head. 'I don't want to read it.'

'You do.'

'Does it mention Mac?'

'Only briefly. Not by name.' When Jess refused to take the phone, Petra sighed and began reading herself. "'*We've all noticed the absence of Lady Jessamine Byron from the public eye these last few months, which comes as no surprise after a rather public meltdown following a messy divorce from Sir Robert Townsend. Now, I assumed she must have been licking her wounds and preparing for the highbrow gala that should have been held this past weekend – in a last-ditch attempt to save her reputation – but when I travelled to the quaint little Scottish village where Byron's ancestral castle lies, I found something quite unexpected—*'"

'Petra, I really don't want—'

Petra ignored her and ploughed on. "'*The gala had been cancelled, but not because the countess was still in hiding. Instead of an extravagant ball, I arrived to find Fort Aileen alive with colour and laughter in honour of a medieval-themed festival, organised by none other than Jessamine herself, who wanted to lift spirits and re-open struggling businesses after a flash flood devastated the village a few weeks ago. Not only that, but Jessamine invited independent artists of all walks of life and has a long history of working with LGBTQ+ charity Shimmer, among many others. A source who wishes to remain anonymous revealed that a sizeable amount of donations in Jessamine's name were made to refurbish the flood-damaged properties around the village.*'"

All right. Perhaps Jess was a little bit interested, if only because she hadn't heard an insult yet.

As though proving it, Petra's voice began to bubble with pride. "'*It is clear that Jessamine Byron has kept herself busy with her work since her split from Sir Robert. More than that, it is clear that she has forged a new path that veers well and truly away from her mother's legacy of beige suits and dull afternoon-tea gatherings.*'" Petra cleared her throat, smirking now. "'*No, while her family socialise and try their best to stay relevant over games of golf or sad soirées with has-been barons, Lady Jessamine has taken a stand. She has committed herself to a far more honourable cause than being a socialite, in order to help others. She has redefined what it is to be a countess, using her title for good rather than evil, and has taken to searching for love that requires no grand wedding or prenups – something the rest of us can only dream of. Farmers are rather dishy, aren't they?"'*

Jess gritted her teeth. 'Why does everyone think Mac is a farmer?'

'It's all the plaid shirts.' Petra shrugged. 'Are you ready for the grand finale?'

Jess waited expectantly.

"'I wasn't convinced either, at first. After all, we nicknamed Jessamine Bunny Boiler Byron after an interview with Sir Robert painted her in a rather unflattering light. However, since then, a new story has unfolded detailing the baron's history of abusive relationships, deceit, and embezzlement. So, who is the real villain? Not Jessamine, by the looks of things! Perhaps we could all stand to learn that not everything is as it seems in the world of spilt champagne and scandal."'

Silence followed. Jessamine furrowed her brows. 'That's it? No remarks about my terrible fringe? No judgements about how tacky costume-themed parties are or how I'm a boring, vapid hag destined to die alone?'

Petra laughed. 'Apparently not.'

It didn't make any sense. Emily could have dished out the biggest scoop of her life. A countess leading a double life would be far more salacious news than acknowledging Jess's philanthropy, her real life here. 'Is it April Fool's Day?'

'It's June.'

'But . . .'

Petra smiled and placed a gentle hand on Jess's shoulder. 'She saw the good you do, Jessamine. It's not that shocking.'

It was, actually. Emily Kingsley had never said a good word about anyone. Her job was to tear people down. And she had never spared Jessamine an ounce of sympathy or kindness when it came to her stories. It made her wonder what her new source had said about Robert. What terrible things had he done to women in a less fortunate position than her?

'She's just found a bigger fish to fry with Robert's misdemeanours,' Jess said cynically. 'Or, she feels sorry for me. She witnessed everything, after all.'

Sympathy crossed Petra's features. 'Whatever the reason, let's just be glad it wasn't a repeat of last time.'

Jess nodded in agreement, but she still felt hollow. Emily could have written a novel on all of her shortcomings and she wouldn't have cared. Not now she'd lost Mac. The things that used to matter didn't anymore, and things she'd never imagined she could have had changed everything.

She didn't care what Emily Kingsley or readers of *Splendour* thought of her. She only cared what Mac thought. And at the moment, Mac didn't think anything good. She looked at Arran, still sitting by the loch and remembered her promise to them.

She needed to find a way to fix it.

Chapter Twenty-Two

Mac sat at the kitchen counter, staring off into space. He'd been doing that a lot recently. Everything just . . . ached. He didn't know how to make it stop. He missed Jess, but he also couldn't bring himself to face her. A small part of him thought she probably deserved a real chance to explain, but every time he thought of all the lies, his stomach lurched as though he was going to throw up.

So he'd been focusing on Arran's adoption, and gardening, and trying not to break. But in the afternoons, when Arran was out on their bike with Liv, and Mac had no flowers left to plant or prune at the castle, there wasn't much to do but wallow.

Mum ruffled his hair and set a mug of tea down in front of him. 'Cheer up, buttercup. I hate seeing you so sad.'

'I know.'

Mac hated *being* so sad. He should have been happy. He was waiting to hear back from Linda about the adoption. His cottage was slowly on the mend. But when he'd called about payment for the refurbishments, they'd claimed it had already been sorted – as with everybody else in town. *She*'d paid for all of it. And now his heart *throbbed*. All the time.

'I'm trying, Mum.'

She watched him carefully. That had been happening a lot lately, too. Like he wasn't a person anymore, just a run-down second-hand car on the verge of spitting out black smoke and breaking down in the middle of the road. 'Have you talked to her yet?'

He shook his head.

'I know we're being angry with her at the moment, and I am completely Team Mac all the way . . . But I think it would help if you did. I think it might give you some closure, or at least some understanding.'

'I just . . . can't.' The same words he'd said to Jess that day. *I can't.* As though everything in him had just given up when the pain had come. 'If she can lie to me about something like this . . .'

'But you're focusing so much on that lie, Mac. What about the festival she threw for us all? What about the love she's shown Arran? What about the way she managed the floods? What about everything the two of you had together? It wasn't all a lie. It sounds like she was just scared. I would be scared if I felt out of place in a village like this. Everyone already knows everyone, and you know how people are about the Byrons.'

He pinched the bridge of his nose, the steam from his tea warming his face.

'Don't you remember your first day of school here?' Mum continued. 'You told everyone your dad was an astronaut because you were worried no one would want to be your friend.'

'Yes, Mum, but I was seven.' He gritted his teeth, hating that he was being short with her. But nobody seemed to understand what this had done to him. 'Jess is an adult. She had plenty of opportunities to tell me.'

'Age doesn't matter,' she replied softly. 'We all get scared sometimes. We all just want to be liked. And Jess . . . She wanted more than anything for you to like her, didn't she? Look at everything she did for you and Arran. Does a title matter when she's become so much more than that to you?'

'Yes,' he muttered.

In truth, he didn't even know what a countess was or what they did. It was just the silly things that broke him: the small ways she lied to keep her story straight while he'd been spilling his soul out for her.

'She made you happy, Mac. All I want is for you to be happy. I think your granddad would have wanted that, too. A lot of people in this town like to hate the Byrons for the past, but your granddad . . . he was just sad he had to stop doing the thing he loved. He would have been glad to see someone trying to heal the past the way Jess is trying to. He would have been proud that if anyone could make amends, stitch the village back together, it would be you and your big old heart.'

'You sound like you're Team Jess,' he pointed out. 'And you're trying to make Granddad, who is no longer with us, Team Jess, too. I don't like that.'

A smile danced on her lips. 'I can't speak for Granddad, but *I'm* Team Mac 'n' Jess. Team Mess.'

And that was certainly what they were. A mess. Mac couldn't think about it anymore, and luckily, he didn't have to. The doorbell rang, and Dad answered it, muttering something about 'Bloody cold callers with their bloody pamphlets.'

The voice didn't belong to a stranger trying to sell them something, though. It belonged to Linda. 'Hello, Mr Douglas. Is Mac about?'

Mac sank lower in his seat, wishing he could disappear. Dread filled his gut until he really did think he might vomit. If it was bad news . . .

'No. I'm not here. I've left the country,' he whispered to Mum. 'I'm in . . . Alaska.'

Too late. Dad had shown Linda in, and she was standing in the kitchen doorway. Strangely, she was smiling brightly. Mac had never noticed she had dimples before.

'Trust me. You don't want to be in Alaska, Mac. Much too cold,' Linda commented. 'This will only take a second. I just wanted to deliver the news in person.'

Oh, God. He was going to puke on her suede pumps. He really, really was. He inhaled shakily. 'OK.'

She beamed. 'Arran's adoption . . . It's being processed.'

The words took too long to register. Mac soaked them up, still feeling hollow – until they hit properly, right in his chest. He whipped up quickly.

'*Seriously?*'

Linda nodded. 'You've been approved! I must say, we've never had so many glowing character references before.'

He froze. 'What?'

'Half of the village chipped in!'

Dizziness scrambled through him, and he clutched the counter for support. He'd only asked a few people for references. Employers and old teachers. The rest . . .

'I . . . I don't know what to say. Thank you, Linda. Thank you so much.'

'Of course. It's well deserved, Mac. Congratulations!'

He felt like his entire body was swimming in thick gloop as he hugged and thanked Linda again and walked her to the door.

'You're going to make a wonderful dad,' Linda whispered, tugging the pocket of his shirt as though they'd been friends for years.

And only then did it really sink in. He was going to be a dad. A proper, permanent dad. Arran was his. They would remain his. Always. They'd never have to worry about getting sent away again, and Mac would never have to feel bad for being late to appointments or burning the pies.

He was a dad. And Arran could finally have a real home.

He ran back into the kitchen and then faltered as though he'd expected to see someone else. His parents hugged him, praised him, cried, but . . . his fingers itched to pull out his phone and call someone else. He hated himself for it. Jess wasn't his person anymore. She wasn't his family. He should have been happy without her, now more than ever.

But he could be ecstatic and still ache, he found. He could be over the moon and under the shadows, all at the same time.

He tried to focus on the light rather than the absence of it. Of her.

*

Mac was practically bursting at the seams by the time he heard the door slam, a sign of Arran's return home. He, Mum, and Dad huddled in the kitchen, Mum with a homemade cake that said *Congralations* (she had forgotten the *t* and *u* when icing) and Dad with a party popper he readied himself with now, hand poised on the string.

Arran walked in a moment later, and they all cheered. Dad's party popper exploded with glittery confetti and Mum broke into tears. As always, though, they were unfazed as their gaze slid to each of them in turn. 'My birthday's in September.'

Mac chuckled. 'We're celebrating something else today, kiddo.'

Arran squinted, trying to read Mum's cake. '"Congralations"? Don't know what that means.'

'It means . . .' Mac braced himself, about to join in with Mum's sobs. He softened his voice, afraid it might break. 'The adoption was approved, Arran. I'm . . . I'm going to be your dad, for good.'

Shock rolled across Arran's features in waves – and then joy. Teary, unbridled joy. Mac had never seen Arran smile like that before. Not once. They'd been depriving the world of something magical, and he hadn't even known.

They dropped their backpack to the floor and ran to Mac, their arms curling around his waist, hands grasping so tightly that Mac could barely breathe. He didn't care. He shook with sobs and laughter as he lifted and twirled Arran – *his* Arran – around the kitchen. He wasn't sure how he'd ever let them go.

'You're happy then, kiddo?' he asked.

Arran nodded frantically. 'I'm happy.'

Mac cradled Arran's head, their long hair tickling his nostrils, as Mum put the cake down to take pictures and Dad snuck a taste of icing with his finger. And it was perfect. Mac realised he wasn't heartbroken at all. His heart would never be broken again as long as he was Arran's dad. As long as he was making them happy.

'Love you,' he whispered.

Arran didn't need to say it back; the way they clung on and emitted nothing but sunlight for the rest of the evening said more than enough. It was all Mac wanted. All he needed.

And if he felt something inside him wilt each time he looked at the empty seat and wished Jess was there, he tried not to let himself feel it for too long.

Chapter Twenty-Three

Sitting on the bench in Bearnard's garden, Jess bristled with nerves. After two weeks of silence since the festival, Mac had finally reached out. She didn't know why, and he hadn't said. He'd simply sent her a message asking if they could talk – suggesting a time and a place – and she was in no position to ask questions.

She fidgeted, jiggling her leg up and down as her stomach churned, until finally the iron gate creaked with his arrival. She stood up and then regretted it when he sat beside her without a word, meaning she resembled a human yoyo. She couldn't talk. Wasn't sure what to say. Wasn't sure if he'd want her to.

'I'm not your charity,' was the first thing he said, so quietly she barely heard. His jaw was set with determination, stubble grown slightly longer, scruffier, than usual.

She frowned. 'I know that.'

'You didn't have to pay for the cottage.'

A stone dropped into her stomach, jagged and cold. She didn't think he'd find out about that. Not so soon, anyway. 'I wanted to. I paid for all the other refurbishments. I wasn't going to leave you out, was I?'

'And the character references? Did you have something to do with those, too?' He kept staring at the fence she'd had put up, the one she was going to surprise him with the night of the fundraiser. She couldn't bear it. Couldn't bear not seeing that warmth in his eyes. He always looked at Arran with unconditional love. With Jess, it had been different. His features had always glittered with amused surprise, like he couldn't believe she was real.

Now, it was like he didn't want to believe in her at all.

'Everybody wanted to help you, Mac. I might have had the idea, but the rest stemmed from nothing but love for you and Arran.' Jess tried to clear the lump from her throat, but her words still came out hoarse. 'It wasn't charity. None of it. If anything, *I* was the charity. I was the one given a family, a home, things I'd never even dreamed of before. Nothing that I give to you could ever outweigh that. Not ever.'

He frowned, leaning back finally. 'Then I have to at least say thank you. Arran . . . they haven't stopped smiling.'

Despite her happiness, desolation settled in her. She no longer got to be a part of that happiness. 'The adoption was approved?'

He looked at her for the first time. There was no familiarity there. Just confusion. As though he'd expected that she'd been the one to personally approve the adoption. As though this was her world, all of it. As though she'd ever had any semblance of control in her life.

'Yes.'

'Congratulations. I'm so happy for you both.' Of course, she'd known the references would give Mac a better chance. She just hadn't known it would make this much difference.

A muscle in his jaw ticked, as if reminding her that the moments were passing and he still hated her.

'Mac . . .' She closed her eyes, desperate this time to keep the tears at bay as she was braced against a mild breeze. 'I am so sorry. You deserve the truth. You deserve honesty. You deserve somebody you can trust, and I wanted so badly . . .'

She couldn't do it. Her voice broke, and she couldn't do it.

Mac pressed his palms on his knees. 'Then why?'

'Because all I've ever been is my title. A countess. It means nothing to me anymore. Nothing. And you . . . you looked at me like I was so much more than that. Like I was a person. And I know how it must sound. I am ignorantly privileged in so many ways, but nobody has ever *seen* me. Not like you do. I felt as though I wasn't even a real person before. I didn't belong anywhere. Then I met you and everything changed. I found out not long after about what my family did to the village, and I was afraid that when you discovered I was a Byron, you'd stop seeing me for me but just as one of them. I couldn't . . . I didn't want to lose you. I was selfish. I just wanted to be Jess. *Your* Jess.' She sniffled, taking a breath and counting to ten just to make sure she didn't crumble. 'I realise now that I shouldn't have to lie to be myself. Who I am is a choice *I* make, regardless of my family's name. I just spent a long time letting other people make the choices for me and it's all so new.'

His chin seemed to wobble, but his expression remained blank. She could feel him slipping through her fingers, drifting away.

But he didn't tell her to shut up. He didn't argue. So she had to explain the rest while she still had the chance. If he was going to walk away, she wanted him to know all of her first.

She pulled her phone out of her bag. Opened an article on *Splendour* from March. Robert's interview with Emily. In quotes at the top of the page: '*Some women are simply impossible to love. Jessamine Byron is one of those women.*'

She didn't dare skim the rest before laying it out on the bench in front of Mac, but enough had been formatted in bold for her to glimpse the worst parts. *Deceitful. Hates children. Secret affairs. Childlike tantrums and meltdowns. Cruel and bitter.* 'This is another reason I was afraid to tell you.'

His brows furrowed as he scanned the screen.

'My ex-husband,' she explained. 'He did an interview after the divorce and said all sorts of awful things about me. Everybody I knew began seeing me that way, though none of it was true. I was cast out of friendship groups and even my mother . . .' She choked on that, unable to finish. 'If my title didn't define me, those words seemed to. *The woman who was impossible to love.* I'm not telling you this as a way of excusing myself, but when I came here, I didn't want *anybody* to know who I was just in case they saw me that way, too. Maybe a part of me was worried some of it might be true. And the thought of you reading this about me . . . I just wanted one person to know me differently. I just wanted *you* to know me differently.'

'I would never have judged you based on this.' He gestured at the screen. 'I don't read tabloids.'

'I know that now. But I suppose when I met you, I was just waiting for the other shoe to drop. When I found out you were a dad and the complete opposite of everything Robert said I was, I wondered if it would just give you a reason to judge me. The way he painted me as selfish and obsessed with wealth . . . those were all things you hated. All things the Byrons were known for here. And then I fell for you, and it was too late to go back. I just wanted things to stay good. It's immature and silly and selfish, but I've never had anything this good before. All of the things I said about my family were true. Nobody has ever cared for me the way you did. And I just wanted to hold on to it for as long as I could, because I didn't want to risk losing you. I could manage the rest of the world believing these things, but you . . . I couldn't bear even the thought.'

Finally, his eyes shone. He closed the article, fingers trembling. 'I understand. I do. But it doesn't change—'

'It doesn't fix what I broke,' she said quickly. 'I know that. I don't expect anything. I don't deserve it. But I . . .' it might have been her last chance to say it, and yet it was an effort to force the words out, 'I'm in love with you, and that was never a lie.'

His face flashed in shock, but Jess didn't understand why. How could he not know how wonderful he was? How catastrophically she cared for him? How could there ever be a world where she didn't love him?

Silence fell across them, leaving her restless. She'd laid herself bare and he had nothing to say. Her skin crawled with humiliation, but still, she kept her gaze lifted, determined to make him *see*.

'Jess . . .' She was sitting down, and yet still her name on his tongue made her knees want to buckle. *Jess*. She was still Jess to him. That was better than nothing. 'How can this work? We started on a lie. I feel like I don't even know you.'

'You do know me. You know I'm a terrible cook, that I never learned to ride a bike. You know I have hay fever and that I drink tea, never coffee. You know my favourite flowers are hydrangeas because they're how we met. You *know* me, Mac. I swear you do.'

'You *hurt* me. I don't know how to come back from it.'

Her face was wet with tears that left her uncomfortable, as though she was drowning in them. 'OK. I have to respect that. I know I do. But . . . I won't stop trying. I can't. I know this is where I'm supposed to be. With you. And I have to keep trying until you ask me to stop. Are you asking me to stop?'

His throat bobbed. Quietly, he answered, 'I don't know. I need more time.'

'OK.' She was trying so hard to be strong, even when her entire body felt torn apart.

She watched as he stood, turned his back and walked away. He stopped at the gate, and hope guttered inside her.

'Arran asked me if you'd come to their party. We're celebrating the adoption and they want you there. It's at the Hairy Coo on Friday night. Six-ish.'

'Do you . . .' She tasted salt on her lips. 'Is that OK?'

'It's Arran's party,' he said again. 'They should at least get to decide who's there.'

He left it at that, his absence turning Jess cold. Still, she couldn't help but hope. Mac could have walked away without telling her. He could have made up a lie for Arran, a reason why she couldn't make it. But he'd invited her anyway.

That had to mean something.

She would make it mean something.

Chapter Twenty-Four

Mac was nervous, and he'd taken to cramming salted pretzels into his mouth at the bar as a way of managing it. The pub was already teeming with people Arran had wanted here. Olivia and Callum, a few other school friends whose parents hadn't minded taking their children to a pub on a Friday night – with Gem enforcing a strict soft-drinks-only policy, of course – and Brodie and Joss, too. Gem had closed the pub to the locals, since they didn't have a separate function room, and she'd also pulled out all the stops with handmade *Happy Arran-doption* banners, a possible hint towards her otherwise well-veiled guilt. She'd even made a personalised playlist with Arran's favourite songs and got out the karaoke machine, with which, unfortunately, Mum was currently entertaining herself by singing ABBA's 'Waterloo'.

Everyone else was here. Everyone but Jess. Mac kept catching Arran looking towards the door. It hadn't sunk in how big an impact she'd had on them until now. It didn't make being angry at her any easier.

Gem eyed him and the pretzels like a disapproving teacher, her One Direction shirt crumpled over Louis Tomlinson's face so that he looked distorted and nose-less. He'd refused to let her little bet trick with Petra and Brodie slide.

'I'm going to start charging you for those,' she said.

He shook his head and said through a mouthful of crumbs, 'Naw y'won't.'

'Try me.' She pursed her lips. 'So. You've forgiven me for keeping Jess's secret.'

He sighed and wiped the salt off his hands, pouting when

320

she spirited the bowl of pretzels away. His stomach was in knots at the thought of Jess walking in . . .

He couldn't even think about it. 'Forgiven, maybe. Not forgotten yet.'

She pursed her lips. 'And Jess? Have you kissed and made up yet?'

'I don't know why everyone is acting like it's just some silly argument. It's not that easy, Gem. I thought you of all people would get that. And, by the way, if the roles were reversed, you'd probably have pushed me off a bridge by now.'

'Yes, but I'm mean and cold. You're Mac. And . . .' she softened her voice, her eyes round and raw and un-Gem-like, 'you're miserable without her.'

'I'm not miserable,' he denied, glaring. 'I'm ecstatic. I have everything I need.'

'You're stress-eating pretzels,' she pointed out.

'They're addictive.' When her stare didn't let up, he puffed out a frustrated breath. 'I'm allowed to be bloody upset about this.'

'I know that. Of course I know that. I just don't want you to miss what's really important.' She leaned across the bar so he had to look down at her. 'Jess would drop anything for you, Mac. If you asked her to walk through fire, she probably would. I've seen her lie and I hated every minute of it, but I've also seen her support you and Arran like she's family. You don't have to forgive the countess, but . . . don't forget about Jess.'

'Jess doesn't exist,' he mumbled, though he wasn't sure anymore who he was trying to convince. He'd turned this over and over in his head for nights on end. If it was all a lie, they couldn't have been that happy together. Could they? What would she gain from stringing Mac along? Everything had felt so authentic, so unexpected, and everything she'd done for him . . . Nobody had ever done those things for him before.

'Speaking of the countess . . .' Gem murmured. A second

later, the sound of a door closing echoed below the blaring music.

'Jess!' Arran's shout was full of joy.

Mac turned around to find her there. Somehow, he expected her to look different. Less like his Jess and more like the countess in those tabloid stories she'd showed him. But if anything, she looked more Jess than ever, with her fringe mussed and her features flushed with colour. Her dress was the same floral, summer style as always, the dresses that always made Mac feel too hot because her thighs were there and he wanted so badly to wrap his hands around them.

'Oop!' Jess exclaimed, as Arran charged at her. Her hands were full with a tray . . . of what looked like pie. She'd made a pie. Not a burnt one, either, but a nice buttery-crusted one with cream and strawberries to top it. In her other hand, a bunch of hydrangeas.

She really knew exactly how to tug on his bloody heartstrings.

Arran pulled her into a hug despite all these things, their face as bright and colourful as fireworks.

Jess giggled and hugged them back once Petra had taken the pie and flowers from her. 'Hello, you. Congratulations. I'm so happy for you.' She said it into their hair, but Mac heard every syllable clear as day. His previously compromised heartstrings snapped. 'I made you pie. Not burnt this time. And the fire alarm only went off once.'

Arran's cheeks swelled with giddiness. 'Thank you. I'm allergic to strawberries, though.'

Jess's face fell. 'Oh, God . . . I forgot about that. How about flowers?'

They shrugged nonchalantly. 'Would rather have a PlayStation, to be honest. Or a motorbike.'

Mac shook his head. Arran was pushing their luck. He'd already told them they wouldn't be allowed to ride a motorbike until they were at least forty, which had not gone down well.

Jess met his eyes across the room, then, and he had to look away. 'Let's, er, stick with the PlayStation.'

Arran smiled and then returned to Olivia and Callum by the karaoke machine. Mum was now dancing to 'Voulez-Vous' – Dad clapping supportively. As entertaining as it was, Mac quickly turned around, losing his nerve as Jess approached. It made no difference. She set the pie and flowers on the bar.

'Hello.'

'I've got to . . . do a thing,' Gem said awkwardly, scratching her neck before joining Brodie and Petra on the other side of the bar.

'You're not getting Arran a PlayStation. They cost a fortune.' Mac crossed his arms. He could barely see Jess over the hydrangeas, almost as though she was hiding in that bush again. It sent a pang through him, and he wished Gem hadn't confiscated his emotional-support pretzels.

'OK. Fair enough.' She slid the hydrangeas closer to him. 'I don't know if hydrangeas are an "I'm sorry" plant or just an "I'm an idiot" plant. I hope both,' she said.

'I think the blue ones mean "quite good at lying" and the purple ones mean "Mac's a gullible numpty".'

'Interesting. The florist just said they symbolise gratitude.' She pushed them away so he could no longer avoid looking at her. 'You're not a gullible numpty, Mac. Please don't ever say that.'

He only hummed, wishing he was as carefree as Mum and her ABBA songs. He was exhausted. Drained. Confused. He didn't know where to go from here because a part of him knew Jess hadn't wanted to hurt him. If she did, she would have done it in far more obvious ways, like breaking up with him or making fun of his embarrassing blunders. Instead, she'd supported him just like Gem had said. She'd been there through every hard moment of his life the last few months. She'd had half the town write him character references for the adoption, for God's sake. None of this would be happening without her.

'I made you a pie,' she offered. 'Well, it was for Arran . . .'

'It's very uncharred.'

'Third attempt. Followed the recipe properly this time. No curdled eggs or milk involved.'

He wanted so badly to laugh, but he was filled with white noise. He didn't know what any of it meant. 'Look, Jess . . . I appreciate everything you've done for Arran and me.'

'Please don't break up with me in a pub,' she begged. 'You really, really don't have to. I know, Mac. I know I've messed it up and there's no way back. I know. You don't have to say it.'

'I wasn't . . .' God, how was it that he felt like the arsehole now? She was giving him those doe eyes, the colour of his favourite wildflowers, and he just . . . he was . . .

He was in love with her, even now. He was woven somewhere along her ribcage, or maybe she'd threaded him through the freckles along her collarbone like a daisy chain. He couldn't cut the stems, couldn't just let go. She'd lied to him, but she couldn't make her regret much clearer. And when she'd told him she loved him in the garden, it had sounded like she meant it.

He didn't know what to do with it.

'I was just going to say that we can at least be . . .'

She winced. '"Friends"?'

He slumped, defeated. What else *could* he say? He needed to be careful now. He couldn't just jump into the deep end with her like last time. She'd only proven it was a terrible idea.

Her gaze burnt a hole in his bowed head.

'It's OK, Mac. You don't owe me anything. I'll take whatever I can get, even if it's just friends.'

Only he owed her everything. For the adoption, for making his heart beat again, for the cottage and the festival and the secret garden he'd waited years to open. Everything had been just out of reach without her. He couldn't quite imagine a world where they didn't talk now. Trying to made him feel empty.

Finally, he lifted his head and tried not to break when he looked at her. 'Can I get you a drink? Only water, apple juice, lemonade, or Diet Coke I'm afraid.'

'I'll have to go with apple juice.' She laughed, and it was musical. Not the cheery notes of ABBA, but that same wistful, haunting harmony that had come from the violinist in the courtyard when they'd danced together. Just before he'd found out. And he . . . he was just the walls it bounced off.

She was a countess. A Byron. Beautiful, confusing, wealthy. And he was just a gardener. Even if they moved past the lying, in what world did that work?

In Rosemire's, an annoying voice niggled at the back of his mind. *Rosemire's and Bearnard's*.

But this wasn't an ancient love story, and their names wouldn't be carved into a bench. He didn't know what it was. He didn't know anything but that they were so different.

So he drank apple juice with her while his heart broke a little bit more, and then knitted itself back together when she went to dance with Arran and their friends. And he knew she was supposed to be in his life, with his family – he just didn't know where he fit in hers anymore.

The night ended with Mac's mum bringing out a cake for Arran, sparklers fizzling on top as everyone clapped. Jess stood outside of it all by the bar, no longer feeling welcome. Mac had been civil, polite, but that didn't mean much. He wasn't the type to be cruel, not like Robert.

She smiled solemnly as she watched Arran enjoy their moment. Mac's dad recorded it all on his phone and Pam began to cry. Mac wore pride like gold, beaming with his hand on Arran's shoulder. In another life, one where Jess hadn't screwed up royally, she would have been by his side.

'He's glad you're here,' Gem muttered from behind the bar. 'Even if he doesn't want to admit it. He wouldn't still be letting you into Arran's life if he thought you meant either of them any harm.'

'But I'll always be a liar to him. You don't get that trust back,' she replied, fidgeting with the straw in her apple juice. The five faces on Gem's T-shirt stared back at her. Jess was quite certain she'd once tried to unknowingly flirt with the curly-haired one at a party, but the memory was fuzzy from all the champagne consumed that night.

'You can try.' Gem offered her a sympathetic smile, which only told Jess just how much of a lost cause she was. So fragile that not even the second most hostile person in the village could bear to dish out her usual deprecating quips. Where was Hamish when she needed him?

'Jess!' Arran called, waving around the sparkler plucked from the cake. Pam fussed, urging them outside, but they said, 'Come and get the other sparkler!'

Jess followed the group through the door, where everyone stood on the cobbles outside the pub, and Arran waved their sparkler as the family crowded around. When they caught sight of Jess, they pushed through to grab her hand and give her the sparkler, getting the other one from their cake. Jess's face heated, both with the sparks and the knowledge that everyone was watching. *Mac* was watching. But she smiled and painted the sky with her sparkler, realising it was the first time she'd ever used one, though she'd always wanted to.

'Watch this,' Arran instructed. They swirled around their sparkler, drawing out letters. *Arran. Mac. Jess. Pam. Stewart. Gem.* Their family. Jess was second on the list after Arran themself. She couldn't help but tear up. Maybe she couldn't have Mac, but she still had Arran. She was still part of their family. It was so much more than she'd ever dreamed of.

She drew Arran a wonky heart in return. They grinned and then their face lit up when they found more sparklers had been lit for their friends. As Arran rushed towards them, Jess was left with her slowly ebbing sparkler. She met Mac's eye, saw that he'd lit one for himself and was steadily approaching.

So, she wrote, '*I'm sorry*'. Her last attempt. The letters disappeared into the night so quickly she wasn't sure if he'd seen them. Not until he curled his own sparkler with, '*I know*'. He offered her a tight smile. And then her sparkler went out all at once, a bit like their relationship, and she was left in the darkness.

When the sparklers had all been extinguished and the cake had been eaten, the kids exhausted, Jess pulled on her jacket. Petra followed, her lips dyed pink from the cake frosting.

'Kids' parties are tiring,' she commented.

Jess nodded, though she missed having the energy of a happy, healthy twelve-year-old, even if she had never been able to use it for fear of being reprimanded by her mother.

'I agree. It's past my bedtime.' She stopped when Petra pulled out her car keys, smirking. 'Aren't you saying goodbye to Brodie, first?'

The two had been watching each other all night. Petra insisted she didn't like him one bit, but Brodie hadn't stopped flirting, and Jess had caught Petra blushing every time he looked her way. Still, she shook her head. 'Nope. Aren't you saying goodbye to Mac?'

'Touché,' Jess murmured, her gaze flitting over to the karaoke machine. Mac was singing a sad Bon Jovi song into the microphone, his voice rough and wavering as he grabbed the air dramatically and did a few leg-guitar solos. As though sensing her, he caught her eye. She nodded and waved him goodbye. He stopped singing.

Unnerved and quite ready to cry into her pillow, she sought out Arran. They were tiredly watching Mac from the corner booth, their head resting against the beer-stained cushions. They brightened as Jess approached.

'I'm off, Arran.' Jess tugged on their curls lightly. 'Thank you for inviting me tonight.'

Their brows set with a frown. 'You and Mac didn't make up, did you?'

She pressed her lips into a thin, wobbly line. 'It doesn't

matter.' She crouched in front of them, grabbing their hands. 'We're both here for you. That's what matters.'

Arran didn't look convinced. She hated that she was the cloud hanging over the celebration.

'It's just better when we're all together,' they mumbled quietly.

Jess felt as cracked as an old teacup. Any moment, all the pain would gush out and she'd have nothing left. She tried desperately to keep it in until she left the pub.

'I'm sorry. I promise I'm trying.'

Arran scooted off the seat to hug her, then, and she almost fell under the weight of them, her calves aching in her squat. But she squeezed back, breathing them in because they smelled so much like Mac, like that night they'd had dinner at his parents' house.

Eventually, they broke apart. Jess stood up on sore muscles, about to wish Arran a final goodnight when her name was called.

She turned around, finding Mac twirling his car keys around his finger.

'Can I give you a lift home?'

Bewildered, she searched the room for Petra. She was still at the bar with Gem, flashing Jess a thumbs-up and mouthing, '*Go*.'

'Er . . .' Jess stuttered. 'Yes. Of course. If that's OK, I mean.'

He gestured to the door and then followed her out into the darkness. The rest of the village was quiet, the lights of the nearby cottages and streetlamps dappling the shadows. She waited awkwardly for Mac to lead her to his truck, and he did. It sat across the road and creaked as they got into it.

Her stomach sank as she fastened her seatbelt and waited. Surely this was it. The final goodbye. The real break-up. The end. But Mac said nothing as he put the keys in the ignition, and Jess didn't dare break the silence. Instead, she focused on the rumbling engine as they headed towards the castle. She remained stock-still, afraid that if she so much as moved, the illusion would shatter like a mirror. She tried not to look at the house she had pretended to live in as they came to the bridge, glad when he didn't comment on it. He just kept driving, over Loch Leannan, where the moon watched over the water like a guardian, painting her an ethereal silver.

The castle appeared, a clump of silhouetted turrets and arched, dimly lit windows. She held her breath as he parked outside, the world stopping with the engine.

It was her last chance. She knew that. She would make it count.

'Can I show you something?'

Mac's forehead wrinkled with uncertainty, but he unfastened his seatbelt and pocketed his keys all the same. 'Aye. I suppose so.'

She hopped out of the truck; the sound of Mac's door slamming cut through the chirps of the crickets. Shakily, she led him into the castle and up the stairs. They stopped when they reached the red rope that separated the visitor's area from the private residential rooms and she unhooked it, letting a puzzled Mac through before putting it back to ensure their privacy.

It was the longest they'd ever gone without talking to each other and the quiet was unnerving, but Jess carried on up the spiralling staircase, emerging into the chandelier-lined hallway where her room was. She took him there first, opening the door and stepping aside.

Mac entered reluctantly as though he wasn't sure he was allowed. His hands were buried in his pockets as he took it all in. The four-poster bed. The bookcase. The walk-in wardrobe and mirrors.

'This is where I live,' she said. The floorboards creaked under her shifting weight. 'This is me. I sleep in that bed and I read those books and I get dressed in front of that mirror. I like candles.' She wandered over to the one on her dresser, a handmade one she'd purchased from the festival last weekend, and wiggled it about. 'My favourites are autumn scents, but I like to keep to the seasons. This one is lemongrass.'

'Jess . . .'

But she couldn't stop. She had to show him every part of her. 'Rufus usually sleeps . . .' she peeled back her curtain to find the cat curled on a pile of pillows in the bay window, 'here.'

Mac's lips curled with a smirk.

'And I started pressing some of the flowers you gave to me,' she admitted. She pulled the scrapbook out of her drawer and flicked over the pages. The first powder-blue hydrangea he'd given her lay flattened and stuck with a piece of tape, labelled with a date because she'd known even then. She'd known she would want to remember the exact moment in time when everything changed. 'I didn't want them to die and be thrown out, so . . .' she flicked to another page; a sprig of lavender he'd plucked from his own garden because she'd told him she was having trouble sleeping one morning, 'I preserved them. Because they're important. Because they feel like pieces of you, somehow.'

She left the book open on her bedside table, smoothing down her dress before nervously walking past him, back into the hallway. She guided him into her study next, unable to meet his intent gaze.

'When I'm not out and about, I work in here.' Her laptop still lay abandoned on the desk. 'Paperwork and planning and meetings. Things like that. I always have a mug of tea next to me, and sometimes, on hot days, I accidentally fall asleep on the chaise longue there.' She pointed to the teal seat, covered in blankets and pillows, before continuing back out the door.

She went to the furthest corner, where an old wooden door was. A key kept it locked, and she turned it now. The fresh air curled around the stone steps and then them, chasing away the indoor warmth as they emerged outside. She let out a ragged breath and began the ascent up to the turret. The peak of the castle. When she reached the top, she turned around, finding Mac behind her, the breeze ruffling his curls, his jaw tight.

'I come here when I need fresh air. I like it because I can see your cottage from here, and if I stand on my tiptoes' – she did, peering over the wall – 'the loch, too. I sometimes see you bringing Arran home from school or Lauren giving one of her birds of prey demonstrations, and it's just . . . nice. It makes me feel small and distant and part of something greater. At peace, I suppose. It was never like that growing up. Just me in a big old house, usually with my tutor. It was always too quiet.'

She was running out of things to say; knew it was time to give it up.

'Anyway. That's me. That's who I am, really. Jessamine Byron, Countess of Cheshire, but mostly just a woman who works and sleeps and tries to be like everyone else. There is nothing more of me to hide, and nothing I'd want to hide. Not from you. And not when I know who *I* want to be.'

Mac chewed on his cheek, inching closer. 'And who do you want to be?'

She shrugged. 'A good person. Someone who helps people.'

Yours. She couldn't say it. This wasn't about begging for his forgiveness or changing his mind. It was just about making sure he knew everything before he gave up for good.

'There's one last thing,' she said, catching sight of that small thatched roof, which wasn't always easy to make out from this distance, but the night was clear. She pointed to it. 'There, across the loch, that's a house. It's mine now. I'm moving out of the castle. I don't want or need a huge place to live. I just need a home. It's pretty and has lots of room for' – she cleared her throat – 'a decent kitchen and a real fireplace. I've never lived completely on my own before. I'm excited. It has a garden, too. A big one. Rufus will like it.'

You might, too.

Finally, surprise flickered across Mac's features. He stared at the cottage for what felt like an eternity. 'What made you decide to stay in Fort Aileen?'

'I think you know the answer to that,' she replied softly. 'You. Arran. And even if you can't ever forgive me, I like it here. I like the village and the people. I like the scenery. I feel right here. I've never felt right anywhere before.'

He deliberated, tilting his head and humming.

Feeling drained suddenly, Jess leaned against the wall, the cold stone digging into her back. She waited again. Always waiting.

Mac's eyes finally locked with hers. 'If I . . .' His voice broke, and he cleared his throat quickly. 'Hypothetically, if we decide to give this another go . . . what kind of life do you see for us?'

'The life we've had for the past few months. Bike rides and picnics and family dinners. Spending time with Arran. Just . . . living. Enjoying every moment, even the silly ones. I might have to travel for work sometimes, but I'd be here mostly, focusing on local charities. You'd be gardening. Arran would be thrilled because they'd get more time with Rufus. That's what I see, I suppose. Or, at least, that's what I hope for.'

It was what she'd been imagining since the moment she'd met him. An extraordinary, ordinary life. A family who knew how to love without judgement. Him, making her laugh like he always did, and making her burn just as often.

'And what about your family? Your social circle and the news articles and the fact you're a countess?'

'I have no interest in ever going back to that life, and the journalist has made it quite clear she no longer has anything to write about concerning me.'

Emily had posted a scathing article about Robert since the one detailing Jessamine's new life. Mother had even tried calling her, no doubt relieved that the Byrons were no longer the villains of the story, but Jess had ignored her. She wasn't interested in going back. She'd said all she needed to, and she no longer wished for an apology from her mother, or for her to change. Better if Mother stayed in London and Jess stayed here, with people she trusted. People who wouldn't cause her pain.

'My title is something I inherited, but my work, my life, is something I get to choose for myself, and I've chosen this. I've chosen Fort Aileen.'

His jaw set, his expression unreadable. Jess felt as though she'd spilt her soul onto the stone floor and he couldn't bear to look at it. Until he did.

'I'm a gardener,' he stated as though she didn't know.

'I'm a countess,' she replied. 'And a charity worker. And a cat mother.'

'So it doesn't bother you that I'm just . . . normal?' He said 'normal' like *his* normal wasn't the most wonderful thing in the world, and she couldn't help but step forward to cup his jaw. He didn't pull away, instead seeming to hold his breath and brush his stubble against her palms like he'd been waiting for her to touch him.

'You're . . . you're everything to me, Mac. You're wonderful and lovely and passionate and you make terrible jokes and I love you. For exactly who you are. And I've been searching my whole life for some "normal". I *dreamed* of finding "normal". But the way I feel for you . . . it's so much more than just "normal".'

A tear slid down his cheek, and then he was kissing her like it was the first time, or the last time, and she didn't know which was true, only that she had missed him so much and she didn't want him to ever let go.

'I can't . . .' he rasped between kisses. The corner of her mouth, her nose, her cheek, her lips. They were the same words he'd repeated over and over the last few weeks. But they were said differently now. Softly. 'I can't pretend I don't love you. I can't walk away.'

'Then, don't,' she begged on a sob. 'Please don't.'

He shook his head, brushing his nose against hers. His lashes were damp, irises dark and glistening. She wanted them to be the first ones she saw in the morning, the last ones to look at her before she went to sleep. She wanted Mac forever, all his rugged gentleness and his sensitivity and his wit. She wanted everything she'd never been allowed to want before, and she wanted it with him.

'God, Jess,' he groaned through gritted teeth. 'I don't want to walk away from you. Not ever again.'

'You won't have to. I swear,' she promised, wiping the damp from his cheek. 'You know all of me now.'

'And I love all of you.' His hands clenched at her hips desperately, as though he was afraid she might slip away. 'You never had to hide from me.'

But she hadn't known then that people could be good and kind and accepting. She hadn't known then that she *could* be loved, that it would ever be possible, because all love had ever been before was ignorance and criticism and barbed sarcasm. She'd never even known that she could love herself, which, despite her regrets, she did now.

She wasn't impossible to love. She never had been.

It was enough to make her cry. She swallowed down the lump in her throat, unable to stop marvelling at him. Every bit of him. He was real. *This* was real.

She didn't need to say it. Didn't need to unearth all of those ugly feelings and doubts that had existed before he'd buried them and planted flowers in her fears. He kissed her as though she was the most delicate thing on this earth; as though he knew she just needed his softness. And, finally, she nestled into his chest where she belonged.

'My jokes aren't terrible, by the way.' His voice vibrated across the crown of her head, his chin pressed into her hair.

She giggled. 'Arran would disagree.'

'You're supposed to take *my* side.'

Jess pulled away to take in the view: him first, and then the starry night sky. 'There's a reason they're called "dad jokes", my love.'

He grinned at that, feigning offence. But she could see the happiness that calling him a dad brought him and squeezed him just a little bit closer. When she shivered, he wrapped his arms around her, his torso pressed against her back as they stared at the crescent moon. She wasn't ready to go downstairs again. She just wanted to stay here, suspended in time and blanketed in silver light and him.

Mac peppered more kisses into her hair, sighing finally, contently, like he could breathe again. 'Come home with me?'

Jess's stomach swooped as though she'd jumped off the highest turret. *Home*. It wasn't the castle. Never had been. It was Mac and Arran.

'Of course.' She twirled around, seeking out his hand. It was warm and rough and safe, and remained entwined with hers as they made their way home together. When Arran rushed out of Mac's parents' house to meet them, joy written all over their features, Jess knew she'd been right to fight for the people she loved.

She belonged here. She would always belong here. She was just grateful they'd chosen her, too.

Epilogue

Eight Months Later

Jess had burnt the pancakes again. Mac winced over her shoulder at the pile of black goo, unable to suppress his chuckle. 'Are they supposed to look like that, love?'

She shot him a glare and he soon shut up, sipping his coffee in peace. Outside, Arran ran around with Pickle, Rufus, and the newest addition to their family, a rescue kitten named Beans. Technically, Beans belonged to Jess, but they were here so often that Arran had taken to pretending otherwise. In her new house by the loch, they all had plenty of space to run around in. The garden was already in bloom – Mac's hard work paying off after months of tending to the plants. A cherry-blossom tree rained down pink petals on the small shed, which had been devoted to his garden tools, and Jess sometimes looked after the vegetable patch by the fence.

It was perfect. Though Mac's cottage had been completely refurbished, they barely spent any time there now. There was more space here, and Arran clearly preferred the company of the cats. Mac was still working tirelessly on Bearnard's garden, even expanding it for more visitors to enjoy. Just as he was certain Rosemire would have wanted.

'Maybe I should make toast instead.' Jess pouted, slumping against the counter and lifting her steeping teabag from her mug.

'And set the smoke alarm off again?' An event that had happened only three days ago. 'Why don't I make breakfast and you make sure Arran doesn't find any more toads to adopt.'

'No. I was on toad duty yesterday.' She lifted her chin defiantly, but Mac could soon fix that. He only had to poke her soft hip and pull her closer, their bellies pressed together and their gazes meeting, to break her sour expression. She broke into a grin, cheesy and wide and breathtakingly beautiful. Mac would never get used to seeing it. He wanted it tattooed all over his skin and painted across the walls.

'What do you fancy doing today?' he asked, which had become a ritual on Sunday mornings. It was their family day, no matter whether it was raining or sunny like today.

She shrugged. 'Anything. Anything but bike riding.'

He smirked. She still hadn't got the hang of that. 'We could go for a drive somewhere. I need to visit Mum first, though.'

She brightened. Her new favourite hobby was singing very badly to Mac's *Now That's What I Call Dad Rock* album while they wound their way through the hills in the truck. Arran usually joined in when they got to Queen.

'Well, before we go . . .' Jess set her mug down and, on her tiptoes, reached for something on the overhead shelf. Mac couldn't catch what it was, her clenched fist immediately hiding it. He frowned, wary. 'I have something for you.'

'Oh, aye?'

'*Aye*,' she mocked. Finally, she unfurled her fingers and revealed a silver key linked to a pastel-green, house-shaped keyring.

Mac examined it. 'I already have a key, love.'

She rolled her eyes. 'Look on the other side of the keyring.'

He turned it over, finding a sentence printed on the house: *Move in with me?*

His heart thumped and then seemed to stop altogether.

'You said yourself Arran prefers it here, and you're always here anyway. I thought maybe it was time . . .' She bit her lip, looking unsure. 'Not a good idea?'

He hesitated for only a second. She was right. Arran loved

it here and there was far more space. They were a family, and it was time they made it official. He just couldn't believe . . .

When he'd met her, he'd been so certain that anybody would run the other way when he told them he was a single dad. But Jess had done the opposite. She loved Arran like they were hers.

'It's a brilliant idea.' He clutched the key as though it was stardust, then pulled her into a hug. She giggled. 'A grand idea. Arran'll be over the moon.'

'I hope so,' she whispered. 'I just want the two of you here always. I want us to be a family.'

'We are,' he promised. 'We have been from the minute we met. Clan Byron-Douglas.'

Despite the Byrons' reputation, everybody had been blown away by Jess's continuous support for local businesses and charities since the festival, and it hadn't taken Mac and the town long to see that she was nothing like her grandparents. His mum had been right: Jess had mended everything the Byrons broke, and he had no doubt his granddad would have loved her just as much as the rest of the Douglases did. She'd made a home here. Had redefined what it meant to be a countess. Mac adored her for that: as both Lady Jessamine Byron and his Jess. He'd been foolish to think he could have one without the other, when both had been there all along. When he'd *loved* both all along.

Her cheeks lined with a beaming smile, and he ran his fingers through her hair delicately. They broke away when Arran returned, and Mac took a smug step back. Arran held a bouquet that he'd picked out for Jess early this morning before she'd woken. In the other hand, a card Arran had made with watercolour paints.

'Surprise!' they shouted now.

Jess frowned. 'What's this for?'

Slightly timid, Arran handed her the card, resting the flowers on the kitchen counter.

'"Happy Mother's Day".' Jess read the card and instantly

teared up. She scanned the inside, which Mac had watched them write. It hadn't been his idea, either. Everyone at school had been making something for Mother's Day, so Arran had done the same for Jess. Instinctively. Without thought. 'I don't know what to say. Thank you so much, Arran.'

She pulled them in for a hug, which was now slightly more awkward as they seemed to have doubled in height over the past year, all long limbs. They'd cut their hair short, too, having begged Mac for permission to dye it dark blue until he'd caved. Arran was happier, though, and it was easy to see. Always smiling, rarely running off to be alone like in the early days, though of course they needed space from time to time. Mac was just thankful he could watch them grow into themself. Just grateful to be their dad.

'Dad picked the flowers,' Arran said, and then blushed. Mac almost dropped his coffee. Arran had never called him that before, and he hadn't expected them to. Mac smiled, not daring to linger too long on the fact in case Arran felt embarrassed. Still, tears stung his own eyes. He could get used to being Dad.

Jess only wiped her tears and smelled the flowers: his favourite roses, fragrant bergenias, pale camellias, and daffodils.

'They're beautiful. Thank you, both,' he said.

'Are we doing something today?' Arran asked. 'I told Callum we were having a barbecue.'

Mac nearly spat out his coffee. 'Eh? A barbecue, at this time of year?'

Arran shrugged. 'That's what coats are for, and Callum really likes burgers.'

'You can't just tell us we're having a barbecue.'

'Well, Gem is bringing the sausages, so . . .'

Mac raised an eyebrow. 'Oh, aye. Who else have you invited?'

Arran gave a teenagerly shrug. 'Everyone, really. Just fancied it.'

'Right. Do you "just fancy" going to the shop and buying the burgers as well?'

Jess's cheeks puffed out, as though holding in a laugh.

'Nah,' Arran said. 'I'll come with you though.'

There went that Sunday drive then. He cast Jess an apologetic look, but she rather unhelpfully said, 'I do like a good barbecue. Besides, we have lots to celebrate.'

'Fine,' Mac grunted. 'Looks like I'm off to the shops, then. Shall I buy us breakfast as well?'

She winced, placing a kiss on his cheek that almost made him forgive her. Almost.

'And dessert, please. I'm craving cheesecake.'

On second thoughts, he'd need more kisses than that – but she'd have to make up for it later. For now, he was going to buy some burgers.

Mac was right. A barbecue in late March wasn't Arran's finest idea. Jess wore her thickest cardigan as she greeted Mac's parents, Callum and Olivia, and Gem. Rather suspiciously, Petra and Brodie entered only minutes apart, both red-faced, Petra's skirt all askew. They were no longer very good at pretending, though they still denied they were . . . whatever they were. It was better Jess didn't delve too deeply into their relationship for her own peace of mind.

Mac tended to the barbecue, hidden by a cloud of smoke. The smell of charring meat wafted through the back garden, and Beans kept trying to crawl up Mac's trouser leg to get a taste. Having served herself a mug of tea – it was too cold for lemonade – Jess sat in one of her foldable chairs by the barbecue and it wasn't long before Pam took the seat next to her, sunglasses perched on her head.

'Happy Mother's Day, love.'

Jess squeezed her hand. 'Happy Mother's Day, Pam.'

Pam was the closest thing to a mother she had now. Her own had stopped trying to call once the Robert scandal had blown over, and though it was sad, Jess hadn't lost anything. She'd only gained and grown since moving here permanently.

'Mac tells me that you asked him and Arran to move in here. Do you think you'll adopt Arran?'

Jess shrugged. They'd had conversations about what the future might hold, but Jess was honoured just to be in their life. She didn't need a piece of paper to tell her what she was to them. Arran was Mac's before anyone else's, and she didn't want to invade that unless it was what they both wanted. Still, that Mother's Day card had her happily perched on cloud nine. Being a mother wasn't something she'd intended, especially not so young, and to a teenager, but Arran had wiggled into her heart and she'd let them. She would always want them to stay there.

'I suppose we'll see,' she said. 'We have talked about fostering more children when the time is right, though. Arran isn't the only child out there who needs a family, and . . . Well, I suppose now we have the space.'

'That's brilliant. I'm ever so happy for you.'

'What are we "ever so happy" about?' Mac appeared, snaking his hand around the nape of Jess's neck. His dad had been coaxed into watching the sausages and burgers instead while humming an Elton John song.

'Everything,' Jess answered honestly, looking up at him. The sound of Arran laughing with their friends filled the air, and beneath it, Petra trying to convince Gem that, no, she did not have a love bite on her neck. It was Jess's definition of perfect, and she wouldn't trade it for anything in the world.

Mac knelt beside her, smothering her with kisses until he reached her neck and she squirmed.

'Dear lord, Mac. There are children about.' Pam tutted.

Mac laughed, his gaze fixed on Jess. 'It's a good day.'

'It's a wonderful day,' she murmured onto his lips, tracing his round jawline with her fingers gently. She'd had a lot of wonderful days in the past year. She hoped to have many, many more.

Want to read more from Rachel Bowdler? Why not try
Honeymoon for One – a sparkling enemies-to-lovers holiday
romance that will have you in fits of laughter!

With her wedding called off, Robin Ellis resigned herself
to spending the holidays with her rowdy family at home.
But then she discovers she forgot to cancel her honeymoon.
Now she is spontaneously jetting off to spend a blissful
few weeks skiing the slopes all on her own.

Romance was far from her mind, until she ran into
standoffish ski instructor, Neve. Despite their rocky start
these two unlikely people can't help but fall for each other
under the starry Canadian skies.

They know that holiday romances don't last, and Robin
has had her heart broken one too many times before. But
can they overcome the distance between them and find a
happily ever after together?

Acknowledgements

As always, I must start by thanking my wonderful agent, Clare Coombes at Liverpool Lit. I'm so grateful to have an agent who supports me the way you do, and I'm endlessly proud of the work you do for underrepresented northern authors.

To my best friends, Leah and Ivy, who put up with my complaining about how difficult and nerve-wracking it is to write a second book for a good few months, and who stuck with me through all of the uncertainty and chaotic drafts until I knew who Mac and Jess truly were. The found family themes in my books are always dedicated to and inspired by you, and I'd be lost without you both.

To the Embla team, who are truly amazing at what they do. I'm so thankful that my books found a home with you – you make traditional publishing feel a lot less scary. Special thanks to my wonderful editor, Hannah, who knew exactly what Mac and Jess's story needed.

To my family, friends, and to Enzo the dog, who is always at my feet when I write – Arran would love you as much as I do (but I don't think I could let them steal you). To Mahlina, who is always so supportive. To the lovely community of readers and reviewers who take time out of their day to choose my books. It means the world to see people enjoying my work and spreading the word – you make the part that comes after writing so worth it. I never really thought about how becoming a writer might lead to me meeting so many new, wonderful people, even if most of them are inside my phone, so I'm very grateful and forever in awe of the readers and fellow authors who have become friends.

Most importantly, though, this book is for the Arrans, the Macs, the Jesses, and the Gems of the world. Whether you know who you are or are still trying to figure that out, I hope this book leaves you feeling a little bit warm and a little bit seen. I'm so lucky to have the space to write the (hopefully) uplifting queer stories I wish I could have read a few years ago – and like Jess and Mac, I think I would have understood myself better much sooner if I had. My books are forever and always for you.

Rachel Bowdler

Rachel Bowdler grew up and still lives just outside of Manchester, on the edge of West Yorkshire. After graduating from the University of Salford with a degree in English and Creative Writing, she became a freelance romance author, focusing on queer, plus-size, and working-class characters. Her only wish is that her words make readers feel warm and fuzzy inside. When she isn't assaulting her computer keyboard or daydreaming about fictional people in her pyjamas, you can find her cuddling and walking her talkative dog, Enzo, venturing out with her camera, wishing it was time to put up her Christmas tree, and painting with watercolours (but not very well!).

About Embla Books

Embla Books is a digital-first publisher of standout commercial adult fiction. Passionate about storytelling, the team at Embla publish books that will make you 'laugh, love, look over your shoulder and lose sleep'. Launched by Bonnier Books UK in 2021, the imprint is named after the first woman from the creation myth in Norse mythology, who was carved by the gods from a tree trunk found on the seashore – an image of the kind of creative work and crafting that writers do, and a symbol of how stories shape our lives.

Find out about some of our other books and stay in touch:

Twitter, Facebook, Instagram: @emblabooks
Newsletter: https://bit.ly/emblanewsletter